Praise for Ukrainian Nights

"Carlson has written a masterpiece of a debut novel, *Ukrainian Nights*, and his gifted pen takes us on a roller coaster ride through love, betrayal, and corruption in New York City and Kiev after the fall of the Soviet Union in 1991. Full of incredible twists and turns, Carlson's story is infused with uncanny knowledge of Ukrainian politics and culture, which was not only intriguing but kept me guessing until the very end--which was well after my normal bedtime!"
    Ward Brehm, author of *Bigger Than Me, White Man Walking, Life Through a Differemt Lens* and *Whispers in Stillness*

"Riveting! Carlson put me in a vice-grip of deception, intrigue, star-crossed love and double cross, and then continued to squeeze harder page after page. I had no idea where he was taking me and was shocked at where I ended up. Today's breathless daily news accounts of political intrigue have nothing on *Ukrainian Nights*."
    John Busacker, author of *Dare to Answer*, and founder of Life-Worth, LLC

"One page in, I couldn't stop reading Pete Carlson's brilliant debut novel *Ukrainian Nights*. Suddenly this year's impeachment hearings made sense. I half-expected Rudy or Lev and Igor to stroll through the pages and end up bloody. I'll never put gas in my car, read the New York Times or hear a Russian accent on the streets of New York quite the same way. A fun read. Give me more."
    John Wirth, Executive Producer/Showrunner of "Wu Assassins;" "Hap and Leonard;" "Hell on Wheels;" T"he Sarah Connor Chronicles"

Ukrainian Nights

Pete Carlson

Minneapolis

Second Edition December 2022
Ukrainian Nights. Copyright © 2019 by Pete Carlson.
All rights reserved.

No parts of this book may be used or reproduced by any means, graphic, electronic, or mechanical, including photocopying, recording, taping or by any information storage retrieval system, without the written permission of the publisher except in the case of brief quotations embodied in critical articles and reviews.

This is a work of fiction. All of the characters, names, incidents, organizations, and dialogue are either the products of the author's imagination or are used fictitiously.

10 9 8 7 6 5 4 3 2

ISBN: 978-1-959770-39-8

Cover and book design by Gary Lindberg

Ukrainian Nights

Pete Carlson

CALUMET
EDITIONS
Minneapolis

"A second chance! That's the delusion. There never was to be but one. We work in the dark—we do what we can—we give what we have. Our doubt is our passion and our passion is our task. The rest is the madness of art."

– Henry James

To my loving wife, Marsha, my family, and all Dreamers

Chapter 1

Another night, another nightmare. Sweat stung Hunter's eyes. Blinking and rubbing them only made it worse. Streetlight from six stories below illuminated his living room just enough to provide a shadowy outline of the small apartment he rented on the top floor. Rain hammered the roof in waves. To keep his mind from returning to the nightmares of Alina's screams—the blood, and then black, sinking silence—he counted the seconds between the lightning flashes and the sound of thunder rumbling in the distance. Rain can be a perfect companion on storm-filled nights. It was the quiet following a storm that scared Hunter the most. His mind would play tricks. He'd hear things, see things that weren't there. The sound of rain on his roof gave him certainty. He knew where he was. What was real.

Sprawled on his couch in a Yankees T-shirt and black boxers, Hunter screwed his eyes shut and conjured a habitual image of Alina, the first and only woman he'd ever loved. There was a period before he met her when he preferred to live alone. Where he could control everything. Where he could keep others from hurting him. But after Alina, he didn't know how to live alone again. As if he lived his previous life in black and white, and then along came Alina in color. He could never go back to black and white, and yet here he was, a colorless ghost surviving on nightmares.

Even though it had been months since the last surgery to rebuild his mangled right hand, the residual pain forced him to sleep on his left side. The Ukrainian mafia had almost destroyed the use of his hand when they shot him. Desperate for sleep, he tossed around for another hour until he gave up. His head pounded from the vodka he'd drunk earlier that evening.

He rose slowly from the couch, not trusting his balance, and walked barefoot across the hardwood floor to the kitchen. Flicking on the light, he rummaged through three drawers before finding two loose Dunhills, one of them slightly bent, and a book of matches. He stepped over to the sink and rinsed out the dirty, high-ball glass he'd left on the counter. After filling the glass with ice and vodka, he cut a lime into green wedges. The sweet smell of limes made him think of Alina. How she had always asked for extra limes when she ordered a vodka. Funny how certain smells triggered instant memories. The bond between a smell and a person or place is indelible. Unique to itself. Forever engrained in our life. All we can do is savor the good ones and try to shake off the bad.

Half drunk and half hung-over, he lit the bent cigarette. Leaning against the counter, he placed the cold glass against his temple to soothe his headache. After a few minutes, he returned to the tattered couch purchased from the previous tenant. Even though he'd lived in this apartment for a year, he had accumulated only a half-dozen pieces of used furniture. The living room was devoid of any art or plants other than a wall full of books and an oak writing desk and swivel chair positioned underneath the single window. While other people his age were busy buying condos, getting married and having children, Hunter was a thirty-year-old bachelor reporter working for the *New York Times*. Living alone, he had nothing to show for his life. His assets included one computer, a female cat that didn't like him, an empty checking account and a few photographs of Alina, his Russian girlfriend, taken the summer they'd spent together two years ago in Kiev, Ukraine, in 1995.

The vodka didn't dull the headache, so he stretched out on the couch and closed his eyes. After a few minutes before acid reflux forced him into a sitting position, he groaned and swallowed hard. Maybe it was from the greasy salo and borscht he'd eaten at a small Russian café near his apartment, or more likely from drinking too much cheap vodka. He reached for the antacid on the coffee table, popped three tablets and tried to relax. He hadn't experienced a full night's sleep since he'd returned from Kiev, mostly because of the nightmares. Tonight was no different. To pass the time, he tilted his head on the back of the couch and used the ceiling as a canvas to paint every detail of Alina's face: the sensual, pouting smile, high cheekbones, and red hair that hung like a curtain of beads over her large dark eyes. He remembered each night after Alina had left for work how he'd encircle her pillow. Placing his face deep into the pillowcase, he'd breathe deeply, intoxicated by the smoky-sweet scent of tobacco and gardenia that always lingered. He loved sleeping with Alina and slowly exploring her body. He loved her parts, the smoothness of the inside of her thighs, the curve of her hips and softness of her full breasts. He liked it best when they were in the dark because he didn't have to look at her red hair, which wasn't real. Under her red hair were the black roots of a Russian girl a long way from her family farm.

The rain stopped, so he decided to go outside for some fresh air and smoke the other cigarette. He dressed, placing a leg holster on his right calf, snapped in the Beretta, and then tightened the straps. After what had happened in Kiev, he never left the apartment without a gun. At first, it felt awkward and always required long pants, but after a few months, he wouldn't think of leaving home without it. His apartment occupied a corner of the top floor of a six-story brick building too old to have an elevator. After he finished dressing, he descended through an open, central stairwell lit by bare lightbulbs at each landing. The paint was peeling on the grey walls, and some of the steps needed repair. He could afford a better apartment, but in a strange way this one reminded him of the flat Alina and he shared in Kiev.

When he reached the fourth-floor landing, Emma McMahon in apartment 4A poked her head out to see who was in the hall. A tiny woman with thin orange hair and a sharp tongue, she was born in this neighborhood around the turn of the century when it was settled primarily by Irish immigrants. At ninety-five, she still had incredible hearing and an insatiable desire to know everyone's business. "Emma, everything's okay," Hunter said, as he passed her door. "Go back to bed. I'm just going out to have a cigarette." Continuing down to the third floor, Italian opera seeped through the paper-thin walls from the DiMaggio's in 3A, while the Gorski's in 3B yelled at each other in Polish as they engaged in a seemingly never-ending fight.

Hunter stepped through the front door and took in the clean night air. He loved the East Village at midnight, especially in May before the weather turned hot and the smell of garbage on the sidewalks permeated the summer air. He flinched when a single gunshot rang out somewhere. He always had trouble determining where sounds came from because his hearing in his right ear was damaged, but he knew the sound of a gun. It triggered a memory that he had relived a thousand times—the searing heat from a gun blast shattering his hand, the loud bang and the acrid smell of gunpowder in his nostrils. He searched the apartment windows in the surrounding buildings on his street, not sure if the gunshot came from his block or the next. After a few seconds without another shot his heartbeat slowed. A man never forgets the sound of a 9mm once he has experienced it at close range.

The street below his stoop glistened with mirrors of silver light. A dozen cars and taxis inched slowly along the street, honking for the traffic to move faster. People meandered along the sidewalks on either side of the road, emptying out of the shops and restaurants, most of which were getting ready to close. Sweet incense tickled the hair in his nose as it drifted up from a Hookah bar adjacent to his apartment. The wind swirled, delivering wisps of garlic, curry and ginger from a dozen ethnic restaurants throughout his neighborhood and reminding him of summer dinners in outdoor cafes in Kiev. To his left, a woman's high-pitched laughter floated out of a patio bar. To his right, someone played a violin near an open window. Hunter sighed and took another drag off his cigarette as two lovers stopped below him and embraced in the middle of the sidewalk; people stepped around them, smiling.

Even though he had to work the next morning, he debated whether to have a drink at a local bar called Jimmy's or go to the Black Sea Club. He glanced at his watch—a quarter past twelve. It was officially Wednesday, May 31, 1997, the second anniversary of the day he had met Alina. Nothing prepared him for what they had experienced, and nothing would ever be the same again. He recalled how they celebrated like silly teenagers the end of each month during their summer in Kiev with an intensity and unspoken sense of urgency that foreshadowed their uncertain future. As he looked down the busy street, he wondered whether Alina was alive or dead.

Hunter crushed the butt of his cigarette on the step, but before he walked back into his building, a woman's voice stopped him. The Russian accent was unmistakable. Her voice floated across the street like a familiar song. His mouth went dry because she sounded like Alina. He strained to find the woman's voice hidden amongst several young adults staggering out of a Karaoke bar. He stiffened when he spotted red hair bobbing up and down in the group at the top as they tried to decide their next destination. The woman wore a short, skin-tight, white skirt with white stiletto heels. She shimmered under a streetlight. Although he couldn't see her face, Hunter moved quickly across the street as the group linked arms, shouting and giggling while attempting to navigate steep steps to the sidewalk. He caught up to the group and tapped the woman on the back of her shoulder.

"Vybachte, ya chuv, yak ty hovoryv ukraïns'koyu movoyu. Zvidky Vy? Excuse me, I heard you speaking Russian."

The woman spun around and focused her drunken eyes on him. "Khto vy? Who are you?"

His heart sank. "Ne zvazhay. Never mind."

She assessed him from head to toe like a dress on a mannequin. "Ve ne Ukrainian. You're not Russian. De vy navchylysya hovoryty umranian? Where did you learn to speak our language?"

Before he could respond, one of her friend's walked over and stepped between them.

"Beat it. She's with us," the man said, pushing Hunter back. He was only an inch taller but thick as a middle linebacker.

Hunter raised his hands in the air. "I don't want any trouble."

"It's okay—he looks harmless," the girl reassured her friend. "I'll be right with you."

Her friend walked away and rejoined the group a short distance away.

Hunter couldn't take his eyes off the woman's face. It was uncanny how she brushed a few strands of red hair away and smiled with the same seductive eyes and pouting, erotic mouth that only certain European women, such as Alina, do so well.

"Shcho vy khochete? What do you want?" she asked.

"Nichoho. Nothing." He shuffled his feet and kicked at a scrap of paper on the sidewalk. "Ya dumav, shcho ty kohos' inshoho. I thought you were someone else." He didn't know what else to say, so he just stood there with her looking at him.

He couldn't explain why he looked for Alina every time he turned a corner, rode the subway, stepped from a taxi, or walked out of a building, stupidly hoping that someday, somehow, she would have found her way to New York. He flashed back to the last time he had seen Alina. He was naked and pinned against a wall with a gun to his head. There was nothing he could do but watch Vladimir Karasov, the head of the most powerful mafia organization in Ukraine, beat Alina bloody and then dragged her out of their flat, leaving a trail of blood along the floor. He tried to forget the terrifying moment when he had suddenly realized that within a few seconds, he would be a dead man. He remembered the loud bang as Karasov's bodyguard pulled the trigger of a 9mm gun—then nothing. He woke up hours later in a local hospital with excruciating pain, his right hand a mangled mess. The following days were a foggy Percocet blur as *The Times* flew him back to a New York City hospital in a private jet. It required two painful surgeries to rebuild his hand. Though he was lucky they hadn't killed him, he would never use his right hand the same way again.

He vowed to Vinny, his childhood buddy and co-worker at the newspaper, how he was going back to Kiev as soon as he fully recovered to kill Karasov and search for Alina. But he never did. Months later, he continued to conjure up endless excuses as to why he couldn't go, but no one believed him anymore. Guilt still gnawed at him. What kind of man abandons the one he loves?

The woman smiled. "Udachi, Ya nadyeyus', vy nashi odyn. Good luck. I hope you find your friend." Then she left him.

Hunter watched the group weave its way down the crowded sidewalk and disappear around the corner. He dreaded returning to an empty apartment, so he stepped off the curb and raised a hand. A taxi pulled up, and he slid into the backseat and immediately wrinkled up his nose. "What the hell is that smell?" Hunter said, trying futilely to open the window. "Hey buddy, your window doesn't work."

The driver shrugged. "I not your buddy."

The driver looked familiar, so Hunter looked at the name on the license attached to the visor. The man had a thick moustache, a scruffy beard, and wore a silver ring in his right earlobe. Hunter had seen him hanging around with a group of Russian and Ukrainian cabbies that took breaks at a popular food stand at the end of his block.

"Yury," Hunter said, "ever consider putting one of those evergreen air fresheners in here?"

The driver looked into his rearview mirror and frowned. "Why I do that?"

"Because your taxi smells like Ray's pizza."

"I like Ray's," Yury said, staring straight ahead. "Where to?"

"Seventh and First Ave, East Village."

Yury grinned. "The Black Sea Club?"

"How did you know?"

"The Black Sea Club is best." Yury kissed his fingers and grinned. "You lucky. I have no money to waste. Since I got married, I can't afford that place. My Sofia, she make nice, fat babies, but sex…" Yury wagged his finger in the air, "no good anymore." He looked up in the mirror again. "You married?"

"No," Hunter said.

"Then you no understand yet." Yury shook his head. "I love Sofia, but at Black Sea Club a man is treated like a man."

Hunter nodded. "I've tried other places in New York, but I always come back to the Black Sea Club. It reminds me of another place I used go to."

"As good as here?"

"Better."

"Really," he said, "And where this place?"

Hunter stared out the taxi window. "A long way from here."

Yury drove east before turning south toward East Village. Even though it was late, the sidewalks teemed with people. The shimmering neon lights reflected off the glass buildings, transforming the streets into a carnival-like atmosphere. The taxi driver played Russian music from a portable CD player on the front seat.

"Yury, where are you from?" Hunter asked.

"Odessa."

"Ever been to Kiev."

"My boss, he live there. Beautiful in summer."

"I wish I was sitting in an outside café drinking vodka along the Dnieper River right now."

Yury pulled up to the curb in front of the Black Sea Club deep into the area they called Little Ukraine. Hunter paid him and walked up several steps to the door of a tall, brown brick building identical to several others along the block. He pushed the buzzer three times and waited. Hunter always felt a twinge of guilt while waiting for the doorman. Ironic, he knew, that two years ago he had been sent to Kiev to write a story about the inhumanity of sex slavery and was so disturbed to discover drug trafficking had exploded during the last five years post-Soviet Union of anarchy. His view was different now. He rationalized there was nothing wrong with the frequency of his visits to the club. Sure, there were bad men all around and other bad places, but the Black Sea Club was not like that. Everyone in the Black Sea Club knew him by name. They liked him. He was important. Since his parents had died when he was ten, he'd been raised by a blur of foster families. He'd lived the last twenty years without ever feeling as if he belonged anywhere. He had never felt that he had a home. Then he met Alina in The Rus' Club in Kiev, and his life was forever changed.

"Yes?" A man's deep voice crackled over the intercom.

"Hunter."

"Just a minute." After a few seconds, the lock clicked, and a big man with a black tattoo on the right side of his neck opened the door.

"Mr. Hunter, welcome back. Please come in."

The lobby was small with a low ceiling, soft orange lights, red walls but no chairs, no furniture. A middle-aged woman in a long black dress walked through a side door. She rushed over and kissed him on both cheeks. "What nice surprise."

"I should've called ahead."

She grabbed his arm and ushered him down the hall. "You forget us, da?"

"I've been busy."

She patted him on the butt. "We fix."

"Is Mila on tonight?"

"Da, yes, I make sure she ready." They stopped before a set of large double doors. The electronic music pulsated loudly from the other side. "You want usual?"

"Sure. Thanks."

She led him into the club and seated him in a red leather booth. It took a minute for his eyes to adjust to the white strobe lights, the rotating blue and green lasers and the flashing, theater track lighting that surrounded the dance floor. Hunter surveyed the smoke-filled room. Clusters of men with young women occupied ruby-colored leather booths that lined the red walls of the lounge. Some booths opened to the dance floor. Others hid behind thin red curtains. It was a slow night. Only a few clients sat on high bar stools at the long mahogany bar. The bartender looked bored and spent most of his time watching two topless girls dance. Hunter didn't see any of the usual girls, so after a quick drink, he moved from the bar to the men's locker room to relax and shower before they took him to Mila.

The manager of the locker room greeted Hunter. Victor was in his seventies, wearing a black bowtie with a white coat that matched his thin, snow-white hair. Bowing politely, he said, "Mr. Hunter, Это приятно видеть вас снова."

"Da," Hunter said. "Ya vyp' yu, Victor, I'll have a drink."

Victor chuckled.

Hunter frowned. "What did you say to me?"

"I said, 'It was nice to see you again.'"

"Damn, I can't believe how fast I'm losing my Russian. It's only been two years since I left Kiev."

Victor ushered him toward a locker and handed him a key. "You just need to come here more often."

Hunter laughed. "Are you kidding? I'm here so much I might as well have my payroll check deposited directly into the Black Sea Club."

"There are worse places to spend your money." Victor had young eyes that smiled, even though time had battered the rest of his body. Bad hips caused him to limp, and age spots speckled his face and hands. He handed Hunter a towel and a fresh white bathrobe.

After showering, Hunter was led into a large lounge. A dozen men in white robes relaxed on full-length lounge chairs circling a large circular, stainless steel soaking pool. Soft Russian music seeped out of the ceiling speakers. The room was warm but not hot. The smell of Eucalyptus and sweat hung heavy in the humid air. Some men drank and watched sports on flat screen televisions, others read the paper or took a nap. Hunter stretched out in an empty lounge chair. One of the junior attendants quickly placed warm towels over him, while another arrived with his vodka on the rocks with a twist of lime.

"I took the liberty of ordering your usual," Victor pointed to the drink tray. "Do you need anything else?"

"No, I'm fine." Hunter took the glass and swallowed a third of the drink.

Victor watched Hunter gulp the drink. "Tough day?"

Hunter shook his head. "The usual."

"What about your boss? Any improvement with him?"

"No, he's still a piece of work."

"Why don't you leave *The Times*? You never sound happy. Maybe you should try something different than working as a reporter."

"You wouldn't understand."

"Try me."

"I love to write. I've always loved to write. It's just that…"

"What?"

"My boss. I owe him."

"Why do you feel that way?"

"He was the one that gave me a chance when no one else would give me a job."

"But the last time we talked, you said he treats you like shit."

"I shouldn't have said that."

Victor paused before he asked, "What exactly don't you like about your work?"

"I don't have time to write."

"I'm confused. You're a reporter, but don't write?"

"I write stupid stuff about park dedications and local Good Samaritan stories. Never anything with real depth or investigation. My boss has me editing most of the work that goes through his office."

"Why would he have you do his work?"

"Because he's a terrible editor. The only reason he got the job was because the previous editor quit without notice. It was a critical time at the paper and nobody else was available. I had just graduated from Columbia about the same time he was promoted. He was way over his head. I was the editor of our university paper, so he hired me to make sure that I'd make him look good."

"So, you do his job, as well as yours?"

Hunter frowned and nodded.

"Sounds to me like he's using you."

Hunter shrugged.

"What would you do if you could write your own job description?"

"No one has ever asked me that before." Hunter looked at the ceiling. "I love history, particularly eastern European history. That was my major in college. I'd love to write a few books and maybe teach someday."

"Then do it."

"I can't."

"Why not?"

"I already told you."

"Hunter, you need to stand up for yourself. You need to stop letting people take advantage of you. Be true to yourself."

"Hah. True to myself?" Hunter took another sip of his drink.

"What happens if I don't have a clue who that person is?"

"Then you're fucked," Victor said, with a straight face.

They stared at each other for a moment and then laughed.

"I love you." Hunter pointed at Victor's chest. "You're amazing."

"My wife would beg to differ." Victor picked up a towel that had fallen off his chair. "Are you hungry? Do want any snacks?"

Hunter shook his head and finished the last of the remaining vodka. Then he swirled the ice cubes in the bottom of his glass and changed the subject. "How did you get to America and find work in the Black Sea Club?"

"In the 70s and 80s, families from Russia and Ukraine started to immigrate to New York. After the Soviet Union collapsed in 1990–91, there was another huge influx of families. Today there are more than 60,000 of us living in the East Village, Brooklyn and Brighton Beach. I came to America because a friend of mine from Ukraine wanted to expand his business interests in New York. He sent me here to keep an eye on his investments."

"What kind of investments?" Hunter asked.

Victor smiled as he picked up Hunter's empty glass and the newspaper.

"Let's just say it involves importing and exporting goods."

"What kind of goods?"

Victor smiled again but didn't answer.

"Okay, I get it."

"Another?"

Hunter nodded. "Sure, why not."

Victor turned away. "I'll be right back. Any special instructions for Mila?"

"Just the usual."

Hunter closed his eyes and relaxed until Victor returned with another drink.

"Let me know when you're ready and I'll bring you to Mila."

Before Victor walked away, Hunter grabbed his arm. "Can I ask you something?"

Victor stopped and turned around. "Of course, anything."

"I'm curious—has the club changed much since you've been here?"

"No, some things never change." Victor paused, as if searching for the correct words. "You see…" Then he stopped. "I'm not sure I can say this in the right way, and I don't want you to misunderstand me."

Hunter waved his vodka in the air. "Go ahead. Don't worry about me."

"Everyone has a story. Everyone has their own reason for coming here." Victor's voice softened. "As I see it, loneliness is the poverty of the soul. Men come here for the things they can't find anywhere else. Think about it. The first thing a man does when he arrives here is remove his clothes. He leaves everything behind in the locker—his job, his fears, his responsibilities, and his failures. He hangs all that baggage on a hook and forgets about it—free from the expectations of everyone else—at least for a few hours. Once a man sheds his clothes and steps into the room with a beautiful woman, he has the freedom to choose. Once the lights are turned off, he can become whoever he wants to be—Napoleon, Rudy Valentino, Cary Grant, Aristotle, or Genghis Khan. It's interesting that after the man and woman make love and lay close enough to feel each other's heartbeat, do you know who that man becomes?"

"I have no idea." Hunter stared at the reflections of light bouncing off the ceiling and mirrored walls surrounding the small pool. "Who does he become?"

Victor smiled. "He becomes himself, his true self, his dream self—the one that lingers with him when he first opens his eyes in the morning, but then, like his pajamas, gets put on the hook in the closet in exchange for his day-self."

Hunter put his finger in his glass and played with an ice cube. "What if a man doesn't like what he sees in himself?"

Victor stopped smiling and waited.

Hunter looked away. "Sorry, it's been a weird night."

"A weird night? Let me guess," he said. "Do you want to talk about her?"

Hunter's eyes widened. "What are you, some kind of a savant?"

"Nope, I know that when a man's upset, it's almost always about one of two things—a woman or money." He grinned. "I had a 50-50 chance."

Hunter laughed and leaned back in his chair. "I saw a woman tonight that could've been a twin of Alina."

"Wasn't she your girlfriend in Kiev?"

"Yes," Hunter sighed.

"Describe Alina for me," Victor asked.

"She has dark eyes that swallow you like a black hole, a laugh that makes you forget who you are, and a Russian accent that would cause a saint to sweat."

"How did you lose a woman like that?"

"I didn't." Hunter swallowed hard. "Someone took her from me."

Victor stared out over the pool and confessed, "I let a girl get away from me once when I was your age."

"Do you ever wonder what happened to her?" Hunter asked.

"Every day," Victor said. "What about you? Did you ever try to contact her again?"

"It's complicated."

"It always is," Victor said. "It's all about choices, isn't it? I made a bad one and regret it to this day."

"Victor, if you had to do it all over again, would you make the same choice?"

"No, I'd go after her."

Hunter took a long drink of vodka while drumming the fingers of his left hand against the edge of the lounge chair. Finally, he spoke. "Here's the thing. She's in my head all the time. I've tried to find someone to replace her, but... I can't."

"We've all lost something that we think we can never replace." Victor's voice softened as he patted Hunter's arm. "If you found it once, you'll find it again."

"I don't think so."

"You will."

Hunter frowned. "How do you know?"

Victor crossed his arms. "Because we're not meant to live alone."

"Bullshit. Except when I was with Alina, I've been alone my entire life," Hunter said. "Okay, tell me, why do guys like me end up in the Black Sea Club, while other guys have a nice house in the suburbs with a wife, two kids and a dog?"

"I don't know," Victor said, rubbing the top of his white head. "But every man that comes to this club is seeking something they can't find anywhere else. This place is an Ark. Men come here to be saved before they drown in loneliness or despair." Victor shook his head. "It's not immoral to desire love, even if you have to pay for it. Many men hide from themselves during the day. They put on a mask, dress the part, go to work, go through the motions. Only when they come here do they find a place where they belong."

"You missed your calling," Hunter said. "You should be a poet or a philosopher."

"No, I'm just an old man who talks too much." He patted Hunter's arm. "I'll be back in a few minutes."

Hunter watched Victor limped away and thought about Alina. After several minutes, the music faded away and everything went black.

* * *

Victor gently tapped him on the shoulder. "Mila's ready."

Hunter raised himself on one elbow. "What?" Dazed, he looked around the lounge.

"You fell asleep. I hated to wake you because it looked like you were having a good dream, but Mila's ready."

"No problem." Hunter rubbed his eyes, blinked several times and struggled to stand up. The vodka was catching up to him.

"Need any help?" Victor asked.

"No, but I could use another drink."

"Are you sure?"

"Yes, I'll be fine." Hunter took a couple of deep breaths. "Just give me a minute."

Victor snapped his fingers at one of the attendants. "I'll have it brought to your room right away. Do you want me to take you to Mila?"

"No thanks, I know the way." Hunter weaved his way down the hall to Mila's room and knocked.

"Come in. It's open."

The room reeked of cigarette smoke and cheap perfume. Mila sat with her legs crossed in a blue chair. Half her face was the same yellow as the light radiating from a small lamp on a table next to her, the other half hidden in a shadow.

Hunter closed the door and sat on the bed. "Can you turn off the light?" he asked. It was better not to see Mila's face. She had a great body, but she wasn't a beauty.

"Whatever you want," Mila said, crushing her cigarette in the ashtray. She stood and let the see-through nightgown float to the floor like a feather, then turned off the lamp and stepped in front of him. His breath quickened as he ran his hands along the contours of her hips. She knelt, slowly unbuttoned his shirt and removed his trousers. With her delicate fingers, she closed his eyelids then moved the soft palms of her hands slowly up and down his bare chest. After a minute, she rolled him onto his stomach.

"Relax now," she whispered. "I be right back."

Hunter lifted his head. "Where are you going?"

She gently pushed his head back onto the bed and walked across the room. "I have a surprise for you."

After a couple of minutes, she returned coated in warm oil. She climbed on the bed and lay naked on top of his back. Slowly, she slid back and forth along the entire length of his body, up and down, quicker and quicker until the oil between their bodies was hot. Hunter didn't respond. He lay still beneath her body as if she wasn't there.

Mila stopped and moved alongside him. "What wrong? I not please you?"

"No, you always please me. Just having a bad night." He rolled over and they lay side-by-side, cooling off on sticky sheets in the dim light. Mila lit two cigarettes and handed one to him.

"Mila, where were you born?" Hunter asked.

"In small village in Ural Mountains."

"Why did you leave?"

"I needed job."

They lay quietly for a few minutes until she asked, "Where's home for you?"

Hunter stared at the ceiling. "Interesting question."

"I not understand."

"You're lucky you have a home."

"Everyone has home."

After a long pause he said, "Not everyone."

Mila looked confused. "What you mean?"

"Nothing." Hunter closed his eyes.

Mila ran her finger along a thin chain that hung around his neck until it came to rest on a small gold cross. "What this?"

"My mother gave it to me. She said the cross was given to her by an angel."

"My grandmother loves angels. She has necklace like yours."

"What about you?" Hunter said. "Do you believe in angels?"

"I gave up on angels long ago." Mila folded her hands across her stomach. "Tell me about your parents."

"My mother was beautiful. A voracious reader. But she never let on how intelligent she was. She could've been a teacher or a college professor." Hunter stopped. "This is boring you."

"No, no," Mila put her hand in the air, "keep on talking. Tell me something most people would never know about your mother."

"Hmmm," Hunter said. "She was a fabulous cook. She could cook anything and make you beg for more. She was a natural in the kitchen. Old school. She always said food was her language of love."

"You a lucky man."

Hunter didn't answer but continued staring at the ceiling.

"What was your dad like?" Mila asked.

"He traveled a lot with work and switched jobs a lot."

"Why?"

"My mother always made excuses for him, but when I got older, I learned that he drank and wasn't good at relationships."

"I know many men like that," Mila said. "What kind of work he do?"

"He loved the hotel business. At one point, he was a junior manager at the Peninsula Hotel. Occasionally, he'd let me go to the office with him. While he worked, I'd roam the halls and pretend that I was a king and the hotel was my private castle. But that didn't last very long before…"

"Before what?" Mila asked.

"I lost my parents in a fire when I was ten."

"That's terrible."

Hunter played with the gold cross with his fingers. "My mother had a premonition. At the time, I didn't understand why she cried when she attached this around my neck. One week later, she died in the fire." He glanced at the cross. "I've never taken it off."

Neither spoke for a long time until Hunter asked, "Mila, have you ever lived with a man?"

"Once, but it not last very long."

"Why not?"

"I don't know. I guess we not good for each other."

"Did he treat you badly?"

Her eyes narrowed. "He use me."

"Do you think he loved you?"

She sighed. "We had different ideas of love."

"Did that make you angry?"

"I hate him, but…"

"But what?"

"Hard to explain. But I love and hate him at same time."

Hunter nodded. "Not much separates love and hate."

They lay in silence again until Mila asked, "You believe in finding special person?"

"Like a soulmate?"

"Yes, yes."

"I used to think that way."

"What happened?"

Hunter shrugged.

"It your fault or hers?" Mila asked.

"Good question."

"Do you still love her?"

Hunter rubbed his face with both hands. "What time is it?"

Mila pointed to her clock radio. "Time to go."

* * *

It was dawn when Hunter crawled into his own bed without taking off his clothes and fell asleep. Four hours later, he walked into the *New York Times* building hoping he wouldn't throw up before he got to a bathroom. Once he reached his floor, he walked straight to the men's room and vomited. Feeling a bit better, he made it to his office, grateful that Tess, his assistant, wasn't in yet. The last thing he wanted was a conversation. He closed the door and slumped into his chair. The office was roughly the size of a large closet. His desk was positioned under one small window and was filled with grey lateral files, bookcases and shelves filled with paperbacks, hardcover books and miscellaneous articles ranging from biographies to European history. Stacks of old magazines, newspapers and a box of used books jammed the space behind the door. He put his head on the desk and hoped no one would bother him for at least an hour.

Hunter hated mornings because they meant the return to the "old" Hunter, the nameless reporter for the *New York Times* who wrote important stories such as restaurant openings and bridge construction. His phone rang. He looked at his watch and knew it was his boss, so he ignored it. He closed his eyes and cursed as he fought off the waves of nausea. It had been almost a month since the last time he got drunk and paid for sex. That damn Russian woman last night that set him off again. He pulled out a warped picture of Alina from his wallet and wondered again if she was dead or alive.

Chapter 2

Hunter stepped off the plane in the spring of 1995 and moved slowly down the jetway toward the main terminal of Kiev International Airport. He gripped his passport tightly as a dozen soldiers with automatic weapons patrolled in starched brown uniforms and tall black boots. Groggy from flying all night, none of the passengers coming off the flight spoke much as they stood in single file waiting to clear customs. Hunter had never traveled outside the United States. New York had a diverse culture, but Kiev was totally different. As he inched toward the front of his line, he noticed that the other lines were moving twice as fast. The unsmiling customs officer in the glass booth closely reviewed the documents of each passenger and asked a lot of questions. Even though Hunter had nothing to fear, his heart raced as he presented his documents. Fortunately, the officer barely looked at him as he stamped the passport and waved him on.

At his hotel, he crashed for several hours and didn't wake up until night. From his window, he could see the city lights reflecting off the Dnieper River. He should've been jet-lagged, but instead, he was wide-awake and pacing around his room. After unpacking, he stretched out on the bed and pulled out a list of brothels and clubs he intended to visit as part of his research on human trafficking and money laundering. The Ukrainian and Russian mafia, made up of former KGB officers, had seized control in 1991 after the Soviet Union had broken apart. It was becoming the largest criminal organization in the history of civilization. Sex slavery and drugs were its major sources of money, but as its control spread beyond the Soviet block and into Asia, it needed more revenue sources. America was the next logical place to go. Once a beachhead was established, it could spread from coast to coast. Hunter's job was to determine how these young women were lured into prostitution and getting into the United States.

Hunter looked at his watch and tried to calculate what time it was in New York City. He had a bad feeling about this assignment. His boss, Cabot, had been looking for compelling story ideas when Hunter's assistant, Tess, complained that the Russians and Ukrainians were taking over Brooklyn. Her friend was in the diamond business and had explained to Tess how diamonds were one of many schemes the Russian and Ukrainian mafias used to move millions of dollars into Brooklyn from overseas. Tess didn't care about the money laundering, but she was furious about the sex slavery and human trafficking. Raised by a single mom in Brooklyn, Tess knew firsthand how men often took advantage of desperate women and homeless young girls. There had been a surge of young Russian, Ukrainian and Asian girls going in and out of the local clubs in her neighborhood. The cops knew it was sex slavery but looked the other way because they were paid off. Tess had challenged Cabot and Hunter to expose the trafficking and protect these voiceless women. "Besides, sex sells newspapers," Tess had said with a flourish. Two weeks later, Hunter had found himself on a plane to Kiev.

The Rus' was the first club on his list. Named after the golden era of Kiev, it was infamous in Eastern Europe for its beautiful women. Hunter dressed in charcoal pants, a blue button-down shirt and a black sport coat. Standing in front of the mirror, he practiced the story that he and Cabot had concocted before leaving New York. He was now Mr. Hunter Smith, the owner of a software company seeking new business partners for expansion into Eastern Europe and Russia. He rubbed his sweaty hands on his pants, checked for his wallet and then put his recorder and a list of questions in his coat pocket. His biggest fear was that nobody would believe this naïve, skinny Italian from Brooklyn was a software mogul. With a sigh, he switched off the light and headed toward the lobby.

A few inquiries with the staff revealed that the Rus' was only several blocks from his hotel, so he decided to walk. The outdoor cafés bustled with people. He stopped to watch a cluster of older men hunched over small tables smoking, discussing the news and playing chess. A man wearing a beret gestured for Hunter to take a chair across from his open chessboard, but Hunter kindly waved off the invitation. As he walked on, Russian music drifted out of open windows. Beeps and honks from countless vehicles added to the cacophony. The scene was very different from New York, yet oddly familiar at the same time.

Two wrong turns added an extra half hour to his walk, but he finally found the Rus' in a drab, two-story building. He entered a small lobby in which everything was painted ruby red. A woman wearing heavy makeup stood from behind a reception desk and approached him and planted a kiss on both cheeks. Time had not been kind to her appearance. Her cheap perfume, Hunter thought, was probably an attempt to cover up an underlying stench of booze and cigarettes. She motioned for him to take a chair at the desk, then presented a menu of services, made an impression of his credit card and asked a series of questions. When he disclosed that he was an executive at a software company, she made a notation.

"Tell me how big?" she asked.

"Are you kidding?" Hunter's eyes widened. "Does it matter?"

"Da," she smiled. "Important to make sure you have right girl." She tapped her pen on the notebook. "So, how big you?"

Hunter's squirmed around in his chair.

"Net, net. No, no, not you big," she laughed. "How big your company?"

Hunter blushed. "We're privately held, but I can tell you that we generate over two hundred million in annual sales."

She wrote down the number on her form. "And what your position?"

"Chief bottle washer."

She looked up, confused. "What?"

Hunter grinned. "I own the company."

"Okay, Okay. You make funny. I understand." She made a few more notes and folded the form in half. She waved at a young woman to approach, handed over the note and whispered something in her ear. The girl nodded and walked through the double doors that led into the club.

"The fees for services, food and drink will be charged to credit card." Then she winked. "For special requests, between you and your girl, you pay in cash or charge it. Okay?"

Hunter nodded. The woman rose from her chair and hooked her arm under his. "I take you in now."

She ushered Hunter into a large lounge and sat him in a round leather booth. The club pulsed with electronic music and laser lights.

"Podozhdite zdes. Wait here," she said.

Hunter leaned closer and tried to use the limited Russian he learned in college. "Ya vas ne slyshu. I can't hear you."

"Da," she said.

Hunter repeated himself, but she obviously didn't understand him. She smiled benignly and walked back to the reception area as he surveyed the club. The room looked like a cheap cocktail lounge in a bad, low budget movie except that young girls in white lingerie were circling around numerous tables of panting men. Four men with beautiful girls caught Hunter's eye. They were seated in a semi-private room partially obscured by a red curtain. One of them, an overweight American, called the girls "darlin'" and "sweetie" in a grating Texas accent as he tried to entice them onto his lap with dollar bills.

A pretty waitress in a very short cocktail dress approached Hunter. "Can I get you something?"

"A beer would be nice."

"What kind?"

"Do you have Heineken?"

"Da," she said.

Hunter pointed toward the men in the semi-private room. "Are those Americans?"

She hesitated, then ignored the question. "Do you want glass or bottle?"

"No, no," Hunter pointed again. "Americans?"

She shrugged. "Ya ne ponimaya. I no understand."

She had spoken perfect English a few seconds ago. "Okay, never mind," he said.

After the waitress left, he watched two young naked women dance on a pole. He tried not to stare too long because the girls looked young enough to be in high school. The longer he sat, the more he regretted coming here. The waitress finally arrived at his table with a beer. She spoke rapidly in Russian and pointed at his table. He had no clue what she had said, so he just smiled and nodded. She set her drink tray on the table and gently pushed him deeper into his seat.

Hunter had never been to a brothel, much less touched a prostitute. This was unreal, sitting in a brothel halfway around the world about to meet a prostitute for the first time.

As he sipped his beer, he noticed a beautiful woman sitting by herself on a barstool, her long legs crossed and one red high heel shoe dangling off her toe. She wasn't wearing lingerie and seemed disinterested in the men around her. Hunter couldn't take his eyes off her.

Suddenly, there was a loud commotion at the main entrance. Two burly men in matching black leather jackets entered the club. They took positions on each side of the door, staring straight ahead with arms crossed. Their short-cropped hair, square jaws, and tattoos reminded him of the thugs in old mafia movies. A few seconds later, an entourage of loud and obnoxious young men and women entered. Everything about them screamed, "Look at me!"

The last to appear was a stocky man over six feet tall with broad shoulders. He wore a black sport coat and a white shirt unbuttoned to the middle of his chest, exposing a heavy gold chain. He cautiously scanned the room before entering. Hunter recognized Vladimir Karasov immediately from a recent picture in a *New York Times* story on the fall of the Soviet Union. Karasov was featured as one of the most powerful men in Ukraine. He looked better in person. Hunter guessed his age at early sixties. Though past his prime, he was ruggedly handsome in a sullen, angry way. The mood in the club immediately changed as he strutted unsmiling into the room with the bearing of a military officer. People quickly moved out of his way. The girls stopped what they were doing and watched the entourage move through the club. Idle waitresses pretended to be busy, and bartenders earnestly wiped down the bar while grabbing dirty glasses and emptying ashtrays.

Karasov barely responded to people who tried to get his attention. He nodded almost imperceptibly to the lucky ones and ignored the rest. The bodyguard leading Karasov snapped his fingers and pointed to a large booth in the corner. Two waitresses quickly set the table with bottles of booze, wine, champagne, glasses and food. Karasov stopped to talk to the beautiful woman with the dangling high heel. They embraced, and he kissed her on both cheeks. She leaned close and said something that made him smile for the first time since he entered the club.

Hunter's waitress passed by and placed another beer on his table.

"Does Mr. Karasov come here often?" Hunter asked.

She didn't understand.

He pointed. "The guy with the long, slicked-backed hair... Karasov."

She avoided eye contact, picked up his empty glass and wiped the table. "Da, yes," she whispered. "Karasov."

Karasov moved on to join the rest of his group. A few minutes later, the receptionist approached the woman in the red dress, chatted briefly and then pointed at Hunter. He immediately looked away, but out of the corner of his eye, watched the woman with the dangling shoe set her drink on the bar and slip off her stool. She was taller than he'd expected—he guessed around six feet with her high heeled stilettos on. She approached him with an intensity that Hunter could feel from across the room. When she reached his table, she paused, studied him up and down as if taking inventory. "I'm Alina," she said in a husky voice. Her eyes were the color of a moonless night.

Hunter couldn't speak.

She held out her right hand. "What's your name?"

He rubbed his sweaty hand on a thigh before extending it to her. "Hunter," he mumbled.

She didn't let go of his hand. "First time?"

He nodded and pulled his hand away.

"Which is it?" she asked. "First time ever or just in a club?"

Hunter blushed and stared into his beer. She stepped closer. Her perfume—a unique blend of gardenia and smoke combined with the salty odor of a woman—made him dizzy.

Hunter pointed to a gardenia in her hair. "I love your flower."

"Thank you. Gardenias are my favorite." She smiled. "Where are you from?"

"The States."

"New York?"

Astonished, he said, "How did you know?"

"Your accent," she said. "We have a few regulars from New York and Texas that come through here on business trips. I've always wanted to go to New York City. It sounds like heaven."

"What's stopping you?"

Alina lost her smile for a second. "Maybe someday. Do you mind if I sit down?"

"No, not at all." Hunter slid over to make room for her.

Alina looked at his empty glass and snapped her fingers at one of the girls. Within seconds a bottle of champagne and two glasses appeared at the table.

Hunter waved his hand. "I don't do champagne."

Alina put her hand on his knee, which was rapidly tapping the floor. "You need to relax," she said. "Let's have some fun."

"I'm just a little nervous."

"Don't worry. I don't bite."

"Ha! I'm not so sure about that," he said.

"Nibble, maybe, but never bite." She leaned closer to him. "Are you going to make me to drink the champagne all by myself?"

Hunter shook his head slightly. "No offense, but I only drink beer."

Alina smiled and patted his hand. "We'll fix that." She poured two glasses of champagne and set the bottle on the table. "Cigarette?" She offered him a pack the waitress had brought with the champagne.

"No, thank you. I don't smoke."

"Really," she said, slowly crossing her long legs, "and I suppose you go to church every Sunday and sing in the choir."

Hunter watched the red dress slide up her thighs as she crossed her legs. One more inch…

"You look good in red," he said hoarsely, trying to force his eyes away from her legs.

"It's my favorite color," she said. "What's yours?"

"It's red now."

She laughed.

"You speak excellent English."

"Part of the job."

"How many other languages do you speak?"

"Five," she said. "What about you?"

"Only one, if you don't consider Brooklyn slang a second language."

"Tell me about yourself. What brings you to Kiev?"

"Business."

"What kind of business?"

"The information industry."

She looked confused. "What does that mean?"

"Software," Hunter said. "We gather and analyze information from various sources and then disseminate it."

Alina nodded. "What kind of software? Who would be your clients?"

"We do a lot of work with banks."

"Do you conduct much business in New York City?"

"Yes, of course," he said. "Why do you ask? Are you thinking of diversifying into the banking business?"

"You never know." She smiled. "What about oil companies?"

"We have a few clients in oil."

"I'm curious, how big is your company?"

"We're global," Hunter bragged. "We just passed two hundred million in sales last year."

"Hmm, a software tycoon," she said. "That's a first for me."

Hunter grinned and lifted his glass in the air. "Well then, we have something in common."

Alina raised her champagne glass and touched the rim of his glass with a clink. "Here's to the first of many firsts."

She slid closer. He wasn't sure, but she seemed to sniff him. She had an unnerving, physical, almost dangerous aura about her. She was a tiger on a hunt, knowing exactly what she was doing to him.

She whispered, "I want to tell you a secret."

"What's that?"

She softly kissed his ear. "Every night with me will be like your first time."

Hunter stopped breathing.

She winked and licked her upper lip. "Are you ready?"

"For what?"

"For an experience you'll never forget."

"Oh, that," he said, his face turning red.

Alina grabbed his hand, led him through a side door and down a long, dimly lit hallway. She unlocked a room and opened the door. Hunter took one step inside and looked around. It was larger than he'd expected and decorated entirely in pink. The air smelled sweet from incense burning in the belly of a miniature gold statue of a Happy Buddha. Alina stepped past him to a dresser and began to take off her jewelry. Without turning around, she said, "Honey, why don't you sit down on the bed and make yourself comfortable."

Hunter sat down on the edge of the bed, folded his hands in his lap and coughed nervously. He pointed to a pretty tierra lying on her dresser. "Where did you get that?"

She picked up the tierra and examined it. "I won a beauty contest a long time ago."

"Wow, a beauty queen."

"Once upon a time," Alina said. Then she stepped in front of him. Slowly, she removed one strap and then the other from her shoulders and wiggled until her dress slipped to the floor. Stunned, Hunter stared at her soft, milky-white body. But when she leaned down to kiss him, he put his hands up in the air and slid several inches away.

"What's wrong?" Alina said.

"I… I can't." Hunter tried to clear his throat and tried to continue speaking, but nothing came out.

She sat down next to him and began to run her fingers through his hair. "I know this is your first time, but you have to relax." She reached over and put her hand in his crotch.

Hunter flinched.

"I won't hurt you," she cooed.

"It's not that," he said. "I have a confession to make."

"I already know what you are going to say."

"I don't think so."

Alina stiffened. "You not one of those weird or kinky guys, are you?"

"No, no, nothing like that." He hesitated. "It's just that…"

She grinned. "What? Do you want me to spank you? Tie you up?"

"I want to talk."

Alina frowned and muttered "shit" under her breath. She reached for a pink robe draped over a chair next to the bed and tied it tightly around her waist. "Okay, but it's the same money."

He reached into his pocket and pulled out his recorder. "I want to ask you a few questions."

Alina shot straight-up and shouted, "Get out!" She pointed to the door. "Get the fuck out of my room right now."

"I only have a couple of questions," Hunter pleaded.

"No!" she barked.

As she moved toward the door, Hunter grabbed her arm.

"Please, I'm not here to cause trouble. I'm a reporter from the *New York Times* doing a background story on the explosion of sex slavery in Eastern Europe."

She jerked her arm away and reached for the door handle.

"Just give me five minutes, and I'll never bother you again."

"Why should I help you?"

Hunter didn't respond. He wasn't prepared for that question.

"Why are you writing this story? Are you here to save us? You're not the first one to come, no pun intended, to our club and pretend you care. You guys are all the same—you're pathetic. You'll write your little story and then leave. We're just another assignment to you."

"That's not true. I want to expose…"

"Expose what? One month from now, you won't remember my name. Nobody gives a shit about us—certainly not a fucking reporter, like you." She put her hand on the door handle again. "Give me one good reason I shouldn't throw you out right now?"

"Look, I have money." Hunter pulled out a roll of American cash from his pocket and held it in the air.

She hesitated, and her eyes narrowed. "How much do you have?"

"A hundred dollars."

"Bullshit," she said, in perfect English and pointed to his roll of dollar bills.

Hunter shrugged. "Three hundred."

"That's not enough."

"How much do I need?"

"That depends. Do you have any Deutsche Marks?"

"No, only American money, but I can get Marks if that's what you want."

She took her hand off the door handle and turned to face him. She folded her arms, leaned against the door and played with the ends of the pink tie around her waist. Finally, she asked, "What's your name?"

"Hunter Smith."

She shook her head in disgust. "I mean your real name."

Hunter rubbed his hands back and forth on his thighs. "Moretti."

"Well, Hunter Moretti," she stood over him with her hands on her hips, "who are you, and what're you really doing here?"

"I told you. I'm a reporter. We're doing a story on human trafficking and sex slavery." He waited. "Can you help me?"

She frowned and then walked over to the table, lit a cigarette and sat down on the bed.

"What makes you think you can make any difference?"

"Maybe I can't, but someone else can if the right people become aware of this horrible problem."

Alina studied him for a long time. "Okay, tell me about yourself."

"There's not much to tell. I've worked at the *New York Times* since college. My boss is one of the editors."

"What kind of connections do you have working for the *New York Times*?"

"Excellent. We're the most prominent newspaper in the country."

"Can you get access to anyone you want—politicians, business, celebrities?"

"Not difficult."

She leaned forward. "What about people in the oil business?"

Hunter nodded. "No problem."

"Bankers?"

Hunter laughed. "Why? Are you thinking of branching out to New York?"

"My boss already has investments in Brooklyn. He's very ambitious."

"I'm sure that I could help. I've heard interesting things about the influx of Russians and Ukrainians in the Brooklyn area. And rumors of lots of young women brought to the United States as sex slaves. They come in through Brooklyn and then disappear into the rest of our country."

Alina ignored Hunter's statement but leaned forward and looked closely into his face. "One last question. Do you have access to the president and members of Congress?"

"Congress, yes." Hunter smiled. "The president... that depends on how much we can help each other."

"How do I know you aren't full of bullshit? You already lied to me about your software company."

"Call the *Times* and check me out. Look, I can help you—if you help me. If you need contacts in New York or anywhere, I can make that happen. I just need to make a few calls and presto." Hunter snapped his fingers.

"Presto?"

"It means people make time for me," Hunter said. "They all want to be my friend because everyone likes to appear in our newspaper."

"You must be a rich man because only people with the right friends get the concessions to do business in our part of the world. Connections dictate how much money you make."

"What about your connections?" Hunter asked.

"Better than you think," Alina said.

"I need real information. Facts to substantiate my story. Can you help me?"

Alina's eyebrows arched up. "And what do I get out of it?"

"A very important friend with connections."

"Hmm..." She tilted her head sideways. "Tempting. My mother warned me to pick my friends carefully."

"She's right, but sometimes you have to take a chance."

Alina smiled and then untied her pink robe again.

Hunter put his hand in the air. "I can't do this."

"Honey, you've already paid for it."

Hunter shook his head.

"Why not?" she asked.

"It's hard to explain."

She straddled him. "Don't you find me attractive?"

"Of course."

"Let me get this straight," Alina said. "You just want information?"

"I need information and the right connections."

"And so do I." She looked at him as if she had found an old penny and wondered if it had any value. Then she stood up, re-tied her robe and sat down in the chair next to the bed. "I have to admit this is a first for me."

"Me too," Hunter said.

She laughed and reached for a pack of Dunhills on her dresser. As she lit a cigarette, Hunter continued to sit on the bed with his hands folded. She seemed deep in thought as she played with her cigarette in the ashtray.

Finally, she frowned and pointed toward the door. "You should leave right now. Take the first flight out of Kiev and never return."

Hunter looked confused.

Alina inhaled deeply and blew the smoke out. "Do you have any idea what you're doing?"

Hunter's eyes darted around the room. "What do you mean?"

"Does anyone know you're here?"

"Only my boss."

Her eyes narrowed. "Anyone else?"

"No."

"Was this his brilliant idea?"

"Yes, well… sort of."

She frowned. "Some boss."

"Why?" Hunter asked.

"You have no concept of who you're messing with."

"I've done some research."

She shook her head. "Riiiight."

"I can take care of myself."

"I bet you can, Sweetie." She chuckled, and then her voice turned edgy. "These people would kill you in a minute if they knew you were a reporter. One word from me and your poor editor would never see you again." She stood up from her chair and held out her hand. "Give me all your cash."

Hunter pulled out $100 out of his pocket.

"That's not enough."

"That's more than the lady at the desk said you'd charge."

"That was before you told me you're a reporter. You'll get charged for my fee on your credit card, but I want additional cash."

"No way." Hunter stood up. "I want your manager. You're trying to screw me."

"Good luck with that." She laughed. "Make sure that you tell them you're an outraged reporter from the *New York Times,* and you're here to do a story about them."

Hunter stared at the floor and then slowly pulled out a roll of bills. "Okay, how much?"

She sized up the roll. "All of it."

"But she said $100!"

They stared at each other until Hunter handed over the roll. Alina reached for the money, but to her surprise, he didn't let go.

"What're you doing?" she said.

"I didn't get my interview."

"You idiot, I just saved your life." She pulled hard, and Hunter let go of the money. "Come back tomorrow night with another $500 in Deutsche Marks, and you'll get your interview." She put his cash in a small box next to the bed and then walked him to the door. "One more thing—next time, no recorder."

"But…"

She interrupted him, "It's my room, so it's my rules."

"Okay, but I want real information tomorrow."

"Trust me. You'll get everything you need."

"Why should I trust you?"

Alina leaned over and kissed him on the cheek. "Because I'm your friend."

Chapter 3

It took Hunter a few seconds to realize he wasn't still dreaming of Alina. The alarm on his desk clock went off. It was set for seven o'clock so he could be in his office before Tess got in. He swallowed three Advil for his splitting headache.

This is crazy, he thought. Maybe I should get out of New York City. A change for the better. Get a fresh start—away from the things that remind me of Alina. I'm sick of sleepless nights. Tired of trying to be what everyone else wants me to be. If I changed my name and disappeared, then maybe I could take a walk without worrying that someone is following me… open my apartment door without fear that someone's inside… sleep without a gun under my pillow. But if I vanished and Alina somehow had made it to New York as we had planned, she'd never find me. I couldn't live with that.

He was fortunate to have built a substantial resume since earning an undergraduate degree in Eastern European history and a master's in journalism at Columbia. Since returning from Kiev, the series of articles that he'd written for the *Times* on human trafficking had won a Pulitzer. Much to the annoyance of his boss, the award had catapulted him from a no-name reporter to a sought-after writer with numerous speaking engagements. His alma mater and a half dozen local colleges and universities on the east coast had contacted him about teaching a course on the era of a post-Soviet Union and the impact on Eastern

Europe. Although Cabot criticized him often and loved to make fun of him as a frumpy intellectual with no real-life experience, Hunter's academic background was ideal for covering the events that followed the collapse of the Soviet Union in 1990.

At first, he wasn't interested in these opportunities. He felt too exposed, too vulnerable. Even his boss didn't know the extent of the undisclosed information he had, evidence that could bring down governments and put some of the most prominent executives of major oil companies in prison. The information he possessed could also get he and Alina killed the minute it became public. It was Tess, his assistant, who had ironically insisted that he visit Ukraine to cover the tragic sex slavery industry in Eastern Europe. Initially, he imagined that he'd write the story at his New York desk based on the research of others. He never imagined that Cabot would actually send him to Ukraine. It seemed like just yesterday that Tess was goading him to be a man and take the assignment in Kiev.

Hunter's desk was covered with stacks of papers, unopened mail, the latest Zagat book of New York restaurants, a Far Side calendar, yellow memo pads, a leather notebook, and a weeks' worth of pink phone messages. He tossed a leftover box-lunch from yesterday into the wastebasket and listened to the first of four messages that Cabot had left. Cabot had no life. He was a short man who barely reached five-foot-two. Extremely insecure, he was always right about everything—just ask him. To make things worse, Cabot was envious of Hunter's natural writing ability.

Hunter booted up his computer as he listened to the remaining voice messages. While the Internet connected, he sipped coffee and skimmed the early edition of the *New York Times*. An article caught his eye: "Wednesday, May 31, 1997. FBI announces the arrest of a Boeing engineer for selling information on the latest fighter plane to the Russians." Hunter stared at the picture of a man in handcuffs hunched under a raincoat. How could he do that for the money? The man looked harmless with a round, friendly face. His graying hair was uncombed and stuck out randomly like Albert Einstein's in that famous picture.

Hunter examined the photograph more closely. The man looked surprised and scared as if he couldn't grasp what was happening. Poor bastard, Hunter thought, only an idiot would get caught doing something like that.

Tess poked her head into his office. "Good morning, Sunshine."

"I'm not your sunshine," he said.

Tess had been his assistant for five years, even though she could barely type and spent most of her time on the Internet. She was the antithesis of a corporate secretary, starting with her long kinky hair that changed color every other month. She bought all her clothes in funky secondhand boutiques in the Village and had a penchant for short leather skirts and large silver jewelry. Hunter imagined that she must own a million pairs of shoes and boots because she wore different footwear every day. Tess was something of an enigma. She was attractive in a simple way—tall and athletic-looking—but for some reason downplayed her looks, wearing her blond hair in a bun or ponytail. Hunter knew she was born in Brooklyn and didn't have any family—her mother had died in a car crash when Tess was eighteen and had lived on her own since. As far as he knew, she didn't have any living relatives.

Tess squinted at him. "How do you feel this morning?"

"I'm good."

"You don't look so good," she said, chomping on gum. "Did you look at yourself in the mirror before you came to work?"

"Yes." Hunter stared at his computer. "I looked fine."

"Are you kidding? You look like shit. I'm always amazed how people can look into a mirror and never see themselves."

"Are you forgetting something?"

"What?"

"I'm your boss."

"So."

"You should show me more respect."

"I'm just trying to help you out. Lord knows you need someone."

Hunter looked up from his computer. "Don't you have something else to do?"

Tess picked up his desk calendar. "Why is today's date circled in red?"

Hunter grabbed the calendar and set it back on his desk. "Never mind."

She thought for a moment, then said, "Kiev. I can't believe it's been two years since you came back. Remember the chaos in the office after you returned home? Whatever came out of those meetings with the FBI agents?"

"Nothing," Hunter said. "Listen, I really need to get some things done."

Tess ignored him. "I remember how tense everyone was when the FBI interviewed you about that American executive who was murdered in Kiev. What a coincidence that you were in Kiev when it happened." She paused. "Wasn't he an oil executive?" She wrinkled up her nose. "No, no, I remember. He was a banker from Brooklyn. I don't remember, actually, but wasn't an oil company somehow implicated in a money-laundering scheme with his bank?"

"I don't remember," Hunter said.

"I do. How could you forget?" She chomped her gum more aggressively. "Anyway, I've been reading all about this Russian mafia stuff. I think it's creepy—but fascinating. I came across an article written in, I think, 1995 by a woman named Claire Sterling. The story caught my eye because that was the same time you were living in Kiev."

"Do you actually read the news? I thought all you did in your free time was watch music videos and sing in Karaoke bars."

"Haha, very funny." Tess playfully poked him in the arm. "Pay attention, and you might learn something from me."

"That'll be a first."

"Ms. Sterling said that the syndication of the 'Moscow-Narco Group' is carried out by a Russian named Strasky, Stravinny, or something like that. Anyway, he makes over five hundred million dollars a year in drug trafficking, then launders the money and reinvests the dollars in legitimate enterprises. I saw another article that appeared in *New York* magazine and described how the Russian mob had received at least forty billion dollars from the United States over the previous two years—all of it in uncirculated hundred-dollar bills still in their Federal Reserve wrappers. The money came to them on flights from New York City five times per week. An official at the Federal Comptroller of the Currency office told the magazine that the laundered currency is used to support organized crime and yet it appears that at least part of the federal government sees nothing wrong with it. It's amazing that this fellow made this statement to the press. Do you know what happened after he disclosed this information?"

"No, what happened?"

"Nothing. Everyone knew it, but they all looked the other way."

"Tess, you're a fountain of information."

"I have a pornographic memory," she explained.

"Photographic."

"Whatever. Point is, important people in power knew that our government was sending forty billion dollars in uncirculated money to the Russian mafia! Aren't you shocked that our own government was involved in this?"

"Not really," Hunter muttered. "Nothing shocks me anymore."

"Well, I am. This is a story somebody should write."

Hunter didn't respond, which made her even more agitated.

"Are just trying to bug me?" she said.

Hunter pointed to his right ear, indicating he couldn't hear.

"Don't pull that on me. You can hear just fine."

"What? Did you say something?"

Tess rolled her eyes and put both hands on her hips.

Hunter thought she looked cute when she was mad. "You're always trying to save the world, but I need to finish this article before noon."

She shook her head. "You guys were cowards. Tell me, who were you more afraid of—our government or the Russian mafia?"

This touched a nerve. "Give me a break!"

"You always complain how your boss never lets you do anything worthwhile. You won all those awards for your articles on sex slavery, but you never pursued the bigger story. What you know could change things on an international level. This could be your chance. You could be the one to make a difference. You're such an amazing person... I don't understand why you can't see yourself that way."

"You don't understand."

"Hunter, these bad guys are already here. Right in our own backyard. Brighton Beach and Brooklyn are their beachheads for everything we stand against—drugs, human trafficking, money laundering—all controlled by the Russian mafia. But you're still acting as if it doesn't exist." She leaned closer to him. "What did those guys in black suits and wingtips say to make you and Cabot so scared?"

Hunter squirmed in his chair. "It's complicated."

"Hunter, you drive me crazy!" She stormed out of his office.

Hunter picked up the framed photo of Alina and glanced at the calendar. It was hard to believe that two years had passed since he returned from Kiev. Hunter recalled that first day back in the office after recovering from a series of plastic surgeries to repair the gunshot wound to his hand.

He hadn't been in any hurry to rehash with Cabot what had happened in Kiev. As he entered Cabot's office, his boss was yelling at someone on the phone and gesturing wildly as he paced. He stopped momentarily to point out the small wooden chairs in front of his huge oak desk—an example of how Cabot showed he was in control. The floor-to-ceiling windows provided a panoramic view of the Hudson River and the New York skyline that Hunter pretended to enjoy while he waited for the call to end.

Cabot finally hung up and sat down on his leather chair. "Goddamn corporate executives," he snarled. "They have no fucking idea what it's like to run a newspaper. By the way, the brass wants to have lunch with you later this week. Congratulations, you're the new 'Golden Boy.' They believe you have tremendous potential." Cabot shook his head. "What a joke."

Hunter crossed his arms. "Thanks for the vote of confidence."

"You know what I mean." Cabot tried to brush it off. "You're so fucking sensitive."

Cabot was Cabot. He wasn't going to change, so Hunter moved on. "How's Leah?"

"Crabby as usual." Cabot played with his cigar. "How's your hand?"

"Okay. Getting better. I'll have some permanent nerve damage."

Cabot leaned forward. "Let me see it."

Hunter gently lifted the bandage off his right hand.

Cabot studied the hand. "Christ, it looks like a Rottweiler got ahold of it."

"Very funny."

"Does it hurt?"

"They gave me some pain pills."

Cabot sat back in his chair and clipped the end of his cigar before shoving it in the corner of his mouth. He lifted a binder containing Hunter's articles from Kiev and held it up. "Where's the rest of the story?"

"So much for welcome home."

"This isn't what we discussed on the phone." He let the binder drop on his desk with a thud. "This isn't why I agreed to let you spend the summer in Kiev. Where are the client lists, the photos, the videos of the big corporate executives and government officials frolicking with underage girls and doing drugs in expensive brothels? That's the story I'm looking for, not this crap about poor young women trapped in prostitution." He leaned forward. "Where are the goods?"

"I told you," Hunter said. "After Karasov beat Alina, his thugs tore apart our apartment looking for any evidence I intended to bring back to New York. They took everything I had."

"How did Karasov and his thugs know you had information on them?"

"They suspected that I got some from Alina. Looking back, I was stupid and asked too many questions. Alina warned me, but I thought she was overreacting. She insisted I hide most of my evidence under floorboards in the bathroom. I didn't believe her until they broke into our flat."

"Did they find it?"

"Yes, I had a friend check after I left. They took it all."

Cabot stared back at Hunter like a poker player trying to decide if his opponent was bluffing. "Do you know what I think?"

Hunter shrugged.

"This is all bullshit," Cabot said. "I think you made up all this crap. You wrote a few feature articles on sex slavery, and now everyone thinks you're great. But what did I get out of it!" His face broke out in red splotches. "I was expecting record newspaper sales from your blockbuster revelations. Maybe a promotion and a raise. But I got nothing. You got a fucking Pulitzer Prize and a bunch of lucrative speaking engagements." His shoulders shook as he pointed at himself. "I should be the one getting the money and rewards, not you, for Christ's sake. I took a big risk sending you to Kiev."

Hunter laughed. "Risk? You were sitting on your ass in this big office while I was walking into a lion's den. You knew how dangerous it was for me to poke the Russian and Ukrainian mafia in the eye with all of the dumb questions you wanted me to ask." He fought to keep from throttling Cabot. "You'll never understand—things over there were very complicated. I did the best I could under the circumstances." Hunter pointed to his hand. "Shit, it almost got me killed."

"Cry me a river."

"You wouldn't feel that way if you saw the damage that human trafficking is doing to thousands of girls."

"Look, I can't change the world. I have a job that I like and want to keep. And you, my friend, are one of the ways that I can pay for my wife's expensive habits."

Hunter chuckled. "So now we are friends?"

"I want more from you. Give me an article by the end of the week that will sell newspapers."

Hunter knew that nothing he did was good enough for Cabot. If he made a mistake, he was criticized. Whenever he did something well, he rarely received any praise.

Cabot pointed to the binder containing Hunter's articles. "I don't get it. You sold me on a box of information that you said would make international news." He raised his hands in the air. "And now you want me to believe all that information is gone. Tell me I didn't spend a fortune just so you could have a summer affair with a prostitute."

Hunter clenched his jaw. "You have a short memory. I never wanted to go over there in the first place. You ordered me to Kiev, remember? I did my part, so give me a break. There are thousands of young women trapped in sex slavery in that part of the world. I wrote about it. What more do you want from me? No one else is lifting a finger to stop the shit going on over there. Not you, not our government, not the Ukrainian government—nobody!" Hunter rubbed his bad ear. "Do you know why?"

Cabot swiveled to stare out the window at the Hudson.

"You know damn well why!" Hunter's pent-up frustration was boiling over. "You knew that before you sent me over there. It's all about money. Corrupt money. There's so much fucking money flowing through Kiev it's hard to believe. Everyone's on the take. And I mean *everyone*. It's all about greed and power. The mafia has control of every important person and key corporation. I did my best. If that isn't good enough for you, then fuck it. Fire me."

Cabot briskly swiveled back to stare at Hunter, then clapped his hands together. "Nice speech." He smacked his hand on the desk. "Goddamn it. I wanted this project to sell newspapers, not win a bleeding-heart award. I gave you a great opportunity."

Hunter stood up. "Are we done?"

"Wait," Cabot growled, "is there any way to contact Alina and get that missing information again?"

"I have no idea if she's dead or alive."

"Maybe you should go back and find her."

"Are you kidding? They'd kill me the minute I stepped foot in Kiev. We're done." He turned and marched to the door.

"Hang on a second!"

Hunter opened the door but stopped and turned to face his boss.

Cabot had opened a file folder and was flipping through some photos as if the previous conversation had never happened. "What do you know about a Brooklyn banker that was murdered while you were in Kiev?"

"Nothing, why?"

"Apparently, he was last seen at the Rus' club."

"So what?"

"So they know Alina worked at the club, and you spent time there."

"Who do you mean, 'they'?" Hunter asked. "I never saw that banker."

"Tell that to the Feds," Cabot said, looking at his watch. "They contacted me just after you returned from Kiev. They'll be here in about twenty minutes to talk you and your goofball buddy, Vinny."

Hunter's stomach suddenly churned.

"Relax," Cabot said. "They just have a few questions. Just don't mention anything about that box of information under the floorboards."

"Did the FBI say what bank the guy worked for?"

"Some small community bank in Brooklyn. What would a banker from Brooklyn be doing in Kiev, and why would he end up dead in the Dnieper River?" Cabot asked.

"Must've had to do with money laundering."

"Damn." A grin spread across Cabot's face. "There's our story. I want you to get right on it."

"No way!" Hunter said, rubbing his ear. "Get someone else. The mafia in Brooklyn and Brighton Beach are controlled by the Russians and Ukrainians. They're ruthless."

Cabot stared at Hunter for a few seconds. "You know, I thought you really had something after I read the first couple of articles you wrote. I thought, 'Damn, the kid has finally got it. This could win you another Pulitzer Prize.' For the first time since you were hired, you wrote with passion. Instead of acting like an intellectual bookworm, you wrote as if you truly cared about something." Cabot rubbed his chin. "I remember how excited you were when you first called from Kiev, especially when you talked about Alina." He paused, then said, "I just don't get it."

"Get what?"

"What happened to you over there?"

"You have no idea."

Hunter closed the door behind him.

Chapter 4

Hunter sorted through his mail. Except for a few marketing pieces, the rest were bills. He stuffed an invoice from a company called "NYC Storage" into his briefcase. He had lied to Cabot about the box of damning information Alina had gathered. It had not been stolen by Karasov. Hunter had brought back the evidence, and it was locked at NYC Mini-Storage. After Karasov's thugs had taken Alina and shot Hunter, they had futilely trashed his apartment, searching for incriminating evidence. Fortunately, Hunter had arranged to have two trunks owned by Alina and several boxes of documents, videos and recordings accumulated by Hunter stored away from his flat.

Alina's trunks contained a who's who list of high-profile businessmen, oil executives and government clients who had engaged in sex, drugs and laundering of large sums of money through Alina's club. Karasov was a shrewd man and knew how to make money and protect himself. He had microphones and video cameras hidden throughout the club so he could document every move of important clients for blackmail purposes. Karasov also saved copies of their credit card receipts and wire confirmations of large sums of money to numerous Cayman bank accounts, evidence of laundering through various fake entities. These documents were his insurance against anyone trying to blackmail or kill him.

For her own protection, Alina had diligently made copies of the same recordings and documents without Karasov's knowledge. She stored them in those two trunks with extra cash she had siphoned off Karasov's operations and key clients.

For months after Hunter had returned to New York, he'd debated whether to write the real story—the story that went far beyond sex slavery. He struggled whether to publish the incriminating evidence and expose the corruption that was transpiring in Ukraine and Russia, including the involvement of the US government. The story would certainly gain instant national attention. Lots of people would go to prison. The story would prove to Cabot and everyone else that he wasn't a fraud. He didn't spend the summer wasting the company's money, drinking vodka all day, and sleeping with a prostitute. But that wasn't possible. He couldn't bring himself to do it because he wasn't sure if Alina was dead or alive. If by some miracle Alina was still alive, Karasov would kill her as soon as Hunter released the information to the public.

Though the images of young girls forced to entertain men in the brothel haunted his nights, he couldn't risk Alina's life. Instead of the full truth, Hunter had produced a sanitized series of articles that satisfied Cabot and won awards but didn't put Alina in danger.

Hunter scrolled through his emails. Since the *Times* had published the series on human trafficking, he had been inundated with messages from kooks. He stopped at a message from someone he didn't know named Carrie. It looked suspicious, but the subject line caught his attention: "Did you save anyone?" Curious, he read the text.

"Dear Mr. Moretti: I read your series on sex slavery in Ukraine. It was very good, but I'm curious, what happened after you left? Did it change anything? Did you save any of the girls? Carrie"

He wondered who Carrie was. On the Internet, you could never be sure, but his curiosity won over his suspicion. He rubbed his fingers together and typed a response.

"Dear Carrie, thank you for your note. I'm glad you liked my series on human trafficking, but I'm not sure what you mean by 'save someone.' I portrayed my experience as honestly as possible. I reported what I saw. I'm not the law. I had no power to change anything. You wouldn't understand, but it was a very complicated situation. H"

He hit the send key and was scrolling through the rest of his emails when a beep indicated that he had received a response from Carrie.

"I thought it was interesting that you used the word, honestly," Carrie had written. "How does a reader know if the writer is honest or not? Are good intentions enough to substitute for honesty, or is there another standard? Carrie"

Hunter quickly responded. "Are you questioning the accuracy of my story or my integrity? H"

Another beep announced Carrie's succinct reply. "Take your pick."

Hunter answered, "I was just trying to do something to help those poor girls." After several minutes without a response, he went to the break room for coffee. When he returned, there was another message waiting.

"Why are you so defensive?"

Hunter typed back, "Defensive? You weren't there. I just wrote the facts." He smacked the send button and reached for a jug of antacid tablets in his drawer.

A few minutes later the computer beeped. "And did your facts make any difference?"

Hunter was fed up with this nonsense. He had an article to submit before two o'clock that afternoon and needed to prepare for a night class he was teaching at Columbia. He tried to concentrate on his work but couldn't stop thinking about Carrie. After lunch, he checked for new emails again. The first one on the list was from Carrie.

"Why did you write this story? Carrie"

Hunter stared at the computer screen. Alina's words echoed in his mind. He remembered exactly where he was when she'd asked him the same question. He was working at his desk in their Kiev flat. She had just woken from a nap, and her red hair was partially covering her sleepy eyes. He hadn't known how long she had been watching him work before she'd asked why he was writing this story.

Hunter leaned back in his chair and stared at the New York skyline, memories of the previous summer flooding back. He recalled landing at the airport, a frightened young reporter barely capable of making his way to the hotel. Initially, he'd struggled to complete simple tasks in Kiev such as currency conversion, much less navigate the complex underworld of the mafia and the sex slave industry. Nevertheless, after three months, he had evolved into a more confident and capable investigative reporter.

So why was he struggling now with how to respond to Carrie? His fingers hovered over the keyboard with indecision, waiting for direction from his brain, which seemed to be waiting for a message from his heart. Finally, he took a deep breath and typed, "I had a very different agenda when I arrived in Kiev. I never wanted the assignment in the first place. I was repulsed by everything when I arrived in Kiev—the dirty hotel, the people desperate for jobs, the decaying city, the bad food. But then I met Alina…" Hunter stopped writing because he couldn't see the blurry letters on the screen. He hesitated, then hit the cancel key, and walked away.

Chapter 5

The next day, Hunter grabbed a cup of coffee from Tess and asked her to join him in his office.

"Tess, can you grab the door?"

"Here we go." She rolled her eyes. "Isn't it a little early to have a serious talk?"

"I'm trying to apologize for yesterday, and you're busting my chops."

"An apology?" She peered suspiciously at Hunter. "Who is this? Must be an imposter. Are you going to say you're sorry?"

"Not sure I have to go that far."

"You should try it sometime. Just takes a little practice. Repeat after me, 'I'm sorry.'"

"Tess, you are the…"

She interjected before he could finish. "…best thing that ever happened to me."

They burst into laughter.

Hunter loved Tess's laugh. It was impossible to stay mad at her. He couldn't help but smile whenever she'd squeeze her eyes, throw her head back and laugh—the same way his mother used to laugh. Hunter was only ten when his mother had died, but he never forgot her joyful laughter.

"Why are you looking at me that way?" Tess said.

Hunter quickly looked away. "I really need to get some work

done."

"Are you okay?"

"Yes," he said. "You've already made a mess of my morning. Now get out of here."

"Okay." She walked out the door. "Yell if you need anything."

Hunter reviewed his Thursday schedule and checked his email and found another message from Carrie: "Since you didn't respond yesterday, I assume that I offended you. If I did, I'm sorry. Carrie"

Hunter typed a response that surprised him with its length. "That's okay. I was just busy yesterday. Have you ever started a project with one idea, only to find yourself swept up in a completely different direction? That's what happened to me in Kiev. I was so naïve. Everything there was upside down. The landscape changed almost daily. Bad was good. Good was bad. Under those conditions, everyone had a little of both. Power was all about control. Self-preservation replaced compassion. The whole country was in anarchy. People were desperate. No functioning government. No jobs. The ex-KGB officers running the mafia understood weakness better than anyone. The most vulnerable are always the women, especially the teenagers and young adults who have no power to protect themselves. Whether by desperation or force, prostitution stripped these girls of everything they owned, including their self-worth and dignity. I tried to explain this tragedy in my articles. You have to see it to really understand how horrendous the situation was for thousands of women. The worst part is no hope on the horizon or anyone who cares enough to stop this tragedy. H"

Carrie responded: "Do you think those girls can ever find someone to love them after what they've been forced to do? Are they damaged goods forever?"

Hunter: "We're all damaged goods. Spiritually, we're only as weak as our secrets. If these women can find the courage, they have to trust someone again—they have to let a man love them for who they are."

Carrie: "But what if every time they attempt to trust someone, they get hurt again?"

Hunter: "Are you speaking from experience?"

Carrie: "No, I just want to understand why it's so hard to find real love."

Hunter: "Some people tend to pick the wrong person to love."

Carrie: "But how do you know if the person you pick is the right one?"

The cursor blinked on and off while Hunter stared at the screen, suddenly at a loss for words.

Carrie: "Are you still there?"

Hunter: "A friend once told me to trust your heart."

Carrie: "What if your heart is a liar?"

Hunter: "Then, you have a problem."

Carrie: "But what if you don't see it? What if you can't see yourself? What would your buddy suggest to fix that?"

Hunter: "My friend is a she."

Carrie: "Someone you loved?"

Hunter: "I thought so."

Carrie: "Did she hurt you?"

The blue cursor blinked like his brain, stuck somewhere between on and off. Finally, he typed: "Why all the questions?"

Carrie: "I have a confession."

Hunter: "Sorry, I'm not a priest."

Carrie: "I'm in your night class."

Hunter pulled his fingers away as if he'd touched a hot stove.

Damn, she's a student in my journalism class, he thought. I'm such an idiot. I wonder how old she is. I shouldn't have this kind of conversation with a female student.

"I have to go," he typed, then turned off his computer and paced around his office before deciding to go out for an early lunch. Outside, he watched hundreds of people hurrying along the sidewalks. He stepped into the moving mass and wondered how he could feel so alone in such a crowd. He'd never felt that way walking the streets in Kiev.

Later that evening, Hunter strolled quickly into the large auditorium of an academic building on the Columbia campus. He was late, sweating, and out of breath. Setting his briefcase on the table, he regretted agreeing to teach a night class in journalism. Standing on the stage, he looked at his name, which he'd just scribbled on the blackboard, and realized that it looked as if a third grader had written it. Embarrassed, he turned to face the class. Two hundred eager students stopped talking and waited for him to speak. He suddenly realized he had no business teaching a journalism class. Writing numerous articles didn't qualify him to impart anything of value to these students. He wanted to give them their money back and go home.

"Let's get started." His voice gurgled as if he had something caught in his throat. "Excuse me." He coughed, took a deep breath and tried again. "Welcome to our second class of the summer session. I was just like you ten years ago. I'm not here to proclaim any special talent or expertise. However, I want to empower you to follow your heart and set a goal to find your passion—find something or someone to love—preferably both."

The students all laughed. "Journalism's not about writing. It's about people—about experiencing the lives of ordinary and extraordinary people and then telling their story. I can teach you the craft, but not the art. You have to find that on your own. Each of you has a story that drives you to write, or you wouldn't be here today. If I asked for a show of hands, I'm positive that all of you would admit that you have a voice that wakes you in the middle of the night—a voice that won't let you get back to sleep. Understand that voice is your soul with a story trying to find its way onto paper. That's what we will discuss this semester."

Hunter stopped for a second and sipped from a glass of water on the podium. "I know this is a journalism class and not creative writing 101, but I want you to take out a piece of paper and write for ten minutes. Don't think about what you're writing. Just let your hand write whatever comes to your mind."

Two hundred faces frowned in confusion.

Hunter raised his hand. "No catch... and don't worry, your writing will not be graded. Just sign your name and set your paper on my desk when you leave."

After ten minutes, he resumed lecturing. "I'm sure that you're wondering why I gave you this assignment. I wanted to remind you of the joy of writing. Sometimes, as journalists, we can lose sight of why we write. So always consider why you do what you do—why it's important to you, and how it can help someone else. Put that into your writing, otherwise, your stories will become academic and boring."

He scanned the room and realized that they probably had no clue what he meant. "Class dismissed. See you next week."

As the students filed out, he packed his briefcase and wondered if Carrie would introduce herself. He waited until the auditorium was empty, but she didn't. It's probably better this way, he thought.

He took a taxi back to the East Village, stopping to pick up dinner for himself and Angel, his cat. Back at his one-bedroom apartment, he flicked on the light and whistled for Angel. She was a stray that he'd found half-dead and abandoned after he returned from Kiev. He'd never owned a pet before, but there was something special about this cat. Besides, he was tired of living alone.

He whistled again, but clearly, she wasn't ready to come out of her hiding place, so he unpacked the food and cracked open a beer. Angel was a red tabby with an attitude. She only let him touch her when she wanted it. In total control, Angel treated Hunter as her pet, not the other way around. He was rather amused by it.

Hunter took another sip of his beer. Pasta sounded good tonight. Hunter loved to cook. There was something about food that made him happy. When you are Italian, cooking is in your blood, and kitchens were a place of love. When he was ten, he remembered how his parents would tease, laugh and smooch in the kitchen like teenagers. His mother believed that food was another language of love. She made a basil pesto pasta that made grown men weep with pleasure, a lemon clam linguini that fostered many dreams, and a three-cheese ravioli so decadent her fans called them "pillows of love."

Hunter missed those meals. Missed his mom. Growing up in foster homes was not the same. Most meals were on his own. There was no laughter in the kitchens.

A stack of essays from class waited for his review after dinner. His students didn't know he had no formal training to teach. The first dozen essays were what he expected. Most of the writers were trying too hard to compose something beautiful or profound. Halfway through the pile, he picked up one that had a single line written on it and no author name: "I read your series. You're a good man."

Hunter quickly sat up. Alina's the only person ever to say that to me, he thought. What if she isn't dead? What if she found a way to get to New York? She still had the fake passport I gave her.

He squeezed his eyes, trying to forget Alina's face covered in blood, her arms reaching out for him to do something, her voice calling his name. This is stupid, he thought. She would've contacted me if she had survived.

He could never forget the whites of her eyes rolled back in her head and the jagged white bone exposed in the wide gashes of her forehead and eye socket. Her bloody face had haunted him every night since he'd returned to New York.

She's gone, he thought, and there was nothing I could've done to stop Karasov. I was pushed against the wall with a gun to my head. I thought I was dead. What would anyone else have done?

Chapter 6

The next morning, Hunter walked through a maze of office cubicles to Vinny's desk. They had grown up in the same Italian neighborhood and had started working for the *Times* the same summer after college. Hunter considered Vinny his best friend.

"Vinny."

"Hey, Hunter… what's up?" Vinny didn't take his eyes off the sports page as he munched on an egg bagel sandwich.

"I see you're hard at work."

"It's Friday." Vinny turned the page and took another bite. "This place is a shithole, and Cabot treats us like slaves."

"Why don't you quit and go somewhere else."

"Because I'd probably have to move from New York. My bride would kill me for taking her away from her crazy mother and goofy sisters." Vinny laughed and took another bite. "What about you? Ever think of taking a job somewhere else?"

"Sometimes."

"So, what's stopping you? Oh right—now you're a big shot."

"Not funny."

"Hunter, the famous author and international reporter. I knew you when you were a nobody from Brooklyn."

"And you're still a mutt from the same neighborhood."

"Can I have your autograph?"

"Fuck you. I'm no different than before."

"Ahh, not true." Vinny waved his finger at Hunter. "The brass upstairs think you're brilliant. I heard they want to groom you for Cabot's job."

"Don't believe everything you hear. Remember when we first met?"

Vinny scratched his head. "Yeah, in first grade… on the first day of school. Your mother held our hands and walked us to school. She was so beautiful. She was always singing something, and she had the best laugh." Vinny sighed. "I loved your mom."

"She loved you too."

"Okay, what can I do for you?" Vinny asked.

"I need a favor."

"Nope."

"What do you mean, no," Hunter said. "You don't even know what I'm going to ask."

"I'm not doing a thing for you until you pay back the money you borrowed and then proceeded to waste on booze and fucking sleazy European women all over New York."

"I should be getting another royalty check soon. I'll pay you back then."

Vinny looked at him in pretended disgust. "How many times have I heard that?"

"But I always pay you back."

"Not the point. You're killing yourself, and I don't want any part of your demise."

"Come on, Vinny, it's not that bad. I need to cut back a little, sure, but you're always so damn dramatic."

"Have you looked at yourself in the mirror lately?"

"Don't start on me again. You're no saint. Who the hell bailed you out when you got caught stealing candy from Jimmy's grocery store?"

"Big deal. We were ten."

"Okay, just forget it." Hunter rubbed his bloodshot eyes.

"Look…" Vinny's voice softened. "I want to help because I'm worried about you. Since you returned from Kiev, you walk around either hung-over or depressed. You eat crap, and you drink like a fish. You never smile, never talk to no one except Tess. When was the last time you laughed at anything? We used to go out and have some beers, but you never want to do that anymore." Vinny stopped for a second. "You're my buddy, but you need help."

"Are you going to lecture me or help me?"

"Okay, no more lectures."

"Good, now help me find Alina."

Vinny rolled his eyes toward the ceiling. "Here we go again."

"No one must know what you are doing," Hunter said.

"I'll help, but listen to me," Vinny said. "We've gone down this road before, and it ended badly. Please, I'm begging you as your best friend, leave it alone and move on with your life."

"I have to know what happened to her."

Vinny frowned. "She's dead, and there's nothing you could've done to save her."

"But what if she didn't die?"

"Hunter, drop it!" He didn't mean to yell, so he quickly lowered his voice. "I'm serious—let's pretend we never had this conversation."

"I can't. There isn't a day that I don't regret going back to find her."

Vinny tilted his chair back and stretched out his long legs. He had the uncoordinated, gangly body of a high school boy that had grown too fast. "Why now? Why after all this time?"

Hunter stiffened.

Vinny squinted at Hunter. "What's wrong? Did something happen to you since yesterday?"

"I think Alina's in New York."

Vinny laughed. "Riiiight! And I still believe in the Tooth Fairy." Vinny stopped laughing when he saw that Hunter wasn't smiling. "You told me she was dead when they dragged her out of your flat in Kiev."

"That's what I thought."

"She's like heroin to you."

"But what if she's really in New York?"

"Even if we assume for a second that she's alive, how would she get here?"

"She hid a fake passport in the false bottom of her purse. I gave her the passport just before Karasov found us in the flat."

"It's been two years since you last saw her," Vinny said. "If she were still alive, she would've contacted you or at least gotten a message to you somehow."

"I know, but there's something else."

"Like what?"

"She talks to me in my dreams."

Vinny sighed. "Goddamn it, not that again."

"This is different."

"Oh, really? What did your psychiatrist say about this shit the last time?"

"That doctor's a quack. She doesn't understand anything."

"And you do?" Vinny shook his head. "You still hear voices?"

"No."

"When was the last time you had a session with your shrink?"

"She just wants to put me on drugs."

"She's trying to help you."

"Like you?" Hunter said.

"Exactly, that's why I'm not giving you another loan. You've wasted all the money from the sale of your story." Vinny pulled a sheet of paper from his desk drawer. "See this? It's a list of dates and dollar amounts of the money you've borrowed from me. Shit, you still owe me six hundred fifty dollars."

"I told you—I'll pay you back."

"Hunter, talk to me. You were doing so well lately, and now this. What happened?"

Hunter looked at his shoes and shifted his weight. "Somebody turned in a note for a class assignment. It could've only come from Alina."

"A note?" Vinny scowled. "What did it say?"

"I was a good man."

"What the hell does that mean?" Vinny leaned back in his chair. "Girls say that kind of shit all the time, especially if they want an 'A' from a certain professor."

Hunter shook his head. "You don't understand. Alina's the only person in the world ever to say that to me."

Vinny rubbed his jaw. "Did you see any girls in the auditorium that looked like Alina?"

"I wasn't looking."

"Tell me what happened in the class?"

"On the second night class of summer session, I asked the students to do a free-write exercise. Later that night, I found the note in the pile of essays. I swear, it looked just like her handwriting."

"This makes no sense. Why would she do that instead of walking right up to you?"

Hunter shrugged and folded his arms. "You're right. I'm just acting stupid."

Vinny got out of his chair and put his arm around Hunter. "I'm your friend, right?"

Hunter nodded.

"I want to help because you've been totally fucked up since you got back from Kiev. Have you forgotten what you were like when you returned?"

Hunter remained silent.

"For Christ sake, you were drunk on and off for almost a year. If you weren't Cabot's Golden Child, he would've fired you long ago. I don't want to hurt your feelings, but you aren't the same Hunter that I knew before you met Alina. You act like an old man. Your jet-black hair went salt and pepper overnight. All you do is work and then disappear at night. It's as if you're paralyzed or stuck in some kind of twilight zone. I know you loved this Alina, but Hunter, buddy—you have to get to on with your life."

Hunter turned toward a large window and looked out over the sea of skyscrapers that dominated a city of over twenty million people. Even if Alina miraculously had made it to Manhattan, he knew he'd never find her unless she reached out to him. He closed his eyes for a second, remembering Alina lying hot and sweaty on white sheets after making love on those long summer afternoons in Kiev.

Everything had seemed so clear back then.

Pete Carlson

* * *

Drifting somewhere between consciousness and his dream-self, Hunter slowly opened his eyes and reached out for Alina, but her side of the bed was already cold. She must've left for the club while he was asleep. She was so different from what he'd expected—so smart, articulate and charming. She knew everything about the sex trade, the money laundering, and the mafia. It would've taken Hunter years to collect this kind of information through other sources. Alina was all he thought about, and he couldn't wait until he saw her again at the club this evening.

Hunter dressed and ordered room service. After dinner, he set the tray in the hall and surveyed the chaos in his hotel room. A pile of dirty clothes occupied one corner, while boxes of research information were stacked high in the opposite corner. Several drafts of his articles were strewn on his desk. He reviewed his notes from the last interview with Alina and noticed that some of the information conflicted with what she'd told him in the previous meetings. Her story had changed. He glanced at his watch. It was only nine o'clock in Kiev, but three in the afternoon in New York. He was long overdue to contact the office, so he placed a call.

"Vinny, hi, it's me, Hunter."

"Hey—how's your trip so far?"

"Interesting."

"I bet," Vinny said. "What a hardship to interview prostitutes all night. I don't know how you do it."

"It's not what you think."

"Oh, really. Hard to believe."

"Listen, I need you to do something for me," Hunter said. "Run a check on a woman named Alina Alan. She told me she grew up on a small farm in Ossetia but attended the Odessa National University in Ukraine. Run the same thing on a guy named Vladimir Karasov. I saw a photo of him before I left. Check with our European office. They must've done a story on him at some point." Hunter switched the phone to his other ear. "Vinny, do it quietly. No one needs to know."

"No problem." Vinny chuckled. "What are they like?"

"What do you mean?"

"You know—European prostitutes."

"You're an idiot," Hunter said. "They're very different than girls in America—very sensual and erotic—something you wouldn't understand."

"Try me... come to papa," Vinny whined. "Remember, I sit in a cubicle all day. Help me out with some good stories."

"I don't have any."

"I read that they're supposedly wild."

"Who are you kidding? You don't read," Hunter said. "You only look at magazines with fold-outs."

"And what's wrong with that? The human body is a work of art," Vinny said. "Tell me, does she moan in Russian when you jump her bones?"

"Alina's not like that."

"That's an interesting way to describe a whore."

"And I'd describe you as a nice asshole from Brooklyn."

"I hear they don't shave their armpits, but they shave their beavers."

"You're sick," Hunter said. "Listen, I'll call you again in a couple of weeks."

Chapter 7

Hunter's first month in Ukraine was a blur. It didn't take long before he was considered a VIP at the Rus'. Most of the staff knew him by his first name, and he loved the attention. In the States, women never noticed him, much less flirted with him. But in Kiev, three or four nights per week, he sat in his usual booth drinking Russian vodka and champagne surrounded by a room full of beautiful, half-naked women. He was living the dream. He was somebody. For the first time in his life, he belonged somewhere.

Alina traveled every other week for two to three days but never disclosed where she went. Whenever Hunter pressed her for an explanation, she brushed him off and told him the travel was business.

Hunter loved to watch Alina work in the club. There was a definite hierarchy to the staff and the girls. Alina was the queen bee in the center of the hive. She would perch on a stool at the bar and supervise the ladies. All the girls pandered to her, making sure they stayed in her good graces. Hunter noticed that Alina rarely mingled with the men. She only entertained a client if he was considered extremely important by Karasov.

One night, Alina was running late, so the hostess ushered Hunter down to her room to wait. Sweet incense and a half dozen fragrant candles created a fragrance that was as intoxicating and mysterious as Alina.

Several minutes later, Alina opened the door and rushed in. "I'm so sorry." She hugged him. "I had some business to take care of."

"What kind of business?"

"We had some new girls starting this week, and I needed to spend some time with them."

"You do that with all the new girls?"

"Yes, why?"

"Just curious."

Alina set her purse on the desk, removed a red wrap and hung it on a hook next to her bed. She turned around. "What do you want to talk about this time?"

Hunter got out a pen and notebook.

"Where do these new girls come from, and how do they get here?"

"They're recruited."

"From where?"

"All over—Eastern Europe, Ukraine, Georgia, Russia, India, Asia."

"Do they come of their own free will?"

"Not exactly."

"Please explain."

"It's complicated." She lit a cigarette. "Let's talk about something else."

"I want to interview some of the new girls."

"No." Alina frowned.

"Come on. I need to find out how they got here. It's important to know their background for my research. This is the main reason I'm in Kiev."

Alina's voice turned firm and cold. "No, I will not allow you to interview them. You can come here every night to dance, eat and drink unlimited champagne, but I forbid you to ask the girls any questions about their past or how they got here."

"What about Karasov? I'd like to interview him."

"Are you crazy? If he knew you were a reporter, you'd be dead before morning."

Hunter frowned. "Then what the hell am I paying you for?"

"Trust me. I know everything, and I can keep you from getting hurt."

"I don't see how this arrangement will work."

"How long have we known each other?"

"Over a month," Hunter said.

Alina sat down on the bed and snuggled up close to him. "You like me, don't you?"

"Of course."

"And do you want to continue seeing me?"

"Yes." Hunter blushed.

She pulled away from him. "Then you should stop coming here."

"Why?" he said, surprised. "Are you trying to get rid of me?"

"On the contrary." She lowered her voice, "I want to suggest a different arrangement. One that is just between you and me."

"What do you have in mind?"

"I can become your consultant."

"Consultant?" Hunter grinned.

"I have a number of unique skills, important contacts, and information you'll never get on your own."

"I'll have to think about that."

She kissed his neck. "You better not think too long, or I might change my mind."

"What about the club? Will anyone have a problem with our new arrangement?"

She jerked her thumb toward the door. "Why should I give them any money? I can cut your expenses in half. You're paying double by coming to the club." She paused for a second to let the suggestion sink in. "I can help you much more if we met somewhere else. There are too many eyes and ears in this building."

"You could come to my hotel," Hunter suggested.

"No," she said. "It must be somewhere safe, where people will not pay any attention to us. As an American, I guarantee you've been observed since you arrived." She chewed on the inside of her cheek. It made her look like a little girl. "I have a friend that's out of the country on business. She's gone for the next three months. Her flat's in a quiet neighborhood not too far from here. It's small and nothing fancy, but we could use it."

Hunter folded his arms because he didn't know what to do with his hands.

"What's wrong?" Alina asked.

"I don't know. Everything's happening so fast."

She glanced at the clock next to the bed. "We still have a half-hour. Let's see if I can convince you." She took his hand and gently pulled him toward the bed. "Remember when we first met, and I promised to give you an experience you'd never forget?"

He nodded, powerless, under a spell he couldn't explain.

"It's time for you to find out what I meant. I will teach you how to make a woman feel good in bed."

* * *

The next day, Hunter called Vinny. It was almost six o'clock Kiev time, and he estimated that it was just after lunch in New York.

"Vinny here."

"Did you get the information I need?"

"Yes, but first, tell me what's so special about this Alina?"

"She's amazing. I'm so lucky to have found her because she's an incredible source of information."

"Well, I know she's good at one thing."

"What's that?"

"Telling lies," Vinny said. "None of the information you gave me checked out. I think she's giving you a ride."

"What?" Hunter said. "Are you sure?"

"She's not who she appears to be."

"I don't believe it."

"She's like a ghost. Our boys in research are having a hell of a time finding information on her. I'd be very careful until I get more information."

"What about Karasov?"

"Just some sketchy information so far. Definitely one of the bad guys. The head of one of the most powerful mafias in Ukraine. From what we hear, he's slippery and very dangerous. He served in World War II with the Ukrainian Freedom Fighters. He was only a kid, barely sixteen when he joined the fight. They fought the Germans alongside the Russians, but the battle lines sometimes were blurry."

"What do you mean by that?"

"There were a number of competing Ukrainian militia groups that clashed during and after the war. They occasionally fought each other for power and the spoils of war. The history of Ukraine is all very complicated between the Germans, Russians, Jews, Poles, KGB and the mafia."

"What happened to Karasov after the war?"

"Toward the end of the war, Karasov realized that Germany was losing, so he aligned with the Russians. After the war, he rose quickly up the ranks of the KGB and became a big shot until the Soviet Union collapsed. The KGB splintered into several regional groups that now make up a loosely aligned mafia that took over and filled the vacuum created by the fall of Communism."

"So, he's now Russian mafia."

"Right. Toward the end of 1992, there's evidence that the Russian mafia took control of almost all the banks and major commercial enterprises. Organized crime now employs most of the working population, kind of like how the Communist party used to control everything. The guys in the CIA call this new social system a 'mafiocracy.' Incredible, huh? The reports indicate that in Russia and Ukraine, there are over five thousand organized crime groups with over a hundred thousand members controlled by an oligarchy of somewhere near two hundred ruthless men. Because of the economic and political meltdown that occurred after the collapse of the Soviet Union, the mafia took control of the fifteen remnant countries that spun off as independent nations."

"Alina was right. This is much bigger than I ever imagined."

"Here's the most interesting thing. Right now, about eighty percent of all commercial businesses, including banking and oil, are either infiltrated, owned or controlled by the mafia. They control almost all the revenue generated by commerce and over forty percent of all the wealth in these countries. Can you believe that?"

"If that's true," Hunter said, "think about the implications of that control of oil and gas over most of Europe. It's incredible!"

"Yet the public is virtually ignorant about this leverage by the Russian mafia. The amount of money involved in the pipeline to Europe must be in the billions annually. This must be one of the best kept secrets in the world. Maybe the biggest consortium of organized crime the world has ever seen. And you're in the middle of it."

"I had no idea," Hunter said.

"Sorry for the history lesson."

"We covered the collapse of the Soviet Union at the *Times*, but I never knew the details of what happened after the communists lost power."

"Listen to me, and don't ever forget this," Vinny said. "Your buddy, Karasov, is head of one of the largest mafia groups in the world, so you be very careful. This is one scary, powerful man."

The phone was silent for a few seconds.

"Thanks for the warning," Hunter said.

"What's Alina telling you lately?"

"She has a list of clients for sale."

"A what?"

"She claims to have a customer list that would rock our government and Europe," Hunter said. "It will expose some very high-profile government officials and prominent businessmen."

"Who cares?" Vinny said. "It's only sex. They'll sweep it under the rug. That stuff won't change anything. There's too damn much money at risk."

"You sound just like Alina."

"Besides, prostitution has been around forever."

"I know, but you should see how many underage girls are trapped in these clubs. Human trafficking should get somebody's attention."

"Not the kind of attention you want. The mafia kills people for a lot less than what you're writing about."

"But Vinny, there's more—a lot more."

"Like what?"

"It's like the Wild West over here. Corruption is a normal part of doing business. The kickbacks, graft and bribery are just commonplace.

So are drugs, money laundering, illegal arms sales… You name it, and I guarantee it's traded in this club."

"That will not get any traction. Within a few days, no one will care or remember."

"What if our government was involved?"

"What are you saying?"

"Nothing yet."

"Are you crazy? Do you know how dangerous that could be?"

"If we put the spotlight on our government, it'll be harder for the mafia to continue running the human trafficking pipeline."

"What kind of spotlight are you talking about?"

"I want you to go to the payphone across the street and call me back as soon as you get there." He gave his phone number.

"What's the big mystery."

"I want you to swear that you'll not talk about this to anyone."

"Come on. You sound paranoid."

"Swear to me. I'm not kidding. Just call from the payphone."

A few minutes later, Vinny called back.

"All right," Vinny said. "So now you can tell me what's the big deal."

"Alina has information that would put many people in prison."

"Like who? Is this about the sex business?"

"Much bigger. I found something I wasn't looking for. This is about corruption in the oil and gas industry in Ukraine. It runs in the billions of dollars every year."

The phone went silent.

"Vinny, are you there?"

"Yes."

"Alina has information that proves there is highly coordinated corruption by our government and prominent oil and gas executives in Texas." Hunter paused. "This goes all the way to our president."

"Shit," Vinny said. "How do you know she's telling you the truth?"

"She promised to deliver to me copies of all the documents that prove what I'm saying."

"Why do you believe her?" Vinny said.

Hunter didn't answer.

"You have to get proof," Vinny said. "You need copies of receipts, photos, recordings, videos…"

"She said she'll give me everything."

"Even if she has the proof, why would she give it to you?"

"She wants money—a lot of money. And she knows the *Times* can pay."

"Why would she risk her life?"

"Because if she can sell this information, she can leave Kiev and disappear."

"I've known you since first grade, but you're a dumb shit."

"Vinny, I can save her."

"What if she doesn't want anyone to save her?"

"That's crazy."

"What if this is who she is? What if she loves the life of champagne and diamonds more than she loves you?"

"You don't understand."

"Maybe *you* don't understand. You can't make her into something you want her to be. She may be addicted to the money and the lifestyle. She's living in luxury compared to everyone else in Ukraine. Do you realize that the average annual income today in Ukraine and Russia is only $2,500 per year?"

"She told me she hates living in Kiev. She hates Karasov and everything he stands for. She wants to leave as soon as possible."

"Hunter, you're so naïve. Who are you really trying to save—you or her?"

"I've got to go."

"Wait, you're a fool if you believe her," Vinny said.

"But what if she's telling the truth?"

"Then she's a dead woman the day after you publish the story," Vinny paused. "Hunter, you're my best friend, but they could kill you too."

"I really have to go."

"What should I tell Cabot?"

"Nothing," Hunter said. "I'll call you again later this week. Remember, from now on, all future calls must be from a random payphone."

"I hope you know what you're doing."

Chapter 8

The taxi ride from Hunter's hotel to the flat of Alina's friend took fifteen minutes. Her flat was in a quiet, residential neighborhood outside of Kiev, yet close to the club. Carrying his bags to the front door, he nodded to an old woman knitting a blue sweater on the stoop. She wore a long summer dress with a matching green babushka and black orthopedic shoes.

"Dobroho ranku. Good morning," Hunter said, pausing in front of her.

Her fingers never stopped knitting, and she didn't smile. Staring at his suitcases and western-style clothes, she suspiciously answered, "Dobroho ranku."

He was surprised at how small the second-floor flat was compared to his one-bedroom apartment back home. It was configured as one great room with dark wooden floors. Two windows faced the street, a queen-sized bed hugged one side flanked by a rust-colored couch, glass coffee table, and two brown side-chairs. Hunter set his luggage down and walked over to examine a white oak desk and wooden chair positioned under the windows. He ran his finger along the oak grain and looked around.

This may work out well, he thought.

The kitchen occupied the opposite end of the flat with barely room for a small table and four wooden chairs. The white enameled appliances were old and rusty. There was no space for a dishwasher.

Hunter could hear voices and footsteps through the paper-thin walls. The only room with a door was a small bathroom that smelled like a backed-up sewer. It didn't take Hunter long to unpack, so he spent the rest of the day trying to catch up on his writing.

The next morning, he found a small market around the corner that was stocked with fresh produce and meats from local farmers. He selected a dozen brown eggs out of a large basket, a loaf of fresh bread, milk, and a handful of fresh-cut summer flowers.

A few hours later, he heard footsteps coming down the hall. The lock clicked, the metal door handle squeaked and the door pushed open. A woman stepped into the room wearing a blue warm-up suit, pink sneakers, sunglasses and a babushka. Startled at first by the intruder, Hunter quickly recognized that it was Alina and rushed over to grab her coat and bag.

She took off her sunglasses, sneezed and wiped her nose. "Thanks, you're sweet."

"Are you getting a cold?"

She shrugged. "Could be allergies."

"How was work?" The words barely left his mouth when he realized the stupidity of his question.

She ignored him and walked over to the couch. "I'm hungry. Do we have anything to eat?"

He kept staring at her. She looked so different than at the club. "What would you like for breakfast?" he asked.

"Eggs would be nice."

"An omelet?"

"Wonderful."

He rushed toward the kitchen and tripped over the bag he had just set down.

"Slow down," Alina laughed. "We have all day." She started to make coffee.

She didn't look as glamorous as in the club, but Hunter liked her much better without the heavy makeup.

Suddenly, she looked up. "What's wrong?"

"Nothing. Why?"

"You're staring at me."

He turned away and focused on cracking the eggs. "I'm just glad you're here."

She leaned against the kitchen counter.

"I know the place isn't what you're used to in New York," she said.

"This will work." Hunter began whisking the eggs into a yellow froth. "I already met one of our neighbors and found a cute market around the corner."

She rubbed her eyes and yawned.

"You look tired," he said.

"I'm okay."

He peered closer and noticed large bruises on her neck. "What happened there?"

Unconsciously, she rubbed the bruised area. "Nothing."

"It's more than nothing." He motioned for her to come closer. "Let me see it."

Alina spun away. "I told you, it's nothing!" she shouted.

"I'm just concerned."

She moved off the counter toward the kitchen table and slouched into a chair. Lighting a cigarette, she stared out the window and said, "Sorry… it was a long night."

"Do you want to talk about it?"

"No, I just need some coffee."

Within a few minutes, he'd finished the omelet and set the plate on the table with toast and jam. He was surprised at how quickly she inhaled the food. "Girl, you eat like a linebacker."

"What's a linebacker?"

"A football player."

"Is that a compliment?"

"It is in America."

"Why don't I believe you?" She smiled, pushed her plate away, and then yawned again. "Anyway, thanks, that was good."

Hunter took her plate to the sink. "Maybe you should lie down and get some sleep."

She sighed. "That might be a good idea. I'll be a lot more fun if I can get some sleep." She walked over and put her arms around him from behind. Hunter twisted around to face her. She kissed him and said, "I'll make it up to you in a few hours."

Hunter watched her undress and climb into bed. For most people, sleep was a refuge, a place to recharge and rest—but not for Alina. He learned over the next two months that on good nights, she'd lie on her back and sleep peacefully until he woke her for work. On bad nights, she'd curl into a ball, her legs and arms twitching and jerking as she argued and swore at the demons that tormented her sleep. During these nightmares, he never knew whether it was better to wake her or let her sleep. He had no idea what she was saying when she screamed in the dark.

She needed her rest since she worked all night, so when the nightmares came, Hunter spooned to the curvature of her naked body and held her close until she stopped crying and drifted off to sleep again. Once she was asleep, Hunter returned to his work. Four hours later, he was still typing on his word processor when she woke up.

"What are you working on?" she asked quietly, her sleepy eyes half-covered by a tussle of red hair.

He stopped typing, walked to the bed and sat down. "Nothing important."

She closed her eyes.

"Bad dreams again?" Hunter asked.

She sighed, reached up and touched his face. "What are you writing about?"

"You." He leaned over and kissed the top of her head. "And how beautiful you look when you sleep."

"Liar." She pulled him on top of her. "I'll give you something to write about."

"Aren't you hungry?"

"Love is food for the soul," she said.

"I can't argue with that." Hunter took off his trousers and slipped into bed. The sheets were warm from her naked body. He tried to roll on top of her, but she stopped him and reached for her purse on the floor. She rummaged inside and pulled out a condom. "Here, put this on." She ripped open a package.

"What's this?" Hunter said.

"Don't argue."

"Why? We've never used one before."

She shook her head. "Silly boy. Just put it on."

Hunter struggled with the condom.

Alina burst out laughing. "What's wrong?"

Hunter blushed and threw up in the air. "This is so embarrassing."

"First time?" she asked. "Let me help you."

* * *

Interrupting the silence after lovemaking, Hunter said, "Tell me about your boyfriend, Karasov."

"He's not my boyfriend—not in the way you're thinking."

"If he's not your boyfriend, then what are you to him?"

"Valuable property. Karasov's very protective of his business assets."

"He calls you an asset?"

"If I cooperate," she said. "If I don't, I become a liability." She paused. "And they take care of liabilities pretty quickly."

"Maybe we should stop seeing each other. I don't want you to get into trouble." Hunter brushed the hair away from her eyes.

"No." Alina reached out and traced her finger along his face. "I don't want to stop seeing you. I can handle Karasov. He's tough, but he has his weaknesses. Everyone does. There will come a day when he won't be around."

"What do you mean by that?"

"He has to pay for the things he's done, the choices he's made."

"Don't we all?" Hunter said.

They continued to lie close to each other, each of them deep in thought. Suddenly, Alina asked, "Are you married?"

"No."

"I bet you have a lot of girlfriends."

Hunter shook his head. "None right now."

"But you're rich, you have a successful job. Many American women would want you."

"Hardly." He pointed at his face. "I'm not exactly George Clooney."

She played with his hair. "I think you're handsome."

"You and my mother are the only ones with that opinion."

"You don't live with your parents, do you?"

"No," he laughed.

"You'd be a huge catch over here," Alina said. "In Kiev, you could have your pick of women."

"Trust me—it's not like that back home."

Alina rolled onto her elbow and played with the curly hair on his chest. "In America, how do you know when you can trust someone?"

"It's the same as here. You need to have faith in the person you trust."

"And what's faith to you?"

"A promise… a hope."

"Hope for what?"

"Happiness," Hunter said. "In the end, isn't that what we all want?"

Alina sighed. "I have to go back to work." She kissed him on the tip of his nose and went into the bathroom to shower.

Hunter was still in bed when she came out of the bathroom and picked up her bag. "I have to go," she said, then sat on the edge of the bed and kissed him. "Have you forgotten something?"

Hunter leaned on his elbow. "What do you mean?"

Her eyes narrowed as she held out her hand. "You're not going be a problem for me, are you?"

"But I didn't get any information today," he deadpanned.

"That's not my fault. You can do whatever you want with the time I spend here—but you still pay."

Hunter rolled out of bed, reached for his wallet on the dresser and handed her one hundred dollars, a discounted price he'd negotiated because she wasn't splitting it with the club.

Alina poured all the stuff out of her purse.

"What are you doing?" Hunter asked.

"The purse has a false bottom. I have to be careful." She held up the money. "This is a bargain for you."

Hunter smiled and walked her to the door. "Same time tomorrow?"

"Yes," she said. "But I can't come every day because people will become suspicious. We may have to get creative, but I think I can sneak away every couple of days without anyone noticing."

"Great. I have to submit a draft of an article to my boss by the end of the week, or he'll cancel my credit card."

"We wouldn't want that to happen. Ciao."

Hunter stepped through the open door and watched her walk down the hall. She was the smartest, most amazing person he'd ever met.

Chapter 9

Hunter, Hunter." Vinny snapped his fingers loudly at his friend. "Hey buddy, you're scaring me with that look. This is exactly why I'm worried about you. You do this all the time, where you just stare off in the distance like you're in a trance or something."

"I'm all right, just a little tired."

"You didn't answer my question. Did you hear anything that I said?"

"What'd you ask again?"

"When will you change your life and stop thinking about that crazy whore in Kiev?"

Hunter turned away from Vinny and stared out the window again. "Those final twenty-four hours in Kiev have haunted me every day for the last two years. I should've done this a long time ago—find out what happened."

Vinny crossed his arms. "Are you sure about this?"

Hunter continued to stare. "You've been a good friend. I don't want you to get involved again."

Vinny took one step closer to Hunter. "What do you mean by that?"

He looked back over his shoulder. "I'm going back to Kiev to find Alina."

Vinny recoiled. "Shit. When?"

"Right after I finish teaching the summer session."

"Don't do this! Once you start this thing again…"

Hunter cut him off. "Let me worry about that."

"Can't help but worry." Vinny put his hand on Hunter's shoulder. "I'm worried that once you go back to Kiev, how will it end?"

"It'll end the way it's supposed to," Hunter said, then turned away from the window and walked through the maze of cubicles toward his office.

* * *

The following week, Hunter arrived early at NYU for his night class. The auditorium was still empty. As he unpacked his lecture notes, he thought about his conversation with Vinny and wondered if he was a little crazy after all. Maybe he imagined things about Alina that were never true.

Students began trickling into the auditorium. Trying not to be obvious, he carefully examined each of the girls that came through the doors, speculating which one might be Carrie, his mysterious student and electronic pen-pal. As Hunter watched the girls take their seats, he remembered what it was like to be in college again. Back then, worries were small—prepare for the next exam, write another fifteen-page paper, get enough sleep and scrape up money for beer.

Everything in Hunter's life changed after he returned from Kiev. His world had been turned upside down. He knew he should stop drinking and wasting money on prostitutes, but he couldn't stop. He had burned through most of his savings and the advances from his articles. Depressed and constantly tired, he hadn't enjoyed a full night's sleep in two years. Alina was in his head every time he closed his eyes, haunting him in his dreams, calling to him from the shadows, or interrupting him while he tried to write. Some days it got so bad he wore a headset to drown out her voice with music.

His day job became a way to pass time until night. The future had no meaning while he was alone. Nothing in New York came close to the friends he'd made in Kiev. Nor the dangerous exhilaration of touching Alina's naked body, or the horror of a gun barrel against your forehead as you realize your next words will determine whether they blow your head off.

Hunter couldn't see the girls entering the upper level of the auditorium, so he tried to adjust the lights to see the back rows better. Instead of making the lights brighter, he accidentally turned them all off. To correct his error, he frantically pushed several buttons that lowered a screen and illuminated an overhead projector. A student jumped up and took over the controls. Within seconds, the lights were on again, and everything was back to normal.

Still flustered, Hunter went up to the blackboard and meekly said, "Welcome back. I hope you all had a good week." He wrote **JOURNALISM** in large block letters and then pointed back to the blackboard. "Who can define this word for us?"

The class sat silent. A few students near the front squirmed within their seats when Hunter looked them.

"No takers? It's not a trick question." He turned back to the blackboard and wrote a second word to the right of the first: **RELATIONSHIPS**. He drew an arrow between the words. "Can someone tell me how these words are connected?" A hand went up in the back row. He shielded his eyes from the bright spotlights and then pointed to a girl with a raised hand.

"They're both about control," the girl said sarcastically. She was wearing a red summer top, a baseball cap pulled down over her eyes and sunglasses.

"What did you say? I can barely hear you," Hunter said, putting his hand behind his good ear. The girl's accent seemed familiar.

A boy near her cut in with, "I think she means who's controlling the bullshit."

"Great," Hunter said. "I didn't realize that we had so many experts with us today." He stepped to the edge of the stage. Looking at the outspoken boy, he said, "May I ask how many articles you have published?"

The boy squirmed and silently looked.

"That's what I thought," Hunter said before stepping back and placing both hands on the podium. "I don't know much about control. However, I do know something about bullshit."

The class skittered with polite laughter for a moment, but the woman in red called out again. "A journalist has the power to rationalize anything he or she writes. Who would know if it's accurate or not?"

He strained to see the face beneath the baseball cap. When he couldn't, he responded in a confident voice: "That's an interesting question, but I think..."

The woman rudely cut him off. "Let me ask you a question. Is it possible to write something worthwhile without having a relationship with your subject?"

"Is this a debate or counseling session?" Hunter was irritated by the interruptions.

Ignoring his remark, the woman said, "You must agree that writers have control over what they convey, and their words have consequences—sometimes serious consequences."

"Yes, but..."

"What happens when a personal relationship you develop in your story conflicts with writing the truth? How do you choose what to write?"

Another hand shot up. A young man halfway up on the left side said, "Excuse me, but I thought relationships were all about love, not control."

A tough-looking, tattooed girl in a leather jacket and silver hoops disagreed. "Obviously, you've never been in a real relationship."

All eyes turned toward the young man she had just slammed.

"Well, sort of." He blushed and jerked his thumb toward the sturdy girl sitting next to him. She slugged him hard in the arm, and the class went crazy.

The woman in red laughed and called down from above, "See! The person with the power controls the relationship."

The students laughed even louder.

Hunter looked at this watch. "I can't wait to hear what comes next, but we need to get back to the main subject." As he pretended to check his syllabus, another hand went up from a different girl in an upper row. Her brown ponytail bounced as she waved both hands to get his attention.

"Yes." He nodded toward the girl.

She adjusted her red glasses and blurted out, "I love the way you write."

Hunter cocked his head. He always had an ear for accents. This girl sounded as if she was from the Midwest, given her long "OOOOs."

"That's nice." Hunter frowned because he had so much material to cover. "But do you have a question?"

"How much human trafficking and sex slavery is continuing unchecked in Kiev?"

"It's still there."

"After your series on human trafficking in Kiev was released, did anyone in Kiev get prosecuted?"

"No," Hunter said, "not to my knowledge."

"Why not?"

"My guess is that they didn't have the evidence to prosecute."

"Is that because no one has the courage to try to stop them?"

"That's not what I said, but if that's your opinion, you're entitled to it."

"So what is the opinion of the poor girls still trapped in Kiev? How do they feel about the lack of evidence while we sit here? We're free to live our lives the way we want to. They are not."

"Prostitution is big business, and the mafia has a lot of power," Hunter said. "Not to mention, someone would be risking their life by coming forward with specific information against them."

"What will it take to stop it?" a different young woman asked.

"The question should be who, not what, has the power to stop it?" the other woman argued.

"Do you have the answer?" Hunter shielded his eyes and pointed to the upper rows. "Or are you just here to moralize?"

"Actually, I do have one last question," the girl responded.

"Thank God," Hunter mumbled while rolling his eyes. "Please, go ahead."

"Do you think the business of journalism is just another form of prostitution, or is it art?"

"It could be both at times."

"Not without sacrificing something."

Hunter doodled on his notebook. "In that case, I suppose it depends on what you are writing about."

"You don't sound so sure."

"Journalism is information—straightforward knowledge and facts."

The woman quickly added, "But journalism is also a business—selling printed information to the public in exchange for money. We're all whores for the right price, aren't we?"

"I disagree." He paused for a second and then continued, "It all depends on your purpose and how you use the information. You can help or hurt people with the power of words."

"Sounds very noble, but what good is that to the poor girls trapped in Kiev?"

Hunter didn't respond.

The woman spoke again, "So, what about you? What was your motivation in Kiev?"

Hunter shuffled his notes on the podium. "We need to move on."

"One last question!" The woman yelled down from above. "How do you know when to write from your head or your heart?"

He resisted the urge to rub his right hand, or what was left of it. He gripped the podium so hard his knuckles went white. The students sensed something wrong and fell silent. Hunter looked down at his notes for a few seconds and then checked his watch. Class was over.

"Someday very soon, each of you will have to answer that same questions for yourself. In the meantime, the assignment for next week is to write a ten-page essay on the topic." The students groaned in unison. "You can thank your classmate in the upper row."

Hunter stepped away from the podium, "That's it for tonight. See you next week." He shielded his eyes from the glare of the stage lights and strained to see the girl in the back row. "Will the girl sitting in the back row who asked all the questions please see me after class?"

A boy yelled down, "She's already gone."

Hunter ran up the steps to catch the girl before she left the building, but a student with a question stopped him. By the time he got to the top, the hallway was almost deserted except for a few lingering students and a janitor mopping the floor with earbuds in place.

Hunter approached the janitor and tapped him on the shoulder. The man removed one of his earbuds.

"Did you see a young woman in a red outfit walk by?" Hunter asked.

"What does she look like?"

Hunter put his hands on his hips and looked down the empty hall. "I'm not sure what she looks like now. It's been two years since I've seen her."

"Is she pretty with a nice smile?"

"Yes." Hunter's face lit up.

"Nice legs and large breasts?"

Hunter grabbed him lightly by the arms. "Yes, yes—did you see her?"

The janitor nodded and smiled. "Yes. In my dreams last night." He laughed and put his earbud back in. "Good luck finding the girl."

Dejected, Hunter gathered up his briefcase and drove home, repeatedly going over the conversation with the girl in red. Inside his apartment, he dropped the briefcase on a table, turned on his laptop and checked his email. A message from Carrie greeted him: "I just wanted to tell you that your class tonight was the best I've attended at NYU. That was such a crazy exchange with the other students, especially with the girl in the back. I love your class."

He lit a cigarette and stared at the screen for a long time. Finally, he responded. "Would you like to meet for coffee?"

The screen remained blank for about a minute then Carrie's response popped up. "Love to. Pick the time and place."

Hunter smiled and leaned back. Just maybe, he thought, something good will happen in my life.

* * *

A month later, Hunter's office door opened so fast it banged into a side chair stored against the wall. He didn't bother to turn around because he knew it was Tess. "Don't you know how to knock?"

Tess approached and leaned against his desk while examining her fingernails. "I didn't want to ruin my new nails. Just cost me twenty bucks." She yawned. "Did you watch the Fourth of July fireworks last night?"

"No," Hunter said, pretending to focus on an article he was writing. "Can't you see I'm busy?"

"Well, I did," she said. "I watched four fireworks displays at the same time on the Hudson River. Awesome!"

Hunter typed something. He knew that if he stopped, Tess would stand there and talk for the next twenty minutes.

She looked over his shoulder at the screen. "What're you doing? Checking your horoscope?"

"Very funny."

"Don't laugh." She had an irritating habit of talking and chewing gum with her mouth wide open. "You should read your horoscope sometime."

"Why?"

"You might learn something about yourself."

"I don't want to know anything about myself."

"What about your future? Aren't you curious?"

Hunter kept his eyes on the computer screen. "I know one thing, if I don't finish this article by four o'clock, I won't have a future here." He glanced at her. "And neither will you."

Tess ignored him and started humming a song while poking around at things on his desk.

Finally, Hunter stopped typing and leaned back in his chair. "Why are you always so happy?"

Tess smiled. "Born that way, I guess. Why would anyone choose to be unhappy?"

"Sometimes, it's not your choice."

"You always have a choice."

"I disagree. We don't always get to pick what happens."

"Boy, aren't we touchy today. No sugar from Carrie over the weekend?" She picked up two pages of an article he had just printed.

"Put that down." Hunter grabbed the papers out of her hand and rearranged his desk into neat piles the way it was before Tess had messed them up. With an air of resignation, he asked, "Okay, what's the matter?"

"I'm bored."

"Thanks for sharing that."

She pulled her gum out of her mouth and looked around as if she was going to squish the wad on the edge of his desk. Hunter quickly pulled the wastebasket out and held it in the air.

"I have a question," Hunter said.

"What color underwear am I wearing?"

"No, a serious question."

She laughed. "Oh boy, here we go."

"You've been here almost five years—and you're still working for me."

"Is there a question in that statement?"

"I was shocked when I looked at your resume, and you had a 3.5 GPA from NYU. You could do anything you wanted, but you play this dumb chick routine and work as a glorified secretary?"

She smiled. "Maybe I feel sorry for you."

Hunter couldn't think of anything to say. Was she serious or what?

"Shit." She smacked herself in the forehead. "I almost forgot. Carrie's on line one."

"Did anyone ever tell you that you have a potty mouth?"

"My boyfriend likes it."

"I give up." Hunter shook his head. "Tell Carrie I'm in a meeting."

"I tried that already."

"Well, tell her again."

"I can't. This is the third time she's called this afternoon."

"What does she want?"

"She wants to know whether you'd prefer meatloaf or pot roast for dinner."

Again, Hunter couldn't find a response.

Tess laughed. "Hold that thought. I'll be right back after I tell Carrie that you'll call her after you finish your piece."

A few minutes later, Tess reappeared and sat on the edge of his desk. "Why don't you want to have dinner with Carrie?"

"Because I'm not big on tater tot hot dish and tuna casserole."

"Aw, come on, she's sweet."

Hunter groaned.

"How long have you been dating?"

"We're not."

She put a finger to her lips. "Don't tell her that. Didn't you meet her last month while you taught your night class?"

Hunter silently went back to typing.

Tess grinned. "I think she's cute. She's not a girl that someone would mistake for pretty, but she seems very nice."

"Don't you have to go somewhere?"

"I like her cute red glasses, but she should do something with that straight brown hair other than wear it in a ponytail." Tess rubbed her chin. "How tall do you think she is—five foot one? She has such unusual proportions, small head, large breasts and pudgy middle." Suddenly she laughed. "And her feet—oh, my God! They're so tiny that I'm sure she must wear children's shoes. But for some reason, it all works."

"Are you done?"

"I think that covers it," she said. "Oh, one last thing, professor, just how old is your student protégée?"

"None of your business."

"Tell me something." Tess folded her arms. "What does a guy like you do at night? Glue model airplanes, fold your laundry, collect stamps?" She cocked her head to the side. "Enlighten me."

"I don't want to spoil your fun."

"Come out with me and my girlfriends some night. I'll show you a different side of New York."

"I don't think so."

"Why not?"

"That would be a waste of time. We're very different kinds of people."

"Is that a bad thing?"

"Look, even if I said yes—and I won't, because I don't do Karaoke—I don't like your music. You like country, I like the Doors. You like Madonna, and I like Yo Yo Ma. You like hummus and celery sticks. I like pizza. See where I'm headed?"

"Okay, no Karaoke, but we could go dancing instead."

"I don't dance."

"Are you serious?" She leaned her head toward him. "Don't tell me you don't know how to dance."

Hunter shrugged.

"But everyone knows how to dance."

"Not me."

"I'll teach you. It'll be fun." Tess grinned and wiggled her finger at him as if he should come with her right now.

Hunter shook his head.

"Look at my eyes."

"Now what?"

"When was the last time you laughed?"

He rolled his eyes and looked back at his monitor. "Don't you have something important to do?"

"I'm doing it." She twisted a strand of her hair around her finger. "I'm preventing my boss from turning into a crabby, impotent bachelor."

Hunter cocked his head to the side. "Impotent?"

"You know what they say… use it or lose it. Carrie's exactly the kind of woman that a guy like you needs."

"And what kind is that?" Hunter said, grabbing the papers out of her hand.

"The marrying kind—she's perfect." Tess started to count with her fingers. "One, she's the future chair of the local PTA. Two, she'll feed you chicken noodle soup when you're sick Three, she'll make at least four fat babies for you." Tess paused. "Shall I go on?"

He had no response.

"Four, she's probably never uttered the F-word. And five, I bet she's never had an orgasm."

"Please stop." Hunter raised his hand. "I don't need a mother. What I need is a woman like… Forget it. You'd never understand."

"Try me."

Hunter tilted back on his wooden swivel chair. "She'd be tall—at least six feet—have flaming red hair, long legs, dark eyes, and full red lips. She'd drink vodka like a fish and talk dirty to me in bed with a thick, sexy European accent."

"Well, well. Straight-arrow, button-downed Mr. Hunter, what have we been watching on television lately?"

"You asked."

"Hmm, there may be some hope for you." She smiled and then frowned. "I'd like your opinion on something."

"First you make fun of me, and then you want my opinion?"

"Okay, okay, I'll take it all back."

He nodded his acceptance of her offer. "So, what's your question?"

Tess looked out the window. "Do you know the difference between lust and love?"

"Why do you ask?"

She turned back to him and wiped away a tear. "I've wasted a significant part of my life lusting after what I thought I wanted instead of waiting for love to come to me."

"What about your boyfriend, Jerry?"

Tess shrugged. "I kicked him out last week."

"I'm sorry," Hunter said. "What was it this time?"

"I caught him cheating."

"Again?"

"He swore he wouldn't."

"And you believed him?"

She shrugged.

"Why did you take him back the last time?" Hunter asked. "You told me that you hated him. I know he's a drummer in a heavy-metal band, but he treats you like shit." Hunter shook his head. "It doesn't make any sense."

Tess twisted another strand of hair around her finger and stared at the floor. "I know," she said quietly. "But he said he loved me."

"So what? That doesn't mean it's true."

They stared at each other for a second. Tess wiped her eyes with the back of her hand and turned toward the door, "Don't forget to call Carrie back."

"Okay, I will." Once Tess left the room, he picked up the phone and called Carrie. "Hi. Sorry—I was tied up in a meeting."

"I've been trying to reach you all afternoon," Carrie said.

"I know. I've been busy." Hunter shifted the phone to his other ear and held it in place with his shoulder. "What's up?"

"Would you prefer meatloaf or pot roast tonight?"

"That's a tough one." Hunter resumed typing again. "To be honest, I'm buried at work and need to take a rain check on dinner."

"Oh no, you can't do that."

"Why not?"

"Because it's our anniversary, and I planned a special dinner."

Hunter winced. "Our anniversary?"

"You didn't forget, did you? It's been one month since we went out on our first date."

"Our first date?" Hunter quickly looked at his calendar. "One month, wow," he cleared his throat. "That's some milestone."

"Exactly how I feel."

Hunter recovered quickly. "Let me take you out to dinner later tonight to celebrate."

"Really? You're the best," she said. "What restaurant? What should I wear?"

Hunter scratched his head. "Uh... I'll make a reservation for eight-thirty at the Union Square Café."

Carrie squealed, "Oh my God, I've always wanted to go there, but it's way too expensive for me."

"You'll enjoy it."

"I don't deserve you."

"Listen, I have to go."

"Love you," Carrie said.

Hunter continued typing on his computer. "I'll pick you up about eight."

"Did she say she loved you?" Tess said, leaning against his door with a fresh cup of coffee.

Hunter threw a pencil at her. "What are you doing, big-ears?"

"I brought you some coffee. And by the way," she drew a finger across her mouth, "my lips are sealed."

"Be careful, you have a mid-year review coming up this month."

"You can save the constructive criticism for someone else." She twirled in a circle. "What you see is what you get."

"I was afraid you'd say that."

"By the way, what did you get Carrie for your anniversary?"

"Get her?" Hunter scratched his head.

"You're so stupid when it comes to women. You have to bring her a gift. Girls expect it."

"Okay. Any ideas?"

Tess folded her arms. "Candy and flowers, of course."

"Great, I'll stop by the Economy Candy Market on my way home."

"But that's a candy store for little kids."

"Are you kidding? It's the best candy store in New York."

"If you're twelve," she said. "You need to buy Carrie truffles and roses."

"I think she'd rather have Fizzies and wax Coke bottles."

"Then, you two sound like a perfect match."

"How so?"

"Because she must be as weird as you."

"Thanks for the compliment," Hunter said. "And close the door on your way out."

Tess saluted and disappeared. The door remained wide open.

***

Hunter stopped at the desk in the lobby of Carrie's gleaming building in Chelsea, an upscale neighborhood. These condos were filled with young models, celebrities and investment bankers, quite different from the artists, aspiring actors, and musicians who dominated his neighborhood in East Village.

"Hunter, my man." Tommy, the doorman, raised his hand for a high-five. "I love that suit on you. It looks like one of those expensive European cuts."

"Thanks, I bought it in Kiev."

"Kiev?" Tommy whistled. "The closest I'll ever get to Russia is Sasha's restaurant over on Seventh Street." He dialed Carrie's apartment. "Miss Carrie, you have a fine-looking gentleman in the lobby." He listened for a second and then laughed as he hung up. "She said to bring the flowers with you, but leave the candy with me. And the door's unlocked."

Hunter held up two empty hands. "Damn, I knew I forgot something. I'll make it up to you next time."

"Miss Carrie's one sweet young lady." He paused and looked around the lobby. "But she's not always what you think she is."

"What do you mean by that?"

"Nothing—just saying."

"Thanks for the advice," Hunter said as he hit the elevator button.

Hunter let himself into her apartment and called out to her.

"Your drink's in the refrigerator," she yelled back from the bathroom down the hall. "I'm not quite ready."

Hunter retrieved his drink and walked to the partially open bathroom door where he could watch Carrie standing on her tiptoes because she was too short to get a close look at her face in the mirror. She was naked except for a white towel wrapped around her head like a turban. She struggled to extract a hair from an eyebrow with tweezers.

"Need any help?" Hunter asked.

Carrie dropped the tweezers in the sink and screamed, "Ahh, get out of here!" She reached for a large bath towel and held it against her chest. "You're not supposed to see me like this. Go wait in the kitchen."

Hunter grinned. "Okay, if you insist."

Twenty minutes later, Carrie rushed into the kitchen and turned around when she reached his chair. "Honey, can you zip me?"

Hunter stood up, lifted her brown ponytail and kissed her neck. She smelled slightly sweet from the baby shampoo she used on her hair. Instead of zipping her up, he reached around and cupped his hands around her breasts. She slapped his hands away. "Cut it out."

He kissed her ear and tried to put his hands around her breasts again. The more she squirmed, the tighter he held her.

"I'm not that kind of girl." Carrie giggled and then turned her head around far enough to give him a quick kiss.

"And what kind of girl are you?"

"A good Catholic girl."

"You don't look Catholic."

"Thank God we don't all look alike."

"I thought all Catholic girls were good."

"Some are better than others."

"How's a guy supposed to tell if you're good and bad?"

"Maybe you'll find out tonight." She twisted around. "Are you going to zip me up?"

As Hunter struggled with the zipper, Carrie wiggled and sucked in her stomach, trying to make herself slimmer. She had never lost the muffin-top that she'd acquired during her sophomore year in college.

"I'm so embarrassed," she said, pulling at her dress and trying to flatten her stomach. "I haven't worn this dress in quite a while."

Hunter yanked a little harder, and finally the zipper went all the way up.

When she turned around, her face was red with perspiration from all her preparation in the hot bathroom. She spun in a circle. "How do I look?"

"Great."

"Are you sure?"

"Absolutely."

She smoothed out her chocolate brown dress. "I can change if you don't like it."

"You look beautiful in brown," he lied.

Carrie stepped closer to Hunter and ran her fingers through his hair. "Hunter, do you love me?"

Startled, he looked at his watch. "We'd better leave or we'll miss our reservation."

They took the subway to Union Square and walked across a plaza toward the restaurant. Halfway across, Hunter looked at Carrie. "You haven't spoken a word since we left your place. Are you mad at me?"

"Yes," she said, staring straight ahead as they walked. "You didn't answer my question."

She refused to look at him, so he grabbed her and began to tickle. "What about now? Are you still mad?"

"Yes, you're terrible."

She tried to squirm away, but he continued to tickle her even more. "How about now?"

"Yes. I mean, no."

He put his hands on her waist, and she threw her arms around his neck and kissed him. "My dad warned me to stay away from older men in New York. He's always worried that some dirty older man will take advantage of me."

"How's that working out?"

Carrie straightened his tie and played with his collar. "My dad knew what he was talking about." She patted his chest and hooked her arm under Hunter's.

A few blocks later, she turned to him and said, "Do you realize this is the first time you've ever taken me out on a fancy date?"

"Fancy date? Is that what we're doing?"

"You know what I mean." She pulled on his arm. "I read that the Union Square Café is one of the top restaurants in New York."

"You'll like it."

When they arrived, the restaurant was packed. Inside, Hunter leaned over to Carrie and pointed. "I love the high ceiling, the contemporary art and the mahogany bar."

"What?" she said. "I can barely hear you."

"Never mind."

The hostess ushered them slowly through the noisy crowd to the bar where they could wait for their table. Carrie stared wide-eyed at everything like a kid in a candy store. "Look at all the cool art," she said.

"You're going to have a sore neck if you don't stop twisting your head around."

Carrie leaned in close and whispered, "I'm looking for celebrities."

"See any?"

"Not yet," she said. "Everyone looks so beautiful."

The bartender gave Hunter a nod. "What can I get you?"

"Do you have any of those warm, spicy nuts left?"

"I'll check, but they're usually gone by this time of night. The cook usually keeps a stash for himself."

"I'll have a vodka on the rocks with a lime."

"What can I get the miss?" He smiled and set a fresh napkin in front of Carrie.

"I'll have a white wine spritzer."

The bartender put his hands on his hips. "I haven't heard that one since college. Where are you from?"

"Minneapolis."

He leaned on the bar. "I should've guessed by your accent. I'm from Minnesota too."

Carrie put her elbows on the bar and leaned forward. "Really, where?"

"Duluth."

"Awesome. I used to go to Duluth with my parents on vacation."

"Ever go to Betty's Pies?"

She nodded. "Always ordered the blueberry."

"My favorite is hot pecan with vanilla ice cream."

Hunter tapped his hand on the bar. "I'm a little parched."

The bartender leaned into Carrie. "We have great cheese curds. You can order them for an appetizer while you wait for dinner."

"Really? Cheese curds?" Carrie said.

Hunter rolled his eyes. "Come on, you guys are killing me." He patted Carrie's hand. "He's kidding."

Hunter jumped as the maître d' tapped him on the shoulder. "Sir, your table's ready. Please follow me."

Their table was near the back of the restaurant. Hunter ordered two New York strip steaks and a bottle of red wine with a French name.

Halfway through dinner, Carrie cut a piece of her steak and sighed. "This is heaven." She pointed her steak knife in the air. "The steak literally melts in my mouth."

"I told you that you'd like this place."

"Everything is so romantic," Carrie gushed. "The flowers, the candlelight, the food…"

"And the company?" Hunter added.

"That's the best part." She leaned over and kissed him. "Thank you for bringing me here." She lifted her glass in the air. "I want to make a toast."

Hunter looked around at the tables next to them. "Do we have to?"

Carrie ignored him. "To us!"

Hunter smiled thinly and touched the rim of his wine glass to hers.

Carrie stared at him, waiting for some response.

Finally, Hunter said, "I can't believe how fast the last month has gone."

"I knooow." Her eyes got big, and she set her glass on the table. "Isn't it funny how life works? I didn't know a soul when I moved to New York last summer and obtained my first job as a reporter for a small magazine in the Village."

"How's that going?"

"Terrible. Up to this point, all I've written are short pieces about local activities and cheap restaurants." Her eyes widened. "However, they gave me a promotion last month."

"Congratulations. What's your promotion?"

"They assigned me to write a story on prostitution and the underside of New York City, the side that tourists don't see. I was shocked to learn how many girls from Ukraine and Russia were shipped into New York—particularly East Village, Brighton Beach and Brooklyn—to work as prostitutes. A friend told me your insight would be helpful. Your story tied in perfectly." She paused to sip her wine. "I felt so sad for those poor girls in Kiev. When I discovered you were teaching a night class in journalism, I signed up immediately. I couldn't wait to meet you. And now, here we are together. Isn't that an amazing coincidence?"

"Amazing," Hunter said.

"My goal is to someday write a real book."

"Do you have any ideas?"

"I'm working on one now."

"What's it about?"

"Way too early to tell, but you'll be the first to know."

"I hate to burst your bubble. It's not all they make it out to be. By the time your book is published, you can hardly recognize it. And the pay is putrid." He grinned. "Pick another career."

Carrie changed the subject. "Do you ever think about your time in Kiev?"

"Sometimes."

"Tell me, what's Kiev like at this time of year?"

"July can be rainy, but the flowers along the Dnieper River and Independence Square are beautiful." Hunter picked up his glass and finished the last of his drink. He knew he wasn't drunk enough to talk about Kiev, so he looked for the waiter to order another vodka.

Carrie looked concerned. "Are you sure you want another one?"

"I am."

"But you had one at my place and two here already."

"You're not my mother," he snapped.

"I didn't mean it that way. It's just that..."

"Just what?" Hunter glared at her.

"Sometimes you drink too much."

He frowned. "I do not."

Carrie sipped her wine spritzer and changed the subject. "I want to talk about your trip. How did you get access to the women in the clubs without anyone finding out you were a journalist?"

"It's a long story."

"Did you have some help?"

"I developed various sources."

"What kind of sources?"

The waiter stepped in between them and set Hunter's new drink on the table. "Do you need anything else?"

"No, we're fine for right now."

"Where did you stay while you lived in Kiev?"

"In a crappy hotel."

"Which one?"

Hunter was feeling interrogated, pressured. "What's with all the questions?" He straightened up and squinted at her. "You read my articles. Everything you need to know is in there."

"I'm sorry. I didn't mean to upset you. It's just that there are some things in your series that confused me." She reached over and touched his hand. "We're having such a lovely evening. I was just trying to make conversation." She played with her fork and then leaned forward. "Would you ever let me interview you for a story about women in prostitution?"

"For your magazine?"

"Yes."

Hunter flinched.

"Don't worry, it's not about you. I'm curious about prostitutes. I've been trying to research why some women make bad decisions even when they know it's not right—even when they know it isn't good for them—yet for some reason, they do it anyway. It's a mystery to me."

"My articles doesn't have anything to do with that."

"I understand that most women are forced into prostitution, but I'm more fascinated by the women who make a conscious decision to use sex for money and some exotic lifestyle."

"You sound more like a sociologist than a journalist."

"All writers are sociologists at some level, aren't they? After all, good stories are about people and their behavior under different circumstances."

"Why interview me? You should be talking to other women."

"Because you were close to it for three months in a way that a woman couldn't experience."

"What do you mean by that?"

"I'm curious about the men who frequent these clubs too." She paused. "I'm interested in their perspective."

"Perspective?" Hunter leaned forward. "Are you insinuating that I used these girls?"

"No, no." She waved her hand in the air. "But you did observe men who went to these clubs and I assume that you talked to them. I just want to know why men would pay money to have sex with women and underage girls when they know damn well they're enslaved by the bastards who own the clubs. How could they enjoy sex with girls young enough to be their daughters?" She paused for a second and shook her head. "That's not love. That just sex. And what's the point of that?" She looked up at Hunter. "What kind of sick men are these?"

"Hard to say," Hunter said as he played with his drink and looked across the room.

The waiter interrupted their conversation. "Can I take these dishes away?"

"Sure, we're done," Hunter said.

After he left, Carrie leaned back in her chair and patted her tummy. Hunter sipped his vodka and shook his head in amazement. "I've never seen such a tiny woman inhale a sixteen-ounce New York strip that fast."

She laughed. "I grew up in a large family. You learn to eat fast or you go hungry."

Hunter leaned toward Carrie. "Tell me, now that you've seen what a gentleman I am, how are my chances looking tonight?"

"For what?" She feigned ignorance.

"Taking advantage of you."

"Sorry, I'm saving myself."

"For me?"

"Maybe." She gave a sly smile.

Hunter crossed his arms. "We've been seeing each other over a month, and I've been a perfect gentleman."

"You're pouting."

Hunter shook his head. "I'm beginning to believe that you were sent here by God to torture me."

"For what? Past sins?"

"We agreed not to discuss my past."

"We all have our secrets." Her shoeless foot found its way to his leg.

Hunter's eyes widened when he felt her foot move slowly up the inside of his thigh. He immediately raised his hand in the air. "Waiter, check please!"

He left a big tip, and they began to navigate the maze of tables toward the exit. As they approached the door, Hunter heard a familiar laugh and stopped, listening carefully.

Carrie looked at Hunter. "What's wrong?"

He slowly surveyed the room but couldn't locate the woman, the source. When a woman laughed again, he followed the sound to a round table in the far corner of the restaurant. At first, he didn't recognize the woman with flaming red hair, but as he looked closer—my God, he thought, it's Alina.

Hunter teetered for a second. Carrie grabbed his arm. "Are you okay?"

He didn't respond—stared in disbelief at Alina. She was stunning in a short, tight red dress. Her red hair was much longer and more sophisticated than in Kiev. He smiled when she laughed again and stood up.

Alina was extremely long from her shoulders to her waist, and the back of her dress opened all the way down to her hips. Hunter stared at the smooth, creamy skin of her back and vividly remembered its touch, its smell. God, she has an incredible body, he thought.

He smiled as she charmed her guests with one of her stories. As she leaned back-and-forth between two men on her left and one on her right, her hands were in constant motion as she held court. Suddenly Alina announced to her companions, "I'll be right back."

"Hunter, what's going on?" Carrie said.

"Excuse me," Hunter mumbled. "I have to say hello to someone."

Carrie gazed at the subject of Hunter's interest. "Who is she?"

"An old friend."

Alina's table was covered with plates of lobster, steak, a rack of lamb, baskets of bread, wine glasses, a large candle centerpiece and two bottles of red wine. Alina didn't see Hunter walking slowly toward her table. The man on Alina's left noticed Hunter, though, and tapped Alina on the arm to get her attention. "Darlin', you have a visitor," he said.

Alina twisted around. "Oh my God, Hunter!" She stood and kissed him on both cheeks and threw her arms around his neck. "What a surprise."

"What're you doing here?" Hunter said.

Alina turned back to her guests. "I'd like you to meet Hunter, a dear friend of mine." Alina waved her hand in a semi-circle. "This is Hank Parrish. He's the CEO of US Oil Corporation, which is based in Dallas." Parrish nodded again and raised his glass to Hunter. She moved on to a heavy-set man stuffed into a pinstriped suit with a drop of brown steak sauce on his yellow tie. He looked uncomfortable as he leaned on the table with both elbows.

"And of course, you know Ambassador Karasov," Alina said.

Hunter took a step back as Karasov thrust out a hand to be shaken. Two years had not been kind to him. He used to be fit and muscular with long, flowing black hair combed toward the back. Now he looked like Buddha in a bad suit. His long hair was replaced by a feeble comb-over that didn't disguise his balding pate.

Karasov stared at Hunter's face. "Moretti, right?"

Parrish turned to Karasov, "How do you know each other?"

"Long story." Karasov smiled and waved his knife in Hunter's direction.

Hunter's mind was reeling. Ambassador Karasov? This must be a joke. He couldn't believe that Alina was alive and having dinner with the man who had ordered his right hand shot off. The same man who, until this moment, Hunter thought had killed Alina, the only woman he'd ever loved.

Alina continued with the introductions by putting her hand on the back of the third man's chair. Hunter stared at the man's wavy, silver hair, gold cuff links and Rolex watch. He thought they might have met before. "Last but not least," she said to Hunter. "I'm sure you've heard of the great senator from Texas, Bob Dixon."

Hunter leaned over and held out his hand. "Have we met before?"

The senator laughed and pumped Hunter's hand. "I don't think so, but my mother always told me that I have a pretty face."

Alina placed her hand on Hunter's shoulder and squeezed. "The senator has been a great friend to Ukraine for many years."

"You bet, Sweetheart!" he said.

As soon as Dixon said "Sweetheart," Hunter remembered seeing the senator in Alina's club. He was drunk and sitting at a large table with other businessmen shouting at several young prostitutes, "Darlin' this," and "Sweetheart that."

You slimy pig, Hunter thought. If the world only knew what a degenerate you are.

Alina noticed that Hunter recognized Dixon and stepped between them. "Hunter, my dear. Where are your manners?" She winked and pointed at Carrie. "Introduce me to your friend."

Hunter spun around. Carrie was standing by herself a short distance from the table. Everyone turned their attention to the tiny girl in a brown dress.

"This is Carrie," Hunter said, not bothering to introduce her further.

Blushing, Carrie adjusted her glasses and waved at the table.

Alina leaned close to Hunter's ear and whispered, "She's a cute little brown thing."

Carrie stepped forward and held her hand out to Alina. "Nice to meet you."

Alina scanned her from top to bottom. "My, what a pretty dress."

At first, Carrie smiled and tugged on the edge of her brown dress, but then stiffened.

Alina smiled, adding, "I'm sure that Hunter told you how we are old friends."

"No," Carrie stared straight into Alina's eyes and didn't blink. "He's never mentioned you before."

Alina slapped at Hunter. "Such a silly boy."

"I didn't know you were in town," Hunter said.

Alina brushed a strand of red hair out of her face. "We must have lunch sometime."

"Seriously? It's been two years, and you want to do lunch?" Hunter said. "Why didn't you contact me when you arrived in New York?"

"I've been so busy."

"How long have you been here?"

"Call me tomorrow." Alina sat down. "We can arrange a time to get together."

"How can I reach you?"

"How rude of me." She reached into her purse and pulled out a business card.

He took the card and read it. "So, what is Euro Consultants?" he asked.

"We offer consulting services to meet the unique needs of our special clients."

Parrish tapped the table. "She's very good at what she does. I'll vouch for that."

Alina reached over and patted his hand. "Thank you, Hank, you're so sweet."

Parrish smiled, sat back and took another sip of his wine.

"What kind of services do you provide?" Carrie said louder.

Unconsciously, Alina played with a gold pendant that hung from a necklace. "Linguistics. I translate languages for…"

Carrie cut her off. "I know what a translator does."

Alina ignored Carrie and turned to Hunter. "I work most of the time at the United Nations for Ambassador Karasov, but I have other clients as well."

Hunter switched his gaze from Carrie to Alina. "I'll call you tomorrow."

Alina reached out and squeezed his hand. "I'd like that." She nodded dismissively at Carrie. "Nice to meet you."

Carrie didn't answer but grabbed Hunter's hand and led him toward the door. Once they got outside, she stopped and leaned forward. Her face was directly under his chin. "Okay, who's that woman?"

"I told you," Hunter said. "An old friend."

She crossed her arms. "You never told me about a friend like her. I'd remember."

Hunter moved a few steps away from the entrance to the restaurant. "I don't want to stand out here and argue."

"We're not arguing. I just asked you a simple question, who is that woman?"

"I'll tell you later." Hunter started to walk down the sidewalk toward Union Square. After ten yards, he looked back, and Carrie was still standing in front of the entrance to the restaurant. "Are you coming?"

She shook her head. "I'll catch a taxi."

"Suit yourself." He turned and walked back to his apartment.

Chapter 10

It was almost four o'clock in the morning. Hunter couldn't sleep, so he took a walk. The block was deserted except for a man in orange coveralls sweeping the sidewalks. Hunter checked his cell phone—three missed calls, all from Carrie. Back home, he slept for a few more hours, showered to sober up, grabbed a coffee on the corner and made it into the office by nine-thirty. Tess was sitting at her desk eating a Cinnabon roll and licking the frosting off her fingers.

"You're late," she said.

Hunter pointed at her sweet roll. "That stuff will kill you."

"I'm not the one with a hole in my stomach. By the way, Cabot was looking for you earlier, and he wasn't happy that you weren't here."

"What'd he say?"

"Get your ass in his office the minute you show up."

Hunter sighed. "Everything's always a frickin' crisis."

"I know." She stuck her finger in the small cup of extra frosting and dug out a large dollop. "But something was different this morning."

"Great." Hunter rubbed his forehead.

"You look like the result of a three-day bender."

"Do you have any Tylenol?"

She dug around in a purse the size of a beach bag and pulled out a small bottle. "Here you go."

"What the heck is in there? You could go on vacation for a week with that thing."

She held the bottle in the air. "Don't laugh. This bag is saving your bacon this morning."

"Thanks. I'll bring the bottle back in a few minutes." Hunter walked toward his office, but before he closed the door said, "Hold my calls for twenty minutes and don't tell Cabot that I'm in yet."

"No problem," Tess said.

Hunter drank three cups of coffee before he could make any sense of his emails. He looked at his watch—10:30 a.m. He couldn't put off seeing his boss any longer. He chomped three Tums on his way to Cabot's office.

The door was closed, and Cabot's secretary, Allison, was busy filing her French nails. She didn't look up when Hunter approached.

"Are you feeling lucky today?" she asked.

"Why?" Hunter said.

She pointed her nail file at Cabot's closed door. "He's been in there with Vinny for a half an hour. And he's been doing a lot of yelling."

Hunter rubbed his bloodshot eyes.

"Rough night?" she guessed.

"Got any coffee?"

"Nope, sorry."

Hunter closed his eyes for a second as another wave of nausea turned his stomach upside down. "Okay, what's the fire today?"

Just then, the door swung open, and Cabot yelled, "Get your ass in here."

Vinny didn't look at Hunter when he pulled up a chair in front of Cabot's desk.

Cabot flicked on the television in the corner of his office. "Watch this video."

A young woman reporter was standing inside the United Nations lobby. "I'm here today with Vladimir Karasov, Ukraine's new ambassador to the United Nations."

Hunter leaped forward and turned up the volume.

The reporter turned to Mr. Karasov. "Mr. Ambassador, welcome to the United States, and congratulations on your new appointment."

Hunter recognized the old man immediately from last night. He wore an expensive black suit and starched white shirt with French cuffs and gold cuff links. The reporter moved closer to get his response.

The camera stayed tight on Karasov while a female interpreter translated his answer into English. "Mr. Ambassador is delighted to visit the United States. He has been a strong partner with the US government and American corporations to promote peace and business in Ukraine and Eastern Europe. He hopes to expand those friendships while he's here in New York."

The reporter asked, "Sir, what's the first order of business in your new position?" The reporter held the microphone up to Karasov for a response.

As the camera zoomed in on the translator, Hunter jumped up and stopped the video. He pointed at the woman behind Karasov. "That's her. The translator is Alina." Then he resumed the tape.

"As you know," Alina translated, "Ukraine has undergone many changes over the last five years. Mr. Ambassador would like to strengthen the relationship between Ukraine and your government and the business community. We have an urgent need to develop our natural gas and oil resources and upgrade our country's infrastructure. We're discussing proposals for a variety of projects and very excited about the prospects of new joint ventures to expedite the development of our gas and oil industries."

The reporter tried to ask another question, but Karasov just smiled, waved at the camera and, walked off. The young reporter looked into the camera and said, "Well, that's all from the United Nations. Ambassador Karasov will be speaking at his first United Nations general assembly in about twenty minutes. Back to you, Chris."

They sat without moving for a few seconds, and then Cabot leaned toward Hunter. "What the hell's going on?"

"What do you mean?"

"How did your whore get here? And how did Karasov become the new ambassador?"

"I don't know."

"How long have you known she was here?"

"Not until last night. I bumped into Alina and Karasov at the Union Square Café."

"You expect me to believe that?"

"Hank Parrish and Senator Dixon were also at the dinner."

Cabot raised his eyebrows. "How the hell do they know each other—and why would they be meeting?"

"I don't know. I was going to tell you about it when I got in this morning."

Cabot looked at Vinny. "How long have you known about this?"

Vinny raised his hands in the air. "All news to me."

Cabot chewed on his cigar. "Well, the shit's hitting the fan here. I had two goons in my office this morning asking a ton of questions about the paper's connection with you, Hunter, and the new ambassador."

"What goons?" Vinny asked.

"Goons from our friendly government. They knew about your interaction with Karasov and the Russian and Ukrainian mafia two years ago. Their questions sounded like something was really bothering them." Cabot stood up and walked over to the window. "OPEC's coming to New York next week, and everyone in the oil business will be in town. The timing suggests all this has something to do with the OPEC meeting. Hunter, you're the so-called Ukraine expert. What do you think?"

"I don't think we should touch this story."

"Why not?" Cabot said.

"For one thing, the Feds must be investigating something serious. Second, these guys in the mafia are really dangerous."

"Vinny, what do you think?"

Hunter glared at Vinny.

"The Russians and Ukrainians are fighting over the Russian pipelines that run through Ukraine," Vinny said. "Most people don't know those pipelines supply most of Europe's oil and gas. If there's a problem, it could affect oil and gas prices for everyone in Western and Eastern Europe, Russia, Ukraine, even the US."

"How big is the problem?" Cabot asked.

Vinny nodded. "A really big deal. The economies in Eastern Europe have suffered disastrous losses since the fall of the Soviet Union five years ago. If energy prices spike, or worse—if the pipeline is disrupted—it could cause another worldwide recession. Karasov could make billions if he could get his hands on the technology and equipment to develop Ukraine's own oil and gas reserves."

"Okay, I want everyone in the conference room in five minutes. We need to move on this story before anyone else gets wind of trouble."

Hunter rushed back to his office and grabbed a notepad for the staff meeting.

"Wait!" Tess handed him a stack of pink messages and a Styrofoam cup of lukewarm coffee.

"Thanks." Hunter flipped through the messages. Two were from Carrie.

"She sounded worried when you didn't return her calls," Tess said. "Did everything go okay last night?"

Hunter looked at his watch. "I'll tell you later. If she calls again, tell her I'm in a meeting, and I'll call around lunch."

"One more thing. A woman called twice while you were gone. She didn't want to leave her name, but said she'd call back later."

Hunter stepped closer to Tess. "What else did she say?"

"Nothing. I think she knew you."

"Get a name and number the next time she calls. I'll be back in an hour."

He walked quickly to the opposite end of the floor. Cabot was standing in front of a large whiteboard writing the assignments with a blue marker and barking out orders. Hunter slipped into an empty seat near the back of the room.

"Nice of you to join us," Cabot greeting sounded like a snarl. "Can I get you anything? A sweet roll, bagel, maybe some tea?"

"Sorry, I got hung up."

Cabot returned to writing on the whiteboard. "Okay, Vinny, you cover the press conference with the mayor. Hunter, I want you to get over to the United Nations and see what you can dig up. Also, check with Senator Johnson on the Foreign Relations Committee, and Senator Abraham, he's the chair of Appropriations. They might have some inside knowledge of what's happening. If they balk at giving you information, get them to respond off the record and then call me."

Cabot spent the next ten minutes listing assignments for the other reporters. Finally, he set his marker on the edge of the whiteboard and clapped his hands together. "Okay, that's it."

Everyone picked up their notebooks and filed out of the conference room.

"Hunter—a moment," Cabot said.

Hunter remained in his seat.

Cabot sat in a chair next to him. "I want you to get on this story. It could be big." He looked around and made sure they were alone. "What's the deal with Alina?"

"What do you mean?"

"Were you surprised when you saw her last night?"

"Shocked."

"What are you doing about it?" Cabot said.

"I plan to call her today."

"Look, she owes you. The least she can do is provide us with access to Karasov."

"I don't know. Unless Karasov has changed, he hates reporters. Remember, he almost shot my fuckin' hand off."

"Don't worry, that was before he became the ambassador. I know his type. He's an ex-KGB guy pretending to be legit," Cabot said. "It's all bullshit. The Russians think the fucking Ukrainians are leaches and always causing trouble. I'm telling you, Karasov's up to no good."

Hunter looked surprised. "Why do you say that?"

"Hundreds of thousands of Ukrainians were slaughtered in World War II. Under the Soviet Union, the Russians believed they were the only ones that took care of the Ukrainians. They fought and died for the Ukrainians in the war, supplied eighty percent of the oil and gas Ukraine needed to survive, and provided food when they couldn't feed their own people. Ukraine's economy has been in shambles for a decade. Since the collapse of the Soviet Union, Ukraine's been controlled by the mafia and a bunch of thugs."

"I know. You're right."

Cabot chomped on his cigar. "That's why I want you to get an interview with Karasov as soon as possible."

"But…"

"No excuses." Cabot said. "Use Alina."

"I don't know if she'll help us."

"That whore of yours is our ticket."

"I'll try." Hunter stood up to leave but hesitated. "I was wondering if I could borrow some money. I'm a little short this month."

Cabot folded his arms. "Again?"

"Just until my next paycheck."

Cabot frowned. "Forget it. You'll just waste it on booze and prostitutes."

"I stopped going to those clubs. This is for some unexpected expenses that came up."

"Bullshit. I told you before—I'm not giving you another dime until you get some professional help."

Hunter threw his hands in the air. "I don't need any help."

"In that case, you're not getting any money."

Hunter stomped back to his office. His cell phone rang as he sat down. He looked at the display—Carrie again. He closed his door and answered, "Hi, Carrie."

"I'm sorry about last night."

Hunter didn't respond.

She began to cry. "I acted like a spoiled brat. I was worried about you when you didn't return my calls."

"My cell phone lost its charge, and I've been in meetings all morning."

"Can you come over for dinner tonight?"

"Sorry, but I'm busy," Hunter said.

"Please. Let me make it up to you." Carrie sniffled. "I'm embarrassed that I ruined a wonderful evening."

"Just stop crying. I hate it when you cry. You don't have to make dinner."

"But I want to."

While Carrie explained why she was so upset, Hunter searched the Internet for any new articles on Ambassador Karasov. The front page of the *Washington Post* had a picture of the ambassador standing in front of the Plaza Hotel. In the background, Alina was holding Karasov's briefcase.

"Well, what do you think?" Carrie asked.

Hunter scrolled down to the story and began to read. "About what?"

"Aren't you listening?" She started to cry again. "About dinner tonight."

"For God's sake, stop crying. Okay, I'll come." Hunter switched to the *Wall Street Journal* to see if they had anything on Karasov.

"Great. See you about seven." Carrie hung up.

Hunter fingered Alina's business card and then called her. After several rings, he got her voicemail and left a message.

* * *

Hunter spent the rest of the day researching information on the fall of the Soviet Union and what had transpired in that region over the last five years. He lost track of the time but remembered at the last minute to buy flowers and a cheap bottle of wine on his way over to Carrie's. When he arrived, he knocked twice and waited for a few seconds before twisting the doorknob and pushing the door open. To his surprise, the room glowed from dozens of candles scattered around the apartment. The soft light cast flickering shadows and danced across the walls. The dining room table was set for a romantic dinner. Carrie was still in the bedroom, so he walked into the kitchen and arranged the flowers in a vase. He didn't hear Carrie come up behind him.

"Did you find what you needed?"

He turned around and smiled. She wore a light blue summer dress, and her brown hair was combed down around her face, a pretty tortoiseshell clipped to one side of her hair.

"Have we met before?" Hunter asked. "I once knew a girl who reminded me of you, but she always wore brown and tied her hair back in a ponytail." Hunter twirled her in a circle. "But you—who are you?"

She blushed, leaned into his chest and played with his tie. "I'm sorry about last night. I know Alina's your friend, but something about that woman rubbed me the wrong way. My mother would kill me if she knew how badly I behaved."

"Forget it." Hunter wrapped his arms around her. "It didn't help that I was so surprised to see her."

"How do you know her?"

"I'll tell you another time." He sniffed the air. "What's that wonderful smell?"

"Beef bourguignon."

"You're kidding." He cocked his head sideways. "I didn't know you could cook like this."

Carrie winked. "There's a lot you don't know about me."

"I'm impressed." He walked over to the stove, took the cover off the pot and took a deep breath. "It smells wonderful."

Carrie shooed him out of the kitchen. "Give me five minutes. Take the wine and wait for me in the living room."

Hunter sat down at the dining room table, poured two glasses of wine and waited for Carrie. After a few minutes, he yelled back to the kitchen, "Are you sure there isn't anything I can do?"

"Why don't you turn on some music?"

Hunter rummaged through her CDs and found some Steely Dan. He hummed to "Reelin' the Years" while looking at family photos on the walls and on tables throughout the living room.

"You have great pictures of your family."

"Thanks," Carrie responded from the kitchen.

"Where are they taken?"

"Minnesota, where I grew up."

"Your family looks like they just got off the boat from Sweden." He picked up a framed photo of her parents and brothers hugging Carrie at her college graduation. "You're a lucky girl."

Carrie brought out two bowls of beef bourguignon and set them on the table. Before they began to eat, Carrie raised her wine glass. "What should we toast to?"

Hunter touched his glass to hers. "To New York."

Carrie added, "To the city that brought us together."

After dinner, they moved to the couch. Hunter leaned back on the sofa cushions. "Thank you. That was a great dinner."

She curled up next to him. "I'm glad you like it, but I have a confession. The beef was an experiment."

"I'm glad that you like to try new things." He set his glass down on the coffee table. "Maybe we should continue experimenting."

She set her glass down too. "Do you have any ideas, professor?"

"A few."

"Are there any laws in the State of New York against taking advantage of students?" Carrie asked.

"That depends." He raised his right eyebrow. "How old are you?"

"How old do you think I am?"

Hunter pulled her over and began to kiss her. "Old enough to know better."

"Good answer," Carrie giggled.

Hunter removed her red glasses and the hairclip. Her hair fell across her face. She put her arms around his neck and kissed him until he scooped her up and carried her into the bedroom where he laid her on the bed and slowly took off her dress. She was tense but still. She shivered as he slipped her panties off.

"Hunter, I should tell you... this is my first time."

He put his finger to her lips. "Trust me."

"But I want this to be... you know... special."

"Carrie, every night with me will be like your first."

"I love you."

Hunter got up to turn off the lights.

"Why did you do that?" Carrie asked. "I want to see your face."

"It's better this way."

"If you say so."

Ukranian Nights

Hunter started slowly—Alina had taught him well. Carrie was a willing student, so eager, trying so hard to please. She rarely opened her eyes, giving him complete control of where and how he explored her body. When he knew she was ready, he took her to that special spot—the spot that Alina taught him—the place that left her gasping as she dug her fingers into his back until she gasped, "Oh, my God."

Once Carrie had caught her breath, she smothered Hunter's face with kisses until he abruptly pulled away and rolled off her.

"What's the matter?"

"Nothing," Hunter said.

"I had no idea it could be like this," Carrie whispered. "Let's do it again."

Hunter rolled on to his side and leaned on his elbow while facing her. He lifted a strand of sweat-soaked hair from her face. "Put that in the book you're writing."

Carrie laughed. "With a footnote referencing you?"

"I always wanted to become famous."

"That was amazing!" Carrie ran her hand along his cheek.

Hunter didn't respond and rolled off the bed. He glanced at his watch and reached for his pants hanging off the back of a chair.

"I have to get going."

She pulled the sheets up over her breasts. "But I thought you could stay with me tonight?"

Hunter stood up and slipped his pants on. "I have to get up early." He grabbed his shirt and sat down on the edge of the bed next to her.

"I love you," Carrie said, and then she grabbed the bedsheet and pulled it up to her neck. Her eyes darted back and forth, searching his face some reaction.

Hunter buttoned his shirt in silence. When he finished dressing, he leaned over and kissed her forehead. "I don't deserve you."

She threw her arms around his neck and squeezed. After a moment, he gently pried her arms off and folded them across her stomach.

"See you tomorrow," Carrie said hopefully.

* * *

Hunter hadn't slept well since he'd seen Alina in the Union Square Café. He couldn't believe that she was living in New York City and hadn't contacted him. This wasn't how he envisioned a reunion; he didn't blame her. He was a coward, and they both knew it. He could've attempted to rescue Alina after Karasov had shot him in Kiev. He could've returned and tried to save Alina, but instead, he saved himself and stayed in New York.

It took Hunter every ounce of energy to make it to the office, where he worked for about an hour before falling asleep on his desk.

Without knocking, Tess poked her head in. "Call on line one."

Hunter didn't look up. "I'm busy."

"I think you should take this one."

Hunter lifted his head. A loose piece of paper stuck to his face for a second before fluttering down. "Why?"

"Because she has a funny accent and insists that she's an old friend."

Hunter stared at the light blinking on his desk phone. "Okay, I'll take it, but close the door and hold my calls until I'm finished."

"Are you all right? You're pale as a ghost."

"I'm fine." Hunter waved her away and picked up the call. "Hunter here."

"Hi, Hunter," Alina said.

"I thought you were dead."

"I know."

"I want to thank you."

"For what?"

"For saving my life. I was sure that Karasov intended to kill me, but at the last second, he looked at you, and something made him stop."

"That was a bad day."

The phone went silent. Hunter struggled to find the right words, but his mind was mush. After two years of imagining what to say at a moment like this, he now drew a complete blank. Finally, he asked, "How long have you been in New York?"

"Just over a week."

"What're you doing here?"

"I'm working for Karasov as his translator."

"You were always good with languages."

"How about you? I read several of your articles. —My, you're famous."

"Not really. I had my five minutes of fame and earned a small bonus. Now it's back to the old Hunter."

"I never thought you were in it for the money."

"I wasn't until I met you."

She laughed. "Don't blame me. Your soul was corrupt long before we met. Hunter, thank you for not disclosing my identity. You saved my life."

"That's not how I remember it."

He heard Russian voices in the background on her phone and for a second was transported back in Kiev.

"Sorry, I have to go."

"Would you like to get together for breakfast tomorrow at Pastis?"

"I've never been there, but I like the name."

"They have fabulous Bloody Mary's."

"Still drinking vodka?" she said.

"I picked up a few bad habits when I was in Kiev."

"Were they all bad?"

Hunter didn't respond.

"Okay," she said, "see you tomorrow."

Hunter didn't get a thing done for the rest of the day. Late in the afternoon, Carrie called about having dinner together, but he made up an excuse about coming down with the flu. He spent most of the evening at home watching old movies and practicing what he would say to Alina in the morning. He didn't know what time it was when he finally flopped onto the bed. His insomnia wasn't about falling asleep—it was about staying asleep.

* * *

Hunter didn't want to open his eyes because he knew that he'd lose Alina again. In his dream, they were intertwined like Siamese twins in the heat of a summer night. Their hot sticky bodies pressed together after making love. Hunter ran his hand down her back and licked the salty sweat off his finger. At his touch, she pushed her hips against him. He tried to stay in this dream, but then he heard a baby crying in the distance. Alina heard it too. She kissed him and whispered, "I love you." Hunter groaned as he slowly became aware of his surroundings, the weight of the comforter on his naked body, a dog barking in the distance, the baby crying, and the smell of frying bacon from the apartment below.

No, please, he thought. Let me stay just a little while longer. He squeezed his eyes tight and tried to go back to her—but she was gone.

Hunter rolled over and draped his right arm across her side of the bed. The sheets were cold and empty. He knew it wasn't rational, but he put his face into the soft pillow next to him and tried to remember what Alina smelled like. A bit of lavender, gardenia, a touch of smoke, and something sweet. After two years, he wasn't sure anymore. He used to be sure about a lot of things, but not now. If you tell yourself the same lies often enough, you began to believe them. The summer he'd spent with Alina seemed no more real now than the scene he had just dreamed. He repeatedly asked himself the same question—did she really love me—as if repetition would change the answer.

He glanced at the blue numbers glowing on the clock radio—4:03 a.m.—and cursed his insomnia. He flicked on the small lamp and reached for his cigarettes. Since he'd returned from Kiev, he had tried several times to quit smoking, but for some reason, he couldn't. He read the label on the package: "…dangerous to your health." He smiled, thinking Alina should have the same label written on her forehead. He lit a cigarette and took a deep drag, trying not to think about it—or about her.

The alarm went off at seven o'clock. Bleary-eyed, he trudged into the bathroom and covered his face in shaving cream. As he shaved, he kept wiping fog off the mirror but flinched when he nicked his cheek. Blood trickled down his face. Staring at his trembling hand, he slowly set the razor down.

He arrived at Pastis thirty minutes early for breakfast with Alina, seating himself on a wooden bench outside the restaurant. What would he say to her after all this time? He closed his eyes and let the sun warm his face until he caught a faint whiff of gardenia. She was standing about four feet away in a simple white blouse with a light blue cotton skirt and a white gardenia pinned above her left ear. A breeze blew her shoulder-length hair across her tanned face. It wasn't as red as he'd remembered—the color was softer, more the color of autumn. She looked perfect except for the scar around her right eye. She'd done a good job of covering it with makeup, but Hunter could still see an outline of the old wound.

He smiled. "How long have you been standing there?"

"Not long." She took a step closer. "I forgot how handsome you looked with your eyes closed."

"You need glasses."

"I see just fine," she said. "It's my memory that I don't trust."

"Some memories can be convenient, can't they?" Hunter shielded his eyes from the sun and stared at her for a moment. "You've changed."

Alina grabbed the edge of her skirt and twirled around. "Do you like the new me?"

"I don't know yet," Hunter said. "I need a minute to get used to the longer hair."

Hunter stood and moved toward her. Alina took two steps and fell into his arms. They held each other for a long time before she pulled her head off his chest and whispered, "When you left Kiev, I never thought I'd see you again."

He rocked her gently for a minute until he noticed several people staring at them. "Come on, let's go inside."

A young hostess ushered them to a table next to the window. Alina hung her purse on the chair and sat down. "This place is perfect."

Hunter ordered two Bloody Mary's and a plate of hot beignets. After the waitress left, Alina grabbed both of his hands and gently rubbed them.

"I can't believe we're here, together in New York," Alina said.

Hunter nodded. "Me too. Where are you staying?"

"The Plaza."

Hunter whistled. "The Plaza. You've come a long way from the Rus' in Kiev."

Alina tried to contain a smile as she sipped her drink. Her tongue slowly licked the celery salt that coated her red lips. Hunter fought the urge to make love to her on the spot.

"You look great," Hunter said.

Alina peered closely at his damaged right hand and gently touched it. "I'm sorry. Sorry about everything."

"It doesn't matter," Hunter said.

They sat in silence for a moment.

"How do you like teaching classes at NYU?" Alina asked.

"How did you know that?"

"I've kept track of you."

"And I thought you were dead."

Alina sighed. "I know, but I couldn't risk contacting you… because Karasov would've ordered you killed."

"What's changed now?"

Alina laughed. "He's gone legit. He discovered that he can make billions using his role as an ambassador to parlay his control over the energy and banking industries in Ukraine. Much more lucrative than drugs and sex."

The waitress came, and they ordered a second round of Bloody Mary's and two French omelets. Hunter felt the vodka slowly taking hold. "Alina, I need to know something."

Alina played with her fork. "Yes?"

"What happened back in Kiev?"

"I made a mistake."

"Was I the mistake?"

She closed her eyes. "No. You were not a mistake."

"Then why didn't you contact me to let me know you were alive?"

"I told you, it was too dangerous."

"Alina, I thought… I thought you were dead after Karasov hit you a second time in the head. What happened after Karasov carried you out of our flat?"

"I don't remember anything after the door exploded and the bodyguards burst into the room," she said. "I woke up in my room, covered in blood and wondering if I was dead or alive. Eventually, they took me to the hospital and told the doctors I'd had a car accident. The girls at the club took care of me until three weeks later, Karasov came to my room and said he was sending me to Moscow."

"Moscow?"

"I'll explain later. But now it's your turn. What happened to you?"

"Not much to tell," Hunter said. "I realized, after they shot my hand, that they weren't going to kill me. They destroyed my writing hand as a warning. I passed out after they left the apartment. A neighbor called the US consulate, and they brought me to the hospital. Once they got me stabilized, a private jet hired by the *Times* flew me back to the States. I was heavily sedated, so I don't remember much of the trip home. I woke up in Cornell hospital and didn't know where I was… or if you were still alive."

"There was nothing you could've done." Alina pushed her hair away from her eyes. "In fact, if you hadn't gone back to New York, they would've killed us both."

"I'm a coward."

"Nonsense," she said. "You were sedated. Let's talk about something else."

"Not yet," Hunter said. "I need to know what happened after I left."

"That isn't worth discussing. You don't know Karasov like I do. He would've killed you if I tried to reach you from Kiev." She paused, then added, "But as I said, things are different now."

"What's really changed?"

"Everything."

"Not quite everything," Hunter said.

"What do you mean?"

"Don't play dumb." Hunter shook his head. "You still have Karasov."

Alina bristled. "Is that what you think?"

"Who's next?"

"What do you mean?"

"He's getting old and fat. How old is he anyway?"

"Sixty-eight."

"There must be another billionaire out there somewhere."

Alina pressed her lips together into a thin line.

"So little time and so many choices," Hunter said.

"You're an asshole."

"Maybe I have my reasons." Hunter looked at her ring finger and pointed. "Why no wedding ring? Doesn't Karasov trust you?"

Alina put both hands on the table and ripped into Hunter with a long string of sentences in Ukrainian.

"Goddamn it, keep it down." Hunter tried to interrupt her because several people had stopped eating and were staring at them. "And speak English."

She glared at him.

"Stop it," Hunter said. "I hate it when you give me that look."

"You haven't changed one bit since Kiev," she said. "It's still all about you."

"What do you mean by that?"

"Where would you be without me? Would you be the man you are now—or the stupid, insecure boy that I met two years ago? Would you have a new life without me?"

"Nice try."

"You have no idea what I've been through since you left." She straightened in her chair. "I've changed."

Hunter regretted what he'd said but was still hurt and angry.

She leaned slowly forward. "I have an important question, and I'm only going to ask you one time." She stared at him seriously. "Do you still love me?"

Hunter's fingers rapidly tapped the table. "Of course, I love you. I'll always love you." He reached over and grabbed her hand tightly. "I love you, but I want to hurt you right now."

"I understand." She looked around the room, then back at him. "Slap me if it'll make you feel better."

"I have a better idea. Why don't we just run away and disappear? America's a huge country. Karasov would never find us."

Alina sighed. "You know I can't—at least not yet."

"Why not?"

She shook her head. "It's just not that simple."

The waitress leaned over Hunter's shoulder and refilled his cup of coffee.

Alina put her hand over her cup. "I'm good."

After the waitress left, Hunter said, "Okay, back to Kiev and Karasov sending you to Moscow."

"He was so angry he still wanted to kill me, but one of his lieutenants convinced him that I was too valuable. They concocted a plan to ship me to Moscow and infiltrate the Stravinsky mafia family."

"Stravinsky? Why do I know that name?"

Alina smiled. "Maybe because he's one of the richest men in the world. Stravinsky owns or controls most of the banks in Russia, and all the oil, gas, and mining resources. He's a very smart but dangerous man who heads the largest mafia family in Russia. When anarchy rose up after the fall of the Soviet Union, Stravinsky recruited many ex-KGB officers. He also put on his payroll thousands of men who had been imprisoned in the Gulags by the Communists. Today, he operates one of the largest organized crime organizations in the world. He literally controls the Russian economy—and his ambition doesn't stop there."

"So Stravinsky and Karasov are competitors?"

"More than that. Bitter enemies. Stravinsky has a unique stranglehold on Ukraine. Until Ukraine can supply its own oil, they'll always be a slave to Russia, which he controls. Karasov has never trusted Stravinsky. He's obsessed with knowing what Stravinsky is doing to undermine his power in Ukraine.

"How do Karasov and Stravinsky know each other?"

"Back in the Soviet Union days, Karasov was the First Deputy Chairman of the KGB, and Stravinsky was the up-and-coming Director of the Federal Security Service of the Russian Federation, which you may know as the FSB. All law enforcement and intelligence, including the secret police, fall under the FSB. Karasov was part of the old regime, while Stravinsky was fifteen years younger and very ambitious. Both of them were obsessed by power and money. Like two dogs, they constantly fought over the same bone."

"This was before the Soviet Union imploded?"

"Yes, and in the aftermath, they both scrambled for power and became even more bitter rivals. Since neither one controlled the army or had enough political power to hold the old Russian Empire together, so it finally broke into pieces along ethnic and geopolitical lines. In the early 1990s, Stravinsky was a senior Russian officer from Moscow who consolidated his power base in Russia by assuming control of the foreign intelligence service, called SVR, and the military intelligence agency, called GRU. Karasov was born in northern Ukraine, so he consolidated his power throughout the region that encompasses Ukraine, Georgia and the smaller independent countries."

Hunter leaned back in his chair. "So Karasov planned to use you to get to Stravinsky."

Alina nodded. "After what happened with us in Kiev, I was expendable. If Stravinsky found out about me, Karasov knew Stravinsky would kill me, so he didn't have much to lose." She paused. "That was my penance for betraying Karasov. If I did a good job, Karasov told me he'd forgive me and bring me back after a couple of years."

"And you believed him?"

"I had no choice," she said. "I spent almost two years in Moscow providing Karasov with vital secrets about Stravinsky's activities. After the cold war ended, many of the top KGB officers moved into pseudo-government positions and the mafia. Initially, Karasov made millions through his mafia, but then he found out that he could make billions—that's billions with a capital B—if he went legitimate and privatized key industries under his control. Sex and drug money was small change compared to what he could make by adding banking and other critical national industries to his portfolio. Stravinsky was a genius at exploiting such opportunities, and I provided Karasov with his playbook on how to do it. Both men ruthlessly took advantage of the desperation so many people experienced after the economy collapsed in 1990. You must understand, Hunter—there were no jobs back then. No money. No government. People will do anything when they are desperate, so it was easy for a few powerful men such as Karasov and Stravinsky to control the country."

"That's crazy. Your story sounds like a movie script written by someone just out of college," Hunter said. "How did you infiltrate Stravinsky? Karasov couldn't deliver you to his doorstep wrapped in a red ribbon."

"I enrolled in linguistics at Lomonosov Moscow State University and put myself in play by attending the right night clubs. Eventually, someone in Stravinsky's organization noticed me. The rest is history."

"The same way you got to Karasov."

"It worked pretty well the first time."

"You're good. But I'm curious about how you got back to Kiev."

"I eventually confessed to Stravinsky that I'd been Karasov's mistress before the old man dumped me for a younger woman. I told him I hated Karasov and wanted to kill him. I also shared with him Karasov's scheme to destroy him and take over his power. At first, Stravinsky was wary, but over time he trusted me. That's when I told Stravinsky about my plan."

Hunter shook his head in bewilderment. "What plan?"

"I told Stravinsky that I wanted revenge. Karasov was a bastard, and I offered to spy on Karasov if he sent me back to Kiev."

"Christ," Hunter laughed. "And he bought it?"

"Not at first."

"What caused him to change his mind?"

She grinned and pushed her hair back. "I have my methods."

"I can vouch for that," Hunter said. "Do you mean to tell me they both still think you're spying against the other one?"

"Like I said, I can be very persuasive."

"It's brilliant—and gutsy," Hunter said. "But what about Stravinsky. Isn't he expecting you to exact your revenge?"

"Now you're beginning to see why I'm here with Karasov. It's taken me a long time to put this plan in place."

"Who's plan—Karasov's or Stravinsky's?"

"Let's just call it Alina's plan."

Hunter rubbed his face and moved his chair closer to the table. "Okay, let me ask some simpler questions. Why did Karasov come to New York right now?"

"To get the Russian boot off Ukraine's neck."

"So why don't the Ukrainians drill for their own oil and gas reserves?"

"You've hit on the main problem. They don't have the expertise or technology. Two years ago, Karasov failed in his attempts to establish business relationships with various companies to do that. When I returned from Moscow, I suggested that he try a different strategy."

"Which was?"

"Which was to establish personal relationships not just with business executives but with important government officials too."

"Personal relationships?"

The corner of her mouth turned up, and she winked. "Money isn't the only thing that men desire."

"What exactly did you do for Karasov during that time?"

"Let's just say that I was in HR—head of recruitment. Queen of entertainment. Director of pleasure. Unfortunately, it didn't work out the way we'd hoped. No matter what we did, the companies continued to beg off at the last minute with some bogus excuses. Karasov knew Stravinsky was pulling strings behind the scenes, bribing or threatening our potential partners not to work for us."

Hunter touched her forearm. "I have to ask you about something else. After I returned to New York, the FBI grilled me about my activities in Kiev. They were very interested in anything I knew about the activities of that Brooklyn banker who was murdered and dumped into the Dnieper River while I was there."

"What did you tell them?"

"The truth."

"And what was the truth?"

"That I didn't know anything."

"Did you mention that he came to our club whenever he was in town?"

"No."

"Did you mention me?"

"No, of course not," Hunter said. "Did you know him?"

"Let's talk about something else.

Hunter ignored her. "What was a small banker from Brooklyn doing in Kiev? The newspaper reported that men like Karasov and Stravinsky were making so much money from human trafficking and drugs that they needed to launder foreign money into US dollars. From what I read, billions of dollars are involved, and they need American bankers to launder the money. Cabot is considering doing an in-depth article on the whole story."

Alina frowned. "That's a bad idea."

"Why?"

"Some things you're better off not knowing."

"Like what?"

"Just drop it, please. I'm trying to protect you."

"Okay." Hunter looked at his coffee cup. "I read there's a huge power struggle within the mafia right now throughout Russia, Ukraine, Georgia and the surrounding independent countries. Is that true?"

"Many men from competing organized crime groups are found murdered every day. It's a very dangerous time in our part of the world. Stravinsky and Karasov are locked in a death struggle."

"What's the deal behind Karasov becoming the ambassador to the United States?"

"He plans to use his new position to strengthen his international power network and gain total control of Ukraine's oil and gas. But he realizes that he can't accomplish that alone. He needs to partner with a major American firm. He doesn't speak very good English, so I convinced him to let me come with him on this trip to develop new contacts in the United Nations, Washington, and with some other key executives. Every major oil company will be here next week for the OPEC meeting, and Karasov's determined to make a deal with one of them."

Alina looked around suspiciously and lowered her voice. "Most people don't know this, but there's a huge dispute between Russia and Ukraine over the pipelines that run through Ukraine to supply Eastern Europe with oil and gas. Russia claims that Ukraine has been illegally siphoning off gas from their pipelines."

"More fuel for the fire?"

"Something like that." Alina crossed her arms. "Remember Bob Parrish, the man you met in the Union Square Café."

"The Texan with the crew cut?"

She nodded. "Parrish wants to meet this week to discuss a deal to provide the technology and equipment Karasov needs to develop Ukraine's own oil and gas reserves."

"Can you cut a deal with him?"

"We'll see. Everything is very preliminary at this point. That would certainly solve part of our problem, but we still have a huge national debt to Russia."

"How can you possibly fix that?"

"More foreign aid from the US."

"How much?"

"Billions."

Hunter shook his head.

"It's possible, I think. Because for the US, Ukraine is critical strategically and politically to offsetting Russia's aggressive push to expand their power in the region. Washington knows how important we can be. Russia currently supplies eighty percent of all the gas that Eastern Europe consumes every year. Most of the foreign government officials and businessmen you saw coming to our club were in Kiev jockeying for a piece of the action. Over the last two years, former Communists, KGB officers, and guys like Karasov are all trying to solidify their power through murder and corruption in their own governments."

"So, that's why Senator Dixon was at dinner with you and Karasov." He reached across and tapped her hand. "You are good at what you do."

Alina smirked. "Thank you."

Hunter leaned forward in his chair. "How did Karasov react when you came back from Moscow?"

"He thought my plan to double-cross Stravinsky was outstanding. He knows that I'm the only one who could pull off something like this." She smiled as she ran her finger around the rim of her water glass. "I've developed a few talents that they don't teach you in school. Besides, why would anyone in their right mind risk becoming a double agent to the two most dangerous men in Eastern Europe?" She laughed. "It would be suicide."

"You're crazy," Hunter said. "Brilliant, but crazy. I'm curious, though. How did Kiev become such a crossroads for this mix of international business and pleasure?"

"Simple," she said. "Kiev's a perfect location because of its proximity to Europe and its lack of police or effective government. You wouldn't believe the deals that were cut in our club, and the amount of money exchanged for services." Alina paused. "The problem was, things were getting very dangerous for me. But then I met you."

Hunter cocked his head to the side. "And America, here I come."

The waitress brought them two espresso coffees. They each took a sip and looked at each other without changing their expression. Finally, Alina set her cup down and said, "It wasn't like that."

"Really?"

"I can explain, but you have to give me more time. I can't go into the details right now."

"Why not?" Hunter looked at his watch. "I have the whole day free."

"Like I said, I'm doing this for your own protection. The less you know, the better."

"What the hell are you talking about? I just spent two years of hell wondering if you were dead or alive."

"I have a plan for us, but I need a little more time." She leaned forward and put her hand on his. "Please?"

Hunter's shoulders sagged and he nodded. "Okay, sure."

"Now I have something to ask you," Alina said. "Why didn't you publish or maybe sell the information I hid in your flat in Kiev? You could've made a lot of money."

"I wasn't sure if you were alive, but I knew that you'd be a dead woman the second I went public with it."

"You'd be rich and famous by now."

Hunter shrugged.

"Thank you." Alina reached out to hold his hand. "I don't deserve you."

"I was afraid you'd say that."

Chapter 11

It was hot, humid and their flat didn't have air conditioning. The sweat dripped off Hunter's face onto his keyboard as he tried to finish his latest piece before a three o'clock deadline. Alina came up from behind him and massaged his shoulders.

"You should take a break," Alina said.

He continued to type without looking up. "I'm almost done, but I need some additional information from you."

"Sure," Alina pulled up a chair and faced Hunter, "Tell me how I can help."

"Let's start with you."

"No." Alina raised both hands in the air. "I thought we agreed that I'd only talk about the mafia."

"We'll get to that, but you've never told me about your background."

She frowned. "You don't need that."

"Yes, I do. It's important to know about you and your family so my readers can relate to how you ended up in Kiev."

"Important for you or your readers?"

He smiled. "Maybe both."

Slowly, she nodded. "Okay."

Hunter picked up his recorder and clicked a button. "Tell me your name and where you're from."

"Alina."

"Your full name."

"Alina Alan. I was born on a small farm in Ossetia."

"Where exactly is that? I get confused on my geography."

"East of Ukraine. On the northern border of Georgia, but below Russia."

"And tell me about your parents."

"There's nothing to tell."

"When was the last time you saw them?"

"It's been a long time."

"Any brothers or sisters?"

"I've changed my mind." She frowned and waved her hand in the air. "Turn off the recorder. My family has nothing to do with this."

"I'm sorry if I upset you."

Alina picked up a pack of Dunhills and lit a cigarette. She took a deep drag and exhaled slowly. "What about you?" Alina asked. "Tell me about your family."

"None." Hunter hung his head. "My parents died when I was young."

"What about your brothers and sisters?"

Hunter looked away. "I'm alone."

It was Alina's turn to look surprised. She stared at Hunter for a moment before she put her cigarette in the ashtray and reached out to take his hand. "Me too."

Hunter sighed and turned on the recorder again. "Let's start over. Tell me about Kiev, the mafia, and the sex slavery industry."

Alina picked up her cigarette and crossed her arms. "After the Soviet Union collapsed, Ukraine became an independent country in 1991, but the economy went into a deep depression. Ukraine was a mess. The last three years were desperate. Everyone struggled to survive. Prostitution and sex slavery exploded, fueled by the fall of communism and a ruined economy. The government had disintegrated, and the mafia had taken control of local police."

"What about the brothels? How does the mafia recruit the girls into prostitution?"

"Easy. Back then, there weren't any jobs for young people my age. I was a student at the Odessa University in Ukraine studying art history and linguistics. During my second year, I lost my part-time job and ran out of money. I was forced to quit school and planned to return home when I saw an ad for a beauty contest in one of the local night clubs. The winner would receive one hundred US dollars. I tried out and won the contest. I was thrilled with the extra money, but even more excited when the sponsors offered me a job as a hostess. They offered me three times what I was making before and said they'd give me enough money to continue school."

"These were the promoters of the beauty contest?"

"Yes. It sounded perfect until they informed me that I'd have to move to one of their clubs in Kiev. I refused because I'd never been to Kiev and didn't know a soul there. But then they offered to pay my moving expenses and subsidize my rent and said I could enroll in the university. I was so stupid," she said, biting her lip. "Once I got settled, they took my passport, what little money I had, and everything else I owned. They told me I had to work off the expenses they incurred to bring me there plus the daily cost of my food, clothing and housing before I could keep any of the money I made."

"Why didn't you just leave?"

"Because they said they would kill my family unless they made thirty thousand dollars off their investment."

"They called you an investment?"

"It's all about making money."

"Did they force you into having sex?"

"They didn't have to. It was obvious that sex was the only way to pay off Karasov. You really don't have a choice."

"What if you don't cooperate?"

"They either shipped you off to some other God-forsaken place or…"—the color drained from Alina's face—"you simply disappeared."

"You mean they kill you?"

"They don't send you on vacation."

"What about the underage girls?"

"Most of them come from Asia." Alina rocked slightly back and forth. "They don't stay long."

"Where do they go?"

"Nobody asks. It's too dangerous."

"But the young ones..."

Alina flared. "You don't understand anything."

"How much does your government know about this?"

"Haven't you heard a word I've said? Who do you think runs our government?"

Hunter took a deep breath. "What about the United States? How much does my government know about this?"

She laughed. "You'd be surprised at the client list we have of American contractors and international government officials. Even some congressmen are regular customers. They love the virgins, especially the young ones."

"Hearing this makes me sick. Anyone that I'd recognize?"

She nodded. "Of course, but we're very discreet."

"Wow," Hunter said. "Can you get me a list of who's been here?"

"Maybe, but the fee will be very high because of the risk."

"How much?"

"Let me think about it."

Hunter turned off the recorder and wondered how much Cabot had known about all of this before he'd sent Hunter to Kiev.

"What's wrong?" Alina asked. "Why did you stop?"

"That's enough for now. You need to get some sleep before you go back to work." Hunter picked her up and carried her over to the bed. They undressed and crawled under the cool sheets together.

An hour later, Alina shot upright into a sitting position and knocked the covers off. She flailed her arms in the air, screaming in Russian and Ukrainian. He didn't understand a word, but her voice made the hair on his arms stand up.

"Wake up!" Hunter shouted, rubbing her back. "You're having a bad dream."

Wide-eyed, Alina stared across the room at someone or something she thought was trying to hurt her.

Hunter sat up and gently put his arm around her. "You're safe. I'm right here."

She wiped her eyes with the back of her hand and slowly turned toward him. She looked as if she didn't recognize him—almost as if she was staring right through him—then laid back down. When he tried to touch her, she turned away and curled up into a ball.

"Leave me alone," she mumbled.

Hunter stroked her hair. "What happened in your dream?"

"I don't want to talk about it."

"Are you sure?"

She didn't respond, only hugged her pillow.

Hunter pulled up tight behind her. Her back was still hot and sweaty from the bad dream. They didn't say anything to each other for a long time. The only sounds in their room came from an occasional shout or car honk from the street below.

"Try to get some sleep," he urged her.

"I can't," she whispered.

"Why not?"

"I'm afraid to go back to sleep. I might dream again."

"Want one of my sleeping pills?"

"No, I have to get up in a couple of hours."

"What can I do?"

"Talk to me," Alina said quietly.

Hunter draped his arm over her. "About what?"

"Anything." She squeezed his hand. "About New York again."

"Where should I start?"

"I don't care, just keep talking."

He pulled a strand of hair away from her ear and kissed it. "The first time you see the skyline of Manhattan at night, you'll fall in love with New York. The lights from the high-rise office buildings cover the city and twinkle like the Milky Way. It's like your first kiss—you'll never forget it."

"Hmmm," she sighed, "sounds nice."

"It's a city that never sleeps, filled with fascinating people from all over the world."

"Tell me about your apartment."

"It's near Central Park with a view overlooking a thousand skyscrapers. Hot and cold water whenever you want it. Electricity that never fails. Air-conditioning twenty-four hours a day, seven days a week."

She purred. "Isn't it amazing how life works."

"In what way?"

"You and me," she said. "What are the odds that we meet?"

"It's crazy when you think about it. I'm from New York, and you live in Ukraine."

"Maybe not as crazy as you think."

"What do you mean?"

"My mother believed that every person you meet in life is sent by God for some reason—each person is a blessing." Alina pulled his arm tighter around her waist. "I never believed that until I met you." She pushed her naked body against him. "Pretend we're in New York, and tell me about all the things we'd do together."

"We'll stroll down Fifth Avenue and shop, stand on top of the Empire State Building at sunset, ice skate in the rink at Rockefeller Center, drink beer until late into the night at McSorley's, an Irish bar in the Village. We'll go to baseball games at Yankee stadium, buy fantastic cheeses and dried Italian meats at Murray's, eat dim sum for hours in Chinatown, and go on romantic picnics in Central Park." Hunter sat up, lit a cigarette and leaned against the wall. He'd never smoked before he met Alina but was beginning to enjoy it. He took another puff. "How does that sound to you for starters?"

Alina kept her eyes closed. "I think you made a mistake. You described heaven, not New York."

He laughed. "Where would you go if you could live anywhere?"

She smiled. "I can't tell you."

"Why not?"

"You'll think it's stupid."

"No, I won't. I promise."

"I dream about living on a small hobby farm overlooking a beautiful glacier lake deep in the mountains. It's far away from the city and the people I never want to see again." She closed her eyes. "For once in my life, I want to feel safe and free."

Hunter kissed her on the neck. "Stand up for a second."

"Why?"

"Just humor me."

Slowly, she stood up. "What are you up to now?"

"I want you to close your eyes for a second." He got out of bed and walked over to his desk. "And no peeking."

Alina giggled and closed her eyes. "This better be good."

Hunter pulled out a small blue box and walked back to Alina. "Okay, you can open your eyes now."

"What's this?" she said, staring at a small box in his hand.

"What does it look like?" He handed the box to her. "A present."

She stared at the box but didn't open it.

Hunter looked hurt. "What's wrong?"

"I don't think this is a good idea."

"You can decide after you open it."

She shook her head. "No."

"Come on, it's just a small present."

"I don't want you to get the wrong impression."

"What? That this is all business?" Hunter said. "Don't worry, I get it."

"I didn't mean it that way. It's just that…"

"If it'll make you feel better," he said, "think of this as a small thank-you for all of your help."

"No one has given me a present in a long time," she said, then opened the box and looked at the gold cross on a necklace. "It's beautiful!" She wiped a tear away from her cheek. "Where did you get this?"

Hunter blushed. "It was my mother's. Let me help you." He moved behind her, draped the necklace around her neck and securing the clasp. "There you go… now you have your very own gold cross. You'll always be safe and free from now on."

She slowly turned around and played with the cross in her fingers. Without warning, she leaned forward and kissed him. He closed his eyes and licked his lips as if they were covered in honey. She kissed him again and then gently moved him back to the bed. As she wrapped her legs around his body, Hunter whispered, "I want you to come home with me."

Her eyes popped open. "What are you saying?"

"I love you." He kissed her hair. "We'll start our own family. New York's a long way from your mountain paradise, but we can take vacations anytime you want." Before she could respond, Hunter described what their children would look like, what their names might be and what they liked for breakfast.

Alina laughed. "My employer wouldn't be very happy."

"So what? Screw Karasov!"

She laughed. "I've done that already."

"I'm serious."

"It wouldn't work." Alina sighed. "Besides, I don't have any documents. They took my passport when I first arrived."

"What if I could arrange new documents?"

"You can do that?"

Hunter grinned. "Let me worry about the passport."

"I love you." She threw her arms around his neck and squeezed.

"I love you too," he said softly. Grabbing the edge of the comforter, he tucked her under the covers and returned to his desk to work.

While she slept, Hunter made a list of things he would have to do to bring Alina back to America. He would need to call in some big favors, but with a little luck, it just might work.

Staring at his computer, he tried to work on his current article, but he couldn't stop thinking about Alina. He looked at his notes scattered all over the room and realized that he could write an entire book on what he was learning from her. This project turned into a bigger story than he ever expected. Not only were American companies directly and indirectly doing business with the mafia, but officials of the United States government were involved. Alina's secret client list could easily become an international scandal. Clearly, in Kiev the lines between pleasure, business and politics were nonexistent. Everyone looked out for their own self-interests because so many business and political interests were interconnected. Billions of dollars were at stake. Companies bartered for various contracts, oil, drugs, arms, political positions and sex was commonplace at all levels of corporations and governments. The more he discovered in Kiev, the more afraid he became for his safety and Alina's.

Three hours later, Alina yawned and rolled onto her side so she could watch him work.

"Did you have a good nap?" he asked.

"What time is it?"

"Almost seven. You better get ready or you'll be late for work."

Hugging her pillow, Alina lay quietly and watched Hunter as he typed. In a low voice, she asked, "Why are you doing this?"

"It was my boss's idea."

"That's not what I meant." Alina sat up and leaned against the headboard.

Hunter's left foot rocked back and forth under his desk. He started to say something but then just shrugged and turned back to the computer.

"You know they'll probably kill you if the *Times* publishes these articles." Alina continued, "They have people in New York."

Hunter pushed his chair back. "I doubt that."

"You don't know them like I do," she said. "These guys are dangerous, especially the Russians. Trust me. They're in Brooklyn."

"Why the Russians?"

"Because to them, it's only business."

Hunter laughed.

Alina crossed her arms and frowned. "What are you laughing about?"

He walked over to the bed and tried to kiss her, but she turned away. "You're so dramatic," he said.

"I'm serious."

"I know you are, and that's why I love you."

Alina put her arms around his neck. "Maybe we should forget everything, sell the information to the *Times* and run away. We can change our names, change our hair color and disappear. Or was that your idea?"

"What about the girls at the club?" Hunter asked. "What would happen to them if we sold the information?"

"The young ones will disappear." Her face turned dark. "They'd probably get sold to clubs in other countries. After a few months, things would settle down and it'd be business as usual."

"So, all of this would be for nothing?" Hunter asked.

"We'd be together."

"But don't you care about the girls?"

"You're so naïve. You Americans are funny people, so full of yourselves. You run around the world trying to fix everything. Some days, you pretend that you're a self-righteous priest, and other days, you're the world's policemen."

"But somebody has to stop these people."

"Do you think your articles will change anything?" Alina said. "These crimes have been going on here for years. Nobody gives a shit. All they care about is making money." She pulled back and searched his face. "Why do you care?"

"I didn't at first." Hunter looked into Alina's eyes. "But now... I have a reason."

"Even if it gets you killed?"

Hunter laughed nervously. "That's only in the movies."

"You're a good man, Hunter Moretti." Alina leaned over and kissed him on each eye. "Stupid, but a good man."

Chapter 12

"Hunter?" Alina tapped his hand. "You didn't answer my question."

He looked across the table covered with the remains of their breakfast at Pastis. Her red hair looked as if it were on fire ignited by the morning sun shining through the window. He blinked his eyes several times to get his bearing.

"What question?"

"Weren't you listening?"

"Sorry," Hunter rubbed his forehead, "what was the question again?"

"Do you still have my two trunks from Kiev?"

"Yes." Hunter squinted at Alina, trying to read her face.

"Where are they?"

"Somewhere safe."

"I need to get something out of one of them."

The breakfast crowd at Pastis was starting to clear out. The waitress stopped by their table holding the check, but she hesitated when they both stopped talking.

"Should I come back later?" she asked.

"No, this is fine." Hunter handed her a credit card.

After she left, they sat quietly for a minute drinking coffee and avoiding eye contact.

"When do you need it?" he finally asked.

"Let me see what Karasov's schedule looks like."

When Hunter set his cup down, Alina pointed to his left hand. "What about you?" she said, touching his ring finger. "Why aren't you married?"

"Never found the right woman."

"And who would be the right woman?"

"Someone I could trust." He regretted that statement as soon as the words left his mouth.

Alina's shoulders slumped slightly. "Do you remember when we first moved to our little flat in Kiev and played house?"

"I remember."

"Remember when you asked me to come back to New York with you?"

"Yes."

Alina's eyes searched his face. "We were happy back then, weren't we?"

Then she abruptly stood up, grabbed her purse off the chair and slung it over her shoulder. "Thanks for breakfast."

Hunter reached out and grabbed her hand. "Alina, if we start this again... how will it end this time?"

"I don't know," Alina said.

He released her hand and watched her walk away.

Not what I expected, he thought. She makes me so happy one minute and yet angry the next. I've never met someone so easy to love and hate at the same time.

Hunter decided to walk back to work. At this time of the morning, the sidewalks were still crowded. Hunter missed Kiev where people moved at a slower pace. Even though Hunter only knew a bit of Russian and Ukrainian, everyone tried to talk to him in the restaurants and stores. People there smiled and wanted to talk to Americans. At the Rus', they treated him like a VIP. Inside the club, he could have anything or anybody he wanted. For the first time in his life, he felt as if he was somebody— someone important.

Hunter continued through several neighborhoods, and not one person paid any attention to him. He was a ghost in his own city— invisible to everyone but his cat and Tess. In New York, he was nobody.

Waiting at a stoplight, a girl passed him who reminded him of Alina. A voice in his head said: Hunter, you're a sap, a loser. You ruined the happiest day in your life. Then another voice—his own—whispered: I didn't intend to hurt her. It just came out that way.

* * *

Tess was already at her desk when Hunter arrived on Monday morning.

"What's wrong?" Hunter asked as he walked into his office and sat down.

She followed him in. "What do you mean?"

"Something's wrong," Hunter said sarcastically. "You've never beaten me into the office in five years."

"I made a mistake."

"Good, don't let it happen again."

"I actually have a different reason why I came in early."

Hunter threw his hands in the air. "Hah, I knew this was too good to be true. I suppose you are setting me up to leave early again. What is it this time? Is your cable man coming? Do you need to get your hair done?"

"It's personal."

Hunter stopped smiling. "Are you okay?"

"Wait a second," Tess tilted her head sideways and leaned forward. "Are you worried about me?"

"No, absolutely not." Hunter shook his head and squirmed around in his chair. "It's just that I have a lot of work today, and I need you."

Tess didn't respond but leaned against the door.

Hunter peeked at her as he pretended to shuffle papers around on his desk. "And I needed to know if I should get help from the secretarial pool."

Tess bent over and laughed in one of those deep belly laughs that only children make. "You're such a terrible liar," she said. "Actually, I had an early dentist appointment. After that, I decided to come to work early to catch up on a few things… but I do appreciate your sweet concern."

Hunter sighed and looked at the ceiling in disgust. "Trust me. It won't happen again. Now get out of my office so I can get some work done."

He spent most of the day interviewing dignitaries at the United Nations. It was after four o'clock by the time he returned to the office and immediately got a call from Cabot, who succinctly said, "I want to see you right now."

As Hunter entered Cabot's office, his boss shouted, "Close the door and sit down."

"Am I in trouble?"

"No." Cabot pulled a large Cuban cigar out of a teak humidor on his desk and shoved it into his mouth. "What did you find out at the United Nations?"

"Nothing yet."

"What do you mean nothing?" Cabot leaned forward in his chair. "I told you to get that interview with Ambassador Karasov."

"I already called Alina about setting up a meeting with him." Hunter played with a pen in his hand. "It's pretty ironic."

"What is?"

Hunter shook his head. "Karasov almost shot my frickin' hand off two years ago, and now you want me to interview him."

"It's not optional. The brass upstairs insists that you obtain an interview with Karasov. They still have the misconception that you're special. That's what pisses me off."

"What?" Hunter said.

"The trip to Kiev was my idea, and you get all the accolades."

"That's not my fault," Hunter said.

Cabot stood up, walked to the window and looked at the New York skyline. "Here's the deal. I need a good story. Sales are down, and I'm getting a lot of pressure from upstairs."

"Karasov never grants interviews to reporters."

"Tell him that you're not a reporter."

"What am I then?"

"You're a writer."

"What should I use as an excuse for a meeting?"

"Tell him we can help his cause at the Capitol with some good press," Cabot said. "These assholes are all the same. They love themselves and will do anything to get in the *Times*."

"Okay, but even if I get the interview, what should I ask him?"

"Ask him why Ukraine has to import eighty percent of their oil and gas from Russia when it has plenty of their own oil and gas. I guarantee that you'll get a great quote from that question. Ukraine's getting into the oil business, and I want you to find out which American oil companies are vying for the contracts." He smirked. "What do you think of Karasov becoming an ambassador?"

"Opinion or reason?"

"Reason."

"Okay—he became an ambassador because the Russian mafia is a huge threat to him and his organization. He needed to figure out a new way to protect himself and increase his power, so he appointed himself as ambassador of Ukraine to the United States. If he can't steal the shit from the Russians, he's going legit and siphoning money from his own country by privatizing key industries and natural resources such as oil and gas."

"That's my boy. One way or another, get that interview!"

Hunter walked back to his office and pulled Alina's card out of his pocket. He was about to call her when his phone rang.

"Hello?"

"Hi, Hunter," Carrie said. "I'm calling to remind you of our date tomorrow night."

"Oh, sure," Hunter said. "What are we doing again?"

"We're going to a coffee house in Tribeca to hear a great writer give a reading. Remember?"

"What time?"

"I'll meet you there at 7:30 p.m."

"Sounds great. See you there."

Hunter hung up and immediately called Alina.

"Yes."

"Am I catching you at a bad time?"

"No, I just finished a meeting. I have fifteen minutes before the United Nations is back in session."

"Are you still mad at me for the things I said at Pastis?" Hunter asked.

Silence.

"I'm sorry about the way I acted." Hunter twisted the cord on his phone. "It's just that everything has happened so fast. Frankly, I'm still in shock that you're here."

"I know, but you have to trust me. I have a plan for us, but I need your help."

"When can I see you again?"

"Let me call you later, and we'll figure something out, but we have to be very careful."

"I almost forgot," Hunter said. "I need a favor."

"What kind of favor?"

"I need an interview with Karasov."

Alina didn't respond.

"Are you still there?"

"Yes, I heard you."

"Well?"

"You know this would be a very bad idea."

"It's not me, it's Cabot. He knows the ambassador's in town."

More silence.

"Just a second." Alina covered the phone and said something muffled to somebody in the room with her. "Hunter, I have to call you back. I need to move outside."

A minute later, his phone rang.

"Alina?" he asked, hopefully.

"What exactly does your boss know about us?" Alina asked.

"Only what I want him to know."

"Okay." Alina paused again. "I'll arrange the interview, but first, I'd like to meet this boss of yours."

"That's a really bad idea."

"But I've heard so many good things about him," she said sarcastically.

"Not funny."

"Here's the deal. If you want the interview, I get to meet Cabot and his wife first."

"And his wife? Why? How should I explain that to him?"

"Tell him I want to meet the people who have been so helpful to you."

"Bullshit. He won't buy that."

"It doesn't matter what he thinks. I want you to invite Cabot and his wife for dinner tonight."

"Why are you insisting on something so stupid?"

"Because I'm an unstable woman… and I'm capable of anything."

Hunter picked up the framed photo of Alina off his desk and stared at her face. "We don't need a dinner to prove that. What do you really want from my boss?"

"More connections," Alina said.

"What if he doesn't want to do it?"

"Then, the paper doesn't get the interview with Karasov."

Now it was Hunter's turn to pause. "Alina, what's going on?"

"Nothing I can't handle."

"Some kind of trouble?"

"Call me when your boss agrees to meet," Alina said and then hung up.

Hunter called Cabot and told him about Alina's request. Cabot was oddly excited. Apparently, he had always wanted to meet Alina.

"Can you make dinner at your apartment for us?" Cabot said.

"I thought we'd have dinner at some nice restaurant and charge it to your expense account. Besides, my place is a pit."

"I can't take us all to a restaurant. I'm way over budget on my expense account."

"How about your apartment?' Hunter said. "It's much nicer than mine."

"No way," Cabot said. "Leah would have a fit. You know how she hates to cook."

Hunter reluctantly agreed and called Alina to confirm the dinner at his apartment. Hunter kicked a wastepaper basket across the floor. Tess poked her head into his office.

"I heard a loud noise," she explained.

Hunter pulled his chair roughly up to the desk and started to write on a document when his pen ran out of ink. He angrily rummaged through his drawers, trying to find a new one. "Goddamn it. Where are all my pens?"

"Take it easy," Tess said. "I'll get one for you." Then she disappeared for a moment and returned with her hands full of pens. "Do you need anything else?"

"No, I'm fine," he growled.

The phone on her desk started to ring. "I have to get that."

A few seconds later, Hunter heard Tess squeal. "You're kidding. The truck is at the end of the block." She paused, then said, "Beth, thanks for the call. I owe you."

Tess rushed into his office and clapped her hands together. "You won't believe it, but Psycho Sara's at the end of our block!"

"Who's Psycho Sara?"

Tess stared him in disbelief. "You don't know Psycho Sara's famous food truck?"

"No," Hunter said, slightly irritated. "So what."

"So what? She's one of the most famous chefs in New York City."

"What is she doing at the end of the block?"

"Grab your wallet and follow me." Tess pulled him out of his chair.

He resisted. "You go without me. She sounds scary. I don't want anyone named Psycho Shirley fixing my food."

"It's Psycho Sara, not Shirley." She pulled even harder until he reluctantly stood up. "You're in for a treat that you'll never forget."

They quickly made their way down to the street, and Tess pointed to the long line at the end of the block. Tess's eyes twinkled with excitement. "She's the queen of food truckers. She's crazy and only cooks whenever she feels like it. She'll pick a place to park for a day, and New York will rush to find her."

Hunter pointed at the truck painted with bright psychedelic flowers. "I'm not sure I want to eat any food coming out of that thing."

"Don't be such a crab. You'll love her."

"I can't wait," Hunter said disinterested.

When they finally reached the truck, Hunter stepped to the window. "I'd like to see your menu."

A woman around forty leaned out of the window. Her hair was psychedelic green and her visible skin was a canvas for tattoos and countless piercings. Psycho Sara glared at Hunter and said, "What did you just say?"

Tess pushed him aside. "Sorry, don't pay any attention to him." She pointed her thumb at Hunter. "He's a rookie."

Psycho Sara gave him one more look over and then disappeared into the truck.

Tess sighed. "Whew! You almost blew it."

"I just asked for a menu."

"She doesn't have a menu. You don't get out much, do you?" She rolled her eyes. "You'd better be grateful for what she gives you, or she'll never serve you again."

"Whatever she's cooking today will be the best lunch you've ever had."

Psycho Sara handed Tess two baskets and said to Hunter, "That'll be $36."

Hunter balked but handed over two twenties. Psycho Sara frowned but took the money and disappeared into the truck. Hunter waited for his change, but when she returned, she ignored Hunter and handed food to the next people in line.

Tess yelled at Hunter. "Come on, the food is getting cold."

"What about my change?" He looked back at the window.

"Forget it. That's your penalty for being such a dork."

Hunter didn't like it, but it didn't appear he had any choice. They found a stoop near the truck to sit on. Tess opened her basket and took a deep breath. "Smell that! Now that's heaven."

Hunter looked at his sandwich. "Looks like a plain meatball sandwich to me."

Tess licked her lips, held the sandwich with both hands and took a huge bite. "Oh, God," she moaned. "This is like an orgasm in a sandwich."

"I've never heard a meatball sandwich described quite that way."

"Shut up and take a bite," Tess said with her mouth full. "You'll see what I mean."

Hunter turned the sandwich this way and that trying to figure out the best way to insert the huge bun into his mouth. Finally, he made his move to come in at an angle to get at least part of the meatball. He took a second quick bite then went all-in with a huge mouthful. The green pesto squirted out of the sides of his mouth, and the gooey, white buffalo mozzarella cheese dribbled down his chin. He looked over at Tess and burst out laughing. She looked like a one-year-old eating her first birthday cake with her hands. Her face was smeared with goop from her sandwich. She didn't let go of her sandwich but tried to wipe her face with the back of her hand.

He pointed at her. "You should see your face!"

Tess laughed. "You don't look any better." She set the sandwich down and wiped her hands with a napkin. Then she took a fresh napkin and gently wiped a glob of pesto off his chin. "You know that's the first time I've heard you laugh since you returned from Kiev."

Hunter held the remaining third of his sandwich in the air. "I will never doubt you again. Best sandwich ever."

Tess dabbed the other corner of his mouth and smiled.

Suddenly, Hunter stood up. "We better get back to the office. I've got a meeting. It's your fault if I dream about that meatball sandwich."

"My pleasure," Tess said.

Chapter 13

Hunter sat through two meetings and then took the rest of the afternoon off to clean his apartment, a task he had ignored for the past two weeks. He was still vacuuming when the intercom buzzed promptly at six-thirty. He was expecting Alina, but Cabot and Leah arrived first. He buzzed them in and a few minutes later greeted them at his door. Cabot breezed past him without shaking hands, leaving Leah standing in the hall.

"What the hell! What kind of place has no elevator?" Cabot complained.

Hunter stepped into the hall and gave Leah an awkward hug. "Hi, Leah. It's been a while."

"I don't know why I'm here," she said harshly as she wiped perspiration from her forehead. "I hate this stupid business stuff."

Hunter unsuccessfully tried to smile. "Let me take your shawl."

Leah handed Hunter a pretty copper shawl and followed Cabot into the living room. She and Cabot looked around as if taking a slow inventory of his small apartment. Leah sniffed, as her gaze moved from his writing desk to an old green couch with frayed armrests, the small dining room table with four mismatched chairs, and across the room to his tiny kitchen. Finally, she wrinkled her nose and sneezed. "What's that icky smell?"

"My feeble attempt at dinner."

"Not that, it's something else."

Hunter shrugged. "I have a cat. Maybe it's the litter box."
Leah sneezed again. "I knew it. I'm allergic to cats."
"Sorry, I'll make sure she stays in the bedroom."
Cabot sat on the couch and crossed his leg over his knee. "I'll have a scotch, one ice cube and no water."
"Leah, what can I get you?" Hunter asked.
Leah sat opposite Cabot on the couch and clutched her purse with both hands.
Hunter looked at Leah and said, "Would you like me to take your purse?"
"No, I'm fine."
"Anything to drink?"
"Do you have any white wine?"
"Of course. I have Chardonnay."
Hunter went into the kitchen to get the drinks.
Leah stared at the bare walls and secondhand furniture. "You could use some decorating. It looks like nobody lives here."
"I'm working on it," Hunter yelled from the kitchen.
"Where's the girl?" Leah said.
"Her name's Alina," Hunter said.
"I thought it was Carrie." Leah glared at Cabot, who squirmed at the other end of the couch.
"Who's Alina? Is she a new client?"
Cabot yelled at Hunter from the couch, "How are those drinks coming?"
Hunter returned with their drinks and sat across from them in a chair he'd bought at a flea market. They stared at each other and quietly sipped their drinks. Leah yawned three times while Cabot's left foot tapping rapidly on the floor.
This may be a long night, Hunter thought. Finally, he broke the silence, "How's the wine?"
Leah made a face. "Too dry for my taste."
"I can get you something else."
"Come on, Leah," Cabot growled. "We just got here, and you're already complaining."

"Well, Hunter asked if I liked the wine. I was being honest."

They sat quietly again, looking at everything in the room but each other.

Cabot glanced at his watch. "Hunter, my boy, when do you think we'll get the interview with Karasov?"

"Maybe Alina can tell us tonight."

"How long have you known this girl?" Leah asked.

"We met a couple of years ago in Kiev. It's a long story."

"I'm not impressed with her so far." Cabot looked at his watch again and frowned. "Do you think she's coming?"

Just then, the intercom buzzed. "There she is. I'll be right back. I'll run down and bring her up."

Alina was standing outside the building's entrance wearing a pretty lime-green, summer dress. Her red hair hung loosely across her bare shoulders. She held up a small bouquet of flowers and a bottle of wine.

"Beautiful," Hunter said.

Alina lifted the flowers to her nose one last time and took a deep breath before handing them to Hunter. "They are beautiful, and I love the smell of summer flowers."

"I was referring to you, not the flowers."

As he reached for the bottle of wine, Alina kissed him lightly on the lips. "I wanted to make a good impression on your boss."

Hunter laughed. "You don't need flowers or wine to accomplish that." Hunter leaned closer to Alina. "Just a head's up. Leah's okay, just a bit stuffy, but working with Cabot has not been easy."

"No problem. I'm used to men like that."

"He's also very insecure, especially around a woman like you."

"And what kind of a woman am I?"

"You know what I mean."

At his apartment door, Hunter took a deep breath and led Alina into the living room. "We made it," he announced more loudly than intended. He set the flowers and wine on the dining room table. Before he could introduce Alina, Leah remained seated as Cabot jumped off the couch and extended his hand.

"Cabot, I'd like you to meet Alina." Hunter said.

Alina stepped closer and fixed her eyes on Cabot. Hunter had seen it many times before. Her body changed, her mouth took on a different shape and her breathing slowed. No man had a chance at this point. It was fascinating to watch Cabot's reaction as Alina extended her hand and pulled him close. Cabot stood with his mouth open and his eyes unblinking as if he was having an out-of-body experience.

Alina held his gaze and his hand longer than necessary and then turned to Leah on the couch. She bent over and held her hand out. "I'm Alina," she said confidently.

Leah slowly let go of her purse and offered a limp hand.

Alina kept smiling, but her eyes narrowed slightly. "I've heard so much about you and Cabot," she said.

Hunter watched the eye contact between the two women. They were like two boxers circling each other before one of them threw the first punch.

"Oh, really?" Leah shared a quick glance at Cabot.

"I understand that you and Cabot have been very helpful to Hunter."

"Yes, yes, we have." Leah smiled thinly. "He's such a lovely boy."

Hunter quickly took Alina's arm and steered her toward an empty chair.

"Alina, come sit by me." Cabot patted the sofa cushion next to him.

Alina left Hunter's grasp and walked to the couch. As she sat down, Leah moved further toward the opposite end.

After several minutes of small talk, Hunter motioned to Cabot. "Why don't you help me in the kitchen while the ladies chat?"

Once they got into the kitchen, Cabot pulled Hunter aside. "I take back everything I said about Alina. My God, she's the most intoxicating and beautiful woman I've ever met." He kept looking back at Alina, who was trying to make conversation with Leah. "She's so much taller than I expected."

A few minutes later, Hunter and Cabot brought out the pasta with garlic bread and passed it around family-style. Hunter poured Alina's wine, Cabot tasted it and licked his lips. "What a wonderful red wine."

"I'm glad you like it," Alina said.

Cabot raised his glass high in the air. "To Alina. You are as beautiful as your wine. Welcome to the United States."

"Thank you. You're sweet to say such a kind thing," Alina said, humorously using an extra-thick Ukrainian accent.

She's really good, Hunter thought. Cabot doesn't have a clue.

Leah coughed and wiped her mouth with her napkin. "Hunter, do you have any more of the white wine?"

Hunter set his napkin on his chair and walked into the kitchen to retrieve the bottle of Chardonnay. When he returned, Cabot and Alina were already deep into a discussion of Eastern European politics. It didn't matter what subject he brought up—art, literature, music, history—Alina proved to be informed and intelligent—a charming conversationalist. To make a point, she'd often put her hand on top of Cabot's hand or forearm, causing him to lose his train of thought. When Hunter interjected a comment, his boss ignored him or cut him off. Every time Alina asked the table a question, Cabot tried to answer before anyone else.

Cabot refilled his wine glass. "How did you meet Ambassador Karasov?"

Alina paused. "It's a long, boring story."

"I have all night," Cabot said, pulling his chair a little closer to her.

Let the games begin, Hunter thought.

Leah rolled her eyes and yawned.

Alina began, "I was a student at the university."

"Which one?" Cabot asked.

"The Odessa National University."

"Odessa? What a small world," Cabot said. "I had relatives in Odessa."

"Which part do they live in?"

Cabot's face turned dark. "They're all dead now, murdered in the Odessa Holocaust—the Odessa Massacre during World War II."

"Don't get him started," Leah said. "He'll complain all night about the Ukrainians that stood by and let the Germans and Romanians slaughter his relatives."

Hunter stood up. "I need a drink." He walked into the kitchen.

"How did you end up in Kiev?" Cabot asked.

"After the fall of the Soviet Union and the economic collapse in Ukraine, I couldn't afford to continue my studies," Alina said. "I needed a job, and a friend introduced me to Mr. Karasov. He was a successful businessman and kind enough to help me."

"Very generous."

"I don't have any family, and he took very good care of me during a very difficult time."

"I'm sorry. No family?" Cabot asked.

"I never knew my parents. I was orphaned at a very young age, so I'm very grateful for Mr. Karasov."

Hunter knew the story wasn't true, but he watched in awe at how brilliantly Alina could weave her fiction.

"He sounds almost like a second father," Cabot said.

Alina sneaked a quick glance at Hunter, who was returning with his drink. "Yes, something like that," she said.

"Who's this Karasov guy anyway?" Leah asked.

"Ukraine's new ambassador," Hunter said.

Cabot reached into the pocket of his sport coat and pulled out a long cigar.

"Montecristo?" Alina said.

Cabot's eyes widened. "How did you know?"

"That's a big dog smoke. Smooth, nice draw—but not for amateurs."

"Care for one? I have an extra."

"Thank you. I'd love one."

Cabot grinned and handed Alina his cigar. He pulled a cutter from a pocket, snipped off the end and opened his lighter. Alina tilted forward and took several draws before leaning back and blowing smoke rings toward the ceiling.

"You're amazing. I've never seen a woman smoke a cigar."

Hunter smiled. She's got him now, he thought. She owns him.

Leah sniffed and played with her fork. "So, what exactly do you do for the ambassador?"

"I'm his translator."

"What do you translate?"

"Leah, don't be an idiot," Cabot said.

Leah frowned and ignored him.

"All kinds of documents from different countries," Alina said. "I speak five languages."

"I see," Leah said, averting her gaze as Alina confidently stared at her.

"Now, Leah—tell me," Alina said. "What do you do?"

Hunter spoke before Leah could respond. "What can I get anyone? More wine, coffee, an after-dinner drink?"

Alina turned back to Cabot. "I'm curious, do you have any connections on the Senate Appropriations Committee?"

Cabot set his wine glass on the table and leaned forward. "Why do you ask?"

"I'd be grateful if you would arrange a meeting with the chair of the Appropriations Committee. Also, I'd like to meet the chair of the Committee on Foreign Relations."

Stunned, Cabot eventually smiled and asked, "Is that all?"

"No. Karasov's looking for a friendly banker. Could you make an introduction?"

"A friendly banker? What do you mean by that?"

"He has some confidential investments in New York that requires…" She paused and smiled. "…let's just say he's looking for someone that can give him a personal touch."

"I'll have to think about that. Anything else?"

"That'll do for starters."

Cabot sat back in his chair and looked at Alina like a poker player trying to read her hand. He poured more wine and swirled it for a few seconds. "Senator Johnson handles Foreign Relations," he said. "He was one of my roommates in college. Senator Abraham's the chair of Appropriations. His committee is the most powerful in Congress." Cabot smiled. "By coincidence, he attends our church."

Alina sat up in her chair with a sly grin. "What a small world."

"I might be able to arrange both meetings, but I want something in return."

"Something like..." Alina wet her lips and leaned closer to Cabot. "...like an interview with my boss?"

Cabot cleared his throat. "Yes—I want Karasov."

Alina winked at Cabot and set her hand on top of his hand. "Interesting how we live several thousand miles apart, and yet we have mutual friends."

Cabot's breath quickened. His face flushed red. "One can never have too many friends."

"Let's celebrate our new friendship," Alina said.

Leah looked at the ceiling and mumbled to no one in particular, "Oh, for God's sake."

Alina ignored her and squeezed Cabot's hand. "In Kiev, we always celebrate with a glass of vodka." She looked at Hunter. "Do you have any, Hunter?"

"Just the thing." He ran into the kitchen, pulled a bottle from the freezer, and returned to the table. "Here we go—real Russian vodka, not the cheap stuff. I've been saving it for a special occasion."

Alina applauded when Hunter returned to the table with a tray and four shot glasses. She filled each glass and then held the tray in front of Cabot. He glanced at his wife, then reached for a glass. "If you insist."

Alina moved the tray to Leah, who frowned and turned her nose up, saying, "I don't drink vodka."

"Try some, you'll like it," Alina said.

"No, thank you. I'll stick to my California wine," Leah said, emphasizing the word California.

Cabot chastised her. "Leah, don't be rude. She's our guest."

Leah shrugged and sipped more wine.

They all stood up, except Leah, who shook her head at the spectacle. Alina held her glass in the air and announced, "Dlya Vashoho zdorov'ya! To your health!"

They touched glasses and swallowed the shot without stopping.

Cabot's eyes watered as he held his empty glass in the air. "Wow, that's strong stuff."

Alina laughed and slapped him on the back. "It's an acquired taste."

They sat down, and Alina announced to Cabot, "Give me a couple of days, but I'm sure I can arrange a meeting with Karasov." She handed him a business card. "I'll call you."

Cabot reached for the card, but she held onto it as she said, "Meanwhile, call me if there's anything else I can do for you. I'm always available to help my friends."

Leah stood up. "It's getting late," she announced as she walked to the door.

Cabot sighed. "I guess we're leaving."

At the door, Cabot thanked Hunter and extended his hand to Alina.

"We're not as formal. In our country, we prefer this…" She leaned forward and kissed him twice on each cheek. "What do you think?"

"I like it better."

Alina turned toward Leah. "It was nice to meet you."

Leah just nodded and walked through the door without a goodbye, and Cabot in tow. After they left, Alina grabbed her purse and lit a cigarette. "Oh, my God, I thought they'd never leave." She took a deep drag and let the smoke out slowly. "So much for your boss." Then she inhaled even longer a second time. "And that Leah! No wonder Cabot's such an uptight asshole. I'll bet you a million dollars his wife hates sex."

"Christ, did you have to lay it on so thick," Hunter said. "Leah's going to kill him on the way home."

"Serves him right for the way he treats her." She flicked the cigarette ash into an ashtray. "I know what men like him want. Trust me, I know exactly what I'm doing." Her eyes softened. "Let me help you clean up."

"Absolutely not. I'll take care of it later." Hunter walked into the kitchen and reached for two highball glasses, some ice and two slices of lime. "Now we can have a proper reunion."

They moved to the couch and sipped on their drinks.

"This isn't how I imagined your apartment," Alina said. "I always pictured your place bigger."

"I had a bigger place on the Upper East Side, but it was too far from work, so I moved to East Village. It's a little Bohemian, but I like it."

"In Kiev, you made it sound like you lived in a palace." Alina looked around the room. "I pictured us living in one of those glass high-rises you described to me. But this…" she shook her head, "this reminds me of our flat in Kiev."

"That's why I took it." Hunter swallowed hard and looked at the floor. "I could fix it up."

"This needs more than fixing," Alina said. "You'd have to demolish it."

Alina took Hunter's glass from his hand and set it down on the coffee table. She kissed him softly, barely touching his lips, then moved closer, caressing his face while kissing his forehead, his eyes and then his lips again. The muffled sound of a phone ringing stopped her, but she didn't move to answer it.

"What's wrong?"

She sighed and pushed away from Hunter.

The phone rang again. "Don't," Hunter said.

"I have to go."

"No, you don't."

She shook her head. "I do, really."

"Is that Karasov?"

She nodded.

"Goddamn it."

"Soon, we won't have to worry about him."

Hunter looked up. "What do you mean?"

"This is what you want, isn't it—for us to be together?"

"Of course, but don't leave now. Make an excuse—say your battery went dead. Tell him anything, but stay with me tonight."

Alina kissed him once more. "I'll call you tomorrow." She grabbed her things and walked out the door.

Hunter poured another shot of vodka. Angel, his cat, scampered to him from behind the couch and rubbed against his leg. "What do you want?" he asked. Angel purred and jumped into his lap. "You only do this when you need something." He pushed her off, drained his glass and went to bed.

* * *

Hunter was already into his third cup of coffee, but he hadn't accomplished anything productive. It was only nine o'clock, and he was already exhausted. He hadn't slept more than a few hours because he kept thinking about his evening with Alina, Cabot and Leah. He tried writing a new article but couldn't sit still long enough to finish it. Frustrated, he pushed his chair away from his desk and walked to the window. It was a cold, rainy morning. He wanted a cigarette, but he didn't want to stand outside and get wet. Alina was supposed to call him before lunch regarding his interview with Ambassador Karasov.

Tess poked her head into his office. "The big guy's on line one."

"Shit." He popped three antacids, chewed for a second and then punched line one on his desk phone.

"Hunter here."

"That was quite the event last night."

"Are you referring to my cooking or my guest?"

"My God, she's something else."

"Now you know why it was so hard to explain Kiev."

"Any luck with arranging the interview with Karasov?"

"I'm working on it."

"In other words, you don't have it."

"Alina's supposed to call me later this morning with the time and place."

"Maybe I should call Alina."

"No, don't do that." Just then, his cell phone began vibrating on his desk. "I think Alina's calling me on my cell. I'll call you right back."

Hunter grabbed the cell phone. "Alina?"

"Karasov agreed to the interview."

"Great," he said. "You made my day. When and where?"

"Today at noon in a restaurant called Shevchenko's at the corner of East 7th Street and 2nd Avenue in the East Village.

"They call that area Little Ukraine. What did you tell Karasov about the interview?"

"That you wanted an exclusive for the *Times*. In exchange, you'll write a flattering article and make yourself available if he needs help in the future."

"Make myself available?"

"Kind of an OUI."

"You mean IOU?"

"Exactly, thank you."

Hunter paused.

"What's wrong?" she asked. "I thought you'd be happy."

"Why did you say I'd help him in the future?"

"Because he never gives anything without getting something bigger in return."

"Does he remember me?"

"Yes."

"After what happened back in Kiev, do we have a problem?"

"No."

Hunter instinctively lowered his voice. "Are you sure? His bodyguard almost shot my hand off."

"Don't worry. I'll be there to translate."

"Why shouldn't I be worried?"

"Because men like Karasov aren't interested in old conflicts unless it affects their business. I paid a heavy price after you left but settled-up with Karasov two years ago. You did your part by not publishing the information I gave you. As far as he's concerned, we're all square unless you do something stupid."

"Any advice for me?"

"Just be careful what you ask him in the interview."

"Why?"

"He's a very suspicious man with a short attention span. Keep the questions brief and to the point. The main reason he's agreeing to the interview is to gain good press and enhance his image. If he senses you're probing into certain areas to make him look bad, he'll be unhappy, and he's very dangerous when he's unhappy."

"What else can I expect?"

"He's very paranoid. It's a dangerous time. Competing mafia groups are killing each other daily. He doesn't trust anyone."

"Even you?"

"You'll have to ask him that question."

"Anything else?"

"I guarantee that he'll ask you for something today."

"Like what?"

"I'll let him tell you. Remember, this is just business to Karasov—nothing personal."

"Easy for you to say. What if he doesn't feel that way?"

"Relax, he needs you. He won't hurt you."

"I hope you're right."

"You mentioned at breakfast that you still have the two trunks?"

"Yes."

"Where?"

"I told you before—somewhere safe."

"In your apartment?"

"Why do you keep asking?"

"Because the information in those trunks could save our lives someday."

"You're such a drama queen."

"And you are so naïve."

"I'll see you at the restaurant," Hunter said.

Chapter 14

A few hours later, Hunter jumped into a taxi and gave the address for Shevchenko's.

"Do you know it?" Hunter asked.

The driver nodded. "Da, yes. It's in my neighborhood."

Hunter recognized the driver's voice. "Yury, it's been a while."

Yury glanced at Hunter in the rearview mirror. "The Black Sea Club?"

"Good memory."

Hunter guessed Yury was somewhere in his mid-thirties. He wore a tight, black T-shirt, but Hunter couldn't stop staring at a bluish tattoo of a rose that covered most of his right bicep and a blue skull on his forearm. Hunter recognized the prison tattoos of the Russian mafia. The skull meant he had killed someone. The last time Hunter had seen those tattoos, he was pinned against the wall by a forearm owned by Karasov's bodyguard. That was just before Karasov dragged Alina away from their flat in Kiev. Hunter wondered how a man like Yury had made it to America.

Yury chewed on a toothpick and glanced at Hunter several times in the rearview mirror as they drove past Chinatown and through Little Italy. Finally, Yury broke the silence, "You been to restaurant before?"

"No, why? Do they have good food?"

Yury shrugged and kept driving. The traffic was bad. It was already hot, well past eighty degrees, even though it was only eleven-thirty in the morning. The backseat smelled like a stale bag of French fries, so Hunter rolled down the window for some fresh air. With another fifteen minutes to kill, he pulled out his notebook and reviewed the list of questions Cabot had given him. He was too nervous to concentrate, so he gave up after a few minutes and put the notebook back into his pocket. Leaning back in the seat, he tried to relax and not think about Karasov.

As the taxi entered the heart of Little Ukraine, Hunter noticed how most of the store signs were written in both English and Cyrillic. Many of the storefronts and sidewalks were partially blocked by mini-farmers markets, racks of cheap clothes, boxes of used books, old furniture, small tables displaying handmade jewelry, sunglasses, fake designer watches and other trinkets. At a red light, a cacophony of street sounds and different languages drifted through his window. Occasionally, he recognized a phrase or a word or two of Russian and Ukrainian, which made him nostalgic for those lazy summer days in Kiev. Through the open window, Hunter savored the smell of sweet sausages, onions and peppers frying.

Yury leaned toward the open passenger window in front. He yelled back and forth to a friend for a few seconds until the light changed. As he drove off, he pointed to his buddy and said to Hunter, "Krascha kovbasa v N'yu-yorku, best sausage in New York."

"Krasche, nizh Italii. Better than in Little Italy?"

"Italians know nothing about good sausage. They drink cheap wine and eat cheesy noodles." Yury thumped his chest and pounded the steering wheel. "Me, Yury, drink vodka and eat real meat." He looked at Hunter in the rearview mirror again. "You Italian?"

"Moretti."

"How you know to speak Ukrainian?"

"I lived in Kiev for a summer," Hunter said.

"You speak Russian?"

"Some, but I know Ukrainian better. By the way, who's the guy running the stand?"

"My cousin, Pavel. He own sausage stand."

"Do you get a cut for all referrals?"

"Zvchayno, of course, we're family." Yury smiled. "We take care of each other."

Hunter stared out the window and wondered what to expect from Karasov as Yury weaved his way through the heavy traffic like a race car driver.

After several more blocks, Hunter said to Yury, "I'll make a deal with you. If you wait for me to finish my meeting, we can stop at your cousin's stand on our way back to my office."

Yury hesitated.

"You can keep the meter running."

Yury still didn't agree until he stopped at another red light. He investigated the rearview mirror. "You seem nice fellow, but…" he wagged his finger in the air above the steering wheel, "but this place no place for tourists."

"Thanks for the advice, but I'll be fine."

"Okay, I wait for you," Yury said. "Da?"

"Da."

They drove four more blocks, and then Yury pulled over to the curb and pointed at the brown building. "There Shevchenko's. Walk downstairs. Restaurant below street."

Hunter stared at the restaurant sign. "Who's Shevchenko anyway?"

"Famous poet and artist in Ukraine."

"Interesting name for a restaurant. I should be back in thirty minutes."

The twelve-story, brick apartment building was one of half a dozen identical buildings on the same block. Hunter walked slowly down several steps to the front door below the sidewalk. Pausing to gather his courage, he took a deep breath and opened the door.

He squinted and blinked several times as his eyes adjusted to the dim light inside the restaurant, which was deserted except for a bartender and one waiter. The main room was long and narrow—approximately thirty feet wide and long enough for a dozen tables covered with red and white checkered tablecloths. If he hadn't known, Hunter wouldn't have been able to tell if it was noon or midnight because no sunlight made its way through the heavy ruby red curtains covering the two windows in front. The only other light came from backlighting behind the bar, several light sconces and small table lamps. Before Hunter could move away from the door, two men in black leather jackets and tight jeans stepped in front of him.

"The restaurant's closed," the big man said in a thick Russian accent.

"I'm Hunter Moretti. I have a meeting with Ambassador Karasov."

The two men exchanged quick glances, and then the first man ordered Hunter to put his hands in the air. Hunter smelled cigarettes and bad cologne as the man patted him down. Once he finished, he looked at his partner and said, "Ochystyty. Clean."

Hunter smiled. "Zvchayno, of course."

The big man was surprised Hunter knew Ukrainian but didn't smile back. He held up his hand. "Pochekay tut. Wait here."

Hunter watched the big guy walk briskly toward the back of the restaurant and stop in front of a semi-circular booth in which a large man in a navy-blue suit was having lunch alone. Hunter recognized Karasov as the bodyguard whispered something to him. Karasov didn't look up but nodded and kept eating.

The big guy waved Hunter to approach. The shorter bodyguard led Hunter through the maze of small tables toward the Karasov's booth. The right wall was covered with dozens of photos—groups of men shaking hands and women hugging someone who appeared to be the proprietor. A middle-aged bartender with thick glasses stood behind the bar, cleaning and polishing the glassware.

As they approached Karasov, Hunter wondered if he'd made a huge mistake. About twenty feet from Karasov's booth, they made Hunter stop again. Two more bodyguards stepped forward and patted down Hunter again and then looked back at Karasov and waited. He barely looked up from his lunch but waved his knife at them to let Hunter approach.

Hunter walked toward the table and stood there waiting for Karasov to acknowledge him. The table was filled with plates of various meats, sausages, cheeses, a basket of bread and a bottle of red wine. Karasov had a white cloth napkin stuffed into the front of his collar. He slouched over his food with both elbows on the table and ate quickly, stuffing more food in his mouth with his fork before he had finished chewing the previous bite. Occasionally he'd pause, wipe his mouth with the back of his hand, and wash down his food with a loud slurp of wine as Hunter watched.

Finally, Karasov grunted and waved his knife at Hunter to take a seat in a chair across from him. The first two bodyguards returned to the front door, while the other two bodyguards remained a few feet away.

"What can I do you for you?" Karasov said, without looking up.

"I'm Hunter Moretti, and I want to thank…"

Karasov cut him off, "I know who you are. You think I don't remember?"

Hunter nervously opened his notebook to look at the list of questions. When he reached for a pen in his coat pocket, his notebook fell, and papers scattered in several directions. The two bodyguards chuckled but didn't offer to help. Karasov shook his head and belched before continuing to eat.

Before he could ask his first question, a waiter appeared with a plate of freshly grilled sausages and more boiled potatoes. After he left, Karasov said, "Begin."

Hunter cleared his throat and said, "Thank you for meeting with me."

"You said that already."

Hunter looked at his notes again and tried to find the first page. Everything was out of order. While attempting to rearrange the pages, he stopped and looked around the room. "Should we wait for Alina?"

"She not coming."

"But she said she would be here to translate."

Karasov stuffed a fork full of potatoes in his mouth. "No translator." He pointed his knife at Hunter. "This between you and me."

This made Hunter even more nervous. "Okay." He glanced down at the unsorted pages. "Can you tell me why you wanted to become the ambassador of Ukraine?" Hunter placed his trembling pen next to the first question and made a check mark.

Karasov set his fork down but kept his knife in his right hand. His upper lip curled slightly. "Tell me why I not kill you right now." Both bodyguards stiffened and took their hands out of their pockets. Karasov squinted at Hunter with eyes the color of a cold winter day. "You fucked my Alina. You tried to hurt my business." Karasov wolfed down a chunk of sausage. "I should've kill you two years ago." He glanced at the bodyguards, and they moved behind Hunter's chair.

Hunter's eyes widened. "But I haven't done anything."

"Do I look like fool?"

"I never said that."

Karasov stabbed a piece of meat and pointed it at Hunter. "Imagine not being here. I could've shot you in Kiev and dumped you in a pit with no marker. Nobody ever find out what happened to you. I could've done that to you." He swallowed the piece of meat and tapped the tip of his knife on the table rapidly. "But I didn't. You know why?"

Hunter shook his head.

"I let you live because I know what kind of shit that woman do to a man. It not your fault. You not first man she seduced." He broke off a piece of bread and soaked it in a pool of brown gravy before stuffing it in his mouth. "We both know this interview is bullshit. Tell me what you want."

Hunter waved his hands in the air and spoke rapidly, "My boss sent me here to interview you. I thought everything was approved by Alina. I didn't want to do it, but my boss made me come."

"You always do what other people tell you?"

Hunter rubbed his sweaty hands together and shifted nervously in his chair.

Karasov's eyes narrowed while he assessed Hunter. After a few seconds, he leaned forward. "You think you smart? You come into my club, my home in Kiev, with your fake name, with your big American money, and you think you take advantage of me?" Karasov's voice sent a chill through Hunter. "You know nothing." He yanked the napkin from his neck. "You think Alina love you?"

The air in the room changed. The guards instinctively moved one step closer to the table.

Hunter stared at Karasov, terrified and speechless.

"You fool. Did you think you steal my Alina and bring back to New York?" He took a swallow of his wine and grunted while gesturing to Hunter's ear. "You lucky boy. To kill you—more trouble than send you home with souvenir."

Hunter unconsciously rubbed his mangled right hand.

"What you want?" Karasov repeated.

"My boss wanted me to ask you a few questions for the newspaper."

Karasov waved his hand in the air. "I don't care about boss's questions. I asking you." He pointed his finger at Hunter's chest. "What you want?"

Hunter hesitated and then blurted out, "I don't know."

"At least you honest. It take courage admit you don't know something. I like that," he said while shoving another forkful of meat into his mouth. "But in life, one has to make real choice, sometimes hard choice." He leaned forward. "You ever make tough choice—kind change your life forever? A choice you no want to make, but had to?"

Hunter resisted the urge to get up and run for the door.

"You know what I talk about?"

The room went silent, and nobody moved. Karasov's fingers tightened around his knife. His jaw clenched, and then he spoke very slowly, "You want fuckin' interview, so answer my question. What you want?"

Hunter noticed that the bartender had disappeared, and the voices in the kitchen were gone. He flashed back to the same helpless feeling he'd had when Karasov had burst into their apartment in Kiev.

Hunter knew his life depended on his next answer.

"I want... I want to know how I can help you," Hunter said.

Karasov burst out laughing. "I underestimate our guest." He looked over at his bodyguards while pointing to his temple. "He not as dumb as I thought." He waved to the closest bodyguard. "More vodka." Karasov didn't take his eyes off Hunter.

The closest guard left for a minute and reappeared with a clear bottle covered in frost from the freezer and two shot glasses. The guard set the tray on the table and poured two shots. Karasov handed one to Hunter. "What should we drink to?"

"Dlya Vashoho zdorov'ya. To your health."

After they downed the shot, Hunter's throat burned and his eyes watered.

"Good?"

"Da, but strong," Hunter said, wiping his mouth with the back of his hand.

The guard immediately filled the glasses again.

Karasov smirked. "How much money she take off you in Kiev?"

Hunter hesitated for a second, then said, "A lot."

Karasov grunted. "Make you mad?"

Hunter grinned. "It wasn't my money. It was my boss's."

Karasov laughed again and raised his glass in the air. "To generous boss."

"And to beautiful women," Hunter said, raising his glass. In unison, they threw their heads back and downed the second shot.

Karasov set his glass down and nodded to a bodyguard. The man quickly pulled out a cigar from inside his coat pocket, trimmed it and handed it to Karasov. As he held the lighter, Karasov took a couple of quick draws to get the cigar lit and then blew grey smoke in the air. Leaning back in the booth, he pointed his cigar to Hunter. "Cuban. You want?"

"Of course," Hunter said.

Karasov waved, and the bodyguard produced another cigar. "Cuban cigars like good woman. They draw you in and leave you wanting more." The guard leaned over and opened a gold-plated lighter. Hunter put the cigar in his mouth, but the end was shaking so badly that the guard had trouble getting the flame on his cigar. Finally, after several attempts, the cigar lit enough for him to keep it going. Then he took a long draw, which relaxed him enough to sit back in his chair.

Karasov poured a third shot and handed it to Hunter. "Now we have proper interview." They quickly drained the shots and set their glasses down.

Hunter picked up his pen again. He felt slightly dizzy, and the vodka made his tongue thick. "What do you want to accomplish while you are in the United States?"

Karasov leaned back in his chair. "I want connections in oil business and your government. You help me?"

"I think so."

"Good." Karasov smiled. "I thought so. You know executives of big oil companies?"

Hunter listed off the presidents of three large American oil companies. "My boss knows all of them."

"Excellent," Karasov said. "Who you know in Washington?"

"My boss went to college with Senator Abraham, chair of the Senate Appropriations Committee. I helped Senator Johnson, chair of the Foreign Relations Committee, run for office. He owes me a number of favors."

"Dobre. Good," Karasov said. "You set up meetings?"

"Da, for you?"

Karasov waved his hand back and forth. "Net, net. Only with Alina."

"Why only Alina?"

"I keep my business secret—rozumity, understand?" Karasov waited for Hunter to respond.

Hunter looked up from his notes. "Why the big secret?"

"The Russkii!" Karasov spit on the floor. "They pig shit. Every year steal billions from us. Every year, try to destroy me."

"Help me understand."

"I explain," Karasov said. "Even though we have more than two billion barrels in oil and gas fields, we not have technology to tap own resources. We forced to import three-fourths of our oil and gas from Russia." Karasov cursed and then added, "Russians extort us with prices that keep our country in debt, so much so we cannot grow own economy."

"What about the money from the huge oil pipelines running across Ukraine to Europe?"

"We don't own pipelines."

Hunter gasped, "You're kidding. Who does?"

"Russians. They pay nothing to cross our land. The pipelines transport most of oil used by Europe. We get nothing." Karasov growled. "That change!" He squeezed his hand into a fist. "I not let Russians control our country again. They killing our economy with greed. You know what average family earn in a year in Ukraine?"

Hunter shook his head.

"Twenty-five hundred dollar." He slammed his fist on the table. "Who live on that?" He hit his fist on the table again. "Your boss spend more on one dinner in New York when he entertain a client." He frowned. "My people suffer. Russians get rich. Nobody in my country have job. Nobody make money because Russian strangle us in debt. We need new relationships for oil equipment and technology."

Hunter wrote down everything Karasov said as fast he could and then asked, "What about the reports of anarchy in Ukraine—daily murders, rampant government corruption, money laundering, drugs and human trafficking?"

Karasov stiffened. "What have do with me?" He was clearly irritated.

"Those problems make it more difficult to get any deals done in Washington."

"Why? What do they care?"

"Because American executives and senators don't want connections with anyone associated with illegal activities."

"Look at me." Karasov's jaw tightened so hard his veins bulged. "Tell me what you see?"

Hunter fumbled around in his chair. "I don't know."

"Do I look like pimp or murder?"

"I never said that," Hunter insisted. But he was thinking: When was the last time you looked at yourself in a mirror?

Karasov pointed his finger at Hunter. "Don't believe everything you read." And then he leaned forward. "You don't know me. I have many enemies. You no idea what it like to save country." He shook his head. "Da, there things that happen, but I do what I need do for

Ukraine. You not understand much. If not for me, Russia would own all Ukrainians. There are sacrifices—choices—to make, but I save my people."

"Besides the oil technology and equipment, what else do you need?" Hunter asked.

"More banking relationships. And your senate approval for more foreign aid." Karasov filled their shot glasses again. "You have senator friends in Washington, da?"

Hunter nodded. "Da."

"We have some contacts in Washington, but need more."

"Like Senator Dixon."

"Da, he's been a loyal friend."

Hunter didn't know how to respond. The last time he had seen the senator in Kiev, Dixon was enjoying a lap dance by a teenager in Karasov's club. The Senator never knew that Hunter was in the club, nor did he know Alina had numerous recordings, receipts and photos of him in compromising positions.

Hunter gathered up his notebook and announced, "I don't think I can help you. This is way out of my league."

Karasov gripped his knife, cut a slice of meat and held it in the air. "That would be unfortunate." He pointed the sharp knife at Hunter. "You want to see Alina again?"

"Yes, but… but I can't do anything illegal."

"No problem." Karasov smiled. "Trust me."

Hunter knew he was trapped. "What exactly do you want me to do?"

"Arrange meetings with executives and Washington officials so we negotiate best deals. Second, good press from *Times* whenever I need. Good for Ukraine. Good for me."

Hunter rapidly scratched the back of his right hand. "That's it?"

Karasov nodded. "We have deal?"

Hunter barely nodded.

"Good." Karasov leaned back and stretched out his right arm.

His bodyguard reached into a coat pocket and handed him a white envelope.

"I want you to have small gift." Karasov held the envelope in his hand for a second and then slowly slid it across the table to Hunter. "For new friendship."

Hunter looked inside. A thick stack of $100 bills was bound by a large rubber band. "What's this for?"

"Appreciation for first article in *Times*."

Hunter pushed the envelope halfway across the table back to Karasov. "I can't take this."

Karasov eyes narrowed. "You refuse gift?"

Hunter's cigar trembled. The envelope sat halfway between them. Karasov waited patiently for Hunter to make a choice.

Karasov spoke first. "Remember conversation about choice?" After several seconds, Karasov tapped his cigar on the edge of the glass ashtray and knocked off the long grey ash. "Okay, if not money, what you want?"

Hunter shrugged.

"You like teaching, da? You want be full professor?"

"How do you know that?"

"I know you." Karasov settled back into the booth and examined Hunter.

Hunter squirmed in his chair, rubbed his sweaty palms on his thighs, stared at his notebook.

"I like you," Karasov said. Then he set his cigar in the ashtray, placed both hands flat on the table and motioned Hunter to come closer. In a low, menacing voice, he said, "But don't ever forget—Alina's mine. After you leave, you be friends again, but you touch her—I kill you." Tiny bubbles of white spit formed in the corners of his mouth. "Then I kill your relatives, your little brown thing, and then I kill your Vinny and Tess."

He stared at Hunter for several seconds and slapped the table.

Hunter and the bodyguards jumped at the sound.

"More vodka!" he shouted. It came. He grabbed the bottle and poured another two shots.

Hunter started to breathe again, and the bodyguards relaxed.

"So," he peered at Hunter, "we good?"

Hunter nodded slowly.

"Excellent!" Karasov smiled and pushed the envelope hard enough to fall into Hunter's lap. He lifted his glass again. "We toast to Alina."

Hunter held his glass in the air and drank it in one gulp.

Karasov looked at his watch. "I must go. I call when I need you."

Hunter held up his notebook. "What about my questions for the article?"

"Call Alina. She give you answers."

Karasov stood up. "Remember what I tell you." And then he walked out of the rear of the restaurant with the bodyguards.

Hunter walked out the front door and up to the street. He shielded his eyes from the bright sunlight and searched for his taxi. Yury pulled up, and Hunter climbed in.

"How was your meeting?" Yury asked.

"Let's go." Hunter stared out the window.

As Yury pulled into traffic, Hunter felt his upper coat pocket and pulled out the envelope. He slowly counted the one-hundred-dollar bills. Jesus Christ, he thought. Five thousand dollars. His hand trembled as he tried to stuff the money back into the envelope. They had only traveled four blocks when Hunter's cell phone rang. He looked down at the caller ID.

"Alina?"

"How was your meeting?"

"Hang on a second." Hunter put his hand over the phone. "Yury, can you pull over?"

The taxi stopped, and Hunter got out to continue his conversation where Yury couldn't hear.

"Why weren't you at the meeting?" Hunter said, pacing around in a small circle.

"Something came up," she said.

"Bullshit. You never intended to come."

"Would you have gone if I'd told you?"

"How can you work for a guy like him? I know he's a big shot, but Christ."

"What did he want from you?"

"I'm supposed to write a glowing article and help you arrange meetings with oil companies and important politicians."

"Is that all?"

"Is there something you're not telling me?"

"No," Alina said.

"I understand Karasov's interest in oil and foreign aid, but what's the deal with Senator Dixon? He's the chair of the Senate Defense Committee."

"They have history."

"What kind?"

"Let's say they have common interests."

"Like beautiful young girls?"

"Hunter, I have to go. When can we meet? Karasov wants me to arrange the meetings with your contacts right away."

"Tonight—meet for dinner at Gramercy Tavern around eight o'clock.

"Perfect. See you later."

Hunter hung up and climbed back into the taxi.

Yury looked at Hunter while adjusting the rearview mirror. "You don't look so good. You okay?"

"Not really." Hunter loosened his tie. Too much vodka and half a cigar made him hot and dizzy. When he unbuttoned his shirt, he found it soaked in sweat. A block later, while idling in traffic, the smell of car exhaust made his stomach do somersaults. He reached out and pounded the back of the front seat. "Stop the car!"

Yury quickly pulled over. Hunter flung the door open and vomited into the gutter. When the retching stopped, he took a deep breath, wiped his mouth with the back of his hand and slowly closed the door. "Sorry, no sausage today. Just drive me back to my office."

Yury nodded and drove. Hunter leaned back and closed his eyes. After another wave of nausea had subsided, he stared at Yury's hairy arms and neck. "Yury, where did you get your tattoos?"

Yury shrugged. "Long story."

Hunter leaned forward again. "Why did you ask about my meeting on our way to the restaurant?"

Yury stared at the road.

"Do you work for Karasov?" Hunter asked.

Yury looked in the rearview mirror again. "Over here, we all do."

Chapter 15

It was almost eight when Hunter walked into Gramercy Tavern, a restaurant near Chelsea. As usual, the place was jammed. He was early, so he pushed his way to the bar and sat down on a high barstool wedged between two couples.

The bartender put down a napkin. "What will it be tonight?"

Hunter could still taste the Cuban cigar. "Not sure. Something different."

He handed Hunter a menu of specialty cocktails. "What do you usually drink?"

"Vodka."

"You like martinis?"

"Of course."

"Okay with some spice?"

"I guess. What do you have in mind?"

"A drink called a Stalingrad. Vodka infused with ginger and muddled cucumbers."

"I like the name—go for it."

While Hunter waited for Alina, he stared at himself in a large mirror that ran the length of the bar. He patted the money envelope in his coat pocket. Maybe it was the slight distortion in the mirror, but he looked different. He changed positions to get a clearer reflection. He played with his hair, turned his head from side to side and then straightened his tie.

The bartender surprised him. "Meeting somebody special?"

Hunter turned red and coughed.

"Ever notice there's a mirror behind almost every bar?" asked the bartender.

"No, but I guess you're right."

"I've watched hundreds of people as they sit at my bar every night. It's funny, but when they think no one's watching, they all look at themselves in the mirror. It's like a giant magnet. They can't help it."

"I never thought about it before."

"It's fascinating to watch their reactions to what they think they see. Everyone's looking into the mirror for a different reason. I make a game of guessing why. Over the years, I've become pretty good at it."

"Okay, hot-shot," Hunter said, "you caught me looking at myself. Tell me what I see."

"Twenty bucks if I'm correct. Free drink if I'm wrong."

Hunter grinned. "Deal."

"You're meeting someone very special." He paused and examined Hunter closely. "You're nervous because she's someone you haven't seen in a long time. You've changed, and you're wondering if she's still the same."

Hunter pulled out a twenty and laid it on the bar. "Goddamn, you're good."

"I should be. This is how I make a living."

"What… by fleecing naïve customers."

"No," he smiled, "by making friends." He placed the twenty-dollar bill under Hunter's glass.

Hunter slid the money out from under his glass and back across the bar. "I insist. I always pay up on my bets."

"The customer is always right." The bartender stuffed the twenty in his shirt pocket, picked up a shiny metal shaker and poured the contents into a martini glass. "Here you go. If you don't like it, I'll drink it."

Hunter carefully lifted the martini and sipped. "This is great."

The bartender patted the bar rail. "I knew you'd like it. I'll check back in a few minutes."

Hunter had a knack for observation too. That was a big reason why his boss hired him out of college. Alina wasn't scheduled to meet him for another twenty minutes, so he played a familiar game. Everyone had a story. He liked to guess what people were doing in the restaurant, who they were and what secrets they might be hiding.

He started with the cute couple sitting next to him. The young woman sat with her back to Hunter but constantly brushed up against him. She was exceptionally long from the waist to her shoulders. The open back of her dress dropped to her hips, exposing the full length of her smooth, olive back. He resisted the urge to run his finger down her spine. Instead, he settled for enjoying the smell of her Jasmine perfume. He could tell she was taller than most women and dressed like many of the twenty-something professionals working in New York. She wore long funky earrings, gold bangles that tinkled together on her wrist and an exceedingly short dress. Hunter tried to imagine what her face looked like beneath her jet-black hair. Careful not to look too obvious, he eavesdropped for a minute. She did all the talking in staccato bursts with a loud, squeaky voice. After listening for a few minutes, he doubted that her face matched the beautiful lines of her body. It almost never does.

In contrast, the young man appeared totally out of her league. He was tall and skinny with disheveled blond hair and thick black glasses that kept sliding down his nose. He wore brown slacks, scuffed-up shoes and a slightly wrinkled dress shirt, the dress code for college students. The young man couldn't decide on a cocktail, so the girl ordered a Perfect Ten martini for him. He had no idea what that was, but he liked the sound of it. Hunter smiled when the young man said something, and the girl leaned over to kiss him on the cheek.

When she turned to ask the bartender a question, Hunter finally caught a glimpse of her. As he'd guessed, her face was dominated by a large nose and dark eyebrows that almost touched. She was average looking, neither pretty nor ugly, but something about her was very sensual. She had an aura about her—something raw and sexual. Hunter noticed how she placed her hand on the young man's thigh and angled her face closer to him when she talked. Hunter couldn't help but chuckle when he saw the young man blush and his breath quicken. It made him think of his high school physics teacher. "For every action, there is a reaction." Women didn't need a physics class to learn that—they were born with that knowledge. Hunter continued to watch them in the mirror. They appeared an odd combination, and he wondered what she saw in him.

The older couple sitting to his right appeared to be in their late fifties. They sat quietly, facing at an angle away from each other toward the open restaurant. The man sat with his back to Hunter, but not touching. He smelled like his boss—a combination of cigar and Old Spice cologne. In the mirror, Hunter could tell that they were losing their battle with age. The gentlemen looked uncomfortable in a suit because he was overweight. His skin hung loosely under his chin, and his grey hair had receded midway to the back of his head. The woman had fared better. Her hair was carefully styled, but Hunter could tell it was colored. She had a pretty smile, but her cheeks had too much foundation, and her lipstick was too bright. She kept picking at the edge of her dress and twisting a long string of pearls around her neck. She didn't look any more relaxed than the man did.

Between long periods of silence, the couple discussed the weather and their latest health issues in low, subdued voices. Hunter guessed that the brown liquor in the man's glass was bourbon or rye, while the woman probably had an Old-Fashioned because of the muddled orange wedge and cherry in the bottom of her glass. They didn't look at each other very often. While they waited for a table, the woman unconsciously tapped her drink with a short straw as she watched the other couples sitting around them.

Hunter thought this is what must happen to lovers when there's nothing left to discover about each other. No dreams left to share, only secret regrets of desires never fulfilled. Funny how love can mean so many different things to different people. I wonder if they still have sex or had they succumbed to an age where passion was only a memory. He stared at the older couple in the mirror. If they had a choice, would they do it all over again?

The young couple was in the spring of their relationship, while the older couple was buried in the winter of their life together. Some people never stop wanting the things they can't have and pine away their lives in regret. Others settle for something less than they desire and live just as miserably.

If I marry Alina, he thought, would we stay like the young couple or end up like the old couple?

The bartender checked with Hunter by pointing to his glass. "What did you think?"

"I'll take another one."

"Thought so."

While Hunter waited for his drink, he looked in the mirror again and thought about what Karasov said in the interview. Despite Karasov's tough façade, Hunter felt sorry for him because he knew the old man was addicted to Alina. She owned Karasov the same way she owned Hunter. In an odd way, he could relate to Karasov. Both had lost their parents at a young age, Karasov in WWII when he was only fifteen. Becoming alone in the world is something most people never experience. He tried to imagine what it would be like to have a real family that cared about him.

Hunter never thought about love when thinking of home. The words "love" and "home" had no meaning together. Home was only for others, not him. He'd spent most of his formative years in foster families and boarding schools. When not at school, home was just a place to come and go from—a place to sleep. He never had a place where he belonged—a home.

Hunter turned to see Alina walk from the entryway toward the bar. She sauntered slowly, as if she was on a fashion runway, aloof yet fully aware of how people were watching her. She looked stunning in a tight red dress and high red heels. Her soft red hair was tied up, exposing her long, milky-white neck, which enhanced a dramatic sense of height and elegance. Hunter chuckled at the reaction of the men staring at her. That was exactly the way he felt when he'd first seen Alina.

Hunter overheard the older man next to him remark to his companion, "Check out the woman coming toward us. You think she rents by the hour or the minute?"

"You'll never know," the woman responded. Her eyes followed Alina across the room.

Hunter glanced at the younger couple. The young man never looked twice at Alina, while the young girl watched every step she took.

Hunter stood up as she approached and held out his arms.

"Sorry I'm late," she said, kissing him on the cheek.

She smelled like a heavy summer night, a thick, intoxicating mixture of perfume, gardenia, heat, and smoke. He took a deep breath and tried to inhale her."

"Thanks. Have you been waiting long?"

"Not really."

"What have you been doing?"

"People watching."

"Anything interesting?"

"People aren't always what they seem if you watch long enough."

Alina took Hunter's seat and placed a small handbag on the bar.

The bartender appeared. "What can I get you?" He couldn't take his eyes off the low neckline of her dress and a simple gold necklace that plunged between her breasts.

Alina pointed at Hunter's glass. "What's he drinking?"

"A Stalingrad."

She looked at Hunter. "Something for old memories?" Then she nodded to the bartender. "I'll have the same."

"Another for you?" he asked Hunter.

"No, I'm fine."

Alina cocked her head. "You're not having another? Is this a new Hunter?"

"No, I'm pacing myself. It's been a long day, and I already have a head start."

Alina stared at the reflection of Hunter in the mirror. "You're cute with longer hair, but I liked it better the way you wore it short in Kiev."

Hunter returned her look in the mirror. "We've both changed."

"This is just like old times."

Hunter glanced around the room. "Slightly different setting."

"There's something we need to discuss."

"Don't worry," Hunter said. "I can arrange all the meetings that Karasov requested."

"We can discuss Karasov later." She played with the leather strap of her purse. "This is about us."

"Is there an 'us'?" Hunter pulled his stool closer to Alina and leaned forward. "Was there ever an 'us'?"

Alina frowned. "That's not fair."

"Fair?" Hunter said. "You used me."

"And what about you? You got what you wanted."

"Not everything."

"Neither did I," Alina's voice rose. "I put my life on the line to help you and look what happened. Did you try to search for me after Karasov beat me?" Alina waited for Hunter to respond. When he didn't, she added, "No, you went home. You came back to… to this," she pointed around the beautiful restaurant, "while I was dragged back to a place worse than hell. I took a huge risk to help you. I helped you write half of your articles, gave you information that you could never have obtained on your own. And yet you abandoned me in a shithole." She stared at Hunter with burning eyes. "Don't talk to me about what's fair."

"Nice speech, but that's not the way I heard it from Karasov today."

"Just what did he tell you?"

"You set me up," Hunter said. "You never loved me. I was just another client."

Alina sat back in her chair and glanced up at the ceiling for a second as if there was a message written above. "And you believe him?"

"Should I?"

"All the time we spent in Kiev meant nothing to you?"

"You're good," Hunter said.

"Excuse me?"

"It's amazing how you can twist things around. Did you really love me in Kiev, or was that all a smokescreen to protect Karasov from a nosy *Times* reporter and obtain a ticket out of Ukraine?"

"What do you want to believe?"

"Why would Karasov lie to me?" Hunter said.

"You didn't answer the question."

The bartender checked on their drinks, and Hunter waved him off.

"What are we doing?" Hunter lowered his voice when he noticed the couples on both sides of them were eavesdropping. "You show up after two years like a ghost, a wisp of smoke, and then you act as if nothing's changed. What are we—friends, lovers, or just business acquaintances? Am I supposed to pretend that nothing happened between us?"

Alina leaned against the bar railing while Hunter's eyes remained fixated on the mirror behind the bar.

Finally, Hunter spoke. "Why didn't you contact me when you got to New York?"

"I couldn't," she said. "I would've ruined two years of planning."

"What do you mean?"

She turned around and faced Hunter. "Because I have set up Karasov, not you. Once we arrived in New York, I knew we'd eventually meet, but I had to make it look like it was completely by accident. Karasov needed to believe that using you to arrange connections was his idea. I was afraid he'd kill you if there were even a hint that I wanted to see you again."

"Karasov told me he knew about us in Kiev. He said you were responsible for containing me until they figured out what to do with me."

"That's exactly what I wanted him to believe."

"What about Stravinsky? What does he know?"

"Only what I want him to know."

Hunter rubbed his head. "I'm confused."

"If we do this right, we can disappear and never have to worry about Karasov or Stravinsky." She reached for his hand. "And we'll never have to worry about money again. That's why you must completely trust me, or you'll ruin everything."

"But…"

"No more questions. Just do whatever I ask because I won't have the time to explain when things start happening."

"What things are we talking about?"

Alina sighed. "Did you hear what I just said?"

They both stared at their drinks for a minute.

"What happened to you today?" Hunter said. "Why didn't you show?"

"I told you. He wouldn't let me come."

"Am I screwed?" Hunter groaned.

Alina shrugged. "We're all screwed in one way or another."

"I'm not sure I can go through this all over again. It was hell not knowing if you were dead or alive over the last two years," he said. "But this… this is even worse. I know you're here, but not being able to touch you is unbearable. They should've killed me in Kiev because now, every time I see you, I die all over again."

"Can we leave and go somewhere?" Alina brushed a tuft of hair away from his eyes. "I don't feel like eating."

"Where?"

"Anywhere. Maybe your place."

Hunter glanced at Alina. "What if Karasov finds out?"

"He'll never know," Alina said.

"Fuck it. Let's go." Hunter's hand slapped the bar. "I'm dead without you anyway."

They walked out of the restaurant into a heavy rain and stood under a blue awning to watch the raindrops cascade off the canvas in shimmering sheets. Hunter gave the doorman a five-dollar bill to flag down a taxi. Soaking wet and giggling, they climbed into the back seat.

Without taking his eyes off Alina, Hunter gave the taxi driver his address. Alina's red hair, wet and plastered against her face, revealed the jagged scar over her right eye. Hunter reached out and touched the scar with his finger. She closed her eyes, and he leaned over and kissed her it. "I love you," Hunter said.

She whispered back, "I know."

By the time they reached his apartment, the rain had turned into a torrential downpour. They held hands, counted to three and dashed through several puddles to the front door of his building. Outside his apartment, Alina turned around and pushed him against the door. Drops of rain dripped into her eyes as she pressed against him, wet and shivering.

"Why didn't you just forget me?" Alina said. "I thought you would marry someone and move on with your life."

"I tried."

"Kiss me," she said.

He kissed her gently at first and then harder and harder until they were out of breath. He stopped and brushed the hair away from her face. "I've dreamed about this moment for two years. I never thought I'd see you again."

They entered the apartment, and Alina rushed to unbutton his shirt. Hunter tried to unzip her dress, but the zipper was stuck. Alina tugged hard on the sleeves of Hunter's soaked shirt because they were sticking to his arms. He unbuckled his belt as fast as he could and tried to step out of his pant leg but tripped when his foot got hung up. They both fell on the floor, laughing and rolling around as they pulled off the rest of their clothes.

"Do you love me?" Hunter asked, pulling off her red panties.

She gently kissed both his eyes. "What does that tell you?"

He carried her naked to his bedroom and laid her on the bed. He slowly stretched alongside her and pulled the sheets over them.

Alina whispered, "Remember my promise? The one I made to you the first time we met in Kiev?"

He nodded in the dark.

"I'm here to keep it."

Hunter closed his eyes, powerless to move, waiting for Alina. She kissed his chest until he couldn't control himself any longer. He flipped her onto her back, and she wrapped her legs around his waist, moaning as he pushed into her.

"Alina, Alina," he cried out.

She gasped, dug her fingers into his back and swore in Russian as they twisted together in ecstasy.

Hunter exploded and lay on top of her, panting and out of breath. "God, I love you," he said, plunging his face into her hair.

She gently caressed him while he caught his breath. After a few minutes, he rolled onto his back and stared at the ceiling. "Remember how we used to make love like this in Kiev for hours."

She lay quietly with her eyes open, staring at the ceiling. "Seems like a lifetime ago."

Hunter rolled onto his side and played with her nipples until they became hard again.

"So, what happens to us now?"

"I don't know," Alina said.

"What if Karasov finds out again that we're sleeping together?"

"He won't."

"But if he does…?"

"Worrying about it doesn't change anything."

"You're right." Hunter kissed her navel. "Close your eyes for a moment. I have something for you."

She closed her eyes for a second, but then opened them. "What are you doing?"

Hunter got out of bed and opened the top drawer of his dresser. "No peeking."

She closed her eyes again.

Hunter opened a familiar-looking blue box and pulled out the necklace with the gold cross that he had given her in Kiev—the same one she'd been wearing when Karasov had shot him. He held the necklace and let the cross swing back and forth.

"Open your eyes now."

Her eyes followed the cross. "My God, where… how… I thought…"

"I found the necklace on the floor after they took you away."

"I never thought that I'd see this again."

Alina sat up. Hunter moved behind her and attached the necklace. "It wasn't very effective the first time, but I'm sure the gold cross will work better the second time."

"It's so beautiful." She looked down and touched the cross. "You're a sweet man. You deserve someone better than me." Her phone started to ring, and she groaned.

"Not again," he said.

"I have to go."

"How do you even know who it is?"

Alina didn't answer. She started to pick up her clothes.

"Please, can't you stay for a little while longer?"

She shook her head.

"Goddamn it."

Holding her shoes, Alina touched his face with her right hand. "Things are going to get complicated."

Hunter wrapped his arms tightly around her. "Hah, so what's new?"

She kissed him one last time and tried to escape his hands.

"I'm not letting you go."

She broke free and slipped on her heels. "I'll call you tomorrow."

As he watched her walk out, doubt made him tremble—doubt about starting down this road again. Doubt about whether she really loved him.

Hunter's phone vibrated on the dining room table. He looked at the caller ID—Carrie. She'd already called three times this evening. Reluctantly, he picked up the cell phone. "Hi, Carrie."

"Where are you?"

"At home, why?"

"I was so worried when you didn't show up at the coffee house."

"Damn." He suddenly remembered that he'd agreed to meet her to hear aspiring writers give their readings. "I'm so sorry. I completely forgot about tonight." He walked into his kitchen and looked in the refrigerator for something to eat while they talked.

"How could you forget? We discussed it this morning."

"I know, but I was distracted by meetings, and then I got tied up with something that made me forget."

"Like what? I've been trying to call you all night."

"A business dinner."

"With who?"

"Clients." Hunter shifted the phone to his other hand and started to make toast. He was starving because he and Alina had left the restaurant without dinner. "You wouldn't know them."

"I just wish you would've called."

"I had my phone on vibrate and didn't see your call until I got home. It won't happen again."

"Well, okay. What are you doing tomorrow?"

"I don't know."

"Can I come over and make dinner for you tomorrow night?"

"I'm not sure," Hunter said. His mouth was full of food. "I have to get ready for teaching my class next week."

"I just want to see you."

"Okay, but we have to do it early because so I can work on my next lecture."

"We'll eat fast, so we have more time to snuggle." When Hunter didn't respond, she added, "I can't stop thinking about the last time we were together. That was incredible."

"I better go." Angel, his cat, rubbed against his leg and purred.

"See you tomorrow. Love you."

Hunter hung up without responding. He made himself another drink, a second piece of peanut butter toast, and then sat at the kitchen table, wondering where Alina was going after she left.

Angel rubbed against him again and purred even louder. "What do you want?" he said, gently stroking her soft fur. "Do you smell my toast or just protecting your turf after you saw Alina?" Angel licked one of her paws and purred again. "Hmmm, so now you love me. Well, don't worry. I wouldn't leave you for her."

Dirty dishes from the dinner with Cabot and Leah were still in the sink. Empty wine and vodka bottles littered the kitchen counter. While he cleaned the dishes, he realized how much he hated the way Cabot looked at Alina. The same way, he guessed, Karasov hated the way Hunter looked at Alina.

* * *

Hunter was late for work the next morning, but he didn't care anymore. Things were different. He felt clear-headed for the first time in two years because he had nothing left to lose. He avoided Cabot all day despite his boss's repeated calls to find out about Karasov. Tess ran interference for him as best she could until Hunter decided he needed to get out of the office and go home.

He regretted having to dine with Carrie again. He knew what she wanted. He was grateful he couldn't see her face in the dark because he could pretend she was Alina. It was only afterward, in the harsh light of reality, that he felt guilty. Carrie was nothing like Alina and never would be. Nobody would.

Tess barged into his office, "I'm outta here. Gotta leave early to take my mom to the dentist. You need anything?"

"No, I'm good. I'm leaving early too."

"My girlfriends are taking me to a new club tonight," she announced. "Why don't you join us?"

Hunter barely looked up. "I don't think so."

"Come on, big boy, here's your chance to prove all the stories about you are wrong."

"What stories?"

"That you're a self-absorbed, reclusive bookworm."

Hunter leaned back and swiveled around to face her. "But what if all those stories are true?"

"I know better," she said, pointing at his chest. "There's another Hunter hiding in there, and I plan on meeting him someday."

"I doubt it."

Tess winked. "You don't know what you're missing."

"Have a good time." He turned his chair back to his computer.

Hunter worked for another half hour, then shut the lights off and headed home. Rush hour had begun. The streets around the Port Authority were clogged with taxis, buses and an occasional police car.

Hunter was walking toward the end of the block to catch a taxi when a long black limousine pulled up. He pretended not to notice and walked faster. The limousine picked up speed, and then, without warning, the rear door opened. Hunter's instinct was to run, but

Karasov shouted for him to get in. When Hunter hesitated, the front door flew open and a large man jumped out, blocking Hunter's way.

Karasov said, "Don't make scene."

The big man put his hand on Hunter's shoulder and guided him into the car. Out of options, Hunter slid into the backseat. The limousine smelled of leather, cologne and cigars.

"Are you going to kill me?" Hunter asked.

"I don't know. Should I?"

Hunter's hands shook so much that he tucked them under his thighs. "Listen, I never touched Alina. We met for dinner at the Gramercy Tavern, and then she went home."

"Relax, you watch too many movies." Karasov laughed. "If I thought you fuck my Alina, you'd already be at bottom of Hudson." Karasov poured Hunter a glass of vodka. "You too smart to make mistake again, da?"

Hunter nodded and drank half the glass in one gulp.

"Izdyty, drive," Karasov ordered the man behind the wheel.

Karasov looked out the window. "I not sure I like New York. It different than I expect."

"What did you expect?"

"I don't know. Everyone in big hurry." Karasov pointed to the crowded sidewalks. "Nobody talk to each other. They push and shove like cattle. Not like Kiev."

"It's rush hour," Hunter said.

Karasov put his face close to the glass and looked up. "Another thing. Buildings too tall."

"What do you mean?"

"Bad, very bad. You can't see sky."

Hunter finished his drink in two gulps.

Karasov saw his glass was already empty. "I make you thirsty?"

"Yes, very thirsty. Truth is you scare the shit outta me."

Karasov laughed again. "This why I like you." And then he said something in Ukrainian to the driver who laughed too. "I like man not afraid to speak truth."

They rode in silence for a few minutes, and then Karasov said, "You know, in Ukraine I control everything. I know all players. But over here," he shook his head, "I not trust anyone. Big disadvantage."

"It's a big town," Hunter said.

"You understand New York. You know right people. You know how game work here, I don't. I don't know good English."

"You have Alina. She can translate anything you need."

Karasov frowned and sipped on his drink. "She good, but I still have problem."

"What's that?"

"I don't know English enough to know someone lying."

"What does that have to do with me?"

"In my country, only friends ask favors."

Here it comes, Hunter thought.

"Are we friends?" Karasov turned and looked Hunter straight in the eye.

"That depends," Hunter said.

Karasov raised his eyebrows. "On what?"

"If I make it to my apartment with all my fingers and toes."

Karasov roared and spilled a few drops of vodka on his pants. He slapped Hunter on the shoulder. "Hah, I knew it!" He tapped the shoulder of his bodyguard in the front seat and pointed at Hunter. "Shcho ya skazhu, baranyna, vyyavlyayet'sya, lysytsi, what I tell you, lamb turn out to be fox."

Hunter looked confused.

Karasov tapped Hunter's chest. "No one dare negotiate with me except you. I like that."

Karasov leaned back in the leather seat and told the driver to take Hunter home. After several blocks, Karasov pointed to a woman on the curb waiting for the light to change. He said, "Look, that woman. She look like Alina, da?"

"Da," Hunter said softly.

"Maybe we cursed?"

"Maybe."

"She like itch that won't go away." He glanced at Hunter. "It feel good at first, only the harder you scratch, the more you hurt."

Hunter nodded.

"I saw what she did to you in Kiev. That why I not kill you. You had no clue. She play games with our soul. She fuck us good and with no regrets." He reached for another cigar and cut the end off. "You not first. I almost killed her in Kiev. I don't know why I stop." He paused to light his cigar. "But after you left, I sent her to Moscow. I try two years to find woman to replace her." He stared out the window. "You college boy. What name of woman on the island?"

"An island?"

"You know—the witch."

"Circe."

"Da, da, that's the one," he said. "Once you hear her voice, drink her potion... well, you know."

"There's no cure," Hunter said. "I've tried... I've tried for two years. I don't sleep well anymore. I'm okay during the day, but at night, that's when she haunts me the most. She's always in my dreams."

"When I first meet her," Karasov said. "I thought she was blessing. She like angel, a gift from God."

Hunter looked at Karasov. "You're the only person in the world that would understand why I wake up in the middle of the night and after two years still smell her empty pillow. Why I still keep her brand of shampoo in the shower. Why I keep the toothbrush she used in Kiev inside a glass on my sink."

Karasov shook his head and stared out the window. "You should forget her."

"I can't," Hunter turned to Karasov, "any more than you can."

Karasov nodded. "You ever wonder?"

"What do you mean?"

"Sometimes I wonder if I pick her or she pick me?"

"Would it change anything?"

"No." Karasov grunted and made another drink. "You know, she like wild horse. I hold reins, I pull, I turn, but never know if I really in control."

While they were stuck in traffic near the Port Authority, Hunter stared out the window of the limousine and recalled the last time in Kiev when he thought he was in control. What a fool I was, he thought. Why did I ever believe that I—Hunter Moretti—could ever save her?

Chapter 16

Through the paper-thin walls, Hunter listened to his neighbors arguing in Ukrainian. Since arriving in Kiev, he continued to pick up a word or two, but for the most part, he didn't understand what anyone said. He had just fixed a second drink when Alina opened the door.

"You're late again," he said.

"Don't start with me. After the way you acted at the club last night, you're lucky I came at all."

"If I'm paying you, I'm not sitting around in this dump all day waiting for you. It was your idea to move here."

Infuriated, Alina said, "What was that?"

"I'm making some changes."

"So, you're making the decisions now?" she snickered.

"I have deadlines. From now on, you show up on time."

"Or what?"

"Or I go back to New York."

Alina stared at him for a second, then her expression softened. She twisted a strand of red hair. "I'm sorry," she whispered.

Hunter cupped his hand around his ear. "I can't hear you."

She raised her voice. "I said I'm sorry. It won't happen again."

"That's better."

"For your information, I was late today because people at the club are wondering why you stopped coming to see me." She set her bag down and walked into the kitchen for something to eat.

Hunter followed behind her. "What did you tell them?"

She reached into the small refrigerator and drank milk out of the plastic bottle. "I told them you left the country on business but planned on returning soon."

"Why did you do that?" Hunter said. "Do you realize what you just did? This means I can't go out in public anymore. If someone sees me, my cover is broken."

"I know," she said. "But I didn't have any choice."

"You could have made up a different excuse." He smacked his hand on top of his head. "Christ, you're so stupid."

She clenched her hands. "Don't ever call me stupid again! You seem to be forgetting that I'm protecting your carcass from ending up in the Dnieper River." She paced in a circle around him. "You dumb ass. You're the one that's stupid. Do you really think you can just waltz into Kiev and do a story on Karasov and the mafia without any consequences?" She picked up her bag and walked toward the door. "This has been a huge mistake. I'm risking my life for what?" She thrust a finger at him. "For you?"

Hunter put his hand on the door so she couldn't open it. "Don't go." He reached out for her free hand, but she wouldn't take his.

"Why should I stay? Give me one good reason."

"Because I'm your ticket to New York."

Alina stepped close to him. "Is that why you think I'm doing this?"

"Don't get so dramatic."

"What's happened to you? You've changed."

"That's for sure," Hunter said. "Since I met you, I've taken up smoking, I drink vodka like a fish and I'm sleeping with a…" He stopped himself.

Alina gritted her teeth and yanked the door open.

"Wait," Hunter reached out and grabbed her arm. "I didn't mean it that way."

She pulled her arm away. "Yes, you did."

"What can I say to make it up to you?"

"Nothing."

"But I love you," Hunter said.

"You don't have any intention of taking me back with you to New York," she said. "Do you think I'm a fool?"

"No," Hunter said.

"That was convincing. I feel so much better now."

"You always twist my words."

"What do you think we're doing here?"

Hunter stepped close. "You tell me."

"You're pathetic. Who do you think you are with all your American money? Do you think you can just buy anything—buy me? I don't need your fucking money... or you for that matter." She slammed the door on her way out.

Hunter kicked his backpack across the floor and sat down at his desk. He looked at all the notes he had taken from Alina. He was furious with her, but he had to admit it was one hell of a story. He thought Alina was the best thing that had ever happened to him, but something was gnawing at him.

Alina didn't return the next day or the day after. He regretted the way he'd acted, but there was nothing he could do but wait for her to return, so he spent most of his time organizing his notes and finishing the remaining articles.

Alina's new Ukrainian passport arrived late in the afternoon. He stared at her passport photo but after several seconds turned away slowly surveying their tiny flat. He knew it was time to go home.

It was after seven that evening when he finished writing the last article and emailed it to the *Times*. He hated eating alone so he had dinner at a crowded café at the end of the block. Lingering over an after-dinner Cognac, he remembered that he had forgotten to call the office yesterday as planned. He walked home and placed a collect call to Vinny at the *Times*.

"Vinny here."

"It's me."

"Hunter, buddy, I'm really glad you called." Vinny sounded worried.

"What's wrong?"

"Everything. George, my friend down in research, called his buddies at the CIA, and they told him that you need to get out of there."

"We were planning on returning soon."

"We?"

"Yes, didn't I tell you? I'm bringing Alina home with me."

"For Christ sake, no! You just asked me to get some information. How is she getting into the country? You told me that Karasov took her passport."

"That's true, but I was able to get a new one."

"How did you pull that off?"

"Some friends owed me some favors."

"You must have some serious friends I don't know about," Vinny said.

"I did a few projects for the government while at Columbia."

"Never knew that."

"Doesn't matter. We'll be heading back in the next week or so."

"You don't have a week," Vinny said. "You don't even have a few days. You've got to leave now."

"Now?"

"I mean today, tonight, first thing in the morning. Now!"

"What's the big hurry? Why are you so riled up?"

"Hunter, did you ever ask yourself why Alina agreed to give you all that information? Why she's taking such a huge risk?"

Hunter replayed the key events over the last couple of months in his head.

"I don't know how to tell you this," Vinny said, "but you can't trust her. Alina's playing you, or maybe going rogue. Either way, it's bad news for you. According to our sources, there's a huge power struggle going on between Karasov and Stravinsky. The competing mafia groups are murdering each other daily. It's like a mini war. Nobody's safe, especially foreign reporters trying to stick their noses into the mafia's business." Vinny was speaking fast. "You need to know that Karasov's faction is particularly dangerous. They'll kill you in a heartbeat if they find out you're writing anything about them, or about the whole sex slavery thing. I mean these guys are nasty."

"Slow down," Hunter said. "What did you mean Alina's playing me?"

"You've been set up... played," Vinny said. "Do I need to spell it out for you? Alina isn't just some floozy. George heard that the boys in the CIA have quite a file on her. She's brilliant, charming and handles a variety of things for the Karasov family."

"I already know that. By why would she set me up?"

"Lots of possibilities, if you stop and think about it. One, take all her unusual questions about your banking connections in New York. I checked with my contacts at the FBI, and they told me the Russians have established a beachhead in Brooklyn for laundering billions of dollars they're making from prostitution and drug trafficking right in our own damn backyard. Two, she wants to sell you the client list for a lot of money and then dump you. Three, she's using you as her ticket to New York to escape from Karasov. Or four, some combination of the above." Vinny stopped for a second, "Shall I go on?"

"No, that's enough."

"By the way, the spooks want to talk to you as soon as you return to the States."

There was a long pause.

"Hunter, what's going on?"

"I'm not sure yet."

"After what I just told you, you still want to bring her back with you?" Vinny asked.

"You don't know her like I do."

"But you know she's lying and..."

"Whose side are you on?"

"Your side," Vinny said quietly. "But..."

Hunter interrupted him again. "I have to go."

"I don't want you to get hurt."

"I can take care of myself."

"I didn't mean it that way."

"Look," Vinny said, "given that you work for the *Times,* George is adamant that you stop whatever you're doing and get out of Ukraine."

"Thanks again for your help."

"Hunter..."

"I can handle it. I'll keep you posted." Hunter hung up the phone and looked at his watch. It was after nine o'clock. He didn't bother to change his clothes before walking straight to the Rus'.

* * *

The usual Rus' hostess sat behind her reception desk looking bored. When she noticed Hunter walk in, she smiled, stood up and threw her arms around him.

"We've missed you." She kissed him on both cheeks and wiped off a residual smudge of bright red lipstick with her thumb. "Where you been?"

"Traveling," Hunter said. "Didn't your hair used to be purple?"

She blushed. "Mr. Karasov didn't like it. He likes red better, so they made me change it." She pulled him closer and whispered. "Don't tell, but it not my real hair—it wig."

Hunter pretended he was astonished. "You're kidding. Your secret is safe with me."

She grinned. "How I help you?"

"Where's Alina? I need to talk to her."

"She's out now, but be back later. She go somewhere with Mr. Karasov. They said they'd be back after ten. Can I get your usual, vodka on rocks?"

"You're the best."

"Da, that they tell me." She hooked her arm under his and ushered him into the club.

"Have seat."

A pretty young waitress in white lingerie arrived at his table with a tray of full of drinks and handed him a glass of vodka. He'd never seen her before. She moved awkwardly in high stilettos and struggled to balance the heavy tray.

"Here," Hunter said, plucking his drink from her tray. "Let me help you."

The tray immediately wobbled as it became unbalanced. She almost dropped it but grabbed the edge of the tray to stabilize it.

"Bravo," Hunter said.

She blushed.

"New at this?" He guessed that she couldn't be more than eighteen years old.

She nodded shyly. Her white lingerie didn't fit her thin, reedy body, but what bothered him the most were her vacant eyes.

"Can I get you anything else?" she said with a thick accent.

"No, I'm fine," Hunter said. "What's your name?"

"Lela," she said flatly, avoiding eye contact.

The girl nervously glanced over to the bar. The bartender was watching them talk as he polished a glass. She quickly wiped up some water on the table with a napkin. "I need to get back to work."

Hunter grabbed her lightly by the arm. She stopped and looked at him.

"How old are you?" he asked.

Her dull eyes shifted back and forth between the bartender and Hunter. The small stack of napkins trembled in her hand. "I have to go."

Lela walked back to the bar, and Hunter never saw her again. When Alina and Karasov finally entered the lounge, he was glad she didn't see him right away. It gave him a chance to observe Karasov in a large booth across the room. Hunter noticed that whenever Karasov spoke, everyone at the table laughed as if on cue. If anyone else tried to speak, Karasov would look away bored. Two bottles of Crystal champagne and several appetizers arrived at their table. Alina poured Karasov a glass of champagne. Hunter loved the way her pretty hands gestured in the air when she talked and the way her mouth moved, exposing her large white teeth when she smiled. God, she was beautiful.

Alina smiled when she spotted Hunter across the room. She hesitated, then leaned over and whispered something in Karasov's ear. He turned and stared at Hunter for a second while fingering a large gold ring on his left hand. Hunter quickly looked down and studied his glass of vodka.

Alina walked quickly over to his booth.

"Are you crazy?" she said, sitting down at his table.

Hunter took a large swallow of his drink. "How's Mr. Big tonight?"

"You need to leave."

"What did you whisper to him?"

"That you're one of my best clients, and you just flew in from New York."

"He's a little old for you, isn't he?"

Alina rolled her eyes.

"Somewhere in his sixties? Can he still do it?"

"You're impossible." She reached over, took a sip of his drink and played with his cocktail napkin.

"I'd love to interview him."

Her head snapped up, and she looked him in the eye. "That's not funny."

"What's he like, anyway?"

"He's your worst nightmare." She stole a look back at her table, but Karasov wasn't paying any attention to them. "What are you doing here?"

"I need to talk to you."

"Not now."

"It's important." Hunter slurred his words. "You and me, we've got things to discuss."

"Not here. Not now." Alina glanced at Karasov and then back to Hunter. "This isn't the time or the place."

"Why not?" Hunter waved his arm in a big circle. A table of girls next to the bar waved back. "They love me here."

"Are you drunk?"

"Not really, maybe just a little," Hunter said. "Hey, what do you care?"

Alina grabbed his hands. "You need to leave now."

"Why? I just got here."

Alina noticed the bartender watching them. She smiled and said in a loud voice, "Sweetie, I'm busy. Why don't you come back tomorrow?"

Hunter's head rolled around, and his tongue sounded like it was stuck in his mouth. "Saaay, you sound like that other girl." He snapped his fingers, trying to remember her name. "Lela, you know, the new girl who brought me my drink earlier."

"What are you talking about?"

"The waitress—her accent." Hunter scratched his head. "Your accent is just like hers."

Alina pretended to snuggle him but hissed in his ear. "You're an idiot. You need to leave, or you'll get us both killed."

"Are you mad at me?"

"I will be if you don't leave right now."

"I don't want to fight. I just wanted to see you again."

"Go home."

He tried to kiss her, but she pulled away and walked back to Karasov's table. Hunter downed the remaining vodka in his glass, took one more glance Alina across the room and staggered toward the door.

* * *

The next morning, Hunter woke up alone in bed with a pounding headache and trying to remember the confrontation with Alina the previous night. He hated the narrow twin beds pushed together. He'd kill to have his king bed from back home. He rolled around the bed, trying to find a comfortable position but finally gave up. He tried to light a cigarette, but his hand was shaking so badly he had to use two matches. It seemed clear that he had to decide about Alina—a decision that could change his life. He had been afraid like this only one other time—at his parents' funeral. He was ten when he'd watched the two caskets lowered into a dark hole in the ground. As he'd walked away from the gravesite, he had realized that he was completely alone. Lying in bed, he tried to shake off the nauseating fear from that terrible day, but he couldn't.

Vinny's warning taunted him. What the hell am I doing? he thought. Have I lost my mind? What idiot would try to smuggle a woman like Alina into the United States with forged documents? Until three months ago, I'd never been to Ukraine, never traveled outside the United States, and never broke the law, but I can't help it. She drives me crazy. My God, she's so beautiful. I can't live without her.

Their flight back to New York was scheduled for tomorrow night. He knew that sometime in the next twenty-four hours, one of three things would happen: He'd end up in jail, he'd be free and clear in New York City with Alina or he'd be dead.

There was no hope of going back to sleep, so he smoked his cigarettes and watched the ceiling fan slowly rotate above his head. Maybe I shouldn't wait for her, he thought. Maybe I should leave for the airport and fly back early to New York without her. I don't need her anymore for the research. I have all the information I need to finish writing the articles.

Rolling out of the sagging bed, he walked to the bathroom. He put his mouth under the faucet, careful not to touch the rusty metal with his lips. The water was warm, tinted slightly yellow and left a bitter taste of iron. He spit again, wiped his mouth, splashed water on his face and then looked at the stranger in the bathroom mirror. Through the small, cracked surface, he examined himself. There wasn't anything he could do about his small eyes, big ears, thin lips and crooked front teeth. He knew he was nothing special and wondered what a beautiful woman like Alina saw in him. When he was a child, his mother used to tell him that he was handsome, but by the time he became a teenager, she had been dead for years, and he understood that she lied. Pretty girls wanted to date tall, handsome boys that played sports, told funny jokes and spent money on them. Even though he was smart, they didn't have any interest in a shy, skinny boy with an empty wallet.

Hunter wiped the steam off the mirror so he could finish shaving. The faucet dripped nonstop, and the bathroom smelled like a backed-up sewer. He brushed his teeth without water and spit out the toothpaste into the yellow-stained sink. He stepped into the shower, careful not to stand too close to the scalding hot water. While he waited for the water to cool down, he reached for Alina's bottle of shampoo and thought about the first time he'd met her in the brothel. He wasn't sure if meeting Alina would turn out to be the best day of his life or something he'd always regret.

After he got dressed, he started to pack his clothes and box up his research materials. He already shipped the two trunks full of Alina's documents and money back to New York. He had one more batch of articles to fax and a couple of last-minute errands to run. He was only gone a few hours, but when he opened the door to the flat, he heard Alina's voice.

"Need some help?" she called out from under the sheets.

Startled, he almost dropped the bag. "Thanks, but I got it."

He set the bag on the table and stood over her. Lying perfectly still, she stared at him.

"When did you get off work?"

"About an hour ago."

"I want to talk to you."

Alina pulled the sheets up to her nose.

"I wasn't sure if you were coming back," Hunter said.

"Me neither."

Hunter sat on the edge of the bed and looked down at her without changing his expression.

"Alina, what happens if you leave Karasov?"

"I'm not afraid of him. Karasov means nothing to me. He's a piece of shit," Alina said. "Somebody will kill him. If not the Russians, it will be one of the other mafia families."

"There is one more thing we need to discuss." Hunter looked down at her face. "I know you've been lying to me."

"What are you talking about?"

"Stop it," Hunter said.

"I'm sorry." Her expression became a confession. "But I have my reasons."

"Not good enough."

"It's complicated." She sat up and crossed her arms.

"When did Karasov find out about us?"

"Shortly after we moved to the flat." Her eyes blinked rapidly to hold back the tears. "I was forced to control you. Keep you from getting any information, but then…"

"But then… we became friends?" Hunter finished the sentence.

Thin lines of tears streamed down Alina's face, running her black mascara. "So now what?" she asked.

"That's up to you."

"I said I'm sorry," Alina said.

"Why should I believe you?"

"If you have to ask that question, then you'll never understand my answer."

"What do you expect me to think?"

Alina looked around the room at the boxed materials and the suitcase in the corner. "When are you returning to New York?"

"Soon."

Alina threw the covers off and stood up. She reached behind her head, unsnapped her necklace and reattached the clasp around Hunter's neck.

"What're you doing?" Hunter asked.

"I want you to remember me."

Hunter looked down at the cross and chain hanging on his chest. He removed it and reattached it around her neck. "I don't need a necklace to remember you."

Alina choked up. "Why not?"

"Because I'll never forget you."

Alina covered her face and threw herself back on the bed. Her shoulders shook as she cried.

Hunter leaned over and gently stroked her hair. "Stop crying. A package came today."

"What kind of package?"

Hunter pulled out her new passport from the drawer in the bed stand.

She quickly sat up and searched his eyes. "Does this mean…?"

Hunter grinned. "Our plane leaves tomorrow tonight at eight."

"Oh, my God!" Alina said. "Are you serious?"

"You must arrive at the airport by five. I want you to go back to the club and stick to your normal routine. Around four, make an excuse that you're sick and need to go to the doctor. Leave the club and take a taxi to the airport. Don't bring anything with you but your purse. Don't talk to anyone. Leave everything. We'll buy what you need when we get to New York." Hunter handed Alina the documents. "Here's your passport and visa. Put them in the false bottom of your purse."

She tucked away the passport and then smothered him with kisses. "Did I tell you how much I love you?"

"I vaguely recall something like that."

"In that case, I better remind you."

They had just begun to make love when they heard muffled voices of men in the hallway, and then heavy footsteps approached their apartment. Hunter and Alina froze when their metal handle squeaked and rattled.

Alina gripped Hunter tightly. "Oh, God… no!"

They didn't have time to move when the door exploded off its hinges and skidded across the floor. Alina screamed as two men from the club stepped in, waving pistols. A few seconds later, Karasov walked into the room. As if on a Sunday stroll, he walked over to the bed and threw off the covers. Naked, Hunter and Alina sat up, trembling.

Karasov said something to Alina in Ukrainian and spat on her. Alina wiped the white glob off her face and frantically waved her arms as she spoke rapidly in Ukrainian. She finished by pointing at Hunter, grabbing Karasov's arm with both hands and sobbing as she kissed his right hand repeatedly. Karasov's face didn't change as she continued to plead. He reached down and dragged her off the bed by the hair. She cried out in pain as she hit the floor. Karasov lifted her head by a fistful of red hair and looked at Hunter.

"You think you pretty smart?" Karasov said, in broken English.

Terrified, Hunter didn't know what to say.

Karasov smashed his fist into Alina's face, and she crumpled. A large man dragged Hunter out of bed and pushed him against the wall. He shoved his forearm under Hunter's throat, held his head firmly against the wall and aimed a 9mm pistol between his eyes.

Karasov lifted Alina's head by the hair again and asked Hunter, "You like bitch?" Then he smashed the butt of his gun into her right eye. Blood spurted down her face before she passed out, but he continued to hold her up by her hair.

Hunter tried to move, but the man shoved his forearm even tighter against his throat.

"She good in bed, da?" Karasov's eyes were wild. He hit her again, only this time so violently that she pitched backward onto the wooden floor. Her nose was smashed in a gross angle toward her left cheek. His fistful of hair pulled straight out of her head. Karasov laughed as he picked Alina up by the hair again, blood gushing out of her nose, eye and forehead. Hunter gagged when he saw white bone protruding through the wide gash over her broken right eye socket. He tried to say something, but the bodyguard's forearm pushed harder against his throat.

"You beg for her," Karasov said to Hunter. "Or you beg for yourself?"

Hunter tried to talk again, but the man was crushing his windpipe. Karasov cocked his pistol and placed it against Alina's temple. Hunter closed his eyes and waited for the blast. When the gun didn't go off, Hunter slowly opened his eyes and found Karasov pointing his gun at him instead of Alina. Hunter felt his leg grow warm. Karasov laughed and waved his gun at the puddle of urine on the floor between Hunter's feet. He said something in Ukrainian to his thugs, and they all laughed.

Karasov walked over to the man holding Hunter against the wall and whispered something in his ear. The man nodded. Then Karasov walked back to Alina and threw her onto the bed. He wrapped her in a white bed sheet and motioned for the other bodyguard to pick her up. The man slung Alina over his shoulder like a roll of carpet and walked toward the door. The sheet quickly turned red from the blood dripping down her right arm.

Karasov paused at the door and nodded to the man holding Hunter. Time stopped—Hunter knew he was a dead man. Everything went into slow motion. At the last second, the man moved the gun and pulled the trigger. The bullet ripped through Hunter's right hand. Another shot turned his hand into a blob of mangled flesh. The concussion blew out his right eardrum, and the acrid smoke filled his nostrils. White sparklers filled his eyes, and the room began to spin. He blinked several times, not believing he was still alive.

When Hunter regained his focus, he saw Karasov standing in the doorway. Although he couldn't hear anything, Karasov's lips formed the words, "Go home."

The thug released his grip on Hunter's throat, and he slid down the wall onto the floor. Hunter carefully put his finger where his hand used to be. It was a sticky, wet glob of flesh, but oddly there wasn't any pain. Hunter examined his bloody red hand as if it wasn't his own and threw up. After catching his breath, he wiped his mouth and tried to focus his eyes on the door. Karasov and Alina were gone, but several neighbors were poking their heads through the doorway. Hunter tried to stand but collapsed after two steps. Lying on the floor, he saw something shiny in a puddle of Alina's blood. He crawled slowly over and picked it up. It was Alina's bloody necklace. He clutched it in the palm of his hand and slumped to the floor. His neighbor, an elderly woman from next door, cautiously entered the room and knelt next to him. Hunter pointed to his desk, "Please, call…" the room began to spin "…the number…" his chest heaved as he tried to breathe "…on the card."

The old woman nodded and put her arm around his shoulder.

"Vy rozumiyete, do you understand?" Hunter begged her. "Laska, please?"

Chapter 17

A car honked. The limo driver slammed the brakes. Karasov and Hunter lurched forward. The driver shook his fist, cursed in Ukrainian. Several minutes later, they pulled up to Hunter's building.

"Life is interesting," Karasov said. He set his drink down and turned to Hunter. "Look at us. You and me. In New York City. Having drink together." He grinned.

Hunter stiffened and gripped his drink.

Karasov looked out the window at the mass of people walking along the sidewalks. "What you think people want more than anything?"

"Money," Hunter said.

Karasov smiled. "Beside money."

"I have no idea."

"Trust," Karasov said. "Trust that friends will help when need them. Trust people do what say they going do. Trust when woman say she love you, she mean it."

Karasov noticed the ice cubes in Hunter's glass shaking. "You okay?"

Hunter quickly finished the rest of his drink. "I'm fine."

"You don't look it." Karasov laughed. "You should be more afraid of Alina than me. People with no guilt or conscience capable of anything."

"What do you want from me?"

"Favor from a friend."

Hunter's head dropped slightly. "Okay, I'll help you. What do you need?"

"Good advice I can trust." Karasov eyes narrowed. "To get things to save my country from Russians. To tell me what to do."

Hunter set his drink down. "Okay, first you need to get some good press. No one knows who you are. Perception is power in New York and Washington. You won't have much success gaining favor or money in Washington if they don't think you're a serious player. I can make you a rock star of the nouveau rich and power brokers who are emerging from the ashes of the old Soviet Union. Second, I'll write an article suggesting you're close to signing a multi-billion-dollar deal with a major American oil company to develop your own oil reserves."

Karasov nodded. "I like that."

"You want the other oil companies to wonder why they aren't invited to the party."

"Party?" Karasov said.

"It's a figure of speech. We want them to panic because they haven't been invited to compete for your business."

Karasov pulled out a large manila folder from his briefcase and handed it to Hunter.

"What's this?" Hunter asked.

"Proposal from Hank Parrish at US Oil Company."

"Is that the same guy you were with at the Union Square Café?"

Karasov nodded. "Read it and tell me what it say. My English not so good. Then use your research department—find what can on Parrish and what his company do in Russia, especially last five years."

"Why me? Why not give it to Alina?"

"You no worry about that. Do what I ask."

Hunter looked at his watch. "Drive me back to the office. If I submit my article within the next hour, it should be in the paper tomorrow. I'll talk to our research department about Parrish."

"Thank you, my friend." Karasov reached into his coat pocket and pulled out a thick white envelope. He handed it to Hunter. "I almost forget. This for you."

Hunter waved his hands in the air. "No."

"Between friends."

Hunter hesitated and rubbed his forehead.

"You insult me?"

Hunter put the money inside his coat pocket. "Okay, only because we're friends."

Karasov motioned to his driver. "Ikhaty nazad v ofis zaka, drive back to Hunter's office."

Hunter got out in front of the *Times* building. He was walking toward the entrance when Karasov yelled at him, waving the large manila envelope through the limousine window. "You forget proposal."

Hunter retrieved the envelope. "Thanks. I'll call you after I review the information."

The dark electric window rose quickly. But before the limousine pulled away, Hunter stared at the distorted reflection of his face in the black rear window. This is crazy, he thought. What am I doing? I'm helping the same guy that almost killed me.

He stared at a garbage can next to him on the sidewalk. For a second, he thought about throwing the proposal in the can, but instead, he turned and walked into his office building.

* * *

It took Hunter longer than expected to finish the article for Karasov, so it was too late to have dinner with Carrie. He called her to reschedule for the next day.

Hunter was in early the next morning. As he worked on more articles for Karasov, Tess popped into his office.

"How did it go with Carrie last night?"

"It didn't. I had to cancel."

"Oh."

Hunter looked up from his computer. "What's with the 'oh'?"

Tess stepped in and leaned against the wall. "I don't know. This is none of my business, but there is something about Carrie that doesn't seem right."

"What do you mean?"

"I can't put my finger on it. She's really pushy, and when she calls here, she asks too many questions about you and what you're working on." Tess stared at Hunter. "She tries a little too hard to be the innocent Midwestern gal. Frankly, I don't trust her. Be careful."

"Tess, are you trying to protect me?"

"I don't want to see you get hurt again."

"That's the nicest thing anyone has said to me." Hunter stood up and gave her a hug. She smelled like warm cinnamon. "Thank you."

Near closing time, Tess yelled from her desk outside his office. "I'm outta here. Do you need anything else?"

"No, I'm fine. Have a good night."

Tess stepped into his office. "I'm meeting some friends down the street for a beer and some country western music at Garton's."

"Country western?" Hunter snickered.

"What's so funny?"

"You don't strike me as a girl who'd enjoy country western music."

She put her hand firmly on her hips. "And why not?"

Hunter pointed at her tall black boots with high heels, her skin-tight, black leather skirt, and her black eye makeup. "Will they let you into Garton's dressed like that?"

"New York loves cross-overs."

"I knew you loved music, but country?"

"Hey, I'm a music junkie—rap, rock & roll, heavy metal, country—I love it all. What kind of music do you like?"

Hunter shrugged. "I'm not much for music."

"Music makes me happy. You should try it sometime." She tilted her head. "Why don't you join us tonight?"

"Thanks, but I have other plans."

"I have a great group of friends."

"I'm sure you do."

"You'd like them." She stepped inside his office and leaned against the door. "We do stuff together all the time."

"That's nice."

"When was the last time you went out with a group of friends?"

Hunter pretended he was busy and randomly moved things around on his desk. "It's been a while."

"Okay, see you tomorrow." She turned to leave but stopped in the door opening. "If you change your mind, you know where we'll be."

It took Hunter another thirty minutes to finish some work. He turned off his computer, glanced back at the box on the floor and then to his manuscript sitting on his desk. The last two years of his life revisited him.

He turned off the lights and walked out. Halfway up the block, he passed Garton's and heard a familiar laugh. He stopped, absorbing the country music that drifted out of the open window. A young man in blue jeans, pointy boots and a tan cowboy hat sat on a high barstool with an old acoustic guitar. He sang in mumbled phrases about some woman that had broken his heart.

Hunter surveyed the crowd and spotted Tess sitting at a round table covered with long-neck beer bottles and bowls of peanuts. She and four girlfriends were singing along with the man. Hunter moved closer to the window and watched until the song was over. He was about to walk away when Tess caught his eye. She smiled, raised her beer bottle in the air, and then threw her head back and laughed. Hunter nodded, but before he could leave Tess, rushed outside and grabbed him by the arm.

"Come inside," Tess begged.

"No, I can't."

"Yes, you can." She started to drag him through the door.

"Okay, but just for one."

When they reached the table, Tess grabbed an extra chair and introduced him to her girlfriends. "This is my good friend, Hunter."

They all greeted him at the same time, inspecting him as carefully as you would pick a Christmas tree. Tess made him sit down next to her. A server asked him, "Honey, what would you like to drink?"

"Vodka on the rocks with a lime."

She slipped her pen into her beehive of bleached blonde hair. "Coming right up."

Hunter grabbed the server's arm before she left. "Sorry, I've changed my mind. Give us another round of whatever beer their drinking."

The waitress came back with cold bottles of Blue Moon and passed them around. After she left, one of the girls, Patty, raised her bottle to the middle of the table. "I want to make a toast."

Everyone raised their bottles until they all touched. Hunter was the last one to touch his bottle to the group.

Tess leaned close to Hunter and whispered, "I'm glad you came."

Hunter smiled. "So am I."

Patty lifted her bottle higher in the air. "To good friends," she said, looking into the eyes of each person's face. "You are the food for my soul."

As she spoke those last words, Tess squeezed Hunter's hand. After a few seconds, Hunter slowly squeezed back.

Maybe Victor had it right—the teacher only comes when you're ready.

Two hours later, Hunter slid into the backseat of a taxi.

"Where to?" the driver asked with a slight Russian accent. He turned his head just enough that Hunter could see the outline of a black tattoo on the side of his neck.

Hunter glanced back at Garton's. He could still hear the country music through the open taxi window.

"Where to?" the cabbie asked again. "I don't have all day."

"Just drive. I need time to think."

* * *

The next night, Hunter arrived home from work and found Carrie sitting on his stoop with two bags of groceries in front of his building. He felt a twinge of guilt. She looked fifteen in a white summer dress, ponytail, sun freckles and leather sandals. She jumped up from the stoop and waved rapidly as if she'd just spotted her best friend.

Tess's lack of trust in Carrie rang in his ears.

"Sorry I'm late. I was stuck on a conference call."

"No problem." Carrie reached up and kissed him before he could say anything else. "I haven't been waiting long." She bent down to pick up her groceries when Hunter stopped her.

"Here," he handed her his briefcase, "let me get those. What are we having?"

She smiled. "It's a surprise."

As they walked up to the entrance, Carrie said, "This is the first time I've been to your apartment."

"It's not much to look at."

They entered the building, and she pointed at the staircase. "No elevator?"

"None of the buildings on this block have elevators. Back when they were built, elevators weren't required."

As they passed the second floor, Carrie craned her neck, looking up and down the stairs. "Been here long?"

"I know it's a little dreary and needs some work," Hunter said, "but I like the location."

"This is different than I expected. How did you pick this place?"

"It reminded me of another place I lived in a long time ago."

Finally, they reached the sixth floor. The lock in Hunter's door tended to stick, so Hunter popped it hard with the base of his hand and twisted the key. After several attempts, it made a loud click, and he pushed the door open.

"The rent must be a bargain here," Carrie said.

"A little over two grand a month."

"You're kidding," Carrie whistled. "That's robbery."

"What do you pay in Chelsea?"

"Too much," Carrie blushed. "My dad still pays my rent until I get a better job."

"Must be nice to have a father like that." Hunter flicked on the light of his apartment and took the groceries into the kitchen.

"He's a good dad—strict, but nice. He wants me to be happy, but he treats me like a baby."

"Typical father."

"I was the last child, a tail-ender, and my dad thought for sure that I was a boy. He had the name all picked out, only it was spelled C-a-r-y, not C-a-r-r-i-e. I was a big disappointment."

"I can't believe that."

Carrie shook her head. "You don't know my dad. He's used to getting what he wants. For example, all four of my brothers are over-achievers. Mark's a doctor, Jim's an investment banker, Tom's a lawyer and Danny's a fighter pilot in the Air Force. And then there's me." She paused. "Funny, Dad has my life all planned out. He wants to marry me off to some nice boy and have five kids."

"Five children?"

"My dad means well. He just doesn't know how to…" She stopped talking and looked away.

"It doesn't matter what he wants—what do you want?"

"I want to become a writer. A real writer," Carrie said. "Father thinks that writing is a complete waste of time. He believes that I should find a good man and settle down. No matter what I did growing up—Girl Scouts, class valedictorian, merit scholar, first chair clarinet—it was never good enough for him."

"I think you should listen to your father. Writing isn't much of a way to make a living. I should know." Hunter laughed. "Besides, the only legitimate writers that become famous are also crazy. And I don't think you're in that category. Sounds like you want respect more than looking for a Pulitzer in literature, especially from your father."

"Maybe there's a little truth in that."

"I understand. Try this on for a pillow thought. 'We work in the dark—we do what we can—we give what we have. Our doubt is our passion and our passion is our task. The rest is the madness of art.'"

"Did you just make that up?"

"No, a crazy but amazing writer named Henry James wrote that just before he died. Growing up with a father like yours must've been very difficult for you." He gave a tired smile. "At least you have a family."

Her shoulders sagged for a second, and then she straightened up. "My mother told me that I was the only one who can make me happy."

"What are you going to do about your relationship with your dad?"

Carrie opened a can of tomato sauce. "I'm going to prove him wrong."

"That's a great idea. I'm all for it."

She smiled and played with the edge of her skirt. "So, what about you. Are you happy?"

"Working on it," Hunter said.

Carrie walked around the apartment, peering at each of the mismatched items Hunter had acquired from the previous tenants and friends. "Wow, this is different. Who was your decorator?" she asked sarcastically.

"You're looking at him."

"What an inspiration to use empty, government gray walls in combination with a few pieces of... well, let's call it eclectic furniture." She ran her hand along the scratched-up dining room table. "It's sooo... I can't find the words... retro minimalist with a psych hospital, institutional feel. Very avant-garde."

"I'm not here very much," Hunter yelled from the kitchen. "But, I love a woman who can appreciate good taste."

She laughed and studied the rest of the living room. "You could use a plant—something green, something living in this place."

"I tried, but I just end up killing them."

"Have you considered a cactus?"

"Very funny," he said while unpacking the groceries.

She sneaked up from behind and ran her fingers through his hair. He turned and let her kiss him for a few seconds, but then pulled back. Compared to Alina, she kissed like a teenager and tasted like bubblegum. He knows he should stop this relationship but doesn't how. Conflict is not his strongest attribute.

"We better start the dinner," Hunter said.

"We could skip dinner and do something more fun," she cooed.

"What did you have in mind?" Hunter said.

Carrie shrieked and jumped into the air. Hunter looked down at the cat rubbing against her bare leg.

"Sorry, I forgot to tell you about Angel—my one connection to the living."

"She's beautiful." When she reached down to stroke the cat's red fur, Angel arched her back and hissed. "Is she always like this?"

Hunter laughed. "Only around other women."

Carrie crossed her arms and pretended to glare at the cat. "So, I have some competition."

"It appears that way."

"How did you pick her?"

"Actually, it was the other way around—she picked me. I found her lying on my building stoop half-dead. I tried to walk around her, but she wouldn't let me pass. Story of my life."

Carrie walked around the kitchen. "What about hanging some pictures on these bare walls… or the refrigerator? You can't kill photos."

"Pictures of what?"

"Let's start with your family?"

"I can't do that."

"You're just like my brother. He's too lazy to buy frames and take the time to hang them on the wall. I'd love to see your family photos. I'll help you pick out some good ones."

"That's not necessary, but I appreciate the offer."

"That's crazy," she said, following Hunter around the kitchen. "I'd love to do it. Just show me where you store your family photos."

Hunter closed the refrigerator and started to wipe down the counter. "I don't have any."

"Then, just grab some the next time you're home."

"That's not possible."

"Why not?" Carrie said, stepping closer to Hunter.

Hunter stopped wiping the counter. "My parents died in a fire when I was young. We lost everything in our house. I happened to sleep at a friend's house the night it occurred. Otherwise, I would've…" Hunter couldn't finish the sentence.

"Oh my God, I'm so sorry."

"That's why I don't have any family photos."

"Do you have any brothers or sisters?"

"I'm an only child. I bounced around in various foster homes until I was eighteen."

Carrie put her hand on his shoulder. "I'm so sorry. I don't know what to say."

"That's okay. I barely remember my parents."

"That must've been so difficult to grow up alone," Carrie said. "I can't imagine growing up without parents and siblings."

Hunter didn't respond.

Carrie stepped closer to him. "What was the worst part for you... growing up?"

Hunter twisted the towel into a tight knot. "I can't remember my parents saying they loved me. I can see their faces, but I can't hear their voices anymore."

Carrie took the towel from Hunter and clasped her hands around his neck. "Well, I love you."

Hunter kissed her and then pulled away. "We better get dinner started or it'll get too late."

"I'm curious," Carrie said. "Why did Cabot give you a job as a reporter at the *Times*?"

"Because he loves to make money," Hunter said. "He hired me after I graduated from Columbia because I was a decent writer, but I didn't have any experience. I was the editor of the university newspaper and finished number one in my class. He believed I'd be a great reporter and that I'd make him look good. The situation was something of a paradox. Although he wanted me to excel so he could take the credit, it turned out he was envious of me as a reporter. He always wanted to be a reporter but didn't have the talent. You see... it's kind of a love-hate thing between us."

"But why did you go to work for him and not somewhere else?" Carrie asked. "I'm sure that you had other options."

Hunter frowned. "It's complicated." He reached for a bottle of wine and started to take off the metal sleeve. "I know this is dumb, but I believed that I owed him because he was the first one willing to take a chance on me."

Hunter twisted the wine opener into the cork and pulled hard until it popped out. Carrie started to say something but changed her mind.

"What?" Hunter said, filling both glasses with wine.

"You don't owe anyone for anything."

Hunter watched Carrie move around the kitchen while she prepared dinner. Occasionally, she'd ask him to grab something for her but otherwise was content to sit back, drink his wine and watch her cook.

"What are you making?"

"Veal scaloppini," Carrie said, placing thin cuts of veal in an egg wash and then dredging them in flour.

"Perfect. I'm Italian," Hunter said. He tried to imagine what it would be like to grow up the way Carrie had—to have a real family and wake up every day to normal people who loved you.

"How's the research coming along for your book?" Hunter asked.

"Terrible."

"Why?"

"Way too much information." Carrie peeled a carrot in rapid motions. "I can't decide what the book is about. It started out as a story about women and love in the 90s. I wanted to explore why it's hard for girls my age to find love on their own terms and not act like a dog waiting for a treat from its master. If you don't marry someone from home or college, it's very hard to meet men."

She stopped peeling for a second and then continued chattering. "About halfway through research, my magazine assigned me to write about prostitution in New York. That took me in a very different direction. But now, I don't know. After I read your articles, I'm tempted to switch and write about the injustice of how easily men can exploit women. The explosion of human trafficking in Europe and Asia is inexcusable."

"I see why you're confused. Those are very different topics."

"Not really. Men make a sport out of controlling women, whether it's for money or love."

"We're not all like that."

She pointed her index finger at Hunter. "Give one example of a brothel where a woman controls a house full of male prostitutes."

Hunter shrugged his shoulders.

"Another thing, I'm sick of my girlfriends who are stuck in long-term relationships waiting for their boyfriends to ask them to marry. This is the twenty-first century, for God's sake. I don't understand why more women don't take control of their lives."

"I think you're over-reacting."

"Most women do make up their own minds about how they want to live their lives and who they love, but too many are trapped by their desire for family approval, or they're paralyzed by their own insecurities."

"Why pick on men? How does that connect to men exploiting women for sex?"

"Have you ever heard of women trafficking men for sex?"

Carrie peeled the carrot so hard that it looked like a thin pencil.

"I think your carrots are ready."

She laughed and threw it in the sink. "See what you made me do?"

Hunter smiled. "Just another example of how men rule." He snuggled up behind her.

"Would you mind if I try to exploit you on the kitchen table?"

"I'm warning you." She threatened him with a vegetable peeler. "If you force yourself on me, I'll have to put you in my book."

"I'll take my chances." He stepped closer. "Why do you want to write a book?"

"So, I can be like you," she said.

"Bullshit," Hunter said. "Give me the real reason."

"You wouldn't understand."

"Try me. Be honest."

"I want to prove my dad wrong." She tucked her hair behind her ears. "I want him to be as proud of me as my brothers. I don't have any fancy credentials yet, and I realize that I can't achieve that goal by working for a small local magazine. I need to find a way to break through, so I'm writing a book in my spare time. I'll do whatever it takes to get my book published."

"Then your dad will love you?"

Carrie stopped peeling the carrot and glared at him. "I thought you'd understand."

"I'm sorry," Hunter said. "That wasn't fair."

"I've wanted to become an author and reporter ever since I took my first creative writing class in high school."

"Be careful what you wish for. It's not as glamorous as you might think." Hunter said. "My advice is to keep writing and trust yourself. Your heart will let you know what the story should be."

"I hope that clarity comes soon because I'm stuck on an important part of the book. Maybe you can help me." She waved the peeler in the air. "Why are people attracted to certain people, especially ones that aren't good for them? Why do some people pick a person to love that's completely wrong?" She resumed peeling. "Funny, isn't it?"

"What is?" Hunter said.

"Funny how often everyone else can see it, but the person herself," Carrie said. "My mother always said that people can't see themselves for who they are—that you only see the 'real' you through the eyes of others."

"I'm not sure we can judge who's right or wrong for someone else."

She shook her head. "I just don't get it. Why would you pick someone to love when you know in your heart that it'll never work?"

"Maybe they never ask themselves that question for a reason."

"Why wouldn't you? It just happens to be the most important decision that a person will ever make. It will affect everything in your life forever."

"Maybe they don't want to go there." Hunter took another sip of wine. "Maybe they're afraid the answer would be something different than what they want to hear. Or maybe they feel trapped by their situation because of fear or family pressure."

"Here's another thing I don't understand." She started chopping an onion and looked at Hunter. "Why do some people love what they can't have—when the one they should love is standing right in front of them?"

"I think we need more wine." As he refilled their wine glasses, his phone vibrated. He pulled the phone out of his pocket and looked at the display. It was Alina.

"Excuse me, I have to take this," he explained, then walked into the other room. "Hunter, here."

"I need to see you right away."

"Why? What's wrong?"

"I can't discuss this over the phone," she sounded frantic. "Can I come over?"

Hunter hesitated. "Ahh, this isn't a good time."

"Do you have company?"

"Just a friend for dinner."

"I see…"

"It's not like that."

"I didn't say anything."

"I don't want you to get the wrong impression."

"Because your friend's a woman?"

Hunter sighed. "I have to go but…" He walked to the farthest corner from the kitchen and said in a low voice, "Come over later. Let's say around 10:30 p.m."

"Thanks. I'll see you in a couple of hours."

Hunter walked back to the kitchen. "How are we coming with dinner?"

"Good."

"When do you think we'll eat?"

"Why? Are you hungry?" She popped the meat in the oven and leaned against the counter with a dish towel slung over her shoulder. "Who called?"

"Just a friend." Hunter grabbed the bottle of wine. "Let's go to the living room until dinner's ready."

Carrie sat down and crossed her legs beneath her.

"Tell me about Kiev?"

"It's all in the articles."

"Your experience was amazing, but I want to hear about all the stuff you didn't write ."

"What you mean."

"Well, the mystery and intrigue with the Mafia controlling the sex and drug business was sickening and fascinating. Did you meet any mafia guys?"

"A few."

"You're kidding!" She leaned closer. "What were they like?"

"Actually, far worse than in the movies. They have a different sense of the value of life. Business, money, loyalty are the only things that matter to them."

"Why did you pick Kiev?"

Hunter explained how it all came to pass after the collapse of the Soviet Union. "In that environment, the drug and prostitution business flourished unchecked."

"Did you ever see business executives from American companies in the clubs?"

Hunter nodded.

"What about government officials?"

He nodded again.

"Who?"

"I can't tell you. It's too dangerous."

"Okay, so tell me about the new ambassador of Ukraine."

Hunter changed positions and crossed his arms. "Why do you ask?"

"What does he think about the mafia? What does he think about the human trafficking and drug trade in his country?"

"I haven't asked him."

"You should interview him."

Hunter laughed. "It would be a short conversation."

"It's ironic how the ex-KGB and mafia guys have morphed into politicians." Carrie shook her head. "What a joke. We launched a space shuttle this year, yet thousands of women are held against their will over there and bought and sold like cattle."

"Can't we talk about something else?"

She frowned. "Somebody should stop them."

"Don't be naïve," Hunter said. "The bad guys have tremendous power, and there are billions of dollars at stake."

"I'm curious, why didn't you name one executive from a major American or international company or any government officials that went to the club?"

"It's not a crime to have a drink in a club like the Rus'."

"So, they were there to play bingo and eat cookies?"

"Before you can accuse someone, you must have indisputable proof. And even if you acquire the proof, then you must decide whether it's worth it or not, because when the mafia finds out it's you..."

Carrie leaned forward. "What?"

"They'll kill you, or if you're lucky..." Hunter pointed to his mangled right hand, "...they just maim you."

Carrie's looked down at Hunter's right hand and gasped. "They did this to you?"

"Like I said, the mafia doesn't like attention," Hunter brushed his hair back over his right ear. "I got too close. I was lucky they didn't kill me."

"You never mentioned anything about this in your series."

"Now you understand why." His eyes narrowed. "Carrie, look at me. You're not thinking of writing about any of this in your little magazine or book, are you?"

"Our readers would find it interesting."

"Didn't you hear anything I said? Do you want the mafia to come after you?"

"It's not right." Carrie crossed her arms. "Think about those poor girls. Somebody must stop them. Evil only exists if we allow it. I can't imagine what it must be like to be forced into prostitution as a human slave."

"Prostitution has been around for centuries. There's nothing you or I can do to stop it."

"Who are these men, these animals, that go to prostitutes for sex? What kind of sick men pay for sex and take advantage of these poor girls?"

Hunter stood and walked back into the kitchen.

"Where are you going?"

Hunter didn't answer. After a minute, Carrie followed him into the kitchen. "I didn't mean to upset you."

"I'm not upset."

Carrie tried to kiss him, but he pulled away and walked over to the freezer for more ice. She sighed and looked at her watch. "We still have ten minutes before dinner's ready." She checked the oven and watched Hunter make a drink. "I'm curious, how did you get access to all the information in Kiev?"

"You don't give up, do you?"

"My dad thinks that perseverance is my best attribute."

Hunter couldn't help but smile. "I interviewed a number of people."

"What was it like to talk to the women, especially the young girls?"

"It wasn't what I expected."

"In what way?"

"Every way," Hunter said. "I expected to feel disgusted by the prostitutes, but they aren't any different from you and me. They're just trapped by evil men who have no morals or regard for life."

"I'd love to see all the research materials you used. Do you store them in your apartment or somewhere else?"

Hunter's hair tingled on his arm. He looked closely at Carrie. "My notes are nothing, just a bunch of scribbles. The rest is a pile of unorganized documents."

"Can I see them anyway?"

"I thought we were talking about your book."

"Mine's boring. Your articles are much more interesting." She picked up two hot pads and pulled the meat out of the oven.

"What can I do to help?" he asked.

Carrie pointed to her wine glass. "I could use a refill."

Hunter looked at the bottle. It was empty, so he opened another one and refilled her glass.

"Tell me about Alina," Carrie said.

"There's not much to tell."

"How did you meet?"

"We met through mutual friends. I needed a document translated, and she came highly recommended."

"I bet." Carrie finished plating the dinner. "Odd, but I can't help believing she's way underutilized simply as a translator. There's something different about her. I can't put my finger on it. Do you know what I mean?"

"I wouldn't know." Hunter glanced at the clock in the kitchen. It was nine o'clock already. "Let's eat. I'm starving."

They moved to the dinner table. Halfway through dinner, Carrie asked, "Can I ask you a favor? Can you get me an interview with Alina?"

Hunter almost dropped his fork. "Why would you want to do that?"

"For my book."

"Why Alina?"

"I'd be very interested in her perspective as an Eastern European woman."

"Her perspective on what?" he asked, cutting his meat rapidly.

"I want to find out what she thinks about love. I'm sure a sophisticated woman like her has seen more things than a girl like me will experience in a lifetime."

"That's not a good idea."

"Why not?"

"I'm sure she's too busy."

"I only need a half-hour." Carrie reached over and squeezed his hand. "Can you at least check with her? Please, for me?"

Hunter carefully searched her face for some clue. Carrie didn't look away, so he relaxed. "What do you want me to say to her?"

"Tell her how much I'd appreciate her time."

"Okay, I'll try."

Carrie grinned. "Thank you!"

Hunter checked his watch again. It was almost nine-thirty.

"What's wrong?" Carrie asked. "You keep looking at your watch. Do you have to do something?"

"I need to prepare for several meetings tomorrow."

Carrie looked disappointed. "I thought we could snuggle and I could spend the night." She grinned. "I brought my toothbrush."

Hunter laughed. "You would make a great Girl Scout—always prepared." He glanced at his watch again. "Can I take a rain check?"

"Okay." Carrie stood up to clear the plates from the table.

"Just leave those. I'll do them in the morning."

"You sure? It'll only take me a few minutes."

"I'm sure." Hunter stood up. "I really need to work on my lecture."

"I don't understand you." She wiped tears from her eyes. "I try so hard, but you push me away."

"That's not true."

"What do you want from me?" she pleaded.

"Nothing."

"Don't you see? I want you to expect something from me. I want to become everything you want me to be." She wiped more tears from her cheeks. "But I can't guess… I can't read your mind. You have to tell me what you need."

Hunter stared at the floor. "I can't."

"Why not?"

"Because I don't know what I need."

Carrie gathered her coat and picked up her purse. When Hunter tried to kiss her, she roughly pushed him away. "Don't you understand? I love you, but this… this doesn't work."

Hunter didn't know how to respond. Finally, he said, "I'll walk you down."

"Forget it," she said. "I can get my own taxi." Then she marched out the apartment and slammed the door.

Hunter sprinted back to the kitchen and started cleaning as fast as he could. Twenty minutes later, the buzzer rang. He took one last look around and opened the door.

Alina burst into the room in tears and threw her arms around him.

"What's wrong?" he asked.

"Everything," she sobbed.

Chapter 18

Alina didn't bother removing her raincoat. She threw a large duffle bag on the dining room table and strode to the window, carefully pulling back the sheer curtain and looking down at the street. It was raining so hard she could only see a short distance.

"What's going on?" Hunter said from behind her.

Alina closed the curtain and leaned against the wall. Shaking, she opened her purse and pulled out a pack of Dunhills. In the process of juggling too many things at once, half the contents in her purse spilled onto the floor. She didn't care. As if in a trance, she slumped and let go of her purse while slowly sliding down the wall. Rocking back and forth, she pulled her knees up and placed her head in her arms. "I had everything planned perfectly," she said. "Now this."

"What are you talking about?" Hunter knelt to comfort her, but she flinched when he touched her. Black mascara smeared her eyes.

She clutched at his shirt. "Do you love me?"

He stroked her hair. "Of course I do."

"Would you do anything for me?"

"You know I would."

"I need you to trust me." Her shoulders shook as she sobbed.

Hunter leaned over and kissed her on the forehead. "I trust you."

She sat up. "Bring me my duffle bag."

Hunter returned with the bag, and she said, "Go ahead. Open it."

He unzipped the bag and froze. "How much is in here?"

She pulled a cigarette out of the Dunhill pack and tried to light it, but the lighter didn't work. She shook it several times, tried again, but still, it failed. She threw it as hard as she could across the room. "Goddamn lighter."

Hunter thumbed through the hundred-dollar bills. "Holy shit!"

"A lot, but still not enough," she said in a hollow, distant voice.

"Where did you get this kind of money?"

"You said you trusted me."

"I do, but this... this... this is a lot."

Alina got on her knees and started to pick up the contents of her purse. "The less you know, the better."

"Are you in trouble?"

"I need you to put the money in one of my trunks along with our other documents."

"Why me?"

"I can't exactly waltz into a bank, hand them a duffle bag full of cash and say I'd like to open an account."

"Where did you get this kind of money?"

"Does it matter?"

"Did you steal it?"

"I earned it," she said, then slammed the last of the contents into her purse. "This is all for us."

"Us?"

Alina nodded and chewed on her lip. "Hunter, I'm trying to protect you. Everything I've been doing over the last two years is to get me to this place... for us... for our future." Her eyes pleaded. "But you have to help me."

"Yes, of course," Hunter said. "But what about Karasov?"

"Don't worry. I'll take care of him." She stood up and took a deep breath. "I need a drink." She pulled away and walked into the kitchen and pulled a frosty bottle of vodka out of the refrigerator. "Where do you keep the glasses?" she yelled over her shoulder.

"Second cupboard, left of the sink."

As Alina approached the cabinets, Angel hissed at Alina and then scampered across the counter and disappeared.

"Where did you get the cat?" she yelled back at Hunter.

"It's a long story." Hunter placed the duffle bag on his desk in the corner of the living room. When he walked into the kitchen, Alina was leaning against the sink holding two glasses of vodka on the rocks with a slice of lime. She handed one to Hunter and pointed toward two empty wine glasses on the counter.

"How's your little brown thing?"

Hunter took a gulp of vodka.

"She seems sweet." Alina said, sipping on her drink. "But, I'm surprised."

"Surprised at what?" Hunter said.

"Why her?"

"What do you mean?"

"Is she a pet or just some toy to play with?"

"It's not like that."

She smiled and tilted her head to the side. "If I remember correctly, you always preferred naughty over nice."

Hunter looked away.

"A word of advice," she said. "Never trust a woman with a cotton candy smile."

"You're not the first person to give me advice about Carrie."

Alina smiled and set her drink down, untied her long raincoat, and wrapped it around Hunter. "Do you remember this?" She began to push her hips slowly against him.

"I vaguely remember something."

She pressed harder and harder.

"Are you sure we should be doing this?" he said between her kisses. "What about Karasov? He'd kill us if he finds out."

"Don't worry." She started to unbutton his shirt. "I find sex is much more fun when it's a little dangerous, don't you?" Alina's cell phone rang. She squeezed her eyes shut for a second and then put her hand inside her raincoat pocket to turn it off. Her voice sounded tired. "I have to go."

"You can't leave without telling me what happening."

Alina pulled the phone out of the pocket in her raincoat. When she looked down at the display, Hunter noticed two large red bruises on her neck. He reached out and touched one. "Tell me what happened?"

"Nothing." She pushed him away. "I bumped into something last night."

"Who did it?" Hunter gritted his teeth. "Karasov?"

Alina shook her head. "Forget it."

"I'll kill him if he touches you again."

"My little tiger." She smiled and touched his cheek. "I need something from you."

"Anything."

She walked into the other room and opened her purse on the table. "I need the box with all the photos, receipts and recordings that I made of Senator Dixon, Hank Parrish and the others."

"Why?"

She reached into her purse and pulled out a thick manila envelope. "I need to put the money and this envelope into the box."

"What's inside the envelope?"

"Nothing you want to know about."

Hunter stared at the large manila envelope and the duffle bag. "Alina, talk to me."

"There's a lot at stake here for everyone."

"Who's everyone?"

She stepped closer to him and searched his eyes. "No more questions. Remember, I'm doing this for us—for our future."

Hunter hesitated and then walked over to his desk. "Okay, but I don't like it."

"When are you going to the storage unit? I'd like to go with you."

"No, it's better that I go alone."

"Give me the address, and I'll meet you there."

"Not a good idea. Karasov might be following you."

"Okay. Did you confirm the meetings that Karasov wanted with the senators and me?"

"I'll send you an email tomorrow with the schedule of interview times."

"Karasov spoke very highly of you after your meeting."

"Hah, I doubt that."

"No, it's true. For some reason, he trusts you."

"We found out we have a few things in common."

"Like what?"

"It doesn't matter."

"You must've had an interesting conversation because he was impressed."

"Interesting is one way to describe it," Hunter said. "Frankly, I was surprised how much he hates the Russians."

Alina found another lighter in her purse and lit a Dunhill. "There are billions of dollars involved in the oil and gas trade. Everyone's out for themselves since the Soviet Union collapsed."

"I know that. Karasov's face got so red when he discussed the Russians that I thought he was going to have a heart attack. It was odd because as fierce and dangerous as he appears, I thought he was going to cry when he told me, 'Those Russian bastards have no heart and no sense of honor. They have no idea what family means. Before the disintegration of the Soviet Union, we belonged to each other. We had centuries of pride in Mother Russia… and now all that's gone.'"

"How touching," Alina said, sarcastically. "Men can rationalize anything. Karasov has no problem looking into the mirror when he shaves every morning because he doesn't see the murderer, the drug trafficker or the man who steals young women and sells them like farm animals." Alina glanced at her watch. "I have to go."

"I almost forgot. Did you see who flew into town today?" Hunter said.

"No, I was in meetings."

"Stravinsky," Hunter said, studying her reaction. "He was interviewed by NBC at JFK airport."

"Christ, everyone has their own fucking agenda." Alina didn't look up as she fidgeted with her purse. "Did he say why he was in New York?"

"No, but he was clearly uncomfortable with the reporters. He wouldn't answer any questions except to say how much he loves New York."

"Interesting, isn't it?" she said. "It feels like a damn International Lion's Club convention with the OPEC meeting in town." She slung her purse over her shoulder. "We're close to agreeing to terms with one of the major oil companies, and Karasov may need your help over the next few days, so stay near your cell phone."

Interesting, he thought. She has no idea that Karasov has given me the same documents to review.

"No problem. I'll make sure that I'm available."

She leaned over and kissed him. "Thanks for the drink."

"When will I see you again?"

"Not sure, just be patient." She gently touched his face. "I can't wait for this to be all over. I'll call when I need you." Before he could protest, Alina put her right index finger on his lips. "Trust me."

"Okay," Hunter said, "but I don't like it."

* * *

After she left, Hunter pulled the curtain back on the window. It had stopped raining. The wet streets glistened like black mirrors. He watched Alina run across the street to a black limousine waiting at the curb. She didn't look back as she stepped through an open door into the backseat. As the limousine drove off, he noticed another car pull away to follow.

The next morning Hunter was in the office when Tess arrived. She handed him a cup of coffee. "How was your night with Carrie?"

"Tess, can you sit down for a minute?"

"Am I getting fired?"

"No, no, I need to ask you about your boyfriend. Why did you decide not to marry him?"

"Hmm, that's complicated."

"Do you want to get married?"

"I don't know. Maybe someday," she said. "I've fallen in love with three men in my life. I picked each one for a different reason. I was young. I picked the first one because I thought he was cute, the second because I desired him." She smiled and licked her lips. "And I lusted for the last one." She sighed. "Silly me, I kept thinking that I picked the perfect man, but not one worked out."

"What happened?"

"It's not enough to pick the right person. You have to *be* the right person for the one you pick."

Hunter leaned back in his chair and put his hands behind his head. "But what if you know that you're the right person for someone, but they don't see it?"

"That's a problem. Are we talking about anyone we know?"

"No—I just want your opinion."

"I'm reading an interesting book about temperament," Tess said.

"You're reading? Really?"

"I'm not an idiot." She scowled. "I do have a brain."

Hunter flinched. "I didn't mean it that way."

"Temperament is how a person's hardwired. You can change your personality, but not your temperament. It's who you are—forever."

"But what if you don't know who you are—much less who she is?"

"Exactly my point—that's why so many people pick the wrong person."

Hunter stared out the window for a minute.

"What are you thinking right now?" Tess asked.

"I'm wondering why, if we all want the same thing, is it so hard to love one another?"

"Trust me," she said. "When it comes to love, you can't change another person… any more than you can change yourself."

Hunter looked at Tess as if he had understood this for the first time.

"What?" Tess said. "Why are you looking at me that way? Do you think I'm wrong?"

Hunter smiled. "You are a special person. I'm lucky to have you as my friend."

Tess blushed.

"I have to ask another question." Hunter motioned to his chair. "Sit here."

Tess looked embarrassed as she settled into his seat.

"Don't worry, I'm not going to embarrass you. Here's my question. You're just like me. We are both alone in this world. Neither of us has any family to complicate things, so if you could have anything you want—your dream life, what would that look like?"

"And money is no object?"

"Sure."

She smiled and closed her eyes. "That's easy. I'd live in a seaside village along a beautiful coast of a lush, mountainous island nobody has heard of. The beaches are powdered-sugar white and the water crystal clear. I'd open a small restaurant and cook only for my friends and neighbors three nights per week. The rest of the time I'd spend sailing and diving in the ocean."

Hunter stared at her.

She frowned. "See? I knew you would think I'm silly."

"No, no, it's not that at all. It's just something I didn't expect," Hunter said. "Have you ever swam in the ocean?"

"Many times. I love to swim. I float as if I didn't have a body, wrapped in the warm womb of the ocean, totally connected to the rhythm of the underwater currents in perfect harmony with hundreds of brilliantly colored fish floating nearby." She paused. "I've never had that feeling anywhere else."

"What feeling is that?"

She closed her eyes. "To feel connected to everything. To totally belong in perfect harmony."

Hunter stared at her until she slowly opened her eyes.

"Sounds absolutely beautiful," he said softly.

Tess shook her head, "Yeah, all in my dreams."

"Well," Hunter smiled. "You never know."

"Now you have to tell me your dream."

Hunter looked at his watch. "I'm sorry, I have a conference call to take."

"Chicken!" Tess said. "You're not getting off this easy. Drinks after work tomorrow?"

"Done." He smiled.

The next morning, Cabot was sitting in Hunter's chair reading the Thursday edition of the *Times* when Hunter walked in. Cabot tapped his watch. "You're late."

"I had to take care of a few things this morning." He set his coat and briefcase on the desk.

"Must be nice to have banker's hours."

Hunter ignored the bait. "How was your trip to DC?"

"Good, it was nice and short. I hate spending that much time with politicians, they're such a slimy group." Cabot played with his unlit cigar. "How was your interview with Karasov last Friday?"

Hunter shook his head. "He's one scary dude."

"Did you write the article for him yet?"

"It's on your desk."

"Great. What does he want from us?"

"Good press."

"That's all?" Cabot sounded skeptical.

"Glowing articles and a favor or two."

Cabot sat up in his chair. "What kind of favors?"

"He didn't say."

"You didn't agree to any favors, did you?"

"He can be very persuasive."

Cabot frowned. "Goddamn it, now he thinks he owns you."

"It wasn't like that," Hunter said. "I told him that I couldn't do anything illegal."

"Shit, you're so stupid."

"I didn't have any choice. He wouldn't give me the interview unless I agreed."

"What's Karasov like?" Cabot asked. "Our sources describe him as one of the most ruthless ex-KGB guys to come out of the Soviet Union."

"He's charming in an odd way, extremely patriotic and hates the Russians with a passion." Hunter paused. "There's something else you need to know. Something big might be going down in New York."

"I know," Cabot said.

Hunter head snapped up. "Where did you hear that?"

Cabot leaned back in Hunter's chair and smiled. "From Alina."

Hunter stopped unpacking his briefcase and stared at his boss. "Alina? When did you talk to her?"

"Relax," Cabot smiled and crossed his arms.

"I just got off the phone with her, and she never said a word about any conversation with you."

"Must've slipped her mind."

"What did you talk about?" Hunter asked.

"Karasov, the Russians, politics."

"You're supposed to go through me."

"Hey, she's a big girl. It's a free world." Cabot smirked. "I didn't contact her, she contacted me."

"I don't believe you."

"I don't care what you believe." He leaned back in Hunter's chair and swiveled slowly back and forth

"What else did she want?" Hunter's face was growing red.

"She's much more ambitious than I thought."

"What do you mean by that?"

Cabot leaned forward. "When Alina and I talked, I had a funny feeling that she was two steps ahead of me. It's as if she had me right where she wanted me, and I don't even know how we got there or where we were going. Ever get that feeling with her?"

"Why did she call you?" Hunter asked.

"She wanted an introduction to 'friendly' bankers in Brooklyn. I asked what friendly meant to her." Cabot grinned. "She said she'd need to have that discussion in person."

Hunter recoiled, and his face tightened.

Cabot laughed, obviously enjoying how he could push Hunter's buttons.

"I told her I would need Karasov's personal information to set up a business account. I was surprised when she said that wasn't possible. She said that she'd prefer to have the account in her name for security reasons." Cabot chewed on his cigar for second. "I got the impression this was a little side venture for our sweet Alina. What do you know about this?"

"Nothing."

"Really?" Cabot's eye narrowed. "You aren't going to do any stupid shit, are you?"

"No, you do enough for both of us."

"Always the wise guy." Cabot shook his head and stood. "I want you to go over to the United Nations and see what you can find out. I'm off to give our good buddy, Senator Dixon, a visit. He owes me big time." Cabot took two steps, then stopped. "Oh, by the way, your girlfriend Carrie was waiting for you in the lobby earlier this morning. She left just before you arrived."

"Carrie's not my girlfriend."

"Whatever."

"What did she want?"

"She didn't say, although we had an interesting conversation."

"About what?"

"A lot of things." Cabot smiled. "Mostly about Kiev. She's smarter than she looks."

"I know."

"She has good instincts and a nose for a story. For example, she believes that people should get credit for what they do. A novel idea, don't you think?"

Hunter squirmed.

"She was especially interested in what happens to a journalist if they're exposed as a fraud or a plagiarist."

"What did you tell her?"

"I told her that she should talk to you because you're an expert in this area." Cabot took the cigar out of his mouth. "I'm curious—I get Alina, but what do you see in Carrie?"

They stared at each other for a few seconds. This conversation had nothing to do with their work relationship. Alina had changed that, and they both knew it.

"I enjoyed our chat." Cabot smiled. "We have to do this more often."

What a fucker, Hunter thought as Cabot walked out.

Hunter tried calling Carrie as soon as Cabot left his office. She didn't answer, so he left a message. When he hadn't heard from her by noon, he left another message and decided to catch Carrie at her office. She free-lanced for a small magazine called *The Big Apple*. Its office was only a short subway ride to Tribeca from the *Times*.

Carrie's office wasn't difficult to find. It was busy with a dozen young people working at beat-up metal desks or running from one end of the room to the other with armfuls of papers. A graveyard of old magazines was stacked in the far corner, along with dozens of boxes containing documents waiting to be tossed or filed.

Hunter looked around for a receptionist, but nobody paid any attention to him. After a few moments, he wandered around the desks looking for Carrie. He paused at a large round table in the middle of the room. A young woman rushing by with her arms full of magazines stopped when she noticed he looked lost. Out of breath, she asked, "Can I help you?"

"I'm looking for Carrie."

The woman looked confused. "I've only been here for two months, but I don't recognize the name. What department does she work in?"

"She's a reporter."

The woman yelled across the room to a heavy-set man that appeared slightly older than the rest. "Stevie, do we have a Carrie working for us?"

He looked up from the document he was reading and adjusted his thick black glasses. "Used to, but she only lasted two weeks before she quit."

"You're kidding," Hunter said. "Do you know where she went?"

"No idea. We liked her. She seemed like the typical mid-western girl from Minnesota—sweet, wide-eyed and naïve, but then..."

"Then what?" Hunter asked.

"I'm not sure how to say this, but she's a girl that knows what she wants. And she knows how to get it."

"Why did she leave?"

"She mentioned something about another project. A book, I think, that she was working on and didn't have the time to do it while she was here."

"What kind of book?"

"Something about exposing our government's involvement with the mafia. Sounded like one of those bad gangster movies. She was never specific, but she said it was big—big enough to make her rich and launch her career as a writer."

"Thanks, sorry to bother you." He started toward the door when he stopped. "Can I ask you one last question?"

"Of course."

"When exactly did she quit?"

He scrunched up his face and rubbed his head. "About two months ago."

"You sure?"

"Yes, why?"

"No reason." Hunter walked swiftly out of the office. He knew it wasn't a coincidence that they'd met in June when he taught his class at NYU. His cell phone vibrated, and he squinted at the display. It was Carrie.

Hunter answered, "Hello."

"I'm glad I caught you."

"I left you messages," Hunter said, harsher than he intended.

"Oh, sorry. I lost the charge on my phone. I stopped by your office this morning to catch you before I took the day off to get some things done. Didn't you get my message? I left it with Cabot."

"He mentioned you stopped by," Hunter said.

"Anything interesting happening today?"

"Interesting would not describe my day so far." Hunter paused. "Hey, I'd love to see your office sometime."

"It's nothing to write home about."

"I could stop by and see your digs."

"Sure, we can arrange that sometime."

"What about tomorrow? It would be fun to see where you work, and we could have lunch."

"I'll have to check my schedule," she said, and then quickly changed the subject. "Why don't we have dinner tonight at your place?"

"Again? You just made dinner for me."

"I know, but it's the only time we see each other. Please, you don't have to do a thing. I'll cook, you can tell me all about your day and then we can snuggle."

"Snuggle?" Hunter said.

"What do you call it?" she said.

"It has seven letters too, but starts with an "F" and ends in "G."

"You're sick." She laughed. "It's been three days since we last made love, and I miss you."

"I'm not sure tonight would work."

"You sound funny. Is something wrong?"

"No. I just have a lot on my mind today."

"All the more reason to let me pamper you tonight. Why don't I stop by and get your key this afternoon? That way, I can have dinner waiting for you when you get home?"

"It could be late."

"I don't care. Come on, it'll be fun. I'll wear a fancy dress like Mrs. Cleaver, and I'll have your paper, pipe and slippers waiting for you."

Hunter knew he was trapped. "Okay, I have to go over to the UN to conduct some interviews. I won't be in for the rest of the afternoon. Swing by my office after four and Tess will have a spare set of keys for you. I need to go. See you about seven."

"Great, see you tonight."

Chapter 19

It was dark by the time Hunter got home. He was shocked when he opened the door to his apartment. The living room glowed with dozens of candles, and the dinner table was set for two.

"Wow." Hunter set his briefcase next to the door.

Carrie stood in the kitchen in a pretty apron covered with flowers and waved a large wooden spoon at him. "Your drink's in the refrigerator."

Hunter walked into the kitchen and opened the door. "What's in the pot?"

"Artichokes," Carrie said while she checked the pot of boiling water. "The man at the store called them passion food because God made them for lovers to share."

"That's one interpretation." Hunter reached for his drink.

"Spoken like a true cynic," Carrie said. "Okay big boy, what's your interpretation?"

Hunter studied her face and explained, "Artichokes are interesting because they aren't what they appear." He walked across the kitchen and leaned against the counter. "Nature is full of paradoxes. Artichokes are hard, unyielding on the outside and protected with needle-sharp points, yet they contain a beautiful purple heart on the inside. Think about that first person who dug an artichoke to find a purple heart deep at the bottom—they must've been shocked." Hunter paused for a second, then continued. "But then there's the Venus Fly Trap—

beautiful on the outside, soft and inviting, yet deadly on the inside. Quite the opposite of the artichoke."

Carrie placed the cover back on top of the pot and folded her arms. "Is there a point to this story?"

"I don't know. I just think it's interesting that looks can be deceiving. You never really know what's on the inside of things." He grabbed her around the waist. "What are you? My purple love or a deadly trap?"

"You'll have to take a risk to find out." She smiled, turned away from Hunter and picked up her glass of wine on the other side of the stove.

"A friend once told me that life is all about risk versus reward." He stopped and stared at Carrie. For the first time, he noticed something was different about her. Gone were the fluffy blouses and brown skirts. She wore a pretty red knit dress that fit her very tightly. His mouth fell open.

She grinned. "Are you okay? You have a funny look on your face."

"Where are your red glasses?"

"I switched to contacts."

He walked around her as if she were a statue. "What happened?"

She blushed and tucked her hair behind her ears. "I have a confession. I really took the day off to have a makeover."

"You... you changed your hair."

"Do you like it?" Carrie tilted her head and played with the loose bangs that hung just over her eyes. Everything was different. Her long brown hair was now short and jet black with deep red highlights. "It turned out a bit shorter than I intended."

"I'm speechless." He looked at her from head to toe. "Why did you do this?"

She poured herself a glass of white wine. "I thought it was time for me to make a few changes in my life."

"Who are you?"

"Who do you want me to be?" She leaned over and kissed the tip of his nose. "I need to finish dinner. Why don't you fix us another drink and take it into the living room?"

He fixed two drinks and walked into the living room. He sat down at his desk, opened the side drawer and reached for the file folder that contained the schedule of meetings he had arranged for Karasov and Alina. All the names were connected to oil and gas, and banking.

"Here we go," Carrie said, holding a platter of artichokes and pasta. "Have a seat at the table."

"I'm impressed. I didn't know you could cook like this."

"It wouldn't be any fun if you knew all my secrets," Carrie said. "I almost forgot, I put your apartment keys in the top drawer of the desk." She casually sipped her wine before adding, "Did you win the lottery or something?"

Hunter stopped chewing his food. "Why?"

"Do you always keep that kind of money lying around in drawers?"

"You looked inside the envelope?"

She played with her food. "I couldn't help it. Some of the money had fallen out of the envelope when I set the keys in the drawer."

"Well, it's not my money," he said.

"Really?" She leaned forward on her elbows with her chin cradled in her hands. "Whose money is it?"

"It's business."

"What kind of business uses wads of cash like that?"

"You wouldn't understand."

"I thought you were in the newspaper business, not banking."

"Very funny," he said. "For as many questions as you ask, you should become a newspaper reporter rather than work for this magazine."

"I'll keep that in mind," she said. "Now, what about the money?"

"See, there you go again. Probing with more questions. You're a natural." Hunter pulled out a cigarette from a pack in his shirt pocket. He lit it and blew smoke off to the side. "It's your turn. Tell me about your job at the magazine."

"Not much to tell." She placed a forkful of food in her mouth.

Hunter waited while she finished chewing. He'd enough experience as a reporter to know when to stop talking. He watched her take a drink of wine without looking at him.

Finally, she said, "I was desperate for work. The magazine wanted someone cheap to write articles. Fifty bucks for every piece they accepted." She frowned. "Doesn't exactly pay the bills."

"Do you like working there?"

"I like the people."

"What are you working on now?"

"Are you done?" Carrie asked as she stood up. "I can clear the plates."

"Yes, thank you."

She walked quickly into the kitchen and started to rinse the dishes. Hunter followed and leaned against the counter, holding his wine glass. "You didn't answer my question."

Carrie's face turned red as she concentrated on scrubbing the dirty plate. "I write about current events, restaurants, concerts, and I do some book reviews.

"What about your other project?" he asked.

She scrubbed the plates faster in the sink. "What other project?"

Hunter put his hand on her shoulder. "Is there anything you want to tell me?"

"No." She flinched and then blew her bangs away from her eyes. Her voice trembled, "It's hard sometimes, but I'm doing the best I can."

"What's hard?"

She set the sponge in the sink and began to cry as she dried her hands on a dishtowel. "I better go. I have to get up early tomorrow."

Hunter crossed his arms. "So that's it? Is that all you're going to tell me?"

"There's nothing to tell."

"You can't change the subject by simply crying. It won't work this time."

"You sound just like my dad," she said angrily, tears suddenly flowing.

"Bullshit. For God's sake, stop crying. You're not a little girl anymore."

She covered her face with both hands. "You wouldn't understand."

"I understand more than you think. I went to your office today."

"You did?" She stopped crying and stared into the sink. Her right foot tapped rapidly on the floor. "Did you talk to anyone?"

"A guy named Stevie."

"What did he say?"

"That you no longer work there."

"Stevie's a dear, but he's dumb as a rock." She shook her head and turned her head sideways to Hunter. "Did you talk to Paul?"

"Who's he?"

"The owner."

"Steve sounded like he was in charge."

"He likes everyone to think that."

"Stevie said you quit. He said you were working on another project."

She dried her hands on the dish towel again. "After working at the magazine for two weeks, it was obvious that I didn't need a desk or an office. I was mainly writing reviews on restaurants, musicians, art exhibits, concerts, and other local events. I could do that out of my apartment. Paul and I agreed there wasn't any need for me to come into their office, so I email him my articles, and then he mails me a check."

"Steve said you quit back in June."

"Like I said, Steve's a nice guy, just not the brightest."

"I'd love to read some of your articles. What editions were they published in?"

"I'll get you some copies, but they don't acknowledge me as the author. These are small pieces scattered throughout the magazine."

"What kind of game are you playing with me?" Hunter asked.

Carrie crossed her arms. "You, of all people, shouldn't be asking me about games. You're the one with the most to lose."

Hunter looked cautiously at her face, examining it as if he was seeing her for the first time. "What do you mean by that?"

"Let's see, where were we? Oh, yes, you wanted to play games with me."

"Who are you?"

"Let's play a new game. Go Fish. I'll guess what cards you have, and you guess mine."

Hunter poured himself another drink. "What do you want?"

"The same things as you want."

"I doubt it," Hunter said. "What do you know?"

"I know you have a drawer full of cash that isn't pocket change. I know that Alina isn't some sweet and innocent friend who happens to be here on a holiday. I know that you spent the summer hanging out in one of the most notorious clubs in Eastern Europe. I did some research on Parrish, Dixon and Karasov." She pointed at Hunter. "Now Karasov—he's a stellar citizen."

"Better be careful here."

"I was going to give you the same advice," she said. "Shall I go on?"

"Be my guest."

"They weren't having dinner at the Union Square Café to celebrate a birthday. I know there are some large deals in the works for oil development in Ukraine, but what I find even more fascinating is the turf war going on between the Russian and the Ukrainian mafia over who controls the money laundering through various banks in Brooklyn and Brighton Beach."

"You don't know what you're talking about."

"So why are Karasov and Stravinsky in New York at the same time?"

"What do you know about Stravinsky?"

"He's the ex-KGB guy who took control of Russia. His mafia is one of the largest and most dangerous in the world."

"You have no idea what you are doing."

"Really?" Carrie said. "And you do?"

Hunter took a big swallow of his drink. "What do you want?"

"I want in."

"What are you talking about?"

"I want in on the story."

"There is no story." He laughed. "You have quite an imagination."

"You sound as patronizing as my dad." Carrie's voice rose. "Look, I know that a deal is in progress. I bet there's a lot of money at stake. I don't want to spoil your fun, but when you get what you want out of this situation and it's all over, I want to write the inside story. You can sanitize it, but this is the kind of story that can launch my career."

"And if I say no?"

She smiled thinly. "Don't underestimate me. There are a number of newspapers that would love to see what I know."

Hunter drained the last of his vodka and set his glass on the counter. "So, what happens now?" Hunter said.

"Nothing." Carrie leaned over and whispered in his ear. "This will be our little secret." She pulled a few inches away from his face. "I'll call you tomorrow."

* * *

The next morning, Hunter fussed with the rusty lock on the storage unit, opened the heavy metal door and stepped inside. The dead air smelled stale and stuffy. He glanced around the small space filled with stacks of boxes, old articles and newspapers. Everything was just as he'd left it after returning to New York. In the rear were the two large trunks that he'd shipped from Kiev just prior to his planned escape with Alina.

With a large wire cutter he'd brought along, he cut off Alina's locks. She had told him the trunks were filled with money and documents that were an insurance policy against threats from Karasov or anyone else. He was shocked when he opened the first trunk. It was filled with hundred-dollar bills and Deutsche Marks—he estimated about one hundred and fifty thousand dollars in neatly stacked bundles. He flipped through one packet of hundred-dollar bills bound by a paper wrapper and noticed a business card on top. The card had a logo of an oil rig with Hank Parrish's contact information.

How far down the rabbit hole does this go? He wondered.

The second trunk was filled with dozens of large manila envelopes, each one filled with incriminating photos, dated cash receipts, audio and video tapes with labels of various businessmen and government officials. Hunter stared at the contents of these trunks and shuddered. He knew that people got killed over a lot less than what Alina had accumulated here.

He rummaged through the second trunk and discovered a grey metal box on the bottom. It was the size of a shoebox with a large steel lock. Hunter snapped the lock with the wire cutter and opened it. To his surprise, it contained dozens of diamonds in various sizes. Obviously, Alina has been planning this for a long time. Hunter knew about the money and the documents, but not the diamonds. No wonder she has been pestering him about the location of the storage unit ever since they'd met again in New York. He suddenly realized the danger he was in. He quickly decided to leave some of the documents here but move most of them and the money and diamonds to a new storage unit in a different part of town. Going forward, he needed to be very careful about everything.

His cell phone rang—Tess.

"Where are you?" she asked. "You missed the Friday staff meeting, and Cabot's looking for you."

"I had to run an errand. I'll be in the office by ten-thirty."

"You better come up with a good excuse."

"What's he upset about this time?"

"I don't know, but two men with identical crew cuts and wearing black suits and shiny wingtips walked into his office after the staff meeting. They closed the door and haven't come out yet."

"I'll be right in."

Thirty minutes later, Hunter arrived at Cabot's office. His secretary pointed to the door with her nail file. Hunter took a deep breath, knocked, and then slowly opened the door.

Cabot was standing next to the window, looking out at the skyline. The two men Tess described were gone.

"You wanted to see me?"

Cabot barely looked at him. "No, I didn't."

"Tess said you wanted to see me as soon as I got in."

"She must've been mistaken. You know how confused Tess can be," Cabot said, without turning away from the window. "I just asked where you were because I didn't see you at the staff meeting."

"She told me that you had some serious-looking visitors this morning."

"Oh, those guys." Cabot glanced at Hunter over his shoulder. His face was drawn and pale. "They were accountants," Cabot said, his voice barely audible. "You know… tax planning stuff."

"Tess said they looked pretty official."

"She has quite the imagination."

"Did you hear the news on the radio this morning?"

"No, I was in meetings."

"Three Russians were found murdered in Brighton Beach last night. They found them stuffed in the basement of an old warehouse."

"So, that's not unusual in New York."

"They were executed—shot in the back of the head. That's the third murder this week. I checked with Vinny, and the word on the street is there's a power struggle going on between competing mafia groups over control of the Brooklyn-Brighton Beach territories."

"It's a dangerous world," Cabot said.

"Are you in trouble?" Hunter asked.

"Me?" Cabot made a face. "No, I'm fine. Just get out of my office and quit bothering me so I can get some work done."

Hunter walked through the bullpen of cubicles. Halfway across the main floor, he stopped and found Vinny with his feet on his desk, tossing a baseball up and down.

"I see you're hard at work."

"Hey, Hunter, where have you been?"

"Cabot has me doing most of his work as well as my own."

Vinny pulled his feet off the desk and leaned toward Hunter. "Come on, I'm dying to know everything about your love life. Must be hard to service two women at the same time."

Hunter's face turned pink. "Did anyone ever tell you that you're an idiot?"

"Once or twice." Vinny grinned. "Tell me what's going on with Alina," Vinny said. "How is she doing?"

"We really haven't had a chance to spend much time together yet. But I need some help again."

"Anything," Vinny said. "I'm at your command."

"I want to know which American oil companies were doing business in the Soviet Union just before the break-up. And who's been the most active in Ukraine over the last two years?"

"Anything specific?"

"Oil and gas drilling. Shale refraction, along with pipeline and refinery construction."

"Anything else?"

"I want you to find out who owns the First National Bank of Brighton Beach."

"Why that one?"

"Just do it," Hunter said, louder than he intended.

"Okay, you don't have to get huffy." Vinny whistled. "What do I look like, the Library of Congress?"

"Sorry, I'm a little stressed out right now," Hunter said. "Oh, one more thing, find out everything you can about Stravinsky."

"When do you need the information?"

"By late afternoon."

Vinny shook his head. "Okay, but you owe me."

"Thanks, you're the best." Hunter leaned toward Vinny and whispered, "Let's keep this between us."

Chapter 20

Hunter couldn't concentrate on work, so he spent the next few hours in his office surfing old articles on Ukraine and Russia after the fall of the Soviet Union. He jumped when someone tapped him on the shoulder.

"Don't you ever knock?" he said to Tess.

"I did," she said. "I knocked twice, but you didn't even look up. Vinny called and said your package was ready."

"Package?" Hunter said. "Oh yeah, tell him I'll pick it up in a few minutes."

His phone rang, and it was Alina.

"Listen, I can't talk very long," Alina said, sounding rushed.

"What's wrong?"

"Things are moving very fast."

"What do you mean?"

"Karasov wants you to meet us tonight and have dinner with Hank Parrish to discuss his latest proposal. I'll send a limousine to pick you up about nine."

"Where are we meeting?"

"The Peninsula Hotel."

"Perfect. I'll see you soon."

* * *

It was after six before Hunter finished work and returned to his apartment. He was tired but excited about the meeting later that evening. He paced, unable to shake the feeling that something wasn't quite right. Something in Alina's voice had bothered him. He read Vinny's summary again. The report outlined a fascinating sequence of events with a motley cast of characters who were involved in the collapse of the old Soviet Union and then the reconstitution of the region into new countries.

Toward the end of the report, he noticed a reference to a Russian company called Volga Oil. Apparently, Volga had hired Parrish's company for several large projects over the previous five years. Hunter vaguely recalled the company name but couldn't remember how or why. He jumped online to the *Times* archives and typed in "Volga Oil." Nothing he found varied from information in the report. As he browsed through various documents, it suddenly dawned on him where he'd seen the company name.

He quickly searched for the Kiev newspaper report on the death of the banker from Brooklyn. *Bingo!* Hunter clapped his hands together. The report revealed that before he was killed, the banker had dined with the president of Volga Oil and two executives from the largest bank in Moscow. Investigators had found no connection with the dinner and the murder.

Hunter set the report aside and called Vinny.

"Hey, Vinny, thanks for the report. I'm curious—who owns Volga Oil?"

"A billionaire named Stravinsky. He tried to hide his ownership by using some shell companies, but I figured it out."

Hunter's stomach turned upside-down. "Are you sure?"

"Yeah, why?" Vinny asked. "You sound worried. What's going on?"

"Thanks for the information. I have to go." Hunter began to pace around the room, and then Vinny called again.

"Hunter, I have more information. Not sure if it's important, but I thought you should know."

"Okay."

"It's about Alina. She was born in Northern Ossetia."

"She told me that a long time ago."

"But that's not where she grew up," Vinny said. "I had to look up Northern Ossetia on a map. It's west of Ukraine and wedged in between Georgia on the south and Russia to the north. South Ossetia was originally part of Georgia until they attempted to become an independent but unrecognized country in 1990. In the years leading up to the collapse of the Soviet Union, the ethnic tensions between Russia, North and South Ossetia, and the Georgians developed into numerous armed clashes that left hundreds dead and created thousands of refugees. Race, nationalism and religion fostered hatred between the ethnic groups. Here's the interesting part—very few Jews lived in that region during those turbulent years, so Alina's parents moved to Odessa, Ukraine, when she was a child to avoid persecution."

"What do you mean, 'avoid persecution'?"

"Her name isn't Alina Alans. Her real name is Alina Robinovich."

Hunter gasped. "You're kidding."

"Isn't that interesting?"

"She never mentioned that she was Jewish," Hunter said. "What about her fake last name? Why Alans?"

"She's very clever, pretending her last name was Alans. The Ossetians descended from the Alans, a Sarmatian tribe that controlled the region around 200 AD. She was pimping you. She knew that you'd never understand she was making a joke out of her last name."

"That doesn't make any sense."

"For some reason, she's hiding the fact that she's Jewish," he said. "Maybe she's protecting something or someone in her past."

"What about her parents and siblings?"

"No brothers or sisters, she's an only child. Her parents were farmers outside of Odessa. At one point, they owned a fair amount of land. The CIA has people on the ground in Odessa, and according to their neighbors, they vanished about the same time Alina left the Odessa National University and went to Moscow. Some of them speculated that they moved to Israel, but I checked with Israeli immigrations, and there's no record of them entering the country. Apparently, the mafia took advantage of desperate Jewish families after the fall of the Soviet Union and went around buying key family properties, paintings and jewelry with the promise to send the money to them once they reached Israel."

"Why would they do that?"

"For many Jewish families, their land was the only asset they owned of any value. During the economic collapse that occurred after the fall of the Soviet Union, many people lost their jobs. The mafia saw an opportunity to exploit that situation by promising cash and passage to Israel."

"What happened to Alina's family?"

"We couldn't find anything definitive. Like many of the Jewish families, some made it to Israel but never received any money. Others simply disappeared."

"I'm curious—how did the CIA track her family down in Odessa?" Hunter asked.

"They got her home address from her records at Odessa National University."

"Well, at least she told me one thing that's true," Hunter said. "Anything else?"

"She left the university after her first year. Apparently, she won a local beauty contest in Odessa, and a month later moved to Moscow."

"Wait a minute—I'm confused. She told me she moved to Kiev."

"The mafia uses a number of techniques to lure girls into forced prostitution. Often, they advertise job openings for hostesses, escorts and waitresses. They promise free airfare, housing, clothes and jobs. But once the girls arrive, the mafia strips them of everything they own and forces them into prostitution. There's a huge market for beautiful young women. They're bought and sold like slaves all over Russia, Ukraine, Asia and Eastern Europe. In Alina's case, the mafia sponsored beauty contests throughout the country to identify beautiful women and entice the winners with promising modeling jobs in major cities like Kiev and Moscow."

"That's incredible. I saw a tiara from a beauty contest on her dresser the first night we met."

Vinny continued, "I'm sure that when she got to Moscow, they forced her into prostitution."

"But how did she end up in Kiev?"

"The CIA found out that she was sold to Karasov. I don't know the price, but the current rate for someone that beautiful could fetch up to thirty thousand dollars. Less pretty girls and the ones addicted to alcohol or drugs are sold for three to five thousand dollars. The mafia's making billions every year off human trafficking. It's disgusting. These desperate girls are simply looking for jobs, and they end up as sex slaves."

"I noticed something odd about Alina after I spent more time with her at the club. She never seemed to sleep with any of the clients. She'd party with the most important customers, but I know that she wasn't having sex with them."

"The CIA found that she had two main roles for Karasov. She's his personal mistress, and they're not sure about this—they think she's what they call a recruiter."

"A recruiter?"

"She recruits young girls to Kiev."

Hunter's stomach churned. "She wouldn't do that. She hates what Karasov's doing to exploit women."

"That's not what the CIA says."

"They're wrong."

"The CIA's report says they assume Alina quickly figured out in Moscow that the fastest way to make money and get out of sleeping with clients was to become a recruiter. They make the most money of any women in organized crime. Alina sounds perfect for the job. She's beautiful, charming and she speaks multiple languages. These are the perfect attributes to lure unsuspecting girls to Kiev. A woman who's good at recruiting is a very valuable asset to men like Karasov. They can make mafia families at least ten times the return on the price of each girl in the first year alone."

Stunned, Hunter was resisting what Vinny was telling him. "That's not what she does. I'd know. I was with her all the time."

"All the time?"

"She traveled with Karasov, but otherwise, she was in the club most of the time."

"How often does she travel? How do you know Karasov's with her?"

"Vinny, shut up," Hunter said. "As usual, you're full of shit."

Hunter set the cell phone down and jumped when the cell phone rang again. He stared at the number flashing in the display. It was Karasov.

What if I don't answer it? he thought. What if I just walked away?

He let it ring three times before answering.

"Are you ready?" Karasov asked.

"I think so."

"Have you reviewed Parrish's term sheet?"

"Yes, I made some changes, but they're minor," Hunter said. "Do you realize the terms in this document are drafted quite broadly? A good attorney could find a dozen ways to back out of this agreement."

"No worry about that."

"You should be. This is a billion-dollar contract over five years."

"I know what I'm doing."

"You have more faith in people than I do."

"Where I come from, handshake more important than signed agreements," Karasov said. "A man's word is bond. And there are consequences if he not live up to agreement. Bad consequences. Tonight we meet Parrish for dinner at the Peninsula Hotel and finish business. You know place?"

"My dad used to work there when I was a kid."

"Good."

"Great. But I need to tell you something."

"Tell me later."

"No, wait…"

Karasov hung up before he could speak. His stomach ached. He chewed on several antacid tablets, but the pain persisted. The car would be here in less than an hour. After pacing around, he walked into the kitchen to make a drink and almost cut himself slicing a lime. He set the knife down and took his drink into the bathroom to get ready. After shaving, he got dressed and went outside to wait for the car. The heat and humidity was oppressive, so he took off his sport coat, wiped his brow and looked up into the sky—no stars, a storm was coming. Finally, he spotted the limousine and walked to the curb. The backdoor swung open, and he was surprised to find Alina in the backseat.

"Hi, Hunter," Alina said.

"I didn't expect to see you. I thought you'd be with Karasov." He stretched out in the seat next to her and wiped the sweat off his forehead. "Ahh, the air conditioning feels good."

Alina slowly crossed her long legs.

"You look beautiful tonight," Hunter said.

Distracted, she didn't answer at first.

"Did you hear me?"

"Oh, yes, thank you." She lit a cigarette and watched people walking along the crowded sidewalk. "I always wondered what it would be like to live in New York. It's so different than Kiev."

"I need to talk to you about something," Hunter said.

"Not now." She continued to stare out the window. "I have too much on my mind about this meeting."

"But, it's important."

"It'll have to wait. We can talk after the meeting with Parrish."

"Will Karasov meet us at the hotel?"

"Yes, he had some things to do first."

"Do you know our agenda?"

"It's our custom to have dinner before we talk business. Parrish has arranged to have dinner in his suite so we can talk in private."

"Did you translate the term sheet for Karasov?"

"Yes, he has a copy."

"Do you think he understands it?"

"Don't understate him. He's very smart."

"I didn't mean it that way. It's just that these documents are drafted very loosely."

"Don't worry. There are more important things."

"You sound like Karasov."

They walked into the lobby of the Peninsula. Karasov was already in the bar having a drink. He nodded to Hunter and kissed Alina when they walked up. "Ready?" he said.

Hunter put his hand on Karasov. "Can I talk to you for a second?"

"Not now."

"But there's something…"

Karasov wheeled around and waved to his two bodyguards before Hunter could say another word. They walked quickly through the lobby and took the elevator to the penthouse suite.

Hank Parrish opened the door with a big grin. He was a tall man, about six-five, with broad shoulders, huge hands, a large head and a long jaw. A small chunk of chewing tobacco bulged inside his lower lip. Dressed in a light blue cowboy shirt with white pearl buttons, blue jeans and pointed cowboy boots, he greeted everyone with a bear hug and ushered them outside to the patio for a drink. A million white lights flickered and sparkled across the New York skyline.

"Quite a view, isn't it?" Parrish said.

Alina pointed to the long lines of pulsating white, red and orange lights from thousands of cars that snaked along the avenues below them. She leaned against the railing. Without taking her eyes away from the view, she said to Hunter, "It's beautiful. Just the way you described it to me in Kiev."

"Once you've seen the skyline from the top of a high-rise at night, you'll never forget New York."

Parrish wiped the sweat off his face. "It's too damn hot and humid to sit out here. Let's go inside and have dinner." He led Alina through the large glass patio doors to a dining table set for four.

The table was covered with a white linen tablecloth, white china, three sets of wine glasses, four place-settings of silver and a beautiful centerpiece of fresh summer flowers.

"Alina, you sit here across from me so I can look at your darlin' face all night." Parrish said. He pointed to a chair immediately to his right. "Ambassador, set yourself down next to me."

Once everyone was seated, Parrish opened a bottle of Bordeaux. "This is my favorite wine, Chateau Petrus '82. I'm fond of that year for two reasons. First, it was the year I hit my first gusher, and second, 1982 was the French vintage of the century. This wine scored a perfect 100 by the wine experts. I only drink it on special occasions."

"I hope this evening warrants the occasion," Alina said.

"Of course," Hank smiled. "We're here to celebrate our new business relationship." He looked at Alina, reached across the table and patted her hand. "Right darlin'?"

Alina nodded and smiled. Parrish didn't notice Karasov frown or see his jaw tighten when he touched Alina. Hunter glanced at Karasov's bodyguards, who stood quietly off to the side. They appeared tense and watched Karasov very closely.

"Alina, how did you and Vladimir meet?" Parrish asked.

"I'll answer that." All eyes shifted to Karasov. "I buy her," he said, without any expression.

At first, Parrish's mouth dropped open. "Yeah, sure you did! And then his eyes moved back and forth between Alina and Karasov. No one spoke. After a few seconds, Parrish burst out laughing and poked Karasov on the shoulder. "Very funny."

Parrish looked at Hunter. "Does he do this to everyone?"

"I wouldn't know."

Parrish slapped his thigh. "Okay, you really had me going there for a second. Game on!"

The doorbell rang. Both bodyguards moved toward the door.

Parrish stood up. "I hope you don't mind, but I took the liberty of ordering our food in advance." He motioned to Karasov's bodyguards. "Go ahead, let them in."

Two waiters in white coats pushed large carts into the room and placed a dozen dishes of food on the table. "I thought you might enjoy some good old Texas cookin', so I had them cook a barbecue for us. We eat family-style back home, so help yourself to the ribs, steak and chicken. I'm partial to the ribs. I think they're the best in the country."

After eating for several minutes, Parrish pointed a rib at Hunter. "Tell me, how do you know these folks?"

"We met a long time ago."

"Really? Where was that?"

Alina interrupted Hunter before he could answer. "Ambassador Karasov met Hunter years ago when Hunter was doing a story on the cold war for the *New York Times*."

Hank's eyes widened. "The *Times*? I didn't know you were a reporter."

Alina patted his hand. "Relax, he's not here for the *Times*."

"Then what are you here for?"

Karasov grunted while shoving a piece of steak in his mouth from the point of his knife, "He here for me."

Parrish looked puzzled. "I don't understand."

Karasov didn't look up but attempted to saw off another piece of steak. Then he growled and hit his knife on the table. Everybody at the table jumped. Parrish stared at Karasov as he barked at his bodyguard in Ukrainian.

Parrish looked at Alina and then Karasov. "What's wrong?"

Alina explained, "He hates dull knives."

"Vladimir, for Christ's sake, all you have to do is ask, and I would've given you another knife."

Karasov just grunted. One of the bodyguards quickly walked over, pulled out a knife out of his pocket, opened the blade, and handed it to Karasov. Everyone stared at the five-inch blade with a white pearl handle.

Parrish whistled. "That's quite a knife."

Karasov ignored him while he resumed cutting his meat.

"Hunter, what are you working on these days?" Parrish asked.

"The OPEC meeting next week."

"Ah, the OPEC meeting." Parrish leaned back in his chair and sipped on his wine. "Let the fun begin. Everyone puts on their best suit and walks around telling each other big fat lies. I don't know why they go through this charade every year. It's nothing but an excuse for a photo op and some fancy dinners in New York."

"I take it you don't like these meetings?"

"It's bullshit because all the deals have been cut long before they get here."

"Not all," Karasov said.

"Thank god." Parrish smiled at Alina. "Right darlin'?"

Alina squirmed in her chair.

Hunter watched Karasov balancing his knife between two fingers. The smooth, silver blade flashed a bright light like a reflecting mirror as it wavered ever so slightly. Hunter was too nervous to eat, so he just listened and pushed his steak around on the plate.

Parrish picked up a long beef rib with both hands and gnawed on the bone. Smacking his lips and licking all five fingers, he leaned across the table toward Hunter. "You aren't eating. Don't you like it?" His mouth was covered in barbecue sauce, which he occasionally wiped away with the back of his hand.

Hunter felt the hair on his neck crawl. I hate Texans, he thought. This guy's an asshole. He's got a big mouth and eats like a pig. Why would Karasov want to do business with this egomaniac?

"The sauce is hard on my stomach," Hunter said.

"That's too bad. You're missing one of life's finest meals."

"I'll take your word for it."

Parrish picked up a large platter and added another steak to Karasov's plate. "Have another. This is my blue ribbon, grain-fed Texan beef right off my ranch. You'll never taste better beef anywhere in the world. I had the meat flown in on my private jet just for tonight."

Hunter couldn't resist throwing his own jab at the senator. "Apparently they had a blind taste test in New York with several of the top chefs in the country. Hands down, they all picked the beef from the Midwest."

Karasov smiled but didn't say anything, while Alina kicked Hunter hard under the table.

Before Parrish could respond, Alina interjected, "Well, I don't know anything, but this is the best steak that I've ever eaten."

"Thank you, darlin'," Parrish said before he resumed gnawing on a bone. After a moment, he paused and pointed the half-eaten bone at Karasov. "Let's get down to business. I reviewed the terms of our deal with my partners, and we need to make a few changes."

Everyone stopped eating and looked a Parrish—everyone, except Karasov, who continued to saw his steak into small pieces without looking up. Karasov stabbed at a piece of steak with his knife in his right hand.

"That would not be good idea," Karasov said, placing the piece of steak in his mouth. "Our deal is good. Good for you, good for me."

Parrish smiled at Alina. "But things change. You know that."

"Like what?"

"Circumstances. People change, business changes, nothing stays the same for very long."

"Some things change, but not me," Karasov said.

Parrish reached for a document on the end of the table and passed it over to Karasov. "I've made the adjustments we need or we have to decline."

Karasov stopped eating. His eyes narrowed into slits so small that Hunter couldn't see his eyeballs. "What you mean decline?" he said, ignoring the document.

The two bodyguards silently moved closer to the table behind Parrish. Alina squeezed her cloth napkin so tightly her knuckles went white.

Parrish picked up his rib again. "We've been offered another contract. You know how it goes. These projects are so large we can only select one to do at a time."

Karasov didn't move. "We have deal."

Parrish dangled the rib between his two fingers. "We had a discussion, and we outlined some terms," he said. "But we didn't execute a deal yet."

"You gave me word."

"But that was before Stravin…"

Hunter had never seen anyone move so fast. Like a bolt of lightning, in one perfect move, Karasov grabbed the back of Parrish's hair with his left hand. Then with his right, he jammed the rib bone still clutched in Parrish's hand into his mouth. Parrish's eyes bugged out, and his face turned red as he choked on the bone.

The bodyguards immediately grabbed both of Parrish's arms and pinned them behind his chair as he gagged on the rib. As he struggled to breathe, Karasov shoved the bone down another inch, and the blood gushed out of Parrish's mouth. Karasov's eyes were wild with rage, and the corners of the senator's mouth were covered in white foam and blood.

Karasov leaned close to Parrish, who was starting to turn blue, and whispered hoarsely in his ear with a devilish grin on his face. "Have some more of your prize-winning ribs." He jammed the bone further down Parrish's throat as he thrashed violently in his chair. Glancing at Alina out of the corner of his eyes, Karasov yanked Parrish's head back, exposing the curved Adam's apple area of his thick neck. Then he picked up his pearl-handled knife and in one swift motion, slit Parrish's throat. The bright red blood sprayed across the table.

Stunned, Hunter looked at the blood dripping off Alina's hair and down her pale face, and then he glanced down at his own white shirt splattered in red. For a moment, Hunter couldn't move. He flinched when something warm and sticky dripped onto his lips. He quickly grabbed a napkin and wiped his face. In shock, Hunter looked across the table at Parrish slumped headfirst on a long rack of ribs, his plate overflowing with a pool of blood mixed with brown barbecue sauce.

Karasov didn't say a word. He sat down and calmly wiped the blood off the knife with his white linen napkin, carefully examining the blade after each swipe until the silver blade was shiny again. Satisfied, he began cutting a piece of his steak with the same knife. He casually chewed his meat for a second and stared into the distance as if no one else was in the room. He casually picked up the bottle of Petrus and refilled his glass. "Anyone care for more wine?" He took a large swallow, swirled it around in his mouth, and nodded toward Parrish slumped in his plate. "He right about one thing... this wine very good." He set the bottle down and continued to eat as if nothing happened.

Alina grabbed Hunter's arm. "Do something!"

Hunter threw his bloody napkin on the table and motioned to the bodyguards. "We have to leave now."

The guards looked at each other, hesitant to move as Karasov brushed back the stringy grey hair that had fallen over his vacant, unblinking eyes. "I not finished," Karasov mumbled while cutting another piece of steak.

Hunter rushed around the table to Karasov's chair. "Yes, you are." But when he touched him on the shoulder, Karasov pointed the pearl-handled knife at Hunter. His eyes were wild again, and for a second, Hunter thought he was dead. "Don't ever touch me again," he said.

Hunter backed away and nodded to Alina to join him on the other side of the room, where he whispered, "You talk to him. We must leave immediately. We need to call your embassy and tell them that the ambassador's sick and needs an emergency evacuation back to Kiev. Order his private jet fueled and ready for take-off in two hours. And one other thing, tell the pilots not to file a flight plan with the tower until the very last minute. We don't want anyone to know anything until we have to."

Alina translated his directions to the bodyguards.

"Alina, you go with him," Hunter said. "Tell the driver not to stop for anything but go directly to JFK. We need to get him on that plane as fast as possible and out of the country. Tell the bodyguards to call your limo driver and have him pull around to the delivery area and wait for us."

"What if someone sees us?" Alina asked.

Hunter smiled. "Don't worry. I know how to get out of here because I used to play here as a kid. I know every inch of this hotel. I know of an old service elevator that's never used except when the hotel is doing some construction. Follow me. We have to go through a small storage room to get to the service elevator door."

The bodyguards approached Karasov and gently spoke to him in Ukrainian. With one on each side of his chair, they looked at Alina and waited until she nodded, then they attempted to lift him up. He shrugged them off at first, but then he relaxed and stood up.

Hunter pointed at Alina. "Get your things and go with Karasov."

"Aren't you coming with us?"

"I can buy you some time. I'll call the police after I know that you're safe at the airport."

"I'm not leaving without you," Alina said. "The bodyguards can take him."

"Don't be stupid," Hunter said. "If you stay, they'll implicate you as a spy and an accessory to murder."

"What about you? What will they do to you?"

"I'll tell the police that I was invited to attend the dinner because we're doing a series on the ambassador at the *Times*. I'll explain that

Parrish became drunk and obnoxious during dinner and became more irrational as the night went on. Then I'll tell them how he went nuts and tried to kill Karasov. I'll assure them it was all self-defense."

"That won't work."

"Why not?"

"You're so naïve. How will you explain why we left and didn't wait for the police? As soon as they realize we left the country, they'll arrest you as an accessory to the murder. Come with us. We'll all go back to Kiev together."

Hunter shook his head. "No, I'd be a fugitive for life, and Interpol will hunt me down."

"I have an idea. The boys can take Karasov to the airport, while we go back to your apartment, get the key to the storage unit, and retrieve everything in my trunks. Once we get out of the country, I can use the documents incriminating US government officials back in Kiev as leverage to negotiate with the CIA to drop the charges. They can use lack of evidence or the self-defense story as a cover for not pursuing charges against any of us." She gripped his arm. "I'm not leaving without you."

"Are you sure this will work?" Hunter said.

Alina nodded. "Trust me."

"Okay, let's go," Hunter said. They hurried down the hall to the storage room. He sighed with relief when the door leading into the service elevator was unlocked. Hunter pushed the button to the basement. The delivery area was deserted, and their limousine was waiting. Once they turned onto the street, Hunter told the driver, "Drop us off at my apartment and then drive to JFK."

They stopped talking and stared at Karasov, fumbling with a crystal highball glass inside the limo. He tried to pour a drink but spilled vodka all over his pants and the leather seat. Alina quickly reached over and took the bottle out of his hands. She spoke quietly to him in Ukrainian and gently patted his hands. She said, "Ne khvylyuytesya, ya polahodzhu vash napiy tak, yak vam podobayet'sya. Don't worry, I'll fix your drink just the way you like it."

Twenty minutes later, the limousine pulled up to Hunter's apartment, and they rushed upstairs before anyone saw their blood-splattered clothing. Inside his unit, he walked into the bedroom and returned with one of his exercise outfits and a long overcoat. "Here, go into my bedroom and put these on."

Hunter stepped into the bathroom, removed his clothes, washed the blood off his face and hands, and stuffed the bloody clothes in a black plastic trash bag. When he returned, Alina was leaning over the sink, trying to rinse the blood out of her hair. She turned off the water and began to cry. Hunter reached for a towel and lifted her face. Her red hair was plastered against her head. He brushed aside the bangs hanging in her eyes and wiped away tears. "Don't worry. Everything will be all right."

"Thank you for taking charge back at the hotel. I panicked. You were the only one thinking straight," she said. "I don't know what we would've done without you."

"We need to leave in five minutes. I'll grab my computer and get the key to the storage unit. You finish dressing." He kissed her and held her face in his hands. "Are you okay?"

She nodded. "I must look like a mess."

"You look fine," Hunter said. "This will all be over soon. Get dressed. I'll be right back."

"Where are you going?" Her voice trembled.

He pointed to the large black trash bag. "Why don't you call the embassy and explain what's happened. I'll be back in a minute."

Hunter ran downstairs and threw the bag of bloody clothes into the neighbor's trash bin. When he returned, Alina was smoking in the kitchen. "We have to go," she said. "They could be here any minute."

"Who's *they*? Who are you talking about?"

"The Russians. I'm sure that Stravinsky's men observed us entering the hotel. They had to know about this meeting. When they don't see us leave, it'll only be a short time before they get suspicious and call the room. If Parrish doesn't answer, they'll send someone upstairs and find out what happened." She started to cry again. "Once Stravinsky learns that Parrish is dead, he's going to move on Karasov."

Hunter grabbed her shoulders and shook her. "Pull yourself together."

Wiping her runny nose, she said, "You don't understand. It will be a deadly free-for-all. Stravinsky will be looking for us, and I'm sure they know where you live." Then she looked at the clock in the kitchen. "We have to hurry."

"What happens when we get to Kiev?" Hunter asked.

She reached up and kissed him. "I have a plan."

"What kind of plan?"

"A permanent one," she said in a strange voice. "No more questions. We must hurry because we have to get the money and the trunks before we go to the airport." Alina's cell phone vibrated. She listened to the message. Her hand was shaking as she turned off the phone. "Stravinsky knows. We have to go."

Hunter grabbed his computer and stuffed it into his briefcase. They were almost ready to leave when they heard a muffled noise outside his apartment door. They froze and looked at each other. Hunter trembled.

The door exploded open. He expected Stravinsky, but instead, several men from a SWAT team rushed in, waving automatic weapons while screaming for them to get on the floor.

Hunter stood still, raised his arms in the air, and yelled, "Stop! What the hell are you doing?"

Several men in black goggles, helmets, bullet-proof vests and boots quickly surrounded them. They shouted and gestured with automatic weapons. "Get down. Get down on the floor and put your hands behind your head. Do it now!"

The closest SWAT member approached Hunter with a gun pointed at Hunter's chest.

"What the hell are you doing?" Hunter cried out. "I'm a reporter for the *New York Times*. You can't do this. Let me see your search warrant."

No one answered him.

Hunter looked down at Alina, who was already kneeling on the floor with her hands in the air. "Are you okay?"

Alina didn't move, but her wide eyes darted wildly around from one SWAT member to the next.

"I want to call my..." Hunter couldn't finish. His back exploded in pain as if he'd been hit between his shoulder blades with a baseball bat. Stunned, he sank to his knees and tried to catch his breath.

From behind, a stern voice yelled in his ear, "Don't move."

"Wait, there must be some mistake!" Hunter pleaded.

More men in black streamed into the room and rushed past Hunter and Alina. A minute later, they reappeared from his bedroom. One of the men spoke into a walkie-talkie, "All clear."

"Who are you?" Hunter screamed at the men swirling around the room. "I demand to see your badges. I know my rights."

The man standing over Hunter pushed him down and pinned his head to the floor with his forearm. "Don't move and shut up!"

Hunter was facing Alina. He tried to reassure her, "We'll be okay. I'll call Cabot."

The man bashed his head against the floor with his fist. "Shut the fuck up. No talking." Two members of the SWAT team patted each of them down for weapons. When they were done, they gave their squad leader the thumbs up. A few seconds later, a tall man in a dark suit walked through the door. "Did you confirm their identities?"

A SWAT member held Alina's purse in his hand. "It's her."

"Okay, get them out of here." He pointed at Hunter and Alina. "You and your team take the guy. I'll take the woman with my squad." He turned toward the doorway. "Bag 'em, and let's roll."

Everything went black as they placed a black cloth bag over Hunter's head. At first, he panicked because he couldn't see or breathe. The bag was hot and smelled like sour sweat, but after a few seconds, he realized he wasn't going to suffocate. Hunter heard his neighbor's voices in the hall as the SWAT team rushed them down the stairs. He yelled through the bag, "Emma, William, help me! Somebody call the police. These men are kidnapping us. Don't let them take us!"

The SWAT leader shouted, "Goddamn it, who forgot the tape? Get the fucking duct tape over his mouth now!"

Hunter tripped when the men tried to pull the black bag off his head. He continued to kick and scream for help until one man placed his leather glove hand tightly over his mouth. "Shut the fuck up." After they taped his mouth shut and recovered his head, two men reached under his arms and roughly picked him up. They led him down the rest of the stairs and threw him on the cold metal floor of a van.

Hunter tried to remain calm and focused on where they were taking him. Although the noise from the van and the bag muffled the sounds, he listened carefully for clues. The sound of the tires changed to a high pitch hum, so he assumed they were crossing one of the bridges, but he wasn't sure which one. Several minutes later, they crossed another one, and after numerous turns, he finally gave up. He had no idea where they were taking him.

Hunter lost track of time, but he estimated that they had been driving for at least thirty minutes when they finally stopped. A man pulled him out of the van and escorted him through a series of doors. He heard elevator doors open and close, and then they descended for a long time before stopping. After a short walk, they entered a room and set him down on a cold metal chair.

Hunter yelled out, "Take the bag off my head and unlock my handcuffs! My arms are killing me."

No one answered him, but he heard footsteps leave the room and a door close. Hunter tried to think straight.

Where am I? he thought. Who were these guys? Obviously, not NYPD. They could be CIA. He tried to shake off a surge of fear. What if they are Russians?

A man's voice startled him from behind. "You've been a bad boy."

Hunter turned his head in the direction of the deep baritone. "I haven't done anything. There has been a huge mistake."

"I don't think so," the voice said.

"Take this fucking bag off my head, I'm suffocating."

"First, you need to answer my questions."

Hunter started to hyperventilate and thrash around in his chair.

"You're just making things worse," the voice said.

Hunter violently shook his head to get the bag off. "You fuckers!" he screamed. His breath came in large gulps.

"Relax. Concentrate, and your breathing will come back."

After a minute, Hunter gave up trying to shake off the bag and slumped forward in his chair.

"Comfortable?" the voice asked.

Hunter violently shook his head. "Fuck you."

"Now, let's start with your arrival in Kiev."

Hunter shook his head again. "I'm not telling you a fucking thing. You can't bust into my apartment, throw us on the floor, refuse to identify yourself, and then expect me to cooperate. This is America, not Somalia. I can't count how many laws you've already broken."

"Are you through?"

"I'm just getting started. I'm a reporter for the *New York Times*. I'm not telling you a thing until you take this bag off and let me talk to a lawyer."

"I was afraid you'd say that."

"What did you expect me to say?"

"It's unfortunate."

"What's unfortunate?" Hunter said.

"I thought you were smarter than this." The voice moved from behind him to in front of him. "But I guess I was wrong."

Hunter gritted his teeth and braced himself for the first blow, but nothing happened. To his surprise, the man's heels clicked on the hard floor as his footsteps moved away from Hunter. The door opened and then closed with a heavy metal clunk.

At least I know they aren't Russian or Ukraine, he thought, because they would've beaten me bloody by now.

Hunter stiffened when he heard the door lock turning. Everything was so black inside the hood that he couldn't discern whether he was dreaming or awake. The door opened, and two muffled voices entered the room. He struggled to stay calm as the voices approached and wondered how long he'd been here.

"If you're ready to talk," the voice said, "we can remove the bag and the handcuffs."

"Fuck you."

"We want to help you."

"I don't need any help."

"You're in big trouble."

Hunter laughed. "You expect me to believe that? You want me to help you, yet you won't tell me who you are or where I am. I'm not telling you a fucking thing. You didn't even read me my rights. You can't do stuff like this. You're breaking the law. You think you can frighten me? You guys are amateurs. I've been shot by worse people than you idiots. You don't scare me for a second."

Hunter was breathing heavily after this rant. For several seconds, no one responded. The only sound came from the sucking noise of his bag expanding and contracting against his face. "Are you finished?"

Hunter didn't move.

"That was quite the speech. Why are you so worked up? It sounds to me like you're trying to hide something."

"You insult me, and then you expect me to help you. Fuck off—I'm not telling you a thing."

The footsteps moved away again. "You're making a mistake."

"No, I'm not. You're the one making the mistake."

"I guess only time will tell," the voice said.

"You're damn right!"

"But here's your problem—you don't have much time."

"What do you mean by that?" Hunter asked.

The door closed, and Hunter slumped in his seat. His arms were killing him from the metal handcuffs. "Guard, guard!" Hunter yelled. "I have to go to the bathroom."

No one responded.

"I have to take a piss."

Still no response. Hunter squirmed around in his chair. "Come on."

Silence.

Furious, Hunter screamed again, "You cocksuckers! Do you want me to piss in my pants? Is that what you want! Is that part of the game?"

The same voice spoke to him from an overhead speaker in the corner of the room.

"Like I said, we want to help you, but we need you to cooperate. Things may get much worse than peeing in your pants."

Hunter weighed his options. He was pretty sure these guys were from some part of our government, probably CIA. Hunter yelled out, "Okay, I'll talk."

The door opened, and two sets of footsteps approached him. The bag was lifted off his head. He squinted and blinked his eyes as they adjusted to the bright white lights. Two men, wearing almost identical black suits, sat across from him. They each carried a large folder and set them on the grey metal table. The taller man looked like a picture of Abe Lincoln with a long, narrow, ruddy face. He nodded to his partner. "Can you get us some coffee?" He looked at Hunter. "Do you want any?"

"Very funny," Hunter said.

The man looked at his partner. "How about you? Would you like some nice hot coffee?"

"I'd love some coffee," said the shorter man. "We could be here a long time."

"You made your point, now let me go to the bathroom."

"Not quite yet."

Hunter peered closer at the man. "You're not the voice. You're not the guy I talked to earlier."

The man folded his hands and placed them on the table. "No, I'm not."

"I want the other guy."

The man frowned. "We're not getting off to a very good start, are we?"

There was something in the man's voice that scared Hunter.

"Let's start over. I'm Bob." He nodded toward his partner. "And this is Jim."

Jim nodded at Hunter. His neck was so thick that he couldn't button the top of his white dress shirt. His black tie was shoved to one side.

"Riiight, Bob and Jim." Hunter scoffed. "And I'm Captain Kangaroo."

Bob's expression didn't change. "Did you still want some coffee?"

Hunter licked his dry lips. He'd never been so thirsty in his life, but his bladder wanted to explode.

"Yes," Hunter said, "I'd like some coffee, but I need to take a piss."

Bob looked at Jim. "Did he say please?"

"I don't think so." Jim leaned toward Hunter and cocked his hand behind his ear. "Did you say please?"

Hunter lurched forward, pulling hard on his handcuffs for a second. Finally, he sat back in his chair and then slowly nodded. "Please."

Jim slapped his thigh. "See? There you go. We were wrong. Of course, Hunter said please. I don't know how we missed it the first time." He stood up and told Bob, "I'll take him to the bathroom."

Bob tossed the key to the handcuffs onto the table. Jim unlocked the cuffs and grabbed Hunter's arm. "Come on, tough guy. Let's go before we have to put a diaper on you." Then he led Hunter out of the interrogation room. They walked down a long, empty hall with white walls and a white tile floor devoid of any sound or people. They passed several unmarked doors until they reached a door marked as a unisex bathroom. Before they entered, Hunter asked, "Where are we?"

Jim didn't respond. He just opened the door and said, "You have five minutes."

When they returned to the interrogation room and found Bob was busy reading through a large file.

"May I ask you a question?" Hunter said after he sat down.

"Sure."

"Why did you arrest me?"

Bob didn't respond.

"Answer me!" Hunter demanded.

Bob calmly closed one folder and picked up another one. "I said you could ask questions, but I didn't say that I'd answer any of them."

"You're a fucking riot," Hunter said.

Bob didn't look up, just continued to read his file.

"There must be some big mistake," Hunter insisted.

Bob raised his hand. "Later. You'll get your chance."

"Who are you?"

He ignored Hunter and continued reading until his partner returned with a pot of coffee and three Styrofoam cups. Jim handed Hunter a cup of coffee. Finally, Bob told Hunter, "You're in a world of shit."

"I don't know what you're talking about." Hunter looked at the mirror window. "I want to call my lawyer."

"Why?" Bob flipped through some photos. "Are you hiding something?"

"No."

"Well, then, why do you need a lawyer?"

"I... I don't know what's going on."

"Relax. Just answer my questions."

Hunter nodded. "Okay."

"Who's the woman you were with?"

"Mary."

"Wrong answer." Bob shook his head. "Let's try again. What were you doing with her?"

"Nothing. We were on our way to dinner when your goon squad broke into my apartment."

Jim frowned and cracked his knuckles. "Do you always go to dinner with your computer, ten thousand dollars in cash and a packed carry-on bag? It appeared that you were taking a trip."

Hunter sized Jim up. "I'm not talking to you. What's your role here anyway? To get coffee and take people to the bathroom?"

Jim's face turned red, and the muscles in his neck tightened. "You little..."

Bob interrupted him, "How do you know Alina?"

"I thought you didn't know her name."

"Just answer the question."

"We're friends through work. She translates for clients at the United Nations."

"Just friends?"

"I barely know her."

Bob sighed and looked at a different file and then leaned forward. "If you tell us everything, we can probably drop most of the charges."

"Most of the charges?" Hunter's eyes widened. "What am I charged with?"

"Espionage. Treason." He sat back in his chair. "We have quite a few things to choose from."

"You think I'm a spy?"

Jim smiled. "That's right, smart guy."

Bob opened another folder containing a stack of photos and spread them across the table. "Look, we have enough evidence to convict you." He pointed at a photo. "This is you having breakfast at Pastis with Alina, a known Russian spy."

"You mean Ukrainian," Hunter said.

"I thought you said you didn't know her?"

Hunter squirmed in his seat but didn't respond.

Bob pointed at another photo. "There you are—getting out of a limousine with Karasov, one of the most powerful mafia leaders in the world." He held up the next one. "Here is a picture of you accepting a large manila envelope containing top-secret documents from him through the rear window of his limo." He set the photo down. "Need I go through the rest?"

"You have it all wrong. I was simply having breakfast with her because my boss, Cabot, wanted me to arrange an interview with her boss, Karasov. I'm a reporter. That's it," Hunter spoke rapidly. "The photo with Karasov—well, we made an agreement that he'd give us exclusive access to him in exchange for some introductions and assistance while he's in New York. The envelope contained a business contract he wanted reviewed by a lawyer I know. I don't have any top-secret documents. You guys are nuts!"

Bob held up his folder of photos. "These pictures, along with the other evidence we have will send you away for life."

"What other evidence? You have no other evidence on me. These photos don't mean anything in court. You can't prove what's inside the envelopes. You guys are full of shit."

"I can only help you if you cooperate with us." Bob paused and then poured another cup of coffee.

"What kind of cooperation?"

"It's not you that we want." He pulled out a picture of Alina and slid it across the table. "She's the one we want."

"But I told you," Hunter said. "I don't really know her. She worked as Karasov's assistant."

"An assistant?" Jim laughed. "I've heard her described as many things, but never an assistant." He tapped his finger on the photo of her. "She's a missing piece in a large jigsaw puzzle. We need you to confirm how she fits in."

"I wish I could help you."

"Don't lie to us," Bob shouted. "We know you met her in Kiev. We know about her connection with Karasov. But there are big blank spots over the last two years where she seemed to have disappeared." He paused. "Where did she go during that time?"

"I have no idea. The last time I saw her was two years ago in Kiev. I was on assignment for the *Times*."

"What was the assignment?"

"Tourism."

"Liar," Bob said. "We want you to tell us everything about her—where you met, times, dates, the people you've seen her with…"

"I don't have to tell you anything."

There was a knock at the door. A man poked his head inside and motioned for Bob and Jim to step out. A few minutes later, they returned and sat down. Their faces wore a faint grimace as they glanced at each other for a second. Then Bob said, "How well do you know Karasov?"

"I don't." Hunter clasped his hands tightly together. "This is all a big mistake."

Bob looked at his partner. "Bag and handcuff him again. I don't have time for this bullshit." He turned and walked out. Jim handcuffed Hunter's wrists behind his back, picked up the bag and tried to place it on Hunter's head. Hunter violently thrashed his head around to avoid the bag. "Don't! Don't put that thing on me again."

"You should know better than to fuck around with my partner," Jim said. "You're nothing but a waste of time." He smacked him hard on the back of the head and slid the bag roughly over his face. "And that is a very dangerous thing to be right now."

Jim started to walk away when Hunter yelled out, "Stop, don't leave. I can't stand this bag. I'm suffocating. I'm ready to talk."

The door closed, and the only sound came from his breathing inside the bag.

When he heard the door open again, he had no idea how long he had been sitting there. He sat up. "Who's there? Can somebody please help me?"

Bob asked, "Is this worth my time?"

"Yes," Hunter said. "Just take this fucking bag off my head."

The bag came off, and the two men took a seat at the table. Bob instructed Jim to remove the handcuffs.

Hunter massaged his wrists as Bob opened a briefcase and picked out a thick folder. "I'm going to ask you a series of questions. I want the truth because I'm only asking you these questions once."

The door opened, and a different man stepped in and walked over to Bob's chair. He leaned over and whispered something in Bob's ear, then Bob nodded and stood. "Looks like you ran out of time."

"Wait, where are you going?" Hunter said. "What do you mean I'm out of time?"

They left the room without another word.

Hunter didn't have any sense of time inside the interrogation room. Without windows or a clock, he didn't know if he had been there for hours or days. He was hungry, tired and scared. He worried about Alina and wondered what they were doing to her.

Suddenly the door swung open. Bob and Jim walked quickly to the table and sat down.

"Hank Parrish was found murdered in his hotel suite," Bob said.

"What does that have to do with me?"

"In addition, Senator Dixon was found dead in his apartment this morning. From the note, it appears a suicide."

"Dixon would never commit suicide," Hunter said. "That note must be a forgery."

"I thought you said that you didn't know him?" Bob tapped his fingers on the table. "You know, these murders change everything."

"Somebody's setting me up!"

"Why don't you do yourself a favor and tell us what we need to know?" Jim said.

"I told you," Hunter scoffed. "I'm not talking to you without a lawyer."

Bob frowned. "Where were you before we picked you up in your apartment?"

"Out for a walk."

"Try again."

"Were you with Parrish at his hotel?"

"I told you. I don't know this Parrish guy," Hunter said. "Somebody's trying to frame me."

Bob slammed his hand on the table. "This is where we stop, and you go directly to prison. Or you can start telling us the truth, and we'll do what we can to help you." He pointed his index finger at Hunter's chest. "You better think carefully about your situation."

"I told you already. I didn't have anything to do with Alina's business activities. I barely know this Hank Parrish."

"Before you answer, I want you to know that unless you help us, we have enough evidence against Alina to get the death sentence. If you cooperate, I think we can reduce the charge to a prison term."

Hunter shrugged his shoulders. "She always told me the less I knew, the better. I didn't think I was doing anything wrong."

"What about Karasov?" Jim asked. "Why did you work for him?"

"Hold on, I told you that I didn't work for him. I just helped arrange a few meetings for him in exchange for an interview."

Bob shook his head. "And for people like Hank Parrish and Senator Dixon?"

Hunter's face turned red. "Call Cabot. He's my editor at the *New York Times*. He'll vouch for me. It was his idea to go to Kiev. He'll confirm everything I told you. He knows Alina."

"We've already done that." Bob held up a thick sheaf of paper in his hand. "Do you know what this is?"

"No."

"It's documentation of your activities for the last two years. We know all about your sick double life in New York—Clark Kent reporter during the day masquerading as a Russian big-shot carousing around the Black Sea club at night."

"Ukrainian, not Russian."

"Who gives a shit?" Bob shouted and slapped his hand on the table again.

"So what," Hunter said. "Sex is not a crime."

"Look, we know you turned bad in Kiev."

"You're crazy."

"We have our sources."

"Like Cabot?" Hunter seethed.

"Cabot told us that he tried to help you when you returned, but you wouldn't listen. You resisted intervention for your alcohol and sexual addiction."

"My boss said that?"

"He also told us that he's never met Alina," Bob said. "In fact, he told us that he fired you two weeks ago."

"That's total bullshit!" Hunter clutched his stomach and doubled over.

"What about your boss?"

"He's a liar. He insisted on meeting Alina when she first arrived in New York. I know they've had meetings and gone to dinner without me." Hunter squeezed his coffee cup, spilling some of the coffee on the floor.

Jim held up a photo taken inside Hunter's apartment. "How does a reporter on your salary end up with two envelopes containing $10,000 in cash sitting in a drawer in your desk?"

"The cash is an advance for my next book."

"Wanna try again?" Jim said.

"Go fuck yourself! Look at you," Hunter said. "You're pathetic. I bet you were a stupid jock in high school and married a cheerleader because you got her pregnant." Hunter shook his head. "How the hell did you ever get into the academy?"

Jim leaped off his chair, but Bob grabbed his arm before he could reach Hunter.

Hunter laughed and crossed his arms.

Bob pulled Jim back into his chair and turned back to Hunter. "Your boss told us that he suspected you became a spy when you went to Kiev. He said you were a different man when you returned. Something had changed."

Hunter muttered, "Fucking piece of shit."

"Tell us why they shot you in Kiev."

"It doesn't matter," Hunter said. "What about Alina? What will happen to her?"

"That all depends on how well you help us, and how much she decides to cooperate."

Hunter turned away from the two men, crossed his arms and stared at the two-way mirror, wondering who was on the other side.

Bob stood and raised his hands in frustration. "You talk to him, Jim. I can't put up with his shit any longer." He walked out of the room.

Hunter and Jim sat in silence for a minute.

"Can I have some more coffee?" Hunter asked.

"No."

"A cigarette?"

"You little shit, not until you start telling the truth."

"I'm innocent. Why doesn't anybody believe me?"

"Because you keep telling us lies."

"That's because I don't trust you guys."

"You better start trusting somebody pretty soon because you're in the crosshairs of some very dangerous men, and you don't even know who's behind the trigger—Stravinsky, Karasov, Alina—take your pick."

"Why should I trust you?"

"You can count on this—if you don't start telling the truth, Bob will be your worst nightmare."

Hunter rubbed his hands on his thighs.

"Let's start over." Jim leaned forward. "You ask me a question, and I'll give you a truthful answer. Then I ask you a question, and you tell me the truth. Okay?"

Hunter nodded.

"Go ahead, what's your question?" Jim said.

"How did you know that I'd be in my apartment with Alina? We were only there for about twenty minutes."

"We had men staked outside. We were also monitoring activities at the airport. An agent called us when they saw the crew refueling Karasov's jet. We checked with the air traffic controllers, and there hadn't been any flight plan filed for that jet, so we knew somebody was going on an unscheduled trip. With the evidence that we already had, we decided to arrest you and Alina, even though Karasov had diplomatic immunity." Jim lit a cigarette and blew out the match. "Now it's my turn. Why don't you have any friends?"

"What? No—I have friends."

"You don't."

"You don't know me."

"You're wrong. We know you don't have friends."

Hunter stiffened. "What are you talking about?"

Jim opened another file. "Tell me about your relationship with Carrie?"

"Don't bring her into this. She has nothing to do with any of this shit."

"You didn't answer my question. Does Alina know you're sleeping with a little slut on the side?"

"Carrie's not a slut," Hunter said. "She's…"

"What?"

"A nice girl."

"You're a little old for her, aren't you? I mean, come on, you're robbing the cradle."

"Fuck you."

He glanced through his file and shook his head. "We've checked her out. Carrie's just like you. On the outside she appears normal, but when you look closer, you realize that she lives alone. No friends—no relationships." He leaned toward Hunter, "What's with you people? You, Carrie and Alina are perfect examples of the Law of Attraction—except you're attracted to each other because misery loves misery. I've never seen a more narcissistic, unhappy and lonely bunch of misfits."

"What do you care?"

"I don't, but if you had good friends, people who cared about you, you would've never gotten involved with this crowd."

Hunter crossed his arms and looked at the ceiling.

Jim went on. "I'm trying to help you."

"Thanks for nothing," Hunter said.

They sat in silence for a couple of minutes, until Jim asked, "What happened in the room with Parrish?"

"It's complicated." Hunter chewed on his lip.

Jim waited for him to continue, but Hunter stopped talking.

"It's hard to know who you can trust." Jim played with his matchbook. "Look at your boss and Alina—you trusted them, and where are they now?"

Hunter sat very still facing the two-way mirror.

"Listen to me." Jim pointed his finger at Hunter. "You're fucked. You're all alone. The only person you should trust is me."

"Why should I trust you?"

"Simple, because I'm the only one who can help you." He took a drag on his cigarette. "Look, I know how you feel."

"No, you don't."

"Yes, I do. You're scared, you're all alone and you don't know who to trust right now," Jim said. "You've told us so many lies you can't keep them straight anymore. You've lied about your relationship with Alina, lied about your dealing with Karasov, lied about Parrish and Dixon, lied about the cash in your drawer, lied about your boss and lied about Carrie. Why should we believe anything you tell us?"

"I'm not a liar," Hunter said.

"When I was in spook school, the first thing they taught us was to guard trust as your most precious possession because if you chose to trust the wrong person, it could cost you your life."

"So, how do you know who to trust?" Hunter asked.

"You don't."

"Oh, great. That's very helpful," Hunter said sarcastically.

"In situations like this, you're forced to take a chance and trust someone because you're fucked either way." Jim looked at his watch. "Think about it. I'll be back in a little bit." He left the room.

Hunter closed his eyes. He's right. He thought. It doesn't matter anymore. Nothing does. I don't care if I go to prison or not. I've lost Alina, lost my job, my life's trashed. Fuck it. They can't hurt me anymore. Nobody can.

Bob and Jim reappeared in the doorway.

"Don't ask me why I'm helping you," Bob said, "but I have a deal to offer you."

"A deal?"

"If you cooperate with us, we'll try to get your charges reduced. For sure, you're a sucker, but I don't believe you're a murderer or a spy. I think you're just a stupid man that was seduced by one of the best in the business. If you tell us everything you know about Alina and Karasov, I think we can get you out of here."

"I'll think about it."

"Don't think too long," Bob said and stood up to leave.

Hunter took a long look at the mirror on the wall and said, "Okay, I'll tell you everything you want to know."

Bob folded his hands on the table. "Go ahead, whenever you're ready."

"I have a box."

The two men looked at each other in surprise. "What are you talking about?"

"I want to trade a box of information for full immunity for Alina and me."

"What kind of information? You're not in a position to negotiate anything."

"Yes, I am."

"What makes you think that?"

"Because I have information that would be very valuable to your bosses."

The two men looked warily at Hunter. "Like what?"

"First, I want immunity in writing from the United States Attorney General."

"Not going to happen," Bob said.

"What if I told you that this information could result in an international scandal?"

"Involving whom?"

"People in the White House, some senators, a number of prominent American business executives, and big-wigs in France, Germany and Italy, just for starters."

"Doing what?"

"Take your pick—kickbacks, bribery, sex slavery, drugs, arms sales, money laundering. The list goes on."

"Do you have proof?"

Hunter laughed, suddenly feeling empowered. "How about photos, receipts, tape recordings, Cayman Island bank account numbers and videos. It's all in a box in storage, but I want full immunity for me and Alina."

"We can't promise anything." They picked up their folders. "We'll get back to you."

Several hours later, they returned with a signed document granting Hunter immunity.

"Must be your lucky day," Bob said.

"Or somebody is very nervous about what I have."

The men glanced at each other. "Where's the stuff."

"Get the keys out of my pants and go to a storage facility called Store-All in Brooklyn. The box is inside unit 88."

Jim stood up. "I'm on it."

Bob walked to the door with Jim, then turned to Hunter. "You better be telling the truth."

Two hours later, Bob returned to the room and sat down at the table.

"Did you find the box?"

"I haven't heard from Jim yet."

"So, why are you here?"

"I thought we'd chat while we wait for Jim to return."

"This is good cop, bad cop?"

"No, that's only for TV and movies," Bob said. "I'm curious. Why did you let yourself get tangled up with people like Alina and Karasov?"

"You wouldn't understand."

"Try me."

Thirty minutes later, the door opened, and Jim walked over to the table and sat down.

Bob looked up. "What did they find?"

"Nothing," Jim said. "There was no box with the information you described. There's just a bunch of crap in the storage unit."

Bob slammed his folder on the desk. "I knew it." He glared at Hunter. "You've wasted my time."

"What?" Hunter gasped. "That can't be! I'm the only one with a key. Were you in the correct unit?"

"Damn," Bob said to Jim. "This guy's a lying sack of shit, and we're back to square one."

Jim cocked his head to the side and asked Hunter, "Does anyone else have a key?"

"Alina." Hunter sighed. "She must've taken my key when I was distracted in one of the meetings we had at my apartment."

Another knock at the door interrupted them. A man motioned for both men to join him in the hallway. They were gone for a long time before they came back. This time they didn't sit down.

"What happened? Have you talk to Alina?"

"Unfortunately, that's not possible."

"Why not? Is something wrong? Where is she?"

"She's on a private jet."

"What?" Hunter said.

Bob glanced at Jim. "Can he really be this fucking dumb?"

Jim shrugged.

"You're an idiot," Bob said. "She threw you under the bus."

"What do you mean?"

"We offered her full immunity and witness protection for you and Alina. You could start a new life somewhere in the United States, all paid for by Uncle Sam. The two of you would've been on easy street for the rest of your lives—if only she cooperated."

"What did she say?"

"She just laughed."

Hunter felt the floor heave. The overhead lights became fuzzy, while the voices faded away. He gripped the edge of the table and blinked at the two men standing across from him.

"What?" Hunter repeated twice.

"She was released four hours ago. Right now, she's drinking champagne on a private jet and giving Stravinsky a lap dance."

"Did you say Stravinsky? You meant Karasov."

"I didn't make a mistake. You did." He laughed. "Why would she choose you? He's a fucking billionaire and the head of Russia's largest mafia family. They're already in the air flying back to Moscow."

Hunter put his face in his hands.

"Don't look so surprised. She wasn't afraid when we arrested her. Apparently, she was laughing in the van when they brought her in. She knew she was too valuable for the US government and Russians to let us keep her in custody. I guarantee she hasn't thought one fucking thing about you since we picked her up."

Hunter bent over and held his stomach. "That can't be true. I know for a fact she works for Karasov. She's his mistress."

"She's also one of the best recruiters in the business. We've tracked her recruitment of innocent girls all over Asia, eastern Europe and Ukraine."

"I never saw her do that. She hated the mafia and the sex slavery. She's only Karasov's pawn."

"Some pawn. Not many pawns can pull off working as a double agent for the Russians."

Hunter laughed and shook his head. "You dumb fucks. That isn't true."

"You're so pathetic, and you don't even see it." Bob said. "Our government just used Alina to complete a spy swap for one of our best CIA agents who the Russians arrested as a spy last year."

Hunter snapped upright. "The Russians? Bullshit. That makes no sense. You mean the Ukrainians."

"Apparently, Stravinsky sold Alina to Karasov so she could spy on his activities for the Russians. She used her access to Karasov to seduce business executives and government officials from Europe and America like Parrish and Dixon."

"Are you telling me she's actually a spy for Stravinsky and not Karasov?"

"Do I have to spell it out for you?"

"You dumb bastards have it all wrong." Hunter scoffed. "It's the other way around. She hates the Russians. Karasov used her to spy on Stravinsky. He sent her to Moscow after I returned to New York two years ago."

"No, you're the one who has it wrong. You've had it wrong from the minute you first met Alina," Bob said. "Alina played you and Karasov like a fucking fiddle."

Hunter slumped forward in his chair.

"We're almost done here," Bob said to the mirror. He pushed his chair back. The door to the interrogation room opened, and another man handed him a note and a small white envelope. He read the note and frowned. "This is against my better judgment, but my boss insisted we give you this."

Bob handed Hunter an envelope. "I guess it was part of the deal that Alina cut before she left. I'm sure it's some coded message for you, but at this point, I really don't give a shit because as soon as you leave here, it's my guess that you'll be a dead man within a month. Karasov and the Russian mafia have a long reach."

Hunter opened the white envelope. Inside, the note read, "Forgive me. Have a Stalingrad martini in the Gramercy Tavern bar for us when you get a chance. Love always, Alina."

"Is this your idea of a sick joke?" He held the note in the air, crumpled it, and then threw it at Bob. "Fuck you guys."

The men picked up their folders and walked out of the room without another word.

"Wait a minute. Is this it? What are you going to do with me?"

"What do you think?" Bob paused at the door and turned around. "I have just one last question. Why did you do it?"

"You wouldn't understand."

"Humor me."

"Because… because I love her."

The two men looked at each other and shook their heads. "Do you really think that she'd pick a schmuck like you over a billionaire?" They didn't wait for an answer and walked out of the room. The door closed with a loud metal clank, and Hunter was alone.

I'm going to prison, but it doesn't matter, he thought. My life's over anyway. Everything Alina told me was a lie. Cabot betrayed me. Karasov's back in Kiev. Carrie's a fake.

Hunter stared at the blank white wall of the interrogation room, unblinking and without expression. He walked over and picked up the note that Alina wrote and put it in his pocket.

They can't hurt me anymore… no one can, he thought. Prison won't be so bad. It can't be worse than living without Alina.

Hunter remembered the newspaper photo of the engineer accused of passing secret documents to the Russians. I wonder if he had the chance, he thought. Would he risk everything again?

An hour later, a man about Hunter's age opened the door. He wore black jeans, a black T-shirt, and a leather jacket. Wrap-around sunglasses dangled from his neck. "Let's go."

"I don't understand."

"Follow me."

"Who are you?"

"Put your hands behind your back."

"Wait a minute," Hunter said. "Talk to Bob and Jim. We were working out a deal!"

"If you don't calm down, I'm going to gag you."

"I want Bob."

"Sorry pal, I'm all you're getting today."

"There must be some mistake."

The man handcuffed Hunter and blindfolded him. "Stand up."

Hunter made no attempt to stand. "I'm not going anywhere until I speak to Bob again."

"Have it your way." The man whistled, and another set of footsteps came into the room. "Pick him up. If he doesn't cooperate, you know what to do."

Hunter slowly stood up and let them lead him out of the interrogation room. They walked for a long time, rode an elevator up several floors before stopping, and then passed through a door into a cold area.

Hunter shivered in his light Polo shirt. "Where are we?"

A car door opened. "Lower your head and slide over," the man said, as they eased Hunter into the backseat.

"Where are you taking me?"

"Just relax."

"Can't we work something out?"

No one responded as the car moved faster.

"I gave Bob everything he wanted. What else does he need from me? He told me they were going to reduce the charges. I know I'm going to prison, but you're making a big mistake. It doesn't have to end like this."

The driver chuckled but didn't answer.

"Come on, somebody talk to me. What more do you want from me? I have money."

"Shut the fuck up," the driver said.

Hunter slumped in the backseat. He never thought things would end like this.

Just as well, he thought, rotting in prison wouldn't be any better. *Alina betrayed me twice. Nothing matters anymore.*

They drove for about a half-hour before the car stopped. The leather-jacket man said, "Watch your head and get out." He grabbed Hunter's arm and led him up a set of stairs, through two sets of locked doors and down a long hallway before taking off Hunter's blindfold and handcuffs. He opened a metal side door and handed Hunter a clear plastic bag containing his wallet, watch and some change.

"I don't understand." Hunter blinked several times and looked at the guard. "That's it? I just walk away?"

"That's it," the man said—and then closed the door.

Dazed and confused, he squinted in the bright morning sunlight and noticed his watch, ten o'clock. Hunter stepped onto the sidewalk and turned in a circle as he tried to get his bearings. To his surprise, he found that he'd emerged from a side door of the New York City police station at Plaza One.

He walked to the front of the building to hail a taxi. Nobody knew what he'd just gone through, and nobody cared either. He shut his eyes for a second to regain his composure, which was ruined by a honk from a taxi.

The window rolled down. "Get in."

Before he could answer, Tess stepped out and gently touched his face with her hand. "Are you okay?"

"I'm not sure," he said. "What day is it?"

"Monday," she said. "Let's go home. You must be exhausted."

"How did you know I'd be here?"

"I was very worried when you disappeared. Nobody knew what'd happened to you. Then I got a strange call from the Russian embassy. They wouldn't give me an explanation explain but told me to pick you up here at this specific time."

"The Russian embassy?"

"Yes, I could barely understand the message because the accent was so thick."

"I'm innocent, Tess. I was framed as a spy for the Russians and Ukrainians."

"I believe you," she said.

"How can I explain what happened to anyone?" Hunter said.

"Based on the secrecy around this whole thing, I doubt anyone will ever know."

Hunter stared at the sidewalk and fought back tears. "I don't know what's wrong with me. I haven't cried since my parents died."

"I'll take you home."

Hunter's apartment looked like a garbage dump. The lock was broken, and clothes were strewn everywhere. The contents of his drawers had been emptied onto the floor. Canisters of sugar and flour had been poured out. Hunter ignored the mess, fed his cat and took a long shower. He sat under the flow of hot water for a long time trying to make sense out of what had happened over the past few days.

He slept for nine straight hours. It was night when he woke up. He didn't feel like eating, so he made a drink and sat down to watch TV. After a few minutes, he turned it off and sat alone in the dark.

He remembered the crumpled envelope and the message he'd been given from Alina. He pulled the note out of his pocket and read it again. He couldn't understand why Alina wanted to hurt him again by telling him to go have a drink at the bar in The Gramercy Tavern, the bar where they had met after his interview with Karasov—and before they had made love in his apartment.

Damn it, he thought, Alina's in a jet at thirty thousand feet giving a fucking billionaire a blow job.

After sulking for several more minutes, he decided to take a taxi to the Gramercy Tavern. He arrived at the bar just before closing. The place was almost empty except for a few patrons lingering over coffee. Hunter sat down at the bar, and a familiar bartender placed a napkin in front of him.

"What would you like to drink?"

"Do you remember me?" Hunter said.

"No," the bartender said with a straight face. But then he grinned. "But I certainly remember the redhead you were with."

Hunter smiled. "I get that a lot."

"A Stalingrad?"

"Of course."

"Good choice. I'm addicted to the drink, but it's rare that anyone orders it. People either love it or hate it. No in-between."

"Some things are an acquired taste."

"Like your red-headed friend?"

"Some things are harder to acquire than others."

The bartender nodded. "I'll be right back." He mixed the cocktail then set it on a napkin along with a sealed manila envelope.

Hunter stared at the envelope for a second and then looked up. "What's this?"

"I don't know. She came in last week and paid me a lot of money to hold this for you."

"How did she know I'd come here and order a Stalingrad?"

"Beats me. She must've had a plan because she gave me specific instructions." He took a cloth to the bar's surface. "You're one lucky man. I'd give my right arm to switch places with you."

"Be careful what you wish for." Hunter fingered the envelope for a long time before he tore the seal and looked inside. The envelope contained photos and a note. Hunter gasped when he looked at the first picture. It clearly showed Alina making love with Cabot in a hotel room. The second one showed Cabot naked and handing Alina money. Hunter unfolded the note attached to the rest of the photographs. "I'm sure you'll find some good use for these."

Hunter didn't need to see the rest of the pictures. A letter was at the bottom of the envelope. He opened it and read: "I'm sorry to put you through all of this. If you're reading this, then my plan for us has failed. I had put in place a sequence of instructions to cut a deal with the CIA that would protect you if we ever needed it. By now, they have copies of a few specific documents relating to certain cabinet members in the White House. I didn't give them everything. The rest are still in the two trunks you have in storage. Be careful and keep them in a safe place. You may need them again. The world is filled with hypocrisy. People really didn't care about all the other corrupt, slimy people or documents that we hold. You may not believe me, but I still love you. Alina."

Stunned, Hunter closed the letter, finished his drink, and then left for home.

* * *

The next day Hunter walked into Cabot's office and closed the door.

"Stop right there!" Cabot yelled. "What the hell are you doing here?"

"Is that any way to greet your friend and favorite reporter?"

"But I thought you were …"

"…going to prison?"

Cabot picked up the phone. "You better leave now, or I'm calling security."

Hunter threw a manila envelope on his desk.

Cabot held the phone to his ear but stared motionlessly at the envelope. "What the hell is this?"

"The first chapter of a new book I'm writing about betrayal. Whether I finish it depends on several things, and I want your opinion."

Cabot pushed the envelope to the corner of his desk with his right hand. "I'll get back to you."

"I want your opinion now." Hunter folded his arms and waited.

"What kind of fucking game are you trying to play?"

"No games," Hunter said, pointing at the envelope. "Just open it."

Cabot set the phone down. His face turned ashen as he saw the first photo. "What do you want?"

"Everything," Hunter said. "Your job, your office—and you out of my life. Think of it as early retirement."

"You can't do this. Once I tell my boss about you, Karasov and your slut Alina, you'll be finished. You'll never work as a reporter again."

"Go ahead, knock yourself out," Hunter said. "March right into your boss and tell your little story. It's your word against my photos."

"I'm calling the CIA. This is blackmail, and you're a Russian spy."

"Really?" Hunter's eyes burned into Cabot. "I just came from them. Hmmm—what would you tell them? That you're just an innocent, married man that somehow ended up in a hotel with a beautiful prostitute who also happens to be a spy for Ukraine. You could explain how she forced you to have sex against your will and then made you give her money, lots of money." Hunter picked up Cabot's phone. "Here, I'll dial the number to the CIA for you."

"You won't get away with this."

"Yes, I will."

"Leah won't believe you. I'll tell her these photos are fakes."

"Good luck with that."

Cabot's hands trembled as he held the photos.

"I'm curious," Hunter said, picking up Cabot's cigar clipper to play with it. "How much of your money did she make off your little pecker?"

"Fuck you," Cabot said.

"Ironic, isn't it?"

"What's that?"

"She got you too."

"What do you want from me?"

"Announce your retirement and insist that I take over your position."

"No way. You're crazy."

Hunter scooped up the envelope and pulled out several more photos of Cabot naked with Alina and spread them out on the desk. "You're right. I'm crazy, unpredictable, and I have very dangerous friends."

"Are you threatening me?"

Hunter smiled. "You have one hour to decide."

Chapter 21

Cabot submitted his resignation, and Hunter was quickly promoted to his position. Two weeks later, the sign painter added Hunter's new title as Editor and Eastern Europe Bureau Chief to the door while Tess coordinated the move from his old office. After the painter left, Hunter stood in the corner of his new office and looked out over the New York skyline.

Tess walked into his office. "Like the view?"

"I'm still pinching myself."

"How does it feel?"

"Dizzy," he said, and then frowned.

"What's wrong? You should be two feet off the ground."

"One last piece is unresolved."

"You mean Carrie?"

He nodded. "I haven't heard anything from her since the CIA released me. No calls, nothing." Hunter noticed Tess smile. "I know that look. What do you know?"

"You don't have to worry about her anymore."

Hunter eyes widened. "Why not?"

"She left New York—permanently."

"How do you know?"

Tess's voice hardened. "She's lucky to be alive and living somewhere far from here."

"Tess—how did you convince her to leave?"

"Never try to blackmail someone another woman loves," Tess said. "Let's just say that I pointed out a few options for her, such as if she tried to publish any of the information that she learned about you, Alina, Karasov, or our government officials, then if the mafia didn't kill her someone else would. I had Vinny arrange a call from one of his buddies, a Federal agent, to make sure she understood the consequences of her folly." She laughed. "The best part was the call that Vinny made to Carrie while pretending he was a member of the Russian mafia! He does a convincing Russian accent."

"Tess, I couldn't have done any of this without you."

Tess walked across the room to him, slipped her hand into his palm and kissed him on the cheek. "We're a good team."

* * *

In early September, Tess and Hunter drank wine at the Boathouse in Central Park. He turned away from watching couples rowing small boats in the pond and looked at Tess on a high barstool. "What are you thinking about?"

"Fall is my favorite time of year." Tess tucked her hair behind her ears. "You look like you're deep in thought."

"I was thinking about how much things have changed over the last few months."

"Amazing, yes." Tess rolled her eyes. "What a summer—you couldn't make this stuff up. I received a note from your boss this morning. Management wants to submit your recent feature for another Pulitzer. Personally, I think you have a good chance of winning another one."

"I'm not holding my breath. Frankly, I'd prefer to stay under the radar for a while."

They finished their wine and walked through the park. Reaching the edge of the water, Hunter looked down at the wiggling image of him and Tess. He wondered what they might look like in ten or twenty years.

They walked further and came upon an intersection that connected several paved paths. A tall, slender woman stood in the middle of the path, staring confused at a guidebook. She wore a low-cut top and red shorts. Hunter couldn't see her face, but there was something familiar about the way she stood. Maybe it the length of her legs or the smooth curvature of her bare back or the way she kept brushing her red hair away from her eyes. She looked up from the map at the same moment he passed. Hunter caught his breath when she smiled. She looked like a clone of Alina.

She waved at him. "Excuse me."

He stopped and pointed at himself. "Me?"

She pointed to her map. "Yes, yes—can you help?"

Hunter glanced at Tess. "Hang on a second, she must be lost." He walked back to the woman. "How can I help you?"

"I try to find Beatles."

"The Beatles?"

"No, not right." She frowned. "Hmmm," struggling to find the words. "Berry fields?"

Hunter laughed. "You mean Strawberry Fields."

"Yes, yes." She pointed to the map. "Image?"

She had long fingers with smooth red nails. Hunter cleared his throat. "Do you mean Imagine? That's a memorial to John Lennon."

"Da, I mean yes. I saw picture in magazine. I love Beatles." She smiled with perfect snow-white teeth.

Hunter just stared at her until she pointed to her map again. "You show me?"

"Where are you from?"

"Odessa."

"I thought so," Hunter said. "I recognized your accent. I love Ukraine."

"You know?"

"Ya provel leto v Kiev."

"Wonderful." She clapped her hands. "You were in Kiev?"

He nodded. "Are you visiting New York on a trip?" Hunter asked.

"No, I move here two weeks ago."

"Really, where do you work?"

"Sorry to interrupt," Tess yelled, "but we're going to be late."

"I'll be right there," he shouted.

The woman smiled. "She's pretty."

Hunter reached for her map. "Here, let me show you." She moved closer and put her head right next to his shoulder so she could see where he was pointing. She smelled like a gardenia mixed with a whiff of cigarette smoke. He put his finger on a small red star. "There! That's what you're looking for."

"Yes, I see it."

Hunter moved his finger along the map. "Follow the path to the second left. Walk fifty yards, and the memorial will be in the middle of a small open square called Strawberry Fields."

"Thank you." She kissed him on both cheeks and then extended her right hand. He reached out to shake it when he realized she was holding a key in her palm.

Hunter felt the warm metal of the key but didn't release her hand. "I don't understand."

"We have mutual friends." She let go of his hand.

Hunter took a half-step backward with the key in his hand.

"Don't be afraid. I won't hurt you."

Hunter backed up even further. "What mutual friends?"

She stared at the sun and the trees surrounding them. "In some ways, this park reminds me of Independence Square in Kiev."

"I'll be damned."

Hunter glanced at Tess, who was watching some kids play.

Putting the key in his pocket, he asked, "What's the key for?"

"P.O. Box 488, Midtown Post Office."

"Who are you?"

"Ciao." She turned back to her map and made a call on her cell phone.

"Ciao," Hunter said, walking away. Halfway back to Tess, his cell phone rang.

"Hunter here."

"Hunter, my boy."

"Who's this?"

"You forget your friend so quickly?"

"Karasov?"

"Da, you like my present?"

"The key or the girl?"

"You can have both."

Hunter didn't respond.

"Are you still there?" Karasov asked.

"Yes."

"Well?"

"For a moment, I thought she was Alina. She could be her twin."

"Amazing, right?" Karasov laughed. "That bitch, she fuck us good."

"Yes, she did."

"Deep down, I always know she bad, but I no care."

"Me neither."

"Well, we have one thing to look forward to."

"What's that?"

Karasov laughed even louder. "I can't wait to see what happen to Stravinsky. That bastard—he have no idea what will hit him."

"How's everything in Kiev?" Hunter asked.

"Good—we do start oil exploration soon." Karasov paused and then added, "I want thank you."

"For what?"

"Saving my ass."

"It was nothing."

"Sorry I leave you in mess."

"It all worked out for the best."

"You take key?"

"Yes."

"In box is first-class plane ticket and cash. I want you come home."

"Home? What are you talking about?"

"Your home is here."

Hunter switched the phone to his other ear. "Vladimir, have you been drinking?"

"Maybe—a little," he slurred.

"We barely know each other."

"You and me—we connected. Always—in past lives."

Hunter laughed. "Now I know you're drunk."

"You come back," he shouted over the phone. "I make you professor at biggest university in Kiev. Maybe you run my newspaper. I make you editor. You never worry about money again. Back here, you have real home. Here you big man, da?"

"I don't know what to say," Hunter said, but then asked, "Why are you doing this for me?"

"I need people I trust. Someone not afraid of me."

"I'm still afraid of you."

Karasov's voice changed, "You and me, we are same. I have no parents, no family. I raised in orphanage. Nobody care about me. I did not exist because I no belong to anyone but me." His voice softened, "So I decide to make my own family. I am, because I belong. *We* are, because we belong to each other. My organization is my family. You understand?"

Hunter looked at Tess thirty yards away and then back to the young woman he'd just met.

"Yes."

"Then you come?"

"I'll get back to you." Hunter hung up.

Tess waved at him twenty yards down the path. "What was that all about?" she asked when he rejoined her.

"Just work stuff."

"No, I meant the girl—woman—whatever she was."

"She was lost," Hunter said. "Just moved to New York and couldn't speak English very well, so I had a hard time understanding her."

"What'd she want?"

"She was trying to find John Lennon's memorial."

"Huh, I did the same thing the first week I was in New York."

They resumed their walk, but after a minute, Hunter glanced over his shoulder. The woman was still standing in the middle of the path. She didn't look surprised when he looked back. She tilted her head slightly and smiled. Hunter heard a noise above him and looked up. A large jet was making its way across the sky. He watched the plane's long, white vapor trail.

They emerged from the park near the Metropolitan Museum of Art. Tess paused to look at some street art. "Look at this," she said, holding up an old map of Manhattan shellacked into a poster. "This would be a great memento of New York."

"Are you leaving New York?"

"You never know, I still dream about my island in the sun."

Chapter 22

Three weeks later, Hunter stood in the corner of his office, staring out over the city from the 48th floor. In the fading light, the people below looked like ants scurrying home from work. He pulled out the key he'd received in the park, turned it over and thought about his last conversation with Karasov.

The door to his office burst open. Without turning around, he knew his visitor was Tess. Hunter smiled and slipped the key back into his pocket.

Tess set a box from a florist on his desk. "You have a delivery."

"From who?"

"Not sure." She pretended to smell the sealed card attached to the flowers and placed it next to the box. "Must be from one of your secret admirers."

"Are they from you?"

"The day I give you a gift, you'll know it's from me." She tilted her head to the side and winked. "And it won't come in a box."

Hunter laughed. "Can't wait."

"What a minute. Did you just laugh?"

"No, something caught in my throat."

"Thought so, because for a second you actually sounded happy."

Hunter smiled. "Sorry to disappoint you."

Tess's desk phone started to ring, and she rushed out.

Hunter peeled back the paper covering the box. Inside was a single gardenia. He inhaled the fragrance of the flower and closed his eyes for a second. Then he walked over to the window and opened the card. The note read: "I'm sorry I didn't have time to explain. Everything happened so fast. Please forgive me. 4009 Lenin Parkway, Apt. #848, Moscow." At the bottom of the envelope was the gold cross necklace he had given to Alina.

Tess entered his office again. "There's a guy with a funny accent on line one."

He raised his hand to acknowledge her. Facing his own reflection in the window, he glanced at the Moscow address one more time and shuddered. He slipped the card into his breast pocket, walked back to his desk and pushed the phone button for line one.

"Hello."

"Is this Hunter Moretti?"

"Yes, how can I help you?"

"This is Juriy Tereshchenko from the *Kiev Post*."

"Did you say Kiev?"

"I understand you worked with Ambassador Karasov when he was in New York recently."

"I don't know where you got your information, but that's not true. I work for the *New York Times* as a reporter. I've never worked for Ambassador Karasov."

"But you know him?"

"I met him a few times."

"Do you know anything about Karasov's activities while he was in New York?"

"Why do you ask?"

"They found him dead three days ago."

Hunter gasped. "What happened?"

"He was shot in the head."

Hunter gripped the phone.

"Can you help us? I'd like to ask a few questions?"

Hunter stared at the gardenia on his desk.

"Mr. Moretti? Are you still there?"

"How did you get my name?"

"What can you tell us about your meetings with him?"

"You didn't answer my question."

"We got your name from a woman named Alina. She's in jail in Kiev for the assassination of Karasov. They caught her trying to board a plane for Moscow at the Kiev International Airport."

"How do you know she did it?"

"The police have a gun with her prints on it. She claims that she was framed."

"What does this have to do with me?"

"She said you have information that could prove she was set up."

"I have to go now." Hunter slowly set the phone down. He put his hand in his pocket and could feel the necklace and Alina's note. Touching the necklace made him shiver.

Tess barged into his office again. "Are you okay?"

"Yes."

"You look funny."

"Must be getting a cold."

"Do you need anything?"

"No, I'll be fine."

Tess closed the door. He stood up and paced. It was almost dark, and the lights of the city spread out beneath his office.

I should walk out of here, he thought, and take a taxi to anyplace but here or home.

He returned to his desk and stared at a large envelope containing the final draft of the manuscript he should've written a long time ago. Clicking and unclicking the end of his pen, he stared at the blank label where he needed to write his publisher's address before sending it by messenger.

Tess came back into his office. "What were you doing?"

"I had to finish making a decision on something."

"Sounds serious," she said.

She set a cup of coffee next to his computer and looked at a large cardboard box on the floor. "What's in this box?"

"A bunch of old stuff."

"What are you going to do with it?"

"Haven't decided."

"You sound just like my mother. She's such a pack rat—can't let go of anything. Need help? I can unpack it."

"No, but thanks."

"Are you sure? I'm good at cleaning up other people's messes."

"This is one mess I need to take care of myself."

"Come on, let me do this," she said, walking around his desk and opened the flaps to the box. "I know you." She paused and pointed a finger at Hunter. "If you don't let me help, this box will still be sitting here a month from now. But I can clean it up in an hour."

Hunter laughed.

"What?" She looked up with unblinking, blue eyes.

"You're incorrigible," Hunter said.

"What does that mean?" she asked, tentatively.

"It means… I don't deserve you."

"I thought so." She broke into a wide grin. "Whatever happened to that crazy Russian ambassador and Alina?"

"He's Ukrainian."

"Russian, Ukrainian, who cares," she said, waving her hands in the air. "We can go to the moon, yet we can't stop those mafia bastards from kidnapping girls and turning them into prostitutes. Somebody has to stop them."

"It's not that easy."

"My dad always said nothing worthwhile comes without risk. Each of us will have a time when we have to make a choice that will change the course of our lives forever."

"He's a wise man."

Tess picked up the large envelope sitting on top of his desk.

"Please set that down," he said.

"It's heavy." She looked at the blank mailing label. "What's in here?"

"Something I've been working on for a long time."

"Feels like one of your manuscripts." She lifted in the air. "Is it finished? Can I read it?"

"No."

"Why not?" She set the envelope back down.

Hunter moved it away from Tess's reach. "I'm trying to protect you."

"From what?" She glared.

"It's complicated."

"Way too complicated for someone like me?"

"I didn't mean it like that. It's only a draft. I promise to let you read it when I'm finished." Hunter ran his hand lightly across the envelope. "Can I ask you something?"

"Sure."

"What would you do if you had information that could put some people in jail but would not really change the proliferation of human trafficking and prostitution in Eastern Europe?"

Tess didn't hesitate. "I'd still print it."

"You sound pretty sure about that."

"Of course. Why wouldn't you?"

"But what if you knew something that was much bigger than human trafficking and sex slavery? What if disclosing this information would change your life forever? What if that decision meant you would lose everything have? And I mean everything. What if it required that you'd have to disappear and never contact anyone you knew ever again? What if you knew in advance that people might be killed because of what you revealed?"

"You're talking about what's in the envelope, aren't you?" Tess arched her eyebrows.

Hunter turned his head away and looked out the window.

Tess bit the corner of her lip. "Do you remember the story about the young boy who saved one starfish by throwing it back in the sea?"

Hunter turned back.

"So let me ask you a question. What if you saved only one girl from that nightmare, would you do it?"

"It depends."

"What if that one girl was your daughter?"

"That's different."

"Why is that different? Every girl that's forced to become a sex slave is somebody's daughter."

Hunter took a deep breath.

"It has to start somewhere. Change only occurs one person at a time."

Hunter put his head in his hands. "I know, but..."

"Look, if you can change the life of one girl, isn't that enough to make it worthwhile?" Tess put her hand on his shoulder. "There's always risk when you try to make a difference."

"You make it sound so simple."

"Doing the right thing is simple." She turned away and started toward the door. "That doesn't mean it's easy. Let me know if you need anything before I leave tonight."

Hunter nodded.

After Tess left, Hunter stared at the blank mailing label for a long time. Finally, he hunched over his desk and filled in the address of his publisher, threw the pen down, leaned back and swiveled around in his chair until it faced the window again.

* * *

Six months later, Hunter walked into a restaurant after a morning of spearfishing. "What are we cooking tonight?"

"I have reservations for fifteen friends and customers. I thought we'd make conk fritters for the appetizer and fresh lobster for the main course. We'll finish with your famous basil lemon sorbet."

Hunter grabbed Tess from behind and put his face in her hair next to a fresh gardenia clipped into a barrette. "You smell marvelous."

"And you smell like dead fish." Tess laughed and tried to pull away.

He turned her around. She was wearing a colorful wrap. "Did I tell you that you look beautiful?"

"Yes, at least three times today."

He touched the gold cross pendant that hung from her necklace and kissed Tess on the lips. She smiled, stood on her tiptoes and kissed him on the nose. "Go wash your hands and then come help."

Pete Carlson

Hunter walked over to the sink in their straw hut and watched the seagulls soar above the blue waves that crashed along miles of a powdered-sugar beach.

Acknowledgements

This novel was born ten years ago in the womb of The Loft Literary Center in Minneapolis, Minnesota. I'm grateful for the patience, collaboration, and instruction provided by nationally known authors and teachers, Carolyn Crooke, Mary Carroll Moore, and Ian Graham Leask. Each provided me with an essential foundation for this novel to grow. I completed a full draft of the manuscript five years ago and then stopped. Doubt is the great Deceiver and I succumbed to those fears. My wife, and Ian's passion for the craft and the art of storytelling, inspired me to finish *Ukrainian Nights* this year, even after multiple attempts to set it aside in frustration. Ian has always been my light and guide on this journey; this work was not possible without his uncanny insights, encouragement and steady advice over the years. In addition, I appreciate the fantastic efforts of Gary Lindberg and the entire Calumet Editions team for adding so much editing value to my raw attempt to write. Writing is humbling and mysterious experience where the words create something that wasn't there before. What a fun and amazing adventure!

About the Author

Pete Carlson was raised in the Minneapolis area, where he graduated with a BSB and MBA from the University of Minnesota. After graduation he began a successful career in commercial real estate investment and development. He has been married to his wife Marsha for 40 years, has three children and three grandchildren, and currently resides in Denver, Colorado.

CPSIA information can be obtained
at www.ICGtesting.com
Printed in the USA
BVHW062337060123
655724BV00006B/174